By Thomas Fleming
from Tom Doherty Associates

WHEN THIS CRUEL WAR IS OVER

Thomas Fleming

FORGE®

A TOM DOHERTY ASSOCIATES BOOK
NEW YORK

This is a work of fiction. All the characters and events portrayed in this book are either products of the author's imagination or are used fictitiously.

WHEN THIS CRUEL WAR IS OVER

Copyright © 2001 by Thomas Fleming

A Forge Book
Published by Tom Doherty Associates, LLC
175 Fifth Avenue
New York, NY 10010

www.tor.com

Forge® is a registered trademark of Tom Doherty Associates, LLC.

ISBN 0-812-57645-4
Library of Congress Catalog Card Number: 00-048444

First edition: March 2001
First mass market edition: October 2002

Printed in the United States of America

0   9   8   7   6   5   4   3   2   1

To Dick, for his help on many books

Europe extends to the Alleghenies, while America lies beyond.
— RALPH WALDO EMERSON

It was evident that the portion of the North lying west of the Alleghenies was in the process of becoming the heartland of America.
— STEPHEN Z. STARR,
The Union Cavalry in the Civil War

Tell them—tell the world that I only loved America.
— JEFFERSON DAVIS

☀
ONE

IN HER BLUE-WALLED BEDROOM on the second floor of Hopemont, her family's redbrick mansion on the Ohio River, Janet Todd sat at a gleaming seventeenth-century marquetry desk writing a letter. Through the French doors that led to the upper porch overlooking the tree-lined front lawn flowed a current of thick warm air. For a month the temperature had hovered around 100 degrees. But Janet seemed immune to the disarray this sort of heat induced in most people. There was not a trace of a wrinkle in her white muslin dress, nor in the overskirt of white lace. Her glossy black hair retained its luxurious wave.

Janet fingered the blue-and-white bow sprinkled with red stars—a variation on the Confederate flag—that she was wearing in her hair. This was not a letter she was eager to write. She took a deep, slow breath and dated it: *July 4, 1864.* For several minutes she sat there mournfully pondering the numbers. Once the Fourth had been a day that everyone in America celebrated with pride.

Dearest Adam, she began.

She pondered these words and tore the paper into shreds. Seizing another piece of paper from one of the many cubicles on the back of the desk, she dated it and began again:

Dear Adam,
  The money and the guns have been guaranteed by our friends in Richmond. It is imperative that you or General Morgan bring your division into the battle beside us. I hope he will be well enough

to accompany you. But his presence is not a necessity. In fact, it might be better if he remained behind. His last visit to these parts did not win him many friends.

The Sons of Liberty are not the bravest fellows in the world. They have avoided military service in either army for three years. But they are very angry men and they will rise and fight if there are trained soldiers on hand to support them.

Orders to undertake this mission will arrive from Richmond. I am merely trying to reinforce them. I've been told General Morgan has a dislike of obeying orders from anyone. But this one comes from the very highest authority, I assure you.

If we take and hold Keyport and the rest of Hunter County, it will release a wave of fury that will oust the tyrants in Indianapolis. With Indiana in our hands, Kentucky and other states will swiftly follow us.

I have hopes of persuading a certain Union major—a West Pointer, no less, with a name that reverberates in the East—to join us. He has been wounded twice and is thoroughly sick of the way the war is being fought by the Union Army's butchers. His late father was a U.S. senator from New Jersey, a Democrat and warm friend of the South.

Janet paused, her pen hovering above the page, while more words rushed through her mind.

What would you say if I resorted to the ultimate persuasion? Will you despise me? I know what your answer will be. My response is: so be it. This war has destroyed so many things. Why shouldn't it destroy love itself?

Janet was tempted to write it, tempted to end once and for all the charade that she was waiting for outsize Adam Jameson to return from the war and marry her. Three years ago, he had used the war to extract a promise from her that she would never have given him under ordinary circumstances. But she had to pretend to be Adam's faithful sweetheart for a few more months. She finished the letter with words that were almost as meaningful to her:

> *However great the risk, you must come. Nothing matters now but victory. Only victory will rescue our dead from a fate worse than death itself—to have died in vain.*
> *With deep affection,*
> *Janet*

She sealed the letter and called, "Lucy!"

"Yes, Mistress?" Lucy said, stepping through the French windows from the porch.

Lucy wore a calico dress that she had cinched at the waist with one of Janet's cast-off leather belts. On her ears she wore a set of cheap jade earrings Janet had given her last Christmas. Janet found these attempts at style mildly amusing. It never occurred to her that by some standards Lucy was attractive. The light-devouring blackness of Lucy's skin barred the idea from her mind.

"Take this letter to the Confederate Post Office. Tell them it should go express to Saltville, Virginia. Hurry. We've got to leave for Keyport the minute you come back."

"I'll run all de way, Mistress," Lucy said.

Instead of dashing out the door, Lucy hesitated, bit her thumb, and said, "'Fore we go, Miz Janet, could you look into my mammy's cabin? She's awful low this mornin'. She sure could use a visit and maybe some of dat medicine de doctor lef' with you."

"I'll go see her while you're gone," Janet said.

"Oh, thank you, Miz Janet. I'm off and runnin'."

This time Lucy darted out the bedroom door and down the stairs. In seconds she was racing across Hopemont's green lawn, ignoring the fierce July sun. Janet watched her with an unstable mixture of approval and concern. The Confederate Post Office was in a cave on the riverbank, two long hot miles away. She did not want Lucy to collapse from heat prostration.

Lucy and Janet had been born on the same day. That coincidence had prompted Colonel Gabriel Todd to make Lucy his daughter's body servant. Janet and Lucy had been raised together, sleeping in the same bedroom, eating at the same table while they were children. Colonel Todd believed this was the best way to create devotion between mistress and servant. As he saw it, Lucy was almost as fortunate as Janet in this conjunction of their stars. She was destined to be a house servant, to eat decent food and sleep in a warm room for the rest of her life. She would never be sold, because her mistress could not imagine life without her.

"Janeykins!" The ragged voice reverberated in the hall. "Janeykins!" The choice of Janet's baby name was a bad sign. Her mother only used it when she was distraught.

In her bedroom, decorated with the ornate mirrors and sensuous gilded furniture she had bought in France on her honeymoon, Letitia Breckinridge Todd sat in dimness and shadow, the drapes drawn. "You're going to Keyport?"

"Yes. I feel—I feel a need to enjoy myself, Momma."

"I want more laudanum."

"Momma, I told you—you must break your dependence on that drug. Dr. Kennedy has warned you—"

"My hip—my hip is a mass of pain."

Four years ago, Letty Todd had been pretty enough and lively enough to play the belle on their annual visits to the races at Lexington, even though she had sons and a daughter of marrying age. Letty had been a fiery participant in the family's political debates, ready and eager to endorse secession, especially when her first cousin, John Cabell Breckinridge, the former vice president of the United States, became a Confederate general. Letty had played no small part in persuading most of the Todds and the Breckinridges to side with the South. Gleefully pitting herself against the influence of Mary Todd Lincoln, she had emerged a clear winner.

Now Letty Todd sat here in semidarkness, drugging herself into hypochondria. Besides laudanum, her only consolation was expensive visits from her spiritualist, Mrs. Virginia Havens, who claimed the power to help her communicate with her beloved dead.

"I'll speak to Dr. Yancey when I get to Keyport. But if he says no, you'll just have to endure it, Momma."

"You're as cruel as your father."

"It's for your own good, Momma. Now excuse me. I have to go see Lillibet. She's too sick to leave her cabin. As you may have noticed from the meager breakfast you got."

"She hasn't been the same since your father sold Maybelle. I sensed that was a mistake at the time. Remember how she reacted when he tried to sell Luther and Tom? They're different, the house servants. More like us."

"Should I give her the medicine Dr. Kennedy prescribed? It doesn't seem to help."

"Try some brandy. More than once I've found that a veritable elixir."

Janet descended the majestic spiral staircase that was Hopemont's claim to architectural fame. The house had been designed by the greatest architect of his era, John Latrobe. In the main floor rooms hung splendid crystal chandeliers, the equal of the ones Latrobe had created for the White House in Washington, D.C. On the outer walls climbed ivy cut from Shakespeare's garden in Stratford-upon-Avon. The shutters were reeded so delicately, they seemed almost an illusion. Touring English and French writers often mentioned Hopemont's Georgian majesty in their travel books.

In the dim dining room, Janet poured two or three ounces of brandy into a glass and mixed it with water. On the walls hung portraits of her grandparents and her Virginia-born great-grandparents, the first comers to Kentucky. All of them gazed at her with the complacent pride of people accustomed to prevailing in life and in love, in peace and in war. Would this be the first generation of Todds to admit defeat? *Never,* Janet vowed.

Outside, the heat was so ferocious, it was like walking into a gigantic furnace. There was not a scintilla of wind. The drought that began on the first of June continued to torment men, women, animals and plants. Janet put up her blue parasol and trudged the quarter of a mile down the dusty road to the slave quarters.

The twenty-five cabins formed a little town, with a main street along which several children scampered after a squawking rooster. Each house had a garden beside it, where the owners raised vegetables they sold either to the kitchen at Hopemont or at the market in nearby Owensboro. A half-dozen calico-clad women were hard at work in these plots, hoeing, hacking away weeds, watering lettuce and other green produce. At the end of the street, Hopemont's parched corn and wheat fields stretched for a mile to a fringe of woods. The long furrows were empty. Colonel Todd gave his slaves a day off on the Fourth of July. Most of the men were visiting friends or wives on nearby plantations, arranging parties that would begin at sundown. No one loved a party more than black folk, Janet mused.

Janet turned into Lillibet's cabin. Hopemont's cook

lay on her narrow bed, her gray hair streeling down both sides of her mournful face. The single room, with the planked wooden floor, was as scrupulously neat as her kitchen at Hopemont. Lillibet was forty-five, but she looked like an old woman. Janet felt a twinge of guilt as she gazed down at her.

"Oh, Miz Janet, I was prayin' you'd come," Lillibet said.

"Lucy told me you were feeling poorly."

"What a pretty dress. Is that new?"

"I bought it last Christmas in Cincinnati. This is the first chance I've had to wear it. No one gives parties anymore."

"It's real pretty," Lillibet said.

"What's wrong?" Janet asked.

"It's my legs, Miz Janet. I just ain't got no strength in my legs."

"The longer you stay in bed, the worse that will get. I brought you some good French brandy. Sip it slowly over the next hour or two and then see if you feel better. Try to stand up and walk a bit. Will you promise me?"

"I'll try, Miz Janet."

"It's the Fourth of July, you know. My father was hoping you'd cook him some of your special beaten biscuits and fried chicken."

"Maybe I can, Miz Janet."

"Drink the brandy now and you'll feel better. I'm sure of it."

Janet leaned over and kissed Lillibet's sweaty cheek. She inhaled the odor of blackness. They were different from white people. But they were similar, too. Their hearts could be damaged or broken. They had hopes and fears—above all the fear of being sold, to begin life again among strangers. Who wouldn't dread such a fate? It was not a frequent fear among Hopemont's slaves, thank God. But when it happened, it often left scars. By now everyone had noticed Lillibet's spells occurred mostly on days that reminded her of her lost daughter. Maybelle had been born on the Fourth of July.

Suddenly Janet was a thousand miles away from this hot cabin, sitting on the broad veranda of the United States Hotel in Saratoga Springs, New York. The year was 1857. It was a sunny August day, but the air was deliciously cool. As they had done in many previous years, the Todds had traveled north to escape Kentucky's brutal summer heat.

Janet was eighteen years old, wearing a sea green walking dress created by a new Paris designer named Worth. Her mother, equally well gowned, sat beside her, waiting for Gabriel Todd and his sons to take them to the races. On Janet's right sat a pert young blond woman in another Worth gown of burnt orange. The dresses created a sort of bond between them. In a Massachusetts accent, the stranger introduced herself as Isabelle Eustis.

Isabelle seemed agreeably surprised to discover Worth's gowns were being sold in Louisville. Janet's mother laughed and joined the conversation, eager to tell the young lady that the latest fashions had been a hallmark of genteel life in Kentucky in her own girlhood.

On Isabelle Eustis's right sat a small, severe older woman who listened to their remarks with pursed lips and a cold stare. She leaned toward them and asked, "Excuse me. Do you own slaves?"

"Why . . . yes," Janet said

The woman stood up. "Isabelle!" she said. "Come with me immediately."

Dismay coursed across Isabelle's oval face. "Momma!" she pleaded.

"Come with me! We don't converse with slave owners. No respectable person would tolerate them in her home."

Isabelle rose and followed her mother down the veranda. Janet felt shame—and anger—throb in her body and mind. She heard her mother say, "Don't mention this to your father. He'll go home directly."

Those painful words, the violent emotions, were as raw now as they had been on that long-ago August day. Perhaps even more intense, standing in the center of this slave cabin, thinking of how many hundreds of hours her mother and she had spent caring for these people when they were ill, calming their fears, soothing their animosities toward one another, sharing their griefs and hopes. *Own slaves.* The words had left an invisible brand on Janet Todd's soul, a wound that still festered.

Back on Hopemont's wide front porch, Janet realized Lucy was too sensible to run two miles to the Confederate Post Office in this heat. The minute she reached the main road, she had undoubtedly slowed to a walk that meant the trip would take at least a half hour. Janet strolled around the house into the garden.

Gray-haired, broad-shouldered Colonel Gabriel Todd, wearing a rumpled white suit and string tie, was stepping into the octagonal gazebo. Janet instantly knew her father was returning from a visit to the family graveyard, a quarter of a mile from the house in the opposite direction from the slave quarters. There, in the shade of a huge cottonwood tree, he had bowed his head before two tombstones—memorials to her brothers, John Randolph Todd and Andrew Lee Todd. At the bottom of each stone was the Latin motto: *Dulce et decorum est pro patria mori.*

Horace, noblest of the Roman poets, had written that line on his farm north of Rome, while his slaves cultivated his grape arbors and his wheat. *It is sweet and honorable to die for one's country.* Horace had been Gabriel Todd's model. He had absorbed his ripe wisdom and his mellow rhythms in his years at Transylvania University in Lexington. He saw himself on Hopemont's broad veranda writing hexameters in praise of those doughty ancestors who had settled Kentucky along with the Boones and the Callaways and the Bullitts. There would be odes to the beauty of the Ohio, to the nobility of the ancient oaks that surrounded Hopemont like hieratic sentinels, yes, even elegies on the brave red men who had resisted the white invasion with musket and hatchet. He had seen himself as a man who would respond with ready courage if his country called him—and his sons would imitate his example.

Gabriel Todd's poetry was an excellent imitation of Horace, good enough to appear in more than one Kentucky and Indiana newspaper. When his country called him to defend her rights in the war against Mexico in 1846, he marched at the head of a regiment and came home with an honorable wound. The Mexican War had been the high point of Gabriel Todd's life, the reason his fellow citizens had sent him to the state legislature as a senator. What could be more nobly Roman? Like Cincinnatus, George Washington's hero, the soldier returned peaceably to his farm and then devoted his accumulated wisdom to his country as a lawmaker.

But the violent antagonisms of America's politics had dissipated this good dream. When the animosity sundered the Union, the dream had become a nightmare. As war loomed in 1861 Gabriel Todd had been one of the many Kentuckians who abhorred the extremists of both sides. He had deplored the idea of seceding from the Union—but he was equally disgusted with the Yankee abolitionists whose rancorous hatred of the South made secession justifiable to many people. As one of the leaders of the state legislature, Colonel Todd had joined the governor in persuading their fellow politicians to declare Kentucky neutral.

Both North and South had been stunned by this unexpected stance. Both sides piously promised to respect the declaration—and promptly broke their word in the name of military necessity. Gabriel Todd soon found neutrality an impossible chimera. Once the Union regiments routed the Southern army and set up a military dictatorship in Kentucky, he lost all sympathy for Lincoln and his government. A Democrat like his father and grandfather, Colonel Todd saw the moralizing industrializing Republicans of the upper Midwest and New England as destroyers of the personal liberty and independence every follower of Thomas Jefferson held dear.

Gabriel Todd did not object when his sons decided to join the Confederate Army. But they had died like too many young Kentuckians, uncertain of the country for which they fought. John Randolph Todd's letters from Alabama, where he had married the daughter of a cotton planter with ten thousand acres and over five hundred slaves, were a litany of disillusion. As a Kentuckian, he had little in common with the radical secessionists of the Deep South, who talked of conquering the North and enslaving the white factory workers. Yet he had become an officer in the regiment his pugnacious father-in-law had raised. John had died two years ago in that explosion of blood and death called Shiloh. His younger brother, Andrew, had died in General John Hunt Morgan's ruinous cavalry foray into Indiana last year.

Death. More than once, Janet had to remind herself that her brothers had succumbed to its terrible finality. They were not away at college or on an extended vacation or living elsewhere with a wife. At times the knowledge seemed to be an effluvia rising in her throat, cutting off her breath. She struggled to remember them as if they were alive.

Thoughtful, earnest Jack, with his love of Sir Walter Scott's poetry and Charles Dickens's prose. Although he was six years older than Janet, he had always treated her with respect, encouraging her to read good books and discussing politics with her as if she were an adult. He confessed to her that his sojourn at Yale had convinced him slavery had to be eliminated eventually.

Ebullient, hot-tempered Andy, three years younger, had encouraged Janet's tomboyish tendencies at first, then sternly tried to eliminate them when she reached her teens. He wanted his "little sister" to marry well, he said—and he even had his eye on the man she might attract, if she concentrated on becoming a Southern belle. Andy never failed to bring her an expensive present—a new pocketbook or a half-dozen pairs of English stockings—if he had a good weekend at the Lexington races.

Janet trembled. It was hopeless. Memory could not give her brothers even a half-life in its feeble world. They were *dead*. Vanished. As if they had never existed, except for those tombstones, which Gabriel Todd had insisted on raising, even though both were buried far away. Janet stood there, thinking of the hundreds of other plantations and thousands of more modest homes where Southern parents and sisters and wives mourned their dead in the same anguished way, struggling to keep them alive in memory's pathetic glow. Recently the Louisville *Journal* had estimated the South had lost 150,000 men, the North 300,000—and the slaughter continued unabated, devouring lives like a monstrous, insatiable Moloch.

Gabriel Todd sat in the gazebo most of the day, steadily consuming a quart of bourbon to dull the pain of his lost sons and an almost lost war. By dinnertime he was often incapable of carrying on a conversation. But at this hour of the morning, he was reasonably coherent.

"Janet!" he called. "Give your ancient father a kiss for old times' sake."

She strolled into the gazebo and kissed him on the lips. He clutched her against him and she breathed his unwashed body odor and the sweetly sour smell of the bourbon on his breath. Why did her mind record these realistic details? It was so unfeminine. Somewhere in the creative process God had become confused and given Janet Todd a man's brain and a woman's body.

"Tell me some good news," he said as he released her. Janet smiled and recited:

> " 'Report of fashion in proud Italy
> Whose manner still our tardy apish nation
> limps after in base imitation.' "

An answering smile brought Gabriel Todd's wide creased face aglow. He responded to those lines from Shakespeare's *Richard II* with another quotation from the same play:

> " 'For gnarling sorrow hath less power to bite
> The man who mocks at it and sets it light.' "

Janet smiled and replied:

> " 'Teach thy necessity to reason thus
> There is no virtue like necessity.' "

Janet and her father had been playing this quotation game for over a decade. Shakespeare was another of Gabriel Todd's literary passions. On their summer trips north, they had never failed to stop in New York to see a performance by one of the great actors of the day, such as Edwin Booth in *Macbeth*. More than once they had gone down the river to Louisville to see a traveling troupe perform *Romeo and Juliet* or *The Merchant of Venice*.

With no warning, Janet's mind lurched out of control. Shocking words rampaged through it. *Has Richard II become your favorite play because it's about a man who thought he was a king and slowly discovered he was a noble fool?*

No! That thought was not only unworthy; it was untrue. Gabriel Todd had done his utmost to undo the blunder of declaring Kentucky neutral. He had helped to create this conspiracy to win the war with an uprising by the Democrats of the West. He had taken the idea to his old friend from Mexican War days, Confederate president Jefferson Davis, in Richmond. Colonel Todd had persuaded the members of the Kentucky delegation in the Confederate Congress to support it. He had recruited his own daughter to become the movement's courier.

"I've written to Adam Jameson," Janet said. "He seems to be in command of Morgan's cavalry at the moment. I told him this time we'll have the money and the guns waiting for our volunteers."

"Good, good."

Hopemont's butler, stooped, big-nosed old Joseph, appeared with a bottle of bourbon and a frosted glass of cracked ice on a tray. He put them on the folding table beside Gabriel Todd and departed without a word. Her father poured a hefty splash into the glass and sipped it reflectively.

"I want to end this filthy war as soon as possible. I want to see you here, with children at your skirts, before I die. You'll have five thousand acres in your name. I'm not pleading Adam Jameson's case if he doesn't stir your feelings, but—"

Janet turned away, a gesture that made it clear she had no interest in the subject. "I'm not sure what you'll get for dinner," she said. "Lillibet's taken to her bed again."

"I know."

"I wish you hadn't sold Maybelle, Father."

"I thought it was for the best, Janet," he said. "I was tryin' to put temptation out of reach of your brothers. She was just too *seductive*. I've been in too many houses where the father has to watch his mulatto grandchildren pickin' his corn or servin' his supper."

"So you've told me."

Was he also putting temptation out of his own way? Janet wondered. Jack Todd had been married and gone to Alabama when Maybelle was sold in 1861. Her brother

Andy made no secret (to Janet, at least) of finding less than respectable women in Louisville and Cincinnati.

Incredible, the way the mind—at least her mind—thrust such ugly questions to the forefront. Would she have cared if her father took Maybelle for his mistress? Her skin was a creamy brown, suggesting that somewhere in the past a male Todd had enjoyed her grandmother or great-grandmother. More than one rumor about slave mistresses was whispered behind fans at Kentucky parties.

"You women don't realize how fortunate you are, not bein' subject to such . . . such . . ."

As if he personified the unmentionable subject Gabriel Todd was trying to simultaneously evade and describe, Major Paul Stapleton leaped into vivid life in Janet's head. He was standing on the ferry dock, smiling in a curiously confident way. His short-brimmed officer's kepi was tilted forward on his head, suggesting a recklessness that the smile reinforced. The strong-boned sunburned face was dominated by eyes that could go from oval innocence to knowing slits in an instant, an epitome of his disconcerting blend of boyishness and maturity. He had his hands on his hips, suggesting a certain impatience with her. Yet his smile suggested he was sure she would satisfy his unspoken desires, sooner or later.

It may be sooner than you think, Major.

There it was again, that rebellious mind of hers, asserting a brazen indifference to conventional morality. Janet walked to the door of the gazebo and said, "Where the devil is Lucy? She promised me she was going to run all the way to the post office."

TWO

STANDING ON THE EDGE OF the sun-scorched court-house square in Keyport, Indiana, twenty-five-year-old Major Paul Stapleton struggled to control his wandering thoughts. A temperature of 106 degrees was turning his blue U.S. Army uniform into a sweat-soaked mess. In his head he was stripping off this symbol of his commitment to a life of discipline and duty and plunging into the wide, cool waters of the Ohio River, a few hundred yards away at the foot of Keyport's jagged bluffs.

On the Kentucky shore, the imaginative major picked his way over the twisted roots of gigantic cottonwood trees exposed by the Ohio's recurring floods. Soon he was on the upper front porch of Hopemont, the most splendid mansion in Daviess County. Through the open French doors he watched a slim black maid slip a chemise over dark-haired Janet Todd's head, flounce it over her breasts and draw it slowly down her sturdy body.

The vision flung Paul back to that boyhood day in Washington, D.C., when he passed the half-open door of his mother's bedroom and saw her dressing for one of her famous salons. Her Negro maid had been pulling a chemise down Caroline Kemble Stapleton's body in the same slow sensuous way. The smile on his mother's face had been strangely contented, as if the mere act of dressing created an inexplicable happiness.

How exotic women were, with their layers of clothes and their oblique elusive emotions. Janet was not as beautiful as his regal mother. Few women were. But Paul was certain Caroline Stapleton would like her, if things advanced to the point where introductions became necessary. They shared a readiness to confront the world with strong opinions. Five minutes with them made it clear that you were in the company of women who emanated pride and self-confidence.

Caroline Stapleton's approval of Janet Todd was important to the major. Although he was far from a momma's boy, Paul tried to avoid quarrels with his formidable mother. His oldest brother, Jonathan, and she quarreled about everything, from his choice of a wife to his Republican politics. For thirty years, membership in the Democratic Party had been as fundamental to the Stapleton family's consciousness as pride in their distinguished bloodline. More than once, Paul had heard his mother refer to Jonathan as "the apostate."

In an hour Paul would be greeting Janet Todd at the Ohio River ferry dock. Who knows how they might celebrate independence before the national holiday expired? In Janet's swift striding walk and quick imperious gestures Paul sensed a wildness that stirred similar vibrations in his own flesh. Marrying a soldier in the middle of a war made no sense—especially if he was wearing a uniform that stirred negative vibrations in the woman's heart. But if the woman discovered the soldier had decided to leave this rear area for one of the fighting fronts, pledging an affection that might grow permanent when the war's acrimony ended—and exchanging proof of that affection—was more than a possibility. Paul had heard enough stories around army campfires to make him hopeful. War repealed all sorts of moral laws.

On the rickety wooden platform local carpenters had constructed before the yellow brick courthouse, an earnest, tired-looking Union colonel named Lawson Schreiber was making a speech: "Our country's future is still at risk, gentlemen. This rebellion remains as formidable, yea, as awesome, as Satan! I've come home here to the county that our president, Abraham Lincoln, honored with his youthful presence to renew the strength of our regiment. I want two hundred volunteers! Don't let the rest of Indiana hear that Hunter County was forced to resort to the draft!"

The regimental band burst into "The Battle Hymn of the Republic." The colonel's shapely sixteen-year-old daughter, Dorothy Schreiber, began trilling the words:

"Mine eyes have seen the glory of
the coming of the Lord;
He is trampling out the vintage where the grapes of
wrath are stored."

Dorothy's voice faltered when she realized not a single person in the crowd was singing with her. The song, written by a New England woman named Howe, was not popular in southern Indiana. Into the square marched a company of the depleted Second Indiana Volunteers, locally known as "Lincoln's Own." The president had spent his young manhood on nearby Pigeon Creek, working at a variety of hardscrabble jobs, before moving on to fortune and fame in Illinois. The Volunteers' blue uniforms were threadbare, and there was little enthusiasm on their faces after three years of hard fighting. At the head of the paltry column, two privates carried a large banner with Lincoln's bearded face on a red background.

Beside Major Stapleton, diminutive Dr. Walter Yancey swigged from a flask and said, "Old Abe on a field of blood. Seems about right, don't you think, Major?" Dr. Yancey's mouth was a wry zero in the middle of his scraggly brown beard. He had at least twenty South Carolina relatives in the Confederate Army.

"Will Colonel Schreiber raise two hundred men?" Paul asked.

"He'll be lucky to raise twenty," said Andrew Conway, the burly black-mustached editor of the local Democratic newspaper, the *Keyport Record*. "Old Abe has sort of lost his appeal hereabouts." Conway was wearing a black-and-white checked suit and a derby set at a cocky angle. The son of a Kentucky congressman, he had crossed the Ohio to become the Democratic boss of Hunter County.

Having grown up in Washington, D.C., and urban New Jersey, Major Stapleton often felt like a foreigner in southern Indiana. The name Stapleton, his late father's fame as a Democratic Party spokesman in the U.S. Senate before the war, carried no weight here. The local folk were complacently unimpressed by big names or big cities east or west. Their world was rooted in the dark loamy soil of the Ohio Valley and they were well satisfied with it.

Paul had tried to tell himself to be satisfied with it too. He had come here under orders from a Union Army major general who happened to be his brother. Major Stapleton had survived two serious wounds in the savage battles of the war's first two slaughterous years. General Jonathan Stapleton said Paul had earned the right to remain out of the line of fire for the rest of the contest.

"One of us has to stay alive," Jonathan said, silencing Paul's attempt to protest his exile. There were no other heirs to the millions of dollars that Stapleton-owned factories, railroads, and banks were piling up in New Jersey's booming wartime economy. But the argument carried less and less weight with Paul as his health improved and newspapers reported West Point classmates like George Armstrong Custer winning fame on the battlefield. He was already at work on a letter to the adjutant general of the army, asking for reassignment.

Dr. Yancey passed his flask to Andrew Conway; he offered it to Paul, who declined it with a brief shake of his head. A lot of homemade Kentucky and Indiana bourbon was going from hand to hand among the three hundred men standing in clusters on the hot cobble-stones. About two-thirds were Democrats like Conway and Yancey, the rest Republicans. Almost every man was carrying a gun.

Several recent recruiting rallies in southern Indiana had degenerated into shoot-outs. Major Stapleton was determined not to let this happen in Keyport. The square was surrounded by the 100 members of Troop A of the Twentieth Indiana Cavalry. On their belts hung billy clubs and Colt pistols. Paul had trained them in the art and science of breaking up a riot before it started. All he needed to do was nod to Sergeant Moses Washington, six feet, two inches tall, with a face like a thundercloud, and they would wade into the crowd, clubs at the ready, pistols even more so.

Jagged white pain lanced through Major Stapleton's forehead. His Gettysburg wound was about to tell him something: *Jesus Christ, Paul, you'd think that Confederate bullet went through your brain. Can't you see your wonderful troopers are more likely to start a riot than stop one? Can't you see the color of their goddamn faces?*

Almost as if he were a secret partner of the wound, Dr. Yancey completed this bitter mental trajectory: "If I were you, Major, I'd request another hundred men. You may find yourself fightin' for your life in a month or two. Tell Lincoln to make them white, this time."

Major Stapleton's eyes roved the impassive black faces of his troopers. "My boys are good soldiers, Doctor Yancey. I've seen to that. They haven't so much as raided a henhouse since they arrived."

"Each one of them could be the reincarnation of Achilles. But they're niggers, Major. Don't you see how inappropriate—to use the mildest word I know—it is for them to be policin' white men?"

"I don't see what their color has to do with it," Major Stapleton said. "They're American soldiers. Every one of them was born in this country. Would you prefer a troop of Germans? Or Irish? Then you'd really have something to complain about."

Flashes of white pain tore through Major Stapleton's head. *How long can you keep lying this way, Paulie?* the Gettysburg wound asked.

I'm not lying. I'm stating U.S. government policy, Major Stapleton replied.

Of course he saw what the color of his troopers had to do with it. But he had to deny it. He was a servant of the federal government. He had spent four years at the United States Military Academy imbibing the West Pointer's creed—duty, honor, country. The war had taught him that duty required a certain amount of somewhat dishonorable lying to sustain the country. Since Gettysburg, however, he had found it impossible to lie to himself. The Confederate bullet seemed to have opened his head to ruthless infusions of honesty.

As the last chords of "The Battle Hymn of the Republic" died away, a voice in the crowd shouted, "Hey, Schreiber, do you think maybe General Early's in Washington by now?"

According to the latest news from the East, General Jubal Early's Confederate Army had routed two Union armies in Virginia's Shenandoah Valley and was marching on Washington, D.C. "I only know what I read in the papers about that problem," Schreiber said.

"Which butcher will these new boys fight for? Old 'Lysses No Surrender Grant?" someone else shouted.

In the last two months, General Ulysses S. Grant had lost 60,000 men in massive assaults on General Robert E. Lee's Army of Northern Virginia, entrenched in the forests of the Wilderness before Richmond. Five of Paul's West Point classmates had died in the fighting. A letter from a classmate who had survived ripped through Paul's head: *All our generals should be wearing dunce caps, including Grant. Haven't we learned by now what happens when you make frontal assaults on an entrenched enemy?*

"Lincoln's Own will continue to serve with the western armies," Colonel Schreiber said.

"Tell us how many you buried after Chickamauga!" someone shouted.

Ten months ago the Union Army of the Cumberland had been defeated by the Confederate Army of Tennessee at Chickamauga Creek, near Chattanooga. Only a desperate stand by General George H. Thomas, the Cumberland army's second in command, had prevented a rout that might have left Kentucky and Indiana exposed to a Southern invasion.

"Are you going to let these traitors ruin this rally?" hissed a voice behind Major Stapleton. He turned to confront the gaunt face and glaring eyes of Captain Simeon Otis.

"Isn't it better to let them have their say?" the major replied.

Like Paul, influential relatives had persuaded the army to send Captain Otis to this theoretically peaceful part of the Union to recuperate. Pneumonia rather than a bullet had laid Otis low. He had yet to hear a shot fired on a battlefield. In Keyport, the Democrats soon nicknamed Otis "John Brown Jr." after the New England–financed fanatic who had raided the Harper's Ferry federal arsenal in 1859 hoping to arm the slaves and start a race war. Harvard-taught hatred of the South and slavery often made Otis's slender frame vibrate with righteous indignation.

Up on the stage, Colonel Schreiber was proudly describing his regiment's performance at Chickamauga. "By the time the rebels gave up the fight, General Thomas himself congratulated me and said he wished he had a dozen more regiments from Indiana."

"Tell us how many you buried. I dare you!" the same voice shouted.

"Our losses were heavy," Colonel Schreiber said. "But I can assure you they died like men, with their faces to the enemy. You can be proud of every mother's son of them."

"Every mother's son of them got what they deserved!" someone else shouted.

"Yeah!" howled another Democrat. "What every nigger-loving one of them deserves."

"Now wait a minute," Colonel Schreiber said. "There ain't a man in this regiment who's fightin' for the nigger. We're fightin' for the Union."

"Do you deny Old Abe's fightin' for the nigger?" someone howled. "Haven't you read his Constipation Proclamation?"

"More like his Diarrhea Proclamation."

"Either way, it's a lot of shit!"

Laughter swept the crowd. Colonel Schreiber wiped his streaming forehead and cheeks with a red handkerchief. "I'm not here to debate politics. I'll be over in Gentry's store, ready to give any man who signs up with us a cash bounty of three hundred dollars."

"Liar or fool!" bellowed a half-dozen voices.

"Liar or fool!" the crowd chanted.

"You've let the Democrats destroy this rally, Major," Captain Otis said. "That regiment won't get ten men now."

Maybe that's ten more than they deserve to get, the Gettysburg wound whispered in Major Stapleton's aching skull. "Then they'll have to go to the draft," Paul said. "Worse things could happen."

"Moreover!" Colonel Schreiber shouted above the din. "Through the generosity of our friend and neighbor, Colonel Henry Gentry, I'm prepared to add a hundred dollars to that bounty for every man who signs up today!"

"Tell Henry to shove his money up Lincoln's ass!" shouted another Democrat.

Working his way toward them through the crowd was Colonel Henry Gentry in the flesh. His big body swayed erratically, as if the arm he had lost at the battle of Shiloh in 1862 had forever unbalanced him. Those who knew him better were inclined to blame bourbon for his wobble. His once-handsome face, with a Roman nose that should have guaranteed dignity, was marred by the sagging cheeks, the jowls, of middle age, compounded by the protruding veins of the heavy drinker. Even now, when he was relatively sober, he had the slightly dazed manner of a man who had barely survived a carriage or railroad accident that had left him in a state of constant apprehension.

"Major Stapleton," Gentry said, "I'm sorry to spoil your holiday. We've got a report that as many as five deserters are hiding out at the Fitzsimmons farm."

Paul stifled an impulse to curse like an Irish sergeant. "We'll be on the road as soon as this meeting is over," he said.

"Maybe when you drag them back in handcuffs you can persuade them to enlist in Lincoln's Own," Dr. Yancey said.

"I wish that were possible, Walter," Gentry said. "But the army doesn't give deserters a second chance."

"What's the difference whether they get shot at sunrise by a firing squad or at moonrise by a rebel?" Andrew Conway said. "Ain't it cannon fodder your murderous friend Lincoln needs?"

"Now, Andy," Gentry said. "You know in your heart Abe doesn't think that way."

"I've engaged to meet your cousin, Miss Todd, at the ferry landing, Colonel," Major Stapleton said. "I hope you can serve as my replacement and express appropriate regrets."

"Now that's the sort of service I'm ready to volunteer for," Dr. Yancey said.

"Precisely why I asked Colonel Gentry," Stapleton said, smiling at the dissolute doctor.

In spite of his size—he was barely five feet—Yancey was known in more than one town along the river as a lothario. Before the war, he and fellow bachelors Gentry and Conway had made frequent trips to Louisville and Cincinnati, where they found ladies of the evening eager to assuage their unwed status.

"Are you aware that Miss Todd is more or less pledged to my nephew, Adam Jameson?" Andrew Conway said. "He's a colonel in Morgan's cavalry. If I were you, Major, I'd sleep with a loaded pistol on my night table. Those boys have crossed the Ohio once. They might do it again, anytime."

"Risks are a soldier's stock in trade, Mr. Conway," Paul said.

"I would say Janet Todd is worth more than a little risk," Colonel Gentry said.

Paul was about to agree when Conway replied with a smile that was almost a sneer. "Come on, Henry. You above all should know what a Kentucky girl can do to a man."

"They're very good at breaking hearts," Gentry said. "I'm sure Major Stapleton knows that's part of the risk."

Had a Kentucky woman broken Gentry's heart? For the first time Paul felt some respect—and even a little sympathy—for this mutilated man. Although Gentry had welcomed Paul into his home and been unfailingly cordial, he spent most of his time in a cellar office getting drunk. He had revealed little or nothing about his personal life, except a boyhood friendship with Abraham Lincoln.

"I like to think broken hearts are like battlefield

wounds," Paul said. "Eventually they heal. And they leave behind a certain vibration of glory."

"Glory!" Conway said. "You must be the last man in this war who believes in that old horse, Major."

"Not at all," Henry Gentry said. "I still believe in it. Especially the kind that's left behind by a broken heart."

"Unbelievable," Dr. Yancey said to Andrew Conway. "Amelia's still got her hooks into him."

The recruiting rally was over. The crowd in the courthouse square had dwindled by half. No one seemed to be going anywhere near the Gentry store, just off the square on Main Street, where Colonel Schreiber waited to pay recruits $400 in federal greenbacks—more than a year's salary for a field hand. Although no shots had been fired, the Democrats had unquestionably won the battle.

It's not your fault. Paul's Gettysburg wound whispered. *It's that idiot in the White House.*

"Sergeant," Paul said to Moses Washington. "Get the men back to camp on the double and saddle up fifty horses. We've got some deserters to catch before we can celebrate Independence Day."

A shadow of uneasiness in the sergeant's eyes suggested he was aware of the incongruity of chasing deserters on the Fourth of July. Major Stapleton was more concerned about the mockery he was certain to hear in Janet Todd's sultry southern voice when she asked him about his latest adventure on behalf of the federal government's quest for victory in this apparently endless war.

THREE

IN THE DARK, DANK ICEHOUSE on Rose Hill, the next plantation down the Ohio from Hopemont, Janet Todd's body servant, Lucy, crouched beside Aunt Rachel, a wrinkled gray-haired slave who was reading aloud the letter to Colonel Adam Jameson by the light of a flickering candle. "Read it one more time," Lucy said. "I wants to get it word for word."

Aunt Rachel was shaking all over; whether from the cold or fear it was hard to tell. But she began reading the letter for the third time. "Faster," Lucy said.

Lucy had asked Miss Janet to teach her to read. But Colonel Todd said no, no, no and no. Niggers who learned to read ran away. Aunt Rachel had learned to read thirty years ago. She was the last slave Mrs. Conway, the old mistress of Rose Hill, had taught to read so they could learn about Jesus in the Bible. Mrs. Conway got a letter from Virginia telling her that her brother had gotten his head chopped off by a slave named Nat Turner. He tried to start a revolution to put the black people on top and the white people on the bottom. If that didn't prove he was crazy, what did? But you could not blame black people for going crazy when you think of what happened to some of them.

Maybe Nat Turner had a sister like Maybelle. Too pretty to let in the house because the white men would be after her and too pretty to work in the fields because she was worth a lot more money working somewhere else. Slaves like Maybelle were a powerful temptation to owners like Colonel Todd. He had two wild sons.

Jack went off to some expensive northern college named Yale and got himself tamed down and married a rich girl in Alabama. But Andy, his younger brother, no one could tame him. He got thrown out of another northern college and ran up gambling debts in Lexington at the races and God knows where else and suddenly Colonel Todd needed money. That's when he took Maybelle to Lexington and let them sell her to a whorehouse in New Orleans.

That was just before the war started and people began thinking of running away because they heard President Abe Lincoln was going to free all the slaves and Colonel Todd said before that happened he'd sell them all to Brazil, they were his property and no damn government was going to touch his property. Before the war no one had run away because Colonel Todd told them white people in the North didn't want niggers in their backyards and he read them stories from newspapers about whites beating up niggers and Lucy asked Miss Janet if they were true and she said yes, that was why it was better to stay in Kentucky and live a quiet life as her body servant.

But every time Lucy thought of Maybelle in that whorehouse in New Orleans and Colonel Todd using the money to pay off Mr. Andy's gambling debts she was tempted to run away and when the war started she didn't want the slave owners to win no matter how much they spouted about lying Yankees and low-down Irish and Germans.

When Aunt Rachel finished reading the letter Lucy would take a dab of honey and seal it good enough to fool the woman who ran the Confederate Post Office in a cave near Hawesville. The Confederates had post offices all over Kentucky in caves and barns. They had riders who carried the mail to Virginia or Tennessee or wherever it was supposed to go, right under the noses of the Union men.

Lucy wished she had someone else to read Miss Janet's letters for her. Rose Hill was run by Rogers Jameson, Colonel Adam Jameson's father. He was the one who told Lucy that Maybelle had been sold to a whorehouse. He said that was always what happened to pretty niggers especially light-colored ones like Maybelle. Rogers Jameson looked forward to getting to New Orleans when the war ended so he could enjoy Maybelle. He said he tried to buy her from Colonel Todd but old Master was too scared of Mrs. Todd to say yes. So the colonel sold her way down south where Mrs. Todd wouldn't know nothing about it.

Whenever Lucy started thinking about that whorehouse she knew what Maybelle was liable to do: kill herself. They had seen their mother try to do it when Colonel Todd said he was going to sell two of their brothers, Luther and Tom, south to help pay the feed bills when the weevil got into the wheat crop. She cut her wrists with a paring knife and bled all over the kitchen. Lucy would never forget the day she came downstairs and found Maybelle mopping up the blood, screaming, "Momma! Momma!" There was blood everywhere. Lucy mopped it up too and Mrs. Todd poured hot wax in the slashes to stop the bleeding.

Colonel Todd changed his mind about selling Luther and Tom. A month later they ran away. No one at Hopemont ever heard from them again. Maybe by now they were in the Union Army, like those troopers in Keyport. A lot of the army's black soldiers were runaway slaves. Anyway, Colonel Todd couldn't get them back even though he tried and damned the Republicans because they wouldn't obey the laws of the United States as passed by Congress.

Sergeant Moses Washington told Lucy the Confederates were the lawbreakers. He was as dark as Lucy, but he could talk a streak about the Declaration of Independence and the Constitution like he was Abe Lincoln in blackface. She had gotten to know the sergeant since Miss Janet started visiting Colonel Gentry's house every other weekend because she was sweet on that Yankee major named Stapleton.

From what Miss Janet just told Adam Jameson, there was more to it than being sweet. But Lucy could tell politics didn't really change what Miss Janet felt every time she looked at Major Stapleton. He was a lot handsomer than Adam Jameson, who always reminded everyone of a bear. That had been his school nickname because when he walked he rocked from side to side as if his legs couldn't carry all his weight. He was strong as a bear too, he could take a log as thick as a man's neck and bust it over his knee. But he wasn't much smarter than a bear, from things Miss Janet said about him walking home from school when they were kids.

Aunt Rachel finished mumbling out the letter through her toothless gums one more time. Lucy recited it back to her and Aunt Rachel sucked her lower lip halfway down her throat and said, "If they catch you they'll whip you silly. I think you's crazy to do this."

"The whole world's crazy, Aunt Rachel," Lucy said.

FOUR

"COULDN'T BE ANY HOTTER IN hell, could it, Major?" Sergeant Moses Washington said.

"I hope not," Major Stapleton said, with a wry grin.

The sergeant returned the grin. Did he know from the Gentry house servants that Janet Todd was coming to the Independence Day party? Did he suspect the major was thinking about the commandment he might soon be breaking with her? Paul hoped not. If anything happened between him and Janet Todd, he would not brag about it, Walter Yancey style. He hoped the sergeant assumed Major Stapleton was referring to past sins of the sort soldiers committed when a weekend pass and a woman of easy virtue coincided.

Captain Simeon Otis, riding on Paul's right, gave them both a severe frown. He undoubtedly disapproved of what soldiers did on weekend passes as vehemently as he denounced slave owners and slavery. He had already hinted to Paul that he thought Colonel Henry Gentry was much too friendly with his slave-owning relatives and friends in Kentucky.

Behind them rode fifty troopers in Union blue. Major Stapleton had made good cavalrymen out of these unlikely candidates for glory. They were all proud of being men on horseback, contemptuous of infantry "creepers." Paul had added to their confidence by arming them with seven-shot Spencer carbines, the gun of choice for sophisticated Union cavalrymen. He was sure he could depend on them in a fight—at least against the sort of ragtag resistance they usually met from deserters.

Moses Washington was the key to this success. He and Paul shared a New Jersey background. The sergeant had grown up in Monmouth County, not far from Kemble Manor, the Stapleton summer home. Washington had been locally famous as a prizefighter, winning matches against white and black opponents. For him to turn up in Indiana in a Union uniform seemed a good omen. It helped Paul accept this assignment.

Paul had made Washington his sergeant and partner in instilling pride and confidence in his fellow blacks, almost all ex-slaves recruited in Kentucky. Granted all this, why did the thought, the fact, of their blackness start a dull ache in his chest around the two-year-old wound he had received at the battle of Antietam?

Paul's emancipation wound, his mother called it, mocking as usual every act of Lincoln's administration. After the Union stand at Antietam forced Lee's army to retreat into Virginia, Lincoln had issued his stunning proclamation, changing the goal of the war from saving the Union to freeing the slaves.

Major Stapleton thrust Caroline Kemble Stapleton out of his mind along with the politics of the war and concentrated on the military task confronting him. Like his friend George Armstrong Custer, he told himself that fighting a war was simpler and more satisfying than thinking about it.

Helpful in this mental maneuver was the western landscape. Although this part of southern Indiana was a series of rippling knolls and dales, each time they crested a rise Paul glimpsed the vastness of the American interior. It was easy to imagine the endless miles of prairie to the north and west, a kind of earthy inland sea stretching to the horizon. In its heartland, America was more than a country; it was a world. Somehow this immensity added an apocalyptic dimension to the war. It was too huge to comprehend, much less control.

In a half hour the red slope-roofed Fitzsimmons

farmhouse undulated in the heat waves rising from the scorched earth. The place looked deserted. There was not even a chicken moving in the yard. Major Stapleton raised his arm and the detachment clopped to a halt. Horses nickered and snorted. Hornets buzzed around a nest in a nearby bush.

"It looks too quiet," Paul said.

"Maybe they knew we was comin' and skedaddled," Sergeant Washington said.

"We should have come by night," Captain Simeon Otis said. "Keyport—the whole county—is infested with traitors."

"Sergeant Washington and I will take twenty-five men in at a trot and surround the place," Paul said. "If there's no one in the house or barn, we'll trample the crops. Captain Otis, take the rest of the troop and set up a blocking position at this end of the property."

By now they were professionals in this dirty business. They knew if deserters heard a detachment of cavalry heading their way, they tried to hide in a farm's surrounding corn or wheat fields. They seldom wanted to go too far from their refuge. They never knew who might betray them. Although these days, with most of the Democrats in Hunter County against the war, they had a lot more friends than enemies.

Captain Otis began stationing the troopers at intervals along the bottom of the field. Major Stapleton, Sergeant Washington and the other half of the detachment cantered up the dusty road to the farmhouse. Paul dismounted and rapped on the door. A tall thin once-pretty brunette opened it. "What do you want?" she asked.

"I'm afraid we have to search your house, Miss," Paul said. "We've got a report that you're harboring deserters."

"Your reporter is a damn liar. Where's your search warrant?"

"We don't need one, Miss. Under the authority granted the military in time of war, we have the right to search and if necessary seize anyone who's interfering with the government's efforts to suppress the rebellion."

"There's no one here but my mother and father and they're both sick. Sick in body and soul since my brother got killed at Vicksburg. Sick of people like you takin' over our country." She glared from Paul to the black troopers. Kentucky Negroes were not popular in Indiana.

Paul sighed and wiped his streaming neck with his kerchief. "We'll give the country back to you as soon as this war's over, Miss."

Paul turned to Sergeant Washington. "Take five men and search the house. Load your guns. I'll take another five and search the barn."

"Why should they load their guns?" the woman asked.

"We had a man almost killed last month by a fellow who fired through a door."

"If I had a gun I'd kill you all," the young woman snarled.

Washington draw his big Colt pistol and ordered five men to load their Spencer carbines. They clumped into the house. Paul led another five men into the dim barn. There was nothing there but two horses munching in feed bags.

Back at the house, Washington soon appeared with his squad. "Nothin' here but what she says, Major," the sergeant reported "Two old sick people upstairs. Cussed us worse than she did."

"Are they in the wheat?" Paul asked the woman.

"I don't know what you're talkin' about," she said.

"I hate to ruin your crop."

"Liar."

"Begin the game, Sergeant."

Washington told Little Eddie, their thirteen-year-old bugler, to sound squadrons left and right. The troopers split into squads and headed for the greenish brown wheat. By now they could perform this routine in their sleep. They took up positions in two facing lines of seven horses each, forming a lane. The remaining eleven men and the sergeant went crunching down the lane between them, cutting a destructive swath but making it impossible for anyone hiding in the wheat to escape the methodical mass of men and horses coming at him.

Watching in the doorway, the young woman began to weep. "Bastards," she said. "You Republicans are all bastards."

"I'm a Democrat, Miss. Born and bred," Major Stapleton said.

"That makes you even more despicable."

Blam. A gunshot. At the far end of the field. *Blam. Blam. Blam.* They weren't Spencer carbines. They were rifles. *Crack* went a carbine. *Crack crack crack blam, blam.* A dozen shots erupted and a swirl of gunsmoke rose in the humid air. The deserters were shooting it out.

"Sabers, Sergeant!" Paul shouted to Washington. "Bugler, sound charge!"

Little Eddie blasted the staccato patter of notes for a charge into the glaring sunshine. Paul leaped on his horse and pounded down the road toward Captain Simeon Otis and his detachment. Two-thirds of the way there he found four troopers riding up the road, their faces cartoons of terror.

"They's ten, maybe twenty of 'em, Major!" one wailed. "They done shot the captain and two or three others of us—"

"Draw sabers and follow me!"

They wheeled their horses and galloped after Paul. He was not at all sure they would be any good in a fight, but he was fairly confident of the men following Sergeant Washington. Paul felt a rush of pleasure. It was his first action since Gettysburg, his first chance to be a soldier again.

Riding in the road, which dipped below the wheat field, he could only see the upper torsos of the troopers and the heads of their horses. Each had his saber ready. They looked as tough and confident as Washington.

"Give them a cavalry yell, Sergeant!" Paul shouted.

"Freedom!" the sergeant bellowed. "Here come the battle cry of freeeeeeedom!"'

"Yeahhhhhhhhhhh!" shouted the troopers. "Yeahhhh-hhhhh!"

Little Eddie managed to rip off another charge call. They surged through the wheat in two lines. The heat, the uncertain footing the horses found among the wheat stalks, slowed everything to a dreamlike pace, as if time itself had faltered in this rural inferno. Shots continued to resound in the fiery distance.

On the road Paul and his four horsemen neared the end of the field two or three hundred yards ahead of the troopers in the wheat. Four men in dust-covered homespun clothes emerged from the side road on horses that belonged to the black troopers. Two fired pistols at Paul and raced off down the road after their friends. The bullets hissed several feet over his head.

"Tell Sergeant Washington to follow me with the rest of the men!" Paul shouted and pounded down the road after the runaways.

The winding road dipped and twisted through the wheat fields, making it difficult to keep the fugitives in sight. Sergeant Washington caught up to Paul after about a mile of hard riding and shouted, "Captain Otis's hurt bad!"

That's good news, whispered the Gettysburg wound. "Anyone else?" Paul asked.

"Fred Clay, Luther Jenkins and Smiley Peters hit too."

"Did we get any of them?"

"One. He's dead."

In another mile they reached a crossroads. Paul reined in his horse and signaled a stop. There was no way to tell from the muddle of hoof tracks in the dust whether the fugitives had turned left or right. "Let's go back and tend the wounded. We'll catch these bastards some other day," Paul said.

Back at the Fitzsimmons farm, they found Captain Simeon Otis slumped against a cottonwood tree, the front of his uniform drenched in blood. He had been hit in the shoulder. "They fired without warning," he whispered. "We never had a chance."

Nearby lay the three black troopers. One, Sam Peters, had been hit in the head. He was barely breathing. The other two, Fred Clay and Luther Jenkins, had leg wounds.

"Captain done run away; that's what he done, Major!" called Jasper Jones, a short stocky trooper who had enlisted in New Jersey with Moses Washington. Jones had a big mouth in more ways than one. His lower lip extended a good inch beyond his upper lip. He jutted his narrow chin at Otis.

"I was wounded. I—" Otis began to weep. "He's right. I ran away. We all ran away."

"Not usn'," said another Clay, whose name was Brutus. He was a brother of the wounded Clay.

Major Stapleton took charge. "Let's not worry about who did what. Let's get the wounded to a doctor. We'll figure out tactics to make sure this doesn't happen again."

Mentally, Major Stapleton rebuked himself. He should have sent Otis to the farmhouse and handled the blocking position himself. But he knew how obnoxious Otis would be to the Fitzsimmonses. Not that his own attempt at civility had made much difference.

He sent Sergeant Washington and two troopers back to the farmhouse to commandeer a horse and wagon for the wounded. They returned with a frightened-looking dark-haired kid in the straw-filled wagon.

"Found this guy hidin' in the hay, Major," Washington said.

"Are you a deserter?" Paul asked. The boy did not look old enough to be in the army.

"I got sick. I came home to see my mother," he said. He began to blubber.

"You can explain it at your court-martial," Paul said.

The deserter crouched in the back of the wagon while they loaded the wounded men onto the straw. They draped the body of the dead skirmisher over the empty saddle of one of the wounded troopers and rode slowly back to Keyport through the ferocious heat.

On July 21, 1864, they would celebrate the third anniversary of the first battle of Bull Run. Major Stapleton found himself remembering his brother, Jonathan Stapleton, confidently predicting that slavery had made the South soft and an army of 75,000 righteous northern men would suppress the secessionist rebellion in three months.

The last time Paul had seen brother Jonathan, he was recovering from a bullet in the knee that had left him with a permanent limp. His hair had turned snow-white, and he had an ugly scar on his right cheek where another southern bullet had struck him during the second battle of Bull Run, knocking out numerous teeth on that side of his mouth. Most of the New Jerseyans Jonathan had recruited for the regiment he raised in response to President Lincoln's call for 75,000 volunteers were dead or wounded. Jonathan was now a major general in command of a division. He recently had confided to Paul that he feared the war might last another five years.

"You know what I think, Major?" Sergeant Washington said. "Them horse thieves wasn't deserters. They was local Democrats. That thing was an ambush. They used this poor sucker we found in the straw as an excuse to shoot us up and steal some government horses."

"I'm inclined to agree with you."

"Could be a sign of big trouble ahead."

Paul remembered Dr. Yancey's warning that he might

soon need another hundred men. "You might be right about that too," he said.

Major Stapleton's agreement with Sergeant Washington was mostly a formality. He did not really think the trouble would be bigger than they could handle. As a professional soldier, he actually liked the idea of a local uprising. It would be an interesting opportunity to develop new tactics and strategies that might prove useful when the army occupied the conquered South. It might also be dangerous enough to impress Janet Todd with his daring, even if she disapproved of his politics.

FIVE

IN THE FRONT PARLOR OF The Grange, the Gentry mansion on the outskirts of Keyport, Colonel Henry Todd Gentry's mother, Millicent Todd Gentry, was playing the grand piano with her usual heavy hand. Her grandniece Janet Todd was singing "The Bonnie Blue Flag" in a lilting contralto. In his cellar office, Henry Gentry asked himself who else but Todds would play—or sing—a Confederate war song in the home of the Union military commander of southern Indiana?

More than once, Gentry had come close to advising his friend Abraham Lincoln not to marry a Todd. Henry's mother had reduced his father to putty before Willard Gentry died of heart disease when his son was nineteen. Henry was not surprised when Abe later remarked in a letter that one *d* was enough for God but not for the Todds. A more high-toned, imperious family never inhabited the earth.

Janet Todd seemed pressed from the same mold. At first Gentry was tempted to warn Major Paul Stapleton of the true proportions of the risk he was taking. Now he was encouraging the match in the name of military necessity. Irony. Gentry had begun to think this war was a story not of blood and iron but of blood and irony.

The colonel swigged from a bottle of bourbon on the desk of his subterranean headquarters. He had moved into the cellar when he returned from Shiloh minus his right arm. It seemed a good place to hide what was left of his body and his self-esteem. Not only was he a military failure—Lincoln's Own regiment had taken casualties of 50 percent at Shiloh—he was a lost soul. He resigned his colonel's commission and stocked the cellar with enough bourbon to keep himself in a permanent state of amnesia.

Gentry could not begin to understand why God had chosen to disfigure Uncle Henry, favorite host of the playgirls of Louisville and Cincinnati. Walter Yancey and Andy Conway, his favorite freethinking partners in sin, tried to cheer him up, but the war had already begun undermining their friendship.

Lincoln had rescued Gentry from oblivion with one of his rarest letters. The president began with a refusal to accept Gentry's resignation as colonel. Next, Abe reminded the self-pitying hero that he had been the worst right-handed horseshoe pitcher in Indiana. Maybe he could do better left-handed. As for the ladies of Cincinnati and Louisville, Abe was sure they would be delighted to learn Gentry was home from the war and had not lost anything *essential*. Finally, in a single pseudopompous sentence, he had appointed Gentry director of military intelligence and chief bashaw for the government in Indiana and signed it: "A. Lincoln, Dictator."

The embattled Republican governor of Indiana, who depended totally on money Lincoln sent him from Washington, had made Gentry the commander of a three-county district along the Ohio. Gentry soon decided Lincoln needed military and political intelligence from the area and used his private funds to create a network of informers.

The intelligence director's cellar office was especially suitable on this particular day. The business he was conducting was subterranean in every sense of the word. In the dim light from the half-window that looked out on the garden, Janet Todd's body servant, Lucy, was reciting her owner's latest letter. Lucy's voice was low and the words were rushed and frightened. She knew what she was risking.

"She say you must come because nothin' matter now but victory. Otherwise the dead won't rest easy."

"But she didn't mention when the guns and money would arrive?"

"No s'r."

"I need a date."

"I'll listen hard, Major. I surely will. What about my sister Maybelle? You found her in New Orleans?"

"I'm trying my best."

"Federal government runs New Orleans now, don't they?"

"I told you—I'm trying to find her. But it isn't easy. They may have changed her name—"

"I won't quit on you if you find her. I swears it 'fore God."

Lucy was not stupid. She could read Gentry's devious spymaster's mind. She could see into the recesses of his hardened heart. Gentry understood, now, why no one in George Washington's army wanted anything to do with spying at first. Nothing corrupted a man faster than intelligence work. To ferret out the truths necessary to win the war, the spymaster lied or told half-truths to almost everyone.

"We need a date. The exact day."

"I'll try to learn it."

"Colonel Gentry! Can you spare me a few minutes?"

It was Major Paul Stapleton, back from the Fitzsimmons farm. Gentry realized the piano had ceased. Female voices rippled behind the major at the head of the cellar stairs.

Terror shredded Lucy's oval face. "Just a minute, Major!" Gentry called. "Let me light you down the stairs!"

He signaled Lucy to vanish. In sixty seconds she had slipped out the storm cellar door into the garden between the house and the barn. Gentry lit a candle and lumbered to the foot of the stairs. Major Stapleton clumped down the wooden steps in his cavalryman's boots and followed Gentry into his office.

"I've got some unpleasant news to report," Major Stapleton said. "We ran into an ambush at the Fitzsimmons farm. Four men, including Captain Otis, have been wounded. We killed one of the attackers. Maybe you can help identify the body."

"What a hell of a thing. On the Fourth of July."

"Another reason why I think it was an ambush," Major Stapleton said.

"Is Otis badly hurt?" Gentry asked.

"He thinks he is. I've sent for Doctor Yancey. I trust he'll treat my troopers as well."

"I'm sure he will."

They went out the cellar door and around to the barn where the troopers had deposited the wounded and the body of the dead ambusher. Gentry stared at the swarthy face of the corpse, the pupils rolled back in final agony. "My God," he said. "That's one of Rogers Jameson's hired men, Frankie Worth."

"Who's Rogers Jameson?"

"He owns Rose Hill, on the Kentucky shore. He runs a big sawmill on this side of the river. He's Andy Conway's brother-in-law—and the chief backer of his newspaper."

"Is he a friend of yours?"

"A friendly enemy would be more exact."

"Is Frankie a deserter?"

Gentry shook his head. "He's a Democrat. You couldn't have gotten him or anyone else in his family into the army."

"I'm in favor of delivering this body to Mr. Jameson—and searching his sawmill and his plantation," Major Stapleton said. "They stole four of our horses."

It was remarkable, Gentry thought, how the major's boyish face could become an inflexible mask when he assumed a military role. Did they teach such transformations at West Point? Or was it an inherited trait?

"That would be a rather cruel thing to do," Gentry said. "Frankie's mother lives just down the road from the sawmill. She might be there."

"The bullets this fellow and his friends put into my men were rather cruel, too," Major Stapleton said.

They faced each other there in the hot barn, the amateur and the professional soldier. "Do I have your permission to conduct a search, Colonel?"

"I think not," Gentry said. "Rogers Jameson is too smart to leave any evidence around—if he's linked in any way with this ambush. I'll send one of my field hands to tell him to pick up the body."

The clop of horses' hooves interrupted them. Coming through the gate of Gentry's property was a massive blond-haired man on a buckboard drawn by two fine white horses. As usual, Rogers Jameson was hatless in the summer sun. His face was tanned a mulatto brown. Beside him was a younger man who could have been a double for the dead Frankie.

"Here he is now," Gentry said. "That's Frankie's twin brother, Pete Worth, with him."

"Isn't this a good argument to conduct a search? He's obviously trying to head one off," Major Stapleton said.

Gentry hurried across the lawn toward the buckboard as Rogers Jameson climbed down from the seat. The sheer size of the man was still intimidating. Jameson was about Gentry's height—six feet—but twice as wide, with shoulders the size of a bull's haunches and a huge head. Years of poling flatboats on the Ohio and Mississippi had given him arms the size of an ordinary man's thigh. Age and good eating had added a layer of fat to his hulking torso, but he still moved with the agility of an athlete. Only one man had ever thrown Rogers Jameson in a wrestling match: Abe Lincoln.

"Does this visit have something to do with Frankie Worth?" Gentry asked.

"Where is he?" Jameson said.

"His body is in the barn."

"Killed by your niggers. How can you face yourself in the mirror each morning, Henry?"

"He was killed by my troopers, sir," Major Stapleton said. He had followed Gentry down to the dusty oval in front of the main house. "Killed after he and his friends fired on them without provocation."

"That's not what Pete here tells me," Jameson said. "They were at the Fitzsimmons farm for a Fourth of July party. Pete here's courtin' Sarah Fitzsimmons. The niggers and their captain, John Brown Jr., just rode up, said they was deserters, and tried to arrest them. Frankie told them to go to hell and they shot him dead."

"That is a complete and total fabrication, sir," Major Stapleton said.

"I have no interest in listenin' to lies told by Abe Lincoln's hired scum," Jameson said. He had his hand on a pistol in a holster on his belt. Major Stapleton had his hand on his pistol. They were seconds away from drawing and firing.

"For God's sake, Rogers, control yourself," Gentry said, stepping between the two men. "There are young women watching us."

Janet Todd and Dorothy Schreiber, both in festive white, were peering out the parlor windows at the confrontation.

"Henry, you've always been an asshole. You were born a two-armed asshole; you'll die a one-armed asshole. Events will soon prove you and your asshole friend Abe are a matched pair."

The insult did not surprise Gentry. Rogers Jameson had been telling people in Hunter County that Henry Todd Gentry was a fool for a long time. The idea had taken root with the pertinacity of ragweed. Hardly surprising, really. It gave a lot of people intense pleasure to think that Henry Gentry, inheritor of 6,000 prime acres on the Ohio, a threshing mill, a thriving general store and a ferry service, was a nitwit.

Jameson and Pete Worth strode to the barn, picked up Frankie Worth's body, deposited it in the buckboard and rode away without saying another word. As they rattled out the gate, Major Stapleton asked, "Why didn't you arrest them both? Are you going to let them bury that fellow without another word?"

"We'll deal with them at the appropriate time and place," Gentry said. Inwardly he winced at the disgust on Stapleton's face. Maybe it was time to explain to this young man why he preferred to play a waiting game with Rogers Jameson and his Democratic friends.

"I almost forgot another matter," the major said. "We caught a deserter. He wasn't involved in the skirmish. Would you like to talk to him?"

"Of course. Where is he?"

The deserter was in the back of the barn in a stall that Sergeant Washington had fitted out as an office. The prisoner did not look more than fifteen years old. Gentry dismissed the trooper who was guarding him and asked the boy his name. "Robert Garner," he said. "I didn't plan to desert. I just come north to see my momma."

"Why did you go to the Fitzsimmons farm?" Gentry asked.

"Joe Fitz' was my friend in the army—the only friend I had—until he got killed at Vicksburg. They made us charge a Confederate battery. A cannonball took his head off. His blood covered me—my hands, my face. Ever since that happened I been sick. I couldn't eat, I couldn't sleep."

"Colonel?" Sergeant Washington loomed in the doorway. "Trooper Bowen give this to me. Says he saw this guy tryin' to hide it in his shoe."

The piece of paper was grimy with sweat and dirt. Gentry opened it and read: " 'I, Robert Garner, do solemnly swear that I will bear true faith and allegiance to the Confederate States of America, and that I will to the best of my ability support its Constitution and its laws, so help me God.

" 'Subscribed and sworn to before me, Post Commandant, at Richmond, Kentucky.

" 'Colonel William C. Danforth.' "

"I don't mean a word of that," Garner said. "I had to sign it to get through the Confederate lines. They control everything in southeast Kentucky."

"What do you know about the men who fired on Major Stapleton's troopers?" Gentry asked.

"I never saw them before. They came to the farm this mornin'. They wanted me to join them. I said I wouldn't do it. I wouldn't shoot a Union soldier. They cursed me for a coward."

Garner began to blubber. "I don't want to shoot anyone. I told them when they drafted me I wanted to work in the hospital. But they wouldn't listen. They gave me a gun."

Gentry sighed. Too many deserters told this story. After three years of slaughter, the Union Army could not afford to inquire where a man wanted to serve. They needed anyone who could carry a gun in the front lines.

"Escort him to the town jail. We'll ship him to Indianapolis for trial on Monday."

Stapleton followed Gentry through the dim barn to the sunbaked yard. "Can you spare fifteen minutes for a private talk?" Gentry asked.

"I want to make sure Doctor Yancey treats my wounded troopers."

"Tell him I'll consider it a personal favor," Gentry said. "I'll wait for you in my office."

Twenty minutes later, Major Stapleton returned looking satisfied. Dr. Yancey, still reasonably sober, was bestowing his considerable medical skills on the wounded black troopers. The man with the head wound had died but that did not seem to trouble Major Stapleton. He had no doubt seen enough casualties at Antietam and Gettysburg and other battles to make death routine. Perhaps they also taught that idea at West Point.

"Sit down, Major. I know you're eager to go upstairs and charm the ladies. But there's some business we ought to discuss first."

"I'm feeling a bit derelict toward Miss Todd—"

"By coincidence, Miss Todd is the business I want to discuss with you."

Stapleton looked wary. He probably assumed that Gentry was in cahoots with his in-laws to snare an heir to the Stapleton fortune for darling Janet. "As a mere observer, I begin to think Janet has some affection for you," Gentry said.

"We've never discussed that idea in a serious way. Mostly we play a game of polite antagonism about the war."

"I'm aware of that. I do the same thing with two-thirds of the people in Keyport. But there's more to Janet Todd than meets the eye, Major. Behind her polite, cheerful antagonism lurks a Confederate agent."

"You're joking."

"I have incontrovertible evidence. She's part of a plot to revolutionize Kentucky and Indiana and take both states out of the war. With them might go Illinois and Michigan and Wisconsin and Ohio. She's been a courier, connecting Confederate agents in Canada to gunrunners in New York and the Confederate secret service in Richmond."

"Remarkable," Major Stapleton said. "I have new respect for her."

"Major—this is a very serious matter. They plan to launch their revolution sometime this summer or early in the fall, before the presidential election. With Lincoln already in trouble with the voters, this thing could have a terrific impact on the outcome of the war."

"What am I supposed to do about it?" Major Stapleton asked.

"I want you to become a Union secret agent, Major. I want you to pretend to lose your enthusiasm for the federal cause. I want you to convince Janet you're in love with her and persuade her to share the details of this plot, especially the date when they plan to launch their armed uprising."

"Colonel Gentry—what you're suggesting is more than a little dishonorable."

"When it comes to winning a war, Major, honor must be sacrificed occasionally, like everything else."

"I'm not sure I agree with that, sir."

"I don't give a damn whether you agree with it, Major. I'm issuing you an order!"

"I'm an officer in the regular army of the United States," Major Stapleton said, his West Point pride vibrating in his voice. "I have severe doubts as to whether I'm required to obey such an extraordinary order from a volunteer officer who is at best on detached duty."

"Why don't you say it? Who's a one-armed cripple."

"I will not say it because I did not think it, Colonel."

Gentry leaned forward in his chair. The major's face dissolved in the dim light into a generic identity. He was all the proud confident young men Henry Gentry had never been able to match.

"Do you want an order from the President of the United States, Major? Your constitutional commander in chief? I can get it. I write Abe Lincoln a letter a week, telling him what's happening in Indiana."

"If he issued such an order, Colonel Gentry, I would think even less of him than I do now."

Gentry glanced at the large framed photograph of Lincoln on the wall. It was taken before he grew his beard. His hair was rumpled; it looked as if he were standing in a prairie wind. The photographer had combed Abe's hair, and he had deliberately mussed it. "I told him otherwise my friends wouldn't recognize me," Lincoln had said.

"Why does everyone in the country think so little of this man? I've known him since we were boys together on Pigeon Creek. I've seen the loathsome cabin he lived in, eighteen to twenty Lincolns sleeping like hogs on the dirt floor. I saw his father, the meanest, stupidest Kentucky dirt farmer this side of Lake Ontario. I was there when Lincoln transcended that ancestral pigsty, when his soul expanded with his body. I saw the wonder and the beauty of the man's spirit when it first flowered."

"Colonel—if I may interrupt you—now you're telling me that this wonderful spiritual being is prepared to write a letter, at your behest, ordering me to traduce the affections of a respectable young woman, in the name of victory? To become a despicable scoundrel in my own eyes and the eyes of any man who discovered it? Is this the kind of war we're fighting? I'm prepared to risk my life in a fair fight at anyone's order. But I absolutely totally refuse to obey this order, even if your noble friend Abe Lincoln comes here and delivers it to me personally!"

They sat there, antagonists, each wearing the blue uniform of the army of the United States. Through Colonel Gentry's brain clanged the alarm bell he had heard a hundred, even a thousand times: *You've messed up again, Henry.* Why was he, reader of uncounted books, never able to find the right words in a face-to-face situation? Always men talked him down, either with frontal assaults à la Rogers Jameson or flanking movements à la Major Stapleton. His mother, Millicent Todd Gentry, his ex-friend Andy Conway and too many others to enumerate did the same thing.

Humiliation. It was impossible to face that word

without deciding it was time to take his service revolver and slowly insert the barrel into his mouth, let his tongue examine the round opening of the muzzle one last time, and pull the trigger. He had made the insertion more than once but something he neither understood nor valued had stayed his trigger finger. Was it Lincoln's spirit, pleading against another desertion?

"I hope, at the very least, Major, you'll conduct yourself like an officer of the U.S. Army and not reveal to Miss Todd even a hint of this conversation," Gentry said.

"Of course."

"Major, you've only been here four months. You don't have any idea how serious this whole thing is. They could do it. They have an organization, the Sons of Liberty, with thousands of men enrolled. Rogers Jameson is one of the leaders. The dissatisfaction, not to say disgust, with the war is so strong, all they need is a show of support from the Confederate Army to rise in strength. Thanks to Miss Todd, they're in a position to get that. In her latest letter, of which I have a verbatim account, she's arranged for four regiments of John Hunt Morgan's cavalry to cooperate with the Liberty men."

"My respect for her grows by leaps and bounds," Major Stapleton said.

"Major," Gentry said. "Don't you realize we could lose this war?"

"A larger question troubles me, Colonel. Whether we deserve to win it."

SIX

CONFEDERATE AGENT. THE WORDS CORUSCATED through Major Paul Stapleton's aching head as he strolled with Janet Todd on the Gentry estate overlooking the Ohio. The river was almost a mile wide here—an inland sea dividing North and South. Would this new knowledge interfere with the onset of love that his brother Charlie called crystallization?

It was a French idea, discovered by Charlie in the outpost of France in the American South, New Orleans. Paul liked it from the moment he heard it, because it made the business of love seem vaguely scientific and impersonal—something that happened to a man whether he liked it or wanted it to happen. He had tried it with one or two women but the demands of West Point and in swift succession the U.S. Army and the war had aborted the experiments before they were even close to maturity. Seeing Janet Todd almost every weekend for the last three months had given him the crucial ingredient, time, for crystallization to occur.

Paul gazed steadily at Janet in her white lace summer dress, white stockings and white shoes. She was not beautiful. But Charlie, Paul's expert on love, had assured him that supremely beautiful women were difficult if not impossible, to love. The essence of crystallization was the slow discovery of new aspects of beauty in the person you desired, discoveries that multiplied the pleasure—and the potential pain—of the experience.

The pain was as important in the equation as the pleasure. For Paul, love was essentially risk—and that redoubled its appeal for a professional soldier. As *Confederate agent* penetrated his consciousness, he saw that it multiplied the risk—and the attraction. It was a new kind of crystallization that Charlie, who had lived and died on risk, would heartily approve.

Janet Todd was not beautiful. But she had thick, lustrously dark hair that seemed to multiply its blackness against her white skin. Her mouth was a bit too wide, but it was strong and expressive—and more than a little knowing. It was a surprisingly worldly mouth for someone who had grown up on a Kentucky plantation. But she had gone to a school in Indiana run by French nuns. Daughters of many wealthy midwesterners, city girls from Chicago, Cincinnati, Detroit, went there. Who knows what young women exchanged in whispers in their rooms over flickering candles? Perhaps sentiments and secrets almost as shocking as those Paul had heard at West Point.

Janet's eyes were brooding blue beneath black brows and long delicate lashes. When she lowered them, she looked unexpectedly vulnerable. A sentence from one of Charlie's letters flashed through Paul's mind: *Nothing is more favorable to the birth of love than a mixture of depression and solitude—and a few infrequent and eagerly anticipated balls.* Was this Fourth of July party the Indiana version of a ball?

They entered the deeper shade of a line of immense cottonwood trees. A modicum of the cool air that filtered up from the river seemed to survive here. The softened light helped Paul admire the strong line of Janet's jaw, the suggestion of willfulness, pride, in the tilt of her head, her remarkably straight back. Her figure was not notably curvaceous. The dress revealed a tantalizing glimpse of breasts that were, at best, average size. But Paul had never been one of those orgiasts who slavered after excess in that department.

A certain broadness in Janet's hips and shoulders

gave her body a compact almost masculine quality. But it was compact with female emotion. Feeling throbbed in her voice, reminding Paul of the lower reaches of the cello.

"You ask me if I'm attracted to you, Major. Of course I am. Every woman in the vicinity is attracted to you. You're dangerously handsome—and rich. What more does one need to set a woman's heart fluttering?"

"You sound as if you dislike this attraction, Miss Janet. As if there were a censor of some sort sitting in judgment on your feelings. Does it have something to do with the color of my uniform?"

"I would consider myself an extremely prejudiced woman if that were the case," Janet said. "As the daughter of a man who called for Kentucky's neutrality, I try not to pass judgment on anyone for the color of his uniform."

"I'm glad to hear that," Paul said.

"But I won't deny I sympathize with the men you spent the better part of the afternoon fighting. To them you represent a *tyranny,* Major. That may be hard for you to understand."

"Not at all," Paul said. "As I've told you, I come from a family of Democrats. My mother wanted my father to do exactly what your father did—urge New Jersey to remain neutral. If a few more border states such as Maryland and Missouri had done it, the war would have stopped before it started. But the senator couldn't bring himself to abandon the Union."

"You know what I really think, Major? Instead of trying to comprehend my ambivalent heart, you ought to pay some attention to poor Dorothy Schreiber. She's *hopelessly* in love with you. She's confided to me that your *coldness* has driven her to the edge of genuine *despair.*"

Paul felt a vibration of pure pleasure. He was well aware of Dorothy Schreiber's infatuation. She was living in the Gentry household. It was the inflections in Janet's voice that produced the pleasure. He loved to hear southern women express themselves. Every important word was colored by emotion.

"Dorothy's only sixteen. Am I to be reduced to robbing the cradle?"

"Women marry at sixteen all the time around here."

"Why haven't you married, Miss Janet?"

She looked away from him. "I told you. I've promised myself to a man who's fighting for the Confederacy."

"But that was only three years ago. I know it's impolite to mention a lady's age, but I've discovered with Colonel Gentry's help that we're both twenty-five. In fact, we came into this world on almost the same day in the year 1839. Where was this Confederate hero between your sixteenth and twenty-second year?"

"He was pursuing me. And I—I was resisting him."

"Poor fellow. He has my deepest retrospective sympathy. Why were you resisting him?"

"Perhaps I disliked the idea that marriage is not only the most interesting event in a woman's life—it's the *only* interesting event."

"So this pledge—if that's not too extravagant a word in the light of what you're confessing—was extracted from you by the war itself?"

"You could say that. I decline to confirm whether your assertion is true or false, or a mixture of both things."

"But I've been told by some people in a position to know that you've hinted this pledge is no longer binding in your heart."

"Until I see the gentleman and discuss it, face-to-face, it must be—unless I met another man who stirred my heart in an unexpected way."

Paul took her hand. It was exquisitely soft and moist. "Miss Janet," he said. "Why can't you abstract the idea of risk and apply it to a professional soldier? A man who doesn't fight for causes—but who summons courage because it's an essential part of his profession. It seems to me a woman's heart could find poignancy in that sort of man. She might admire his devotion to duty and honor for their own sakes. She might want to share his determination to challenge fate in the name of glory, without the least illusion that glory is anything more than the tinsel of the season. It seems to me that two people, pledged to each other that way, would focus all the emotions of love with the sort of intensity created by a magnifying glass held up to the sun. They might achieve a love that would all but consume them—with joy, with pleasure, with a happiness that approaches salvation."

"Major—you are absolutely amazing. How did someone born in New Jersey learn to talk like a southerner? If I closed my eyes, and added a touch of accent, those words could be coming from the lips of a dozen men I know."

"I had a southern roommate for four years at West Point."

"Where was he from?"

"Georgia."

"So he's probably fighting General Sherman at this very moment."

"Possibly."

The Gettysburg wound fired a bolt of pain through Paul's skull. *You are getting to be a really gifted liar, Paulie. To hear you now, you felt next to nothing when you walked Thomas Jefferson Tyler to the steamboat dock for his journey south.*

Not true, not true, I remember everything: the beads of perspiration on Jeff's upper lip, the tears dampening the lashes of his lowered eyes. We were beyond words, beyond politics, beyond anger, beyond fate itself in a world of absolute emotional purity.

"What?"

"I asked you, What is your roommate's name?"

"Tyler. Thomas Jefferson Tyler. We called him Jeff."

"You were fond of him?"

"I loved him."

She was wide-eyed. Was it amazement or a species of wicked hope? For a moment *Confederate agent* became an impenetrable barrier between them. But Paul thrust it aside with the reminder that he had known from the start this woman supported the South.

"Everyone in the class loved him. He was generous, honest, true in every imaginable sense of the word. Even the most obnoxious abolitionists had to confess that Jeff Tyler was as close as any of us came to moral perfection. It utterly baffled them that he could own slaves and yet attain such a spiritual ascendancy."

"Yet you have no sympathy for the cause that Jeff Tyler is risking his life to defend?"

"On the contrary, I have enormous sympathy for Jeff Tyler's cause. For your cause. What made our farewell so heartbreaking was the knowledge we shared—and expressed—as professional soldiers, the night before we parted, that the South couldn't win the war."

He raised her hand to his lips. She permitted him. It was the sort of proof he was seeking. It added passion to his words. "That's why I feel capable of offering you my affection, Miss Janet—even though I'm wearing the wrong uniform. I believe I've been chosen to console you for the Confederacy's inevitable defeat."

She freed her hand and stepped back a pace, as if she no longer wanted to be too close to him. "How can you say that when Lincoln's own party loathes him so much, they almost refused to renominate him? When the Democrats of Kentucky, Indiana, Illinois and Ohio are rising in a virtual *mass* of rage and disgust against Republican tyranny?"

"Wars aren't won by politics and politicians. They're won by soldiers with the training to organize and concentrate superior force. I was General John Reynolds' aide until he was killed at Gettysburg. He was the finest soldier in the Union Army, and his loss remains a tragedy. I sat at his dinner table and listened to him predict and describe in detail the defeat of the South—a fact that saddened him as much as it distressed me. He even predicted the precise strategy that General Grant and General Sherman are pursuing at this moment—battering attacks on the Confederate armies in Virginia to hold them in place while Sherman executes a vast flanking movement to penetrate the heart of the Confederacy from the west."

"Why did you decide to become a professional soldier, Major?" Janet asked.

The question threw Paul off balance like an unexpected attack on an exposed flank. He groped for an answer. "My grandfather was a West Pointer. He was killed in Canada in 1812. My father fought in Mexico. Soldiering was in my blood, so to speak. But I suppose the real reason was—"

"What?"

"It offered a life that had nothing to do with politics."

He was shocked by the bitterness in his voice. Why was it seeping into his soul after all these years? As the youngest brother he had tried to remain neutral as his brother Jonathan denounced the South as a region of slave drivers and his brother Charlie defended it as the last bastion of gentility and honor against the crude commercialism of the North where everything had a price. While their mother watched, Sibyl-like, defending neither side but subtly demonstrating in a thousand ways that she agreed with Charlie—and their senator father spouted remonstrations and appeals to George Washington's ideal of an indissoluble union.

Paul tried to remember how moved he was by West Point's motto, Duty, Honor, Country. How he believed it promised him a kind of spiritual haven in which he could escape the quarrels and contradictions that had ravaged the Stapleton family. For a while he had found it in the military academy's mathematical and scientific approach to war. But soon the quarrel between North and South was raging in the barracks and the classrooms; insults far worse than any exchanged by Charlie and Jonathan echoed in the crisp air and the brotherhood of the corps collapsed into fistfights and duels with swords and pistols.

Suddenly the Gettysburg wound was mocking him again. *Is there a sort of calculus of honor being devised here? Duty requires seduction and lies and honor requires confession and truth? Is this whole thing a moral experiment, the sort of game Charlie liked to play with women? If duty is given a value of one and honor is given a value of one is the result zero? Will that entitle you to do as you please, Charlie style? Plunder her pathetic little secrets, take your pleasure, and depart? What about country? How does that fit into the equation?*

A steamboat plowed downriver, a gleaming white mass in the late-afternoon sunshine. A huge American flag flew from its stern. "I never see one of those boats without thinking of my brother Charlie," Paul said. "The last time I saw him, I was getting on a steamboat at New Orleans."

"Did he stay there when the war began?"

"He was dead by then. He was killed in 1859, trying to make Cuba the thirty-fifth state."

"Your family fascinates me, Major Stapleton. One brother a martyr to the South, another a major general in the Union Army."

"Charlie was a martyr to the Union, in our eyes. We thought making Cuba a state would placate the South and keep them in the Union. My father put up most of the money for the expedition. But someone in a high place betrayed them. The Spanish took no prisoners."

"The Union, the Union. I'm sick of this invocation of the Union. My father began the war using the word as if it were a sacred chant. Now the mere mention of it torments him. Would you have Charlie die for Lincoln's kind of Union? One created by bullets instead of ballots?"

"In order to graduate from West Point we were required to take an ironclad oath of loyalty to the federal government."

"But is it the same federal government to which you swore your allegiance? A government that has converted the war into a crusade to free the blacks, after teaching them to hate the whites?"

"As a citizen I deplore that. But as a professional soldier my political opinion is irrelevant."

The emotions that played across Janet Todd's face were an exquisite blend of sympathy and desire. "Major—listen to me. I'm telling you that the constitution—the government—to which you swore allegiance has ceased to exist. Lincoln and the Republicans have annihilated it. We're in a new world, where force and risk are the only arbiters of the future."

As soon as women embark on abstract reasoning, they create love unconsciously. Another of Charlie's gems of amorous wisdom. But what did it mean? Did reasoning women create love in themselves? Or in their lovers? For the moment, Paul only knew it was another step in the process of discovering the remarkable dimensions of this woman's mind and heart.

"Your logic, Miss Janet, has a certain irresistibility. Are you prepared to live on risk? That seems to make you susceptible to the flattery of a professional soldier."

"I'm prepared to love a professional soldier who lives on risk for my sake. That man—I would love with my whole soul."

Paul felt the tremor of a fresh wholly original crystallization in his flesh. A woman who *wanted* him to live on risk. The idea had enormous resonance in his soul.

Back home in New Jersey, while he was recuperating from his Gettysburg wound, he had been forced to endure the lamentations of his brother Jonathan's wife. She orated endlessly on how determined she was to persuade Jonathan to quit the war. His next wound would be fatal. For a while it had only stirred sardonic amusement, thinking of Major General Stapleton listening to these cries of woe in the bedroom when he limped home from the battlefield. But in retrospect the tears of the Union hero's wife had grown distasteful.

By now twilight was seeping across the Ohio, like a flood of darkness from the South. Janet Todd was a white ghost beneath the cottonwood trees. The dwindling light made it easier to speak the final seductive words: "I think you should be the first to know I'm planning to return to the fighting front as soon as possible. Honor doesn't permit me to linger here in safety any longer. If I thought the risks I'll face there were for your sake, it would transform them in a way that would make the fear of another wound a mere trifle."

Without warning, without invitation, Janet Todd kissed him. As that strong pliant mouth pressed his lips, Paul knew that crystallization had been occurring in Janet's heart too. She loved him beyond politics, perhaps even beyond risk. But his Gettysburg wound insisted on whispering, *Confederate agent.*

SEVEN

HENRY TODD GENTRY SAW HER hesitating in the doorway, her behemoth of a husband glowering behind her. "Amelia—Rogers!" he called, careening toward them. "I was hoping you'd come—"

Amelia Jameson brightened marvelously, although a patina of sadness remained beneath the exquisite smile. "I told my husband I wasn't going to let a war stop me from going to a Gentry party," she said. Her russet hair still retained its sheen, the face its Grecian cast, although her complexion was no longer the pure snow of a japonica.

Before Gentry could speak, his mother's bulk dispersed them like a steamboat on a collision course with canoes. "I'm *so* pleased you've come, Amelia *darling*," she said. The dewlaps protruding over Millicent Todd Gentry's high-necked lace collar virtually vibrated with the intensity of her emotion. Her large square face, powdered a garish white, was distorted by a totally insincere smile.

Rogers Jameson and Gentry exchanged glances. Were they both marveling at the talent women had for concealing hatred behind elaborate courtesy and the rhetoric of affection? Millicent Todd Gentry had never forgiven Amelia for jilting her son.

Gentry decided he was attributing too much intelligence to Rogers Jameson. He was probably thinking the same triumphant sentence he had been caressing in his primitive forebrain for the last thirty years: *She's mine,*

Gentry, and there's not a goddamn thing you and your money can do about it.

Out in the garden, beneath a tent festooned with red, white, and blue bunting, Jimmy Hemings's fiddle band was striking up his theme song, "Muckymoss." For a moment Gentry was back thirty-five years, his arms around Amelia Conway, dancing to the plaintive strains of that old Welsh song. In the darkness outside the tent, Rogers Jameson was watching, envy on his fleshy face. Gentry had made the mistake of savoring that envy. He had assumed that God was in his heaven waiting to unite elegant Amelia Conway, descendant of one of Virginia's First Families, and Henry Todd Gentry, heir to one of the largest fortunes in Indiana.

> *Time! What an empty vapor 'tis!*
> *And days how swift they are:*
> *as an Indian arrow—*
> *Fly on like a shooting star.*
> *The present moment just is here*
> *Then slides away in haste,*
> *That we can never say they're ours,*
> *But only say they're past.*

How often had he heard young Abe Lincoln recite that poem? But Henry Gentry had paid no more attention to it than he had paid to Abe's warning that Rogers Jameson was going to lure Amelia Conway out of Gentry's arms. In those days, Henry Gentry had felt immune to disasters, disappointments, losses. He was destiny's darling, with his head crammed full of Sir Walter Scott and his pockets full of money.

How could Rogers Jameson, who seldom had a nickel left after one of his flatboat trips to New Orleans, who could barely sign his name, much less read Sir Walter Scott, possibly entice Amelia Conway into abandoning Henry Gentry? Granted Rogers had, as his name suggested, some vague claim to descent from George Rogers Clark, conqueror of Indiana and Illinois in the days of 1776. But the old warrior had died drunk and forgotten and his descendants had been left with nothing but their muscles to rely on.

Lincoln had wrinkled that lean already ugly face into a grimace: "He's goin' to tell her all men are created equal, Henry. And her hypocritical old Democratic daddy's gonna smile and say, 'That's my boy.'"

When Gentry returned from his senior year at Harvard College, he discovered that Lincoln was right. The Democrats' rant about equality, which left four million black men and women under the lash from Kentucky to the Rio Grande, could also melt the female heart. Especially when it was combined with a set of magnificent muscles, a permanent suntan and a gift for crude flattery.

Also not to be discounted were Rogers Jameson's assaults on the pretensions of fake pioneers like the Gentrys, who had arrived from the hated East with enough money to buy up all the best land and support politicians in Kentucky and Indiana who dared to say the Democratic Party was a collection of swindlers and incompetents. That was why Gentry's grandfather had named his mansion The Grange, in memory of the New York estate of Alexander Hamilton, the great foe of the founder of the Democratic Party, Thomas Jefferson.

Gentry had thought it was no more than a charming aberration when Amelia lectured him on Jefferson's call for universal democracy and rebuked Gentry for his "aristocratic" notions. She particularly deplored his tendency to imitate Lincoln's caustic criticism of Democrats. Too late he realized she was rationalizing her attraction to Rogers Jameson and echoing her father's hostility to the Gentrys and their conservative politics.

"What can I get you to drink?" Gentry asked.

"Whiskey," Rogers Jameson said.

"Have you opened any of your wonderful wines?" Amelia asked.

"We have a Montrachet fifty-four on ice—and a Latour fifty-two on the sideboard."

Gentry poured a glass of Montrachet for Amelia and asked his black butler, Peter, to bring Rogers Jameson a whiskey. The behemoth accepted it without so much as a grunt of thanks and strolled over to Dr. Walter Yancey. "How's John Brown Junior doin', Walter?" he asked. "You chop off any arms or legs yet?"

"He's almost certain to recover and give you another shot at him," Yancey said.

"Don't that prove there's no God?"

"It would certainly suggest that he's not paying attention to his business."

Gentry led Amelia into the garden. On the dance floor, Major Paul Stapleton was waltzing with Janet Todd. The glow of delight on their young faces made him wince. Did it also disturb Amelia? "When I see those two I hear the sound of wedding bells," he said. "But I've been wrong about that sort of thing before."

"They do look terribly pleased with each other," Amelia said pretending to have no idea when Gentry heard those earlier wedding bells.

"Except that Cousin Janet is a passionate supporter of the Confederacy. I wonder how—or if—they can resolve that contretemps."

"This dreadful war can't last forever."

"There are people around here who are trying to prolong the war, I'm afraid. You must know that."

Amelia continued to gaze at Major Stapleton and Janet Todd as they cavorted across the floor with a half-dozen other couples in a lively square dance. "I pray to God they won't succeed," she said.

Her favorite younger brother, Eddie, had been killed at Shiloh. He was one of the few Democrats in the ranks of Lincoln's Own. Gentry had recruited him.

"I'm glad to hear that. I've been afraid—ever since Eddie died—that your dislike of me had turned to hate. I'm not sure I could bear that."

"Hate you? How could you even think such a thing, Henry?"

"War does terrible things to people's feelings. Could you believe thirty years ago that so much hatred would be swirling through Kentucky and Indiana? The days of our youth begin to seem more and more like a sojourn in Eden to me. Our little personal quarrels that caused us so much heartbreak recede to the level of the trivial, the childishly innocent."

"Isn't everyone innocent at a certain age?" Amelia said.

"I think we exceeded the natural tendency by a vast American distance."

"I never thought of your friend Lincoln as innocent. He always looked too lean, too hungry."

"You think he's proving that as president? His hunger was for power?"

"I don't know. I'm a mere woman. But it seems to me he could have ended this war a dozen times. Why didn't he say to the people of the North at some point—after Fredericksburg or Chickamauga or some other Union defeat—'Fellow citizens, we have tried to force our southern brethren to submit. But they refuse. I now see that the contest will engender undying hatred between the two sections if we persist. Here are my terms for an honorable settlement.' "

"He could have done that. But by then he owed a debt of honor to the dead—and the wounded. He had to prove that they hadn't bled in vain."

"So he could get re-elected?"

"So he could face them in the middle of the night. Can you imagine Abe's dreams? His waking nightmares? Those legions of ghostly faces parading through his bedroom? I pity him, Amelia. I wish you did too."

"I pity the dead—and the wounded."

For a fraction of a moment she glanced at his empty sleeve. Henry Gentry's soul almost leaped its fleshly moorings. Mingled with pity and regret was there a fragment of their original love in her eyes? Some echo of their happiness before the democratic serpent slithered into their garden hissing, *equality*?

"When Lincoln receives a wound, maybe I'll pity him too."

"Amelia, I could show you letters that reveal a hundred thousand wounds. One for every death."

A mistake. That extravagance only invigorated Amelia's youthful dislike of Abraham Lincoln. "That man has been a bad influence on you, Henry. I sensed it from the day I met him. I *sensed* that in some strange way, he would come between us. His peculiar *hatred* of the Democratic Party—I can remember him mocking it back then, when we were barely twenty. He especially mocked *rich* Democrats. He said they were the biggest hypocrites on earth. He was insulting my *father* and you just sat there, smiling."

What could he say? He agreed with every word Abe said? Colonel Augustus Conway *was* the biggest hypocrite, if not on earth, certainly in Kentucky, where he ran for office, and in Indiana, where he was often a stump speaker for other Democratic candidates. He poured rotgut bourbon and gaseous rhetoric down the throats of the voters so he could go to Washington and orate in the "Cave of Winds," as Lincoln called the House of Representatives, about the greatness of Thomas Jefferson while he cut deals with railroads and land speculators and Indian agents that made him rich enough to turn Rose Hill into an ornate imitation of a European palace.

Gentry tried to make a joke of Amelia's diatribe. "Now—at last—I find out why you broke our engagement. It was Lincoln's fault. He's been blamed for everything else under the sun. Why not this ultimate blunder?"

"I'm *serious,* Henry. There was an arrogance about that man—an intellectual arrogance. He communicated it to you."

Gentry wanted to tell her that if anything, it was the other way around. He had not needed Lincoln to make him arrogant. He had only needed his mother, Millicent Todd Gentry, a woman who was convinced that everyone with Todd blood was superior to the rest of the human race. But he chose conciliation over the truth.

"Maybe he did, maybe he did."

On the dance floor the young folks continued to prance, and the music swelled to Jimmy Hemings's call:

> *"Take your partner, twirl her around.*
> *Kiss her twice if she makes a sound.*
> *Bees in the honeycomb, cows in the creek,*
> *Men are strong and women are weak!*
> *The preacher says that kissing is wrong.*
> *But men are weak and women are strong!"*

Watching Paul Stapleton and the other smiling young men twisting and turning their laughing partners, first with their left hands, then with their right, Gentry was suddenly back on the battlefield at Shiloh. The southern boys charged the Union lines howling like young wolves, incredibly indifferent to death. Soon there were several hundred bodies on the sunken road in front of Lincoln's Own regiment. An acrid cloud of gunpowder scorched Gentry's lungs. But he was exultant. His men were holding their ground. The air was full of hissing bullets but only a few members of Lincoln's Own had gone down.

The Confederate attack faltered and a Union colonel rode up on a white horse and shouted, "Now is the time! Charge them!" Colonel Gentry seized his sword and strode out on the road among the Confederate dead. "Follow me, men!" he shouted. He was racing toward glory, toward the thought that Amelia Jameson would wonder why she had failed to marry such a hero, the man who won the battle of Shiloh.

Gentry had gone only a half-dozen steps when a bullet struck his right arm midway between the elbow and shoulder, literally breaking it in two, shivering and splintering the bone down to the elbow and upward to within two inches of the shoulder joint. The bullet struck with such force that it spun him around and sent his sword flying. As his men rushed past him into an apple orchard on the other side of the road, where a Confederate cross fire massacred them, Colonel Gentry stumbled to the rear, clutching his smashed arm. A half hour later he was in a field hospital under chloroform, dimly aware of the rasp of the saw as the surgeon cut off the arm near the shoulder.

"I would love some more of this wonderful wine," Amelia said.

Gentry gazed into the still-beautiful face for which he had sacrificed his arm. At a party five or six years ago, he had seen, beneath carefully applied powder, the shadow of a bruise on Amelia's cheek. He had heard rumors of Jameson snarling drunken insults at her, telling her she was not as good in bed as the sluts he enjoyed in New Orleans.

Gentry snatched a glass of Montrachet off a tray that the butler was carrying to guests sitting at tables around the dance floor. Amelia sipped it and said, "The Sons of Liberty. What do you know about them, Henry?"

For a moment Gentry was too flabbergasted to speak. "They're a secret organization," he finally said. "I wish I knew more about them."

"Rogers has joined them. He says they're going to win the war for the South. How could they do that?"

"I have no idea."

"I'm afraid it might be dangerous. He tells me Adam is playing a part in their plans."

The possibility of turning Amelia into an informer blazed in Henry Gentry's mind. But he could not speak. Why? He was urging Major Paul Stapleton into Janet Todd's arms in the hope of planting an informer in Hopemont. But he could not violate the purity of his betrayed love for Amelia Conway. It lay there in the past, battered by time but ultimately beautiful, like the classic statues Lord Elgin had discovered in Greece.

Gentry struggled to disregard the rage and humiliation he had felt when Amelia jilted him. He consigned to oblivion all those expensive women with whom he had sought consolation in Cincinnati and Louisville. A man had to cling to something pure and true, even if, like so many other things in this disintegrating American heartland, it was irretrievably lost.

EIGHT

"I'M TELLIN' YOU AGAIN, TRANSFER youself and y'men outta here. They gonna kill every last one'f you."

In the dark rear of the Gentry barn, with the sound of the whites' Fourth of July celebration in the distance, Sergeant Moses Washington tried to concentrate on what Janet Todd's slave, Lucy, was telling him. There was a revolution coming in Indiana and Kentucky, led by Democrats. It made sense. Those looks of hate blacks got when they walked down the main street of Keyport—the insults flung at them by boys. Today's ambush at the Fitzsimmons farm.

But Sergeant Washington did not like the idea of running away. Lucy was a slave nigger, after all. Running away was slave talk. Sergeant Washington's people had been free in Monmouth County, New Jersey, for almost a hundred years. He tended to have a low opinion of slave niggers, although he felt sorry for them. All the men in the troop, except for his New Jersey sidekick, Jasper Jones, were slave niggers. He and Jasper had long since agreed that they were a poor grade of human being. Not one could read or write. They were incredibly ignorant. Most of them had never seen a book or a newspaper.

Still, the slave niggers made good soldiers. They had obedience ground into their bones. Major Stapleton said that was more important than being smart. When the bullets started flying, the important thing was to obey orders. The sergeant saw no need to run away. Major Stapleton had told him that their seven-shot Spencer carbines gave them the firepower of a full Confederate regiment.

Besides, what could he do to transfer his men? Sergeants did not transfer soldiers in the United States Army. Only generals did that.

"Where did you hear all this?" Washington asked.

"Aunt Sophie, our washwoman at Hopemont, got a son who's a house servant at the Jameson place. He says they got a plan all worked out. When Colonel Adam Jameson and his Confederate cavalry come, the Democrat Sons of Liberty is headin' for you and your boys. They gonna kill all of you. No surrender. Why don't you go kill them first?"

"On your say-so? We should just cross over the river to this man's farm and shoot him to pieces? You can't do that in a civilized country, girl."

"Who says this is a civilized country?"

"I'll talk to the major about it."

"The major? He on the dance floor lookin' down Miz Janet's dress. She gonna have him so dizzy in a day or two, he won't know which end of a horse is which."

"How do you know so much?"

"I keeps my ears and eyes open. That's what I'm tellin' you to do, if you don't want to get killed. That shootin' at the Fitzsimmons place is just the beginnin' of big trouble for you."

"Water! I needs water."

Fred Clay, one of the wounded, was burning up with fever. Dr. Yancey said he might have to take his leg off if it got any worse. Sergeant Washington thought Yancey looked too eager to start cutting. But what did he know about medicine? Clay was on a bed of straw in one of the stalls. Washington gave him his canteen and returned to Lucy.

She moved against him in the dark, black against lesser blackness. She had taken off her dress. "I wants you real bad," she said. "Don't you want me? They won't even give you time off to go to a whorehouse in Cincinnati. Lots of black whores in that town. I heard Miz Janet's brothers talkin' about them before they got themselves killed."

Sergeant Washington's mouth went dry with desire. It had been four months since he had a woman. Four long dry (or wet, if you counted his dreams) months since he arrived in Keyport and became a sergeant, thanks to Major Stapleton. Lucy was a good-looking woman, even though she didn't seem to know it.

Lucy put his hand on her breast. "I know I ain't beautiful and you can probably get a lot better-lookin' women where you come from. But I'm here and willin'."

"Put your dress on, girl," Sergeant Washington said. "I made a promise to Major Stapleton when he 'pointed me sergeant. I said I'd set an example to our men. How can they respect me if one comes in here and finds me ass-naked in the hay with you?"

"You northern niggers is crazy," Lucy said. "You think you're as good as white folks. Maybe gettin' yourself killed is the only way you'll learn the truth."

"There's all kinds of truths," Washington said. "The one I'm tryin' to prove is a black soldier is as good as a white soldier. That's why I joined the army. Jasper Jones and me heard a speech by a man named Fred Douglass. He's half-white, but he's proudest of his black side. He told us we had a chance to prove to the whole country that black people deserve the vote and a lot more by joinin' this fight."

Lucy thrashed back into her dress. "Only truth I know is my sister Maybelle's in a whorehouse in New Orleans gettin' fucked seven times a night. Is it because I'm so damn ugly? Is that why you don't want me?"

She ran the words together so fast Washington had a hard time untangling them. "I want you all right. You're not ugly. But I been given responsibility. I got to show a black man can handle responsibility."

"How long that gonna take? Eight, ten years? Then the white man's gonna let you have some satisfaction?"

"I'll get satisfaction when I decide I want it. Get out of here now before I whip your silly ass."

Lucy scuttled out a side door and Sergeant Washington stopped to check on the feverish Clay. Jasper Jones was sitting with him. "Don't let that cracker doctor cut off his leg, Moses," Jasper said.

"I'll talk to the major. Maybe find another doctor."

"Get him some whiskey," Jasper said. "Whiskey kills fever."

Outside, the troopers were chowing down on chicken and ham from the Gentry kitchen. The major had made sure they got a share of the white folk's feast. But there was no whiskey. The major had made that a standing rule. They were drinking champagne mixed with apple juice—strong enough to make the boys cheerful but not crazy.

Sergeant Washington decided to go over to the party and see if the major could give him some whiskey for Private Clay. There were about a dozen couples on the dance floor. The band was playing a waltz and everyone was moving in a slow way that reminded the sergeant of dances at the seaside New Jersey hotel where he had worked before he joined the army. There was no sign of Major Stapleton.

The sergeant found Colonel Gentry talking to a tall sad-eyed woman and a big, heavyset man. "What's this?" the man said. "Are niggers invited to this shindig?" He was drunk.

"Of course not," Gentry said. "What brings you here, Sergeant?"

"Lookin' for Major Stapleton, Colonel. One of the wounded men could use a little whiskey. I wanted to get the major's permission."

"He's off in the trees with Miss Todd."

Why couldn't Gentry give him permission? It was his

whiskey. The colonel let Major Stapleton handle all the military details. He acted like his lost arm had disqualified him from being a real soldier.

Washington soon reached the grove of cottonwood trees at the far end of the property. Twice figures loomed up in the darkness and he said, "Major?" but they turned out to be other couples, kissing and panting like stallions and mares in heat. On the third try it was the major all right—and he was doing the same thing. He had his arms around Janet Todd and his lips were on her mouth. She let out a little shriek when Washington said, "Major?"

"What the hell do you want, Sergeant?"

Washington apologized and explained Private Clay's desperate need for whiskey. "Tell Colonel Gentry it's okay," the major said.

Back at the dance floor, Washington found the band was playing "Yankee Doodle." The big man who had cracked wise about niggers at the party was roaring out a song while Colonel Gentry stood there with a sad smile on his face.

> *"Yankee Doodle is no more*
> *Sunk his name and station*
> *Nigger Doodle takes his place*
> *And favors amalgamation.*
> *Nigger Doodle's all the go*
> *Ebony shins and bandy*
> *Loyal people all must bow*
> *To Nigger Doodle Dandy."*

Something strange started happening inside Sergeant Washington's head. The words that Major Stapleton had laid on him, *responsibility, leadership, example,* dissolved in a churning inner wind, a kind of spiritual hurricane. Maybe it had something to do with refusing Janet Todd's slave, Lucy. Maybe he could still feel, almost breathe, how much he had wanted her. Maybe it was just these lying sneering words.

Suddenly Sergeant Washington was out on the dance floor, putting his full weight behind a punch that sent the singer flying twenty-five feet. The sergeant stepped over him, walked to the bar and poured a half-bottle of Kentucky bourbon into his canteen. No one said a word while he stalked back to Private Clay with the whiskey.

NINE

RISK. THE WORD ECHOED AND re-echoed in Janet
Todd's head. He was a soldier who lived on risk. He ad-
mired other people who lived the same way. Her tongue
moved slowly across her bruised lips. He loved her—he
had almost confessed it out there in the darkness beneath the cottonwoods. He had been on the brink of saying the words and she had been ready to reveal—or at
least imply—what she was prepared to do if he under-
took for her sake a risk considerably greater than the
battlefields of Virginia or Georgia. To her chagrin they
had been drawn back to the dance floor by cries and
shouts to find Dr. Yancey kneeling beside Rogers Jameson, diagnosing a badly broken jaw. Major Stapleton
had been forced to respond to the outrage among the
guests by arresting Sergeant Washington and confining
him in the Keyport jail.

Downstairs, a clock chimed 2:00 A.M. A desultory
breeze rustled the leaves of the cottonwood trees outside
her window. It did nothing to stir the hot thick air in
Janet's bedroom. At midnight, as everyone went to bed,
Henry Gentry had reported that the temperature still
hovered at ninety degrees.

Was Major Stapleton awake, perhaps wondering what
she would do if he tiptoed into her room? Had she communicated her willingness to him by some sort of mental or spiritual telegraph lovers shared?

When she was fourteen Janet had watched a stallion
cover a mare. Her father had invited her to the occasion.
He said it was part of her education. He wanted her to

remember it as an image of male desire. He hoped it would make her more understanding, more compassionate, toward men.

She heard his oblique criticism of her mother. Letty Todd had not been more understanding, more compassionate, toward Gabriel Todd's desires. After their fourth child, a boy, was born dead, she had moved into a separate bedroom. At night, her door was closed to her husband. Behind her gaiety, the buoyant party manner she displayed in Lexington, there was this silent secret refusal. Janet's brothers never said a word about it to her. They left her to puzzle over love and the other mysteries of life while they rode off to gamble and cavort in Lexington and other cities where young men and fast women gathered.

What had happened between Gabriel and Letty Todd? Had her mother found sexual love disgusting? Was there a similar secret waiting to be discovered in Major Stapleton's bedroom? Some sort of repulsive ritual that no educated woman could tolerate? Would he take her the way the stallion had covered the mare? Crude wild thrusts from behind while she whimpered and snuffled half in ecstasy, half in terror?

At St. Mary-of-the-Woods, the Indiana school where Janet had spent two happy years, love and marriage had been one of the favorite topics after the lights were extinguished. Her roommate, Clara Daly, an Irish-American from Chicago, confided that she planned to stay single. Her mother had given birth to twelve children before dying in her thirteenth pregnancy. Maybe that was all Letty Todd was trying to avoid, behind her closed door.

Were there better ways to avoid pregnancy? One girl from Detroit, with a talkative older brother, said coitus interruptus was the best way, even if it was condemned in the Bible. No lover worthy of the name wanted to get a respectable woman pregnant.

Wait. Janet struggled to rein in her careening mind.
Think. Paul was not going to tiptoe into this room. He
knew Lucy was sleeping at the foot of the bed. This
might be the last time she would see him. He was
mailing his letter to the adjutant general tomorrow. He
had implied that the response would be swift. West
Point officers were a relatively rare and valued commodity.

Think. There was only one solution. She would have
to tiptoe into his room. There was no need to worry
about pregnancy. She sensed Paul would instantly understand she was risking it to prove how much she loved
him. He would respond to her daring, confident that he
had the money and the family name to proffer a wedding ring the moment one was needed. Long before that
became necessary, the larger risk she would ask him to
take for her sake would succeed or fail.

She was buoyed by knowing she was ready to marry
him, by the certainty that they could be happy in a
postwar world that included an independent South,
even if they did not choose to live there. She had been
attracted to him from the moment she saw him, in spite
of his blue uniform. There was a sadness in his eyes
that stirred an echo in her own soul. They were both
children of the war, even if she had never seen a battlefield.

The war was like the Ohio in flood, ripping away
chunks of the banks, toppling majestic old trees. The
war tore away chunks of lives; it shattered faith in a
benevolent God; it left desolation in its wake—but it
also left freedom. There were no certainties, only the re-
morseless unfolding of the future and a chance—a
hope—that a woman could find a place for herself in it.

The clock downstairs bonged once. Two-thirty. *Do it,*
whispered an alien voice in Janet's head. It was not
Day-Janet, the dutiful obedient daughter. It was Night-
Janet, the new woman who was emerging from the

war's rampage, a creature who moved through a world of unstable hopes and dangerous secrets in search of a new self.

Janet swung her legs out of the bed and listened for a long moment. The only sound was Lucy's deep breathing. She was asleep on her pallet at the foot of Janet's bed, as usual. If Lucy woke up, she would say nothing, even if she guessed where Janet was going. Lucy was totally devoted to her. At times she seemed almost part of her.

Gathering her blue silk nightrobe around her, Janet tiptoed into the hall. One, two, three doors to Paul's room. She tried the knob. It moved noiselessly in her hand. She opened the door just enough to slip inside, without arousing a rusty hinge.

To the right, on a desk in the corner, a small oil lamp created a yellow glow and left the rest of the room in virtual darkness. Major Stapleton sat at the desk, naked from the waist up, writing a letter. The major had the physique of a Greek or Roman statue—a broad firm chest covered with curly blond hair, sloping muscles in his arms, a solid neck. Just above the nipple on the left side of his chest was the scar of the wound he had received at Antietam. It was an ugly red blotch, with a web of bluish lines all around it.

For a moment, Janet could do nothing but stare at the scar in dismay. *Damaged*. The word resounded in her head. She felt as if she were looking at one of those extraordinary marble statues Lord Elgin had discovered in Greece that had been marred by a clumsy workman or a puritanical hater of nudity in art. It was much worse than Paul's head wound. She had seen the ridge of scar tissue beneath his blond hair. He had joked about how the doctors had opened his skull and closed it with a metal plate. Somehow this chest wound seemed more awful. Was it because it was concealed? Or because it was so close to his heart? Did it suggest more than disfigurement?

Paul gazed at Janet in undisguised astonishment. "What do you want?" he asked in a hushed voice.

"I've come—to let you know just how much I care for you," Janet said. "To show you—that you're not the only one who's willing to risk something."

He leaned forward and blew out the oil lamp. His chair scraped on the floor as he stood up. In a moment he loomed over her. "You're sure?" he said.

"If you are," she said.

"I've never been more certain of anything in my life. I was writing a letter to my mother, telling her about you—"

"I want you to share a risk that means a great deal to me. A risk connected with the war. I hope you'll do it as wholeheartedly as I'm prepared to share my—my affection—with you."

He drew her to him for a long surprisingly gentle kiss. "Only if you understand something *vital*. Loving you takes precedence over everything else. No matter what I think or say about this other risk, loving you will come first. I want you to love me that way. Can you—will you?"

It was not unfolding like the scenario Janet had imagined. Where was the swelling savagery of male desire, the brutal thrusts? She had assumed the pledge of partnership, the words of endearment, would be exchanged later, when she had demonstrated how richly she was prepared to reward him. She had to answer him without hesitation.

"I'll try. With all my heart."

"Oh, Janet."

Paul kissed her again and slipped the nightrobe from her shoulders. His hands roved her body and found the straps of her nightgown. He slid them down her arms and the silken cloth fell to her feet. Naked, she sensed he too had shed the underclothes he had been wearing.

"I'm so *honored*—this is so *precious*," he said.

His hands continued to rove her body. She felt a wildness, like the beat of invisible wings, rising inside her. She *wanted* him. She wanted to be that violated humiliated mare. She was unafraid, moving past her mother's refusal with a faith in her capacity to survive the worst imaginable shame.

Major Stapleton lifted her in his arms and carried her to the bed. Suddenly his fingers were in truly forbidden territory. He was touching her in a way that transcended any and all expectations. The beating wings multiplied enormously inside her body until they threatened to pound her heart to pieces.

"I love you," she whispered. "I love you love you love you."

Where had that dangerous word come from? Not once but four times. It seemed to exist outside Janet's will, her intellect. Suddenly he was above her, pressing her into the soft mattress with his body. His tongue roved her mouth. "Janet, Janet, Janet," he whispered.

A flash of white pain as he tore her hymen and he was within her—but there was still nothing of the stallion's rampage. *He's a lover,* whispered Night-Janet in shock and dismay. *He was in loving control.* Long slow thrusts sent whirring flights of azure pleasure up her belly into her breasts.

A fist pounded on the door. "Major Stapleton!" cried Colonel Gentry in a hoarse gasping voice. "You'd better get downtown immediately with your troopers. There's a mob gathering. They're threatening to lynch Sergeant Washington."

"God*damn* it!" Paul hissed.

Coitus interruptus whispered a voice in Janet's head. Was it Day-Janet, mocking her? Paul rolled out of the bed, found Janet's night robe and nightgown and pressed them into her arms.

"Send a servant to wake up the bugler," Paul said to

Gentry. "Tell him to sound boots and saddles. I'll be there in five minutes."

"Are you dressed?" Paul whispered to Janet.

"Yes," she said, pulling the nighrobe around her.

He lit the small lamp on the corner desk and began putting on his clothes in the shadows just beyond its glow. "You should be able to get back to your room. I'll take Gentry with me."

In no more than three minutes Paul was in his uniform. She watched him strap his holstered pistol around his waist. He strode across the room and kissed her. "I love you," he said. "You love me. Nothing else matters."

He was gone into the night. Janet waited five minutes and slipped into the silent hall. In her bedroom, Lucy was awake. "Oh, Miz Janet, I feared you was sick," she said.

"It's so hot. I took a walk around the grounds."

Outside, the metallic notes of the bugle rang out, summoning Major Stapleton's black troopers from sleep. Lucy ignored it and persisted in her puzzlement.

"Would you like a drink of cold water?"

"No. Don't worry about it."

"Yes'm."

Lucy waited a strategic moment. "Major Stapleton's a handsome man, ain't he."

"Yes."

"He sure seems crazy about you."

There was no need to tell Lucy anything. But another kind of need was exploding in Janet's body and soul. She had to tell someone what was happening to her. Who better than Lucy? It was almost like talking to herself.

"Major Stapleton loves me. He's going to help us win this war."

"That's powerful news, Miz Janet."

"Don't mention it to a soul."

"I won't say a word to no one," Lucy promised. "I means, it's a sort of military secret, ain't it?"

Janet laughed and gave Lucy a fierce hug. "Yes. That's what it is. A wonderful military secret. Not even Major Stapleton knows it yet."

TEN

DOWN KEYPORT'S MAIN STREET PAST a dozen dark storefronts Major Paul Stapleton led his troopers at a brisk canter, in a column of twos. Riding beside him, Colonel Henry Gentry found himself admiring the major's military judgment. A gallop might have triggered panicky gunfire. A canter exhibited exactly the right amount of determination. Riding two-men-abreast converted them into a column a half-block long, making them look formidable.

They could see the mob now. At least a dozen of them were carrying torches that cast a fluctuating glare over their enraged faces. From their mouths came a guttural chant: "Give us the nigger! Give us the nigger!" The implications of that refrain made Gentry's brain congeal. Was this all Lincoln had to show for three years of war and a half-million dead?

About a hundred men swirled before the darkened courthouse. The sheriff of Hunter County, gaunt Monroe Cantwell, stood in the doorway with two deputies, horsefaced Lew Mason and graybearded Pete Grumbach. They had shotguns leveled on their hips, but their faces revealed little enthusiasm for the task of defending Sergeant Moses Washington, downstairs in the basement jail.

"Give us the nigger," the mob chanted. "Give us the nigger *now!*"

Sheriff Cantwell had sent a messenger racing to Gentry's door urging him to call out the troopers. As the ranking Union officer in Hunter County, Gentry was the ultimate authority. The state was divided into military districts because the Republican governor, Oliver Morton, had no confidence in Democratic officials. They in turn were inclined to abandon all attempts at law enforcement and let the army take the heat when the populace grew restless.

"Sound platoons right oblique," Major Stapleton told the bugler.

As the brisk notes resounded against the storefronts, the column split into two files. One took up a position on the south side of the courthouse, facing Main Street, the other on the east, facing Court Street.

"Sabers!" called Major Stapleton. With a simultaneous shiver of steel, ninety-six gleaming sabers slid from their scabbards and were hefted erect in the torchlight. The display of weapons evoked a howl of fury from the mob. Most of the rage was directed at Gentry.

"Now we know the whole truth about you, Henry. You're nothin' but a goddamn nigger lover!" one man bellowed.

"What're you gonna do, Henry? Sit there with these niggers for the rest of the year? The minute they go away, we're comin' back!" roared another man.

"Give us the nigger, Henry!" about half of them shrieked in unison.

The whole mob quickly adopted it: "Give—us—the—nigger—Henry!"

"Give'm to us or you better get asbestos shingles for your house!" shouted another man.

Several men in the rear of the mob fired pistols in the air. Some of the cavalry horses reared and almost bolted. It occurred to Gentry that cavalry was not the best answer to this situation. A company of infantry with fixed bayonets could disperse these bullies in five minutes. "Give—us—the—nigger—Henry!" roared the entire mob. A half-dozen more guns went off. Horses reared and backed and whinnied.

At the edge of the torchlight, in the shadow of the shuttered Canaday Saloon, Rogers Jameson sat in a chaise beside his brother-in-law, newspaper editor Andrew Conway, giving a semi-legitimacy to the mob. Walter Yancey had wired Rogers' fractured jaw, making it difficult for him to give one of his patented rabble-rousing speeches. But Jameson was demonstrating that no one, above all a black man under Henry Gentry's command, could humiliate him with impunity.

"Tell them if another gun goes off, I'll order my men to charge them," Major Stapleton said.

Gentry dismounted and walked up on the courthouse steps beside Sheriff Cantwell and his deputies. "Listen to me!" he shouted. "I know why you're angry. I was angry myself when Sergeant Washington punched Rogers Jameson. The sergeant committed a serious breach of the peace and he's going to pay for it. I'm going to report him to headquarters in Indianapolis. The army will punish him. The code of military justice doesn't permit any soldier to attack a civilian."

"Give us the nigger, Henry! Shut your stupid mouth and give us the nigger!" the mob howled.

At least a dozen more guns went off. One of the horses at the end of the line facing Main Street bolted, carrying his trooper into the night at a wild gallop. The mob roared with laughter. "These niggers are findin' out there's more to ridin' a horse than sittin' in the saddle!" one man bellowed.

"You've got two minutes to clear out of here!" Major Stapleton shouted. He took out his watch and began counting. "Thirty seconds—sixty seconds," he said.

The bugler sounded another burst of notes. The line of troopers facing Court Street wheeled and rode into Main Street. The mob now faced two arrays of drawn sabers. "You're a nigger-lovin' bastard!" howled one Democrat.

"One minute and thirty seconds," Major Stapleton said.

At a wave of his hand, the Court Street line began moving toward the mob. The rioters backed away, several tripping over their own feet and scrambling up to continue the retreat down Main Street. In another sixty seconds, they were a block away, their shouts and insults feeble echoes.

"I'm glad someone in your army knows what he's doin', Henry," Sheriff Cantwell said.

"I thought they might listen to reason," Gentry said.

"Reason?" Cantwell said. "No one's listened to reason since your friend Abe Lincoln decided he knew more than God and started this miserable war."

"I think those fellows who fired on the flag at Fort Sumter had something to do with starting the war, Monroe," Gentry said.

"Nobody buys that line of shit anymore, Henry," Cantwell said. "I don't believe even Republicans buy it. Only ass kissers of Abe like you are still spoutin' it."

Major Stapleton joined them on the courthouse steps. "I'm sorry, Colonel. I had to take charge before half our horses ran away."

"I understand, Major."

There was simply no end to the humiliation that God seemed determined to inflict on his not very faithful servant Henry Gentry. First the Almighty had lopped off his arm and now He was amputating whatever shreds of manhood Gentry could claim for staying in uniform. Major Stapleton obviously despised him as much as Sheriff Monroe Cantwell and most of the other citizens of Hunter County.

Gentry nodded his agreement as Major Stapleton announced he was going to station ten troopers with carbines in the courthouse until they heard what

Indianapolis wanted to do about Sergeant Washington. At the major's insistence, Gentry went downstairs with him and assured Washington that they would do everything in their power to guarantee his safety.

"I'm real sorry I lost my temper, Colonel," Sergeant Washington said.

"Personally, I'm glad you slugged the bastard, Moses," Major Stapleton said. "But I'm worried about how the army will react."

"I understands, Major," Washington said. "I understands."

They left him hunched on his cot in the corner of his cell. A few cells away, someone called, "Colonel Gentry!" It was Robert Garner, the deserter they had captured at the Fitzsimmons farm. "Have you written to my momma?"

"I sent her a telegram but it was returned. She's not at that address."

"Oh. She was sick. Maybe she moved in with friends."

"I don't know what else I can do," Gentry said.

Garner began to blubber. "Don't let them shoot me, Colonel. I didn't mean that Confederate oath—"

Gentry rode back to his house through the sunrise with Major Stapleton and the black troopers. They arrived as Millicent Todd Gentry came out on the porch to say good-bye to Janet Todd and Lucy, who looked longingly at Gentry. Did she have something else to tell him? Maybe it did not matter. Gentry felt battered, almost physically beaten, by the hatred the mob had flung at him.

Down in his cellar office, Gentry picked up a letter he had been writing when the messenger from Sheriff Cantwell arrived:

Dear Abe:
   The state of Indiana is on the brink of sliding

across the Ohio into the Confederacy. This is a hell of a message to send you on Independence Day. From the start of this thing, we agreed I would tell you the truth as I saw it no matter how much it hurt. An awful lot of chickens are coming home to roost, Abe, looking more and more like vultures. There isn't a Democrat I know who isn't either a secret Southern sympathizer or an outspoken peace at any price man. The number who are ready to reach for their guns and join an armed uprising grows by the day.

Abe, I told you last year the Emancipation Proclamation was your biggest blunder yet. Maybe it won you support in New England—but why did you have to appease those self righteous bastards? The Yankees aren't going to quit the war. They know they have to win or face the vengeance of the South—and maybe the West. I'm told there isn't a man in Sherman's army or any other army where westerners are fighting who wouldn't rather shoot an abolitionist than a rebel, if he was given half a chance.

It seems to me you have to say something—do something—to show the people of the North that you have no intention of inflicting two or three million freed ex-slaves on them as the price of victory. You've got to announce a program to give them land in the west—set them up like the Indian tribes on reservations. Or lay out the details of the plan you mentioned to me last year—send them back to Africa or to some Caribbean island like Santo Domingo, which is half black already.

If you made that part of your reelection campaign, I think we would be able to reduce the disaffection among the Democrats by 50 percent.

If you pursue the course that the ultras put in the platform at the Republican Convention last

month—total abolition and the unconditional sur-
render of the South—I can't answer for the conse-
quences here in Indiana.

With statesmanship, Abe, this thing can be de-
fused short of the brutal application of force. These
are my neighbors, my friends—and your old neigh-
bors and friends—the Bradys, the Cantwells, the
Conways. Some of them have lost sons in the war.
The nightmare has driven them a little crazy. I
know you never dreamt the thing would last three
years—and no end in sight. Neither did I, old
friend. What I'm urging you to do is avoid the worst
consequences of that blunder—the sowing of per-
petual hatred between Democrats and Republicans
in Indiana, Kentucky, and the rest of the Midwest.

There may be no hope of changing the hatred
between the Old North and the Old South. But we
can, we must do something to prevent that hatred
from penetrating our country's heartland.

As ever,
Henry

Colonel Gentry took his bulky Colt pistol out of the
desk drawer and checked the chamber. It was loaded.
Maybe tonight he would do it. Maybe there was no
other way to convince his friend the president that Gentry took his predictions of doom seriously, that the letter
was not what Abe used to call a Gentry effusion—a
mere exercise of the forebrain. Maybe his corpse would
convince Abe that this lamentation came from the heart,
the belly, the bowels.

Clumping steps on the cellar stairs. A man in cavalry
boots. Through the dimness loomed Major Paul Stapleton, a solemn expression on his handsome face. "I've
thought over your proposition, Colonel. I'm prepared to
work with you to infiltrate the Sons of Liberty. But you
must understand one thing. I'm in love with Janet Todd.

Under no circumstances can she be prosecuted for her part in the conspiracy. She must be protected at all costs—even if that involves lying, subterfuge, the destruction of incriminating evidence."

"Agreed," Colonel Gentry said. What difference did any of that make to a man who had consigned his ruined soul to eternity?

Major Stapleton held out his hand. Colonel Gentry stared into his young face. He could see the line of scar tissue beneath his blond hair, where the doctors had trepanned him to extract the Gettysburg bullet. Love, an emotion that had caused Gentry nothing but pain and indignity, was animating the major's face. He was prepared to continue fighting this baffling, tormented struggle in its name.

What could Gentry say? He was doomed to failure and humiliation? No, he would sound like a madman. He shook Major Stapleton's hand.

"I liked your performance down there at the courthouse," Stapleton said.

"You did?" Gentry said.

"I was afraid one of those fellows would put a bullet through you. Didn't the thought occur to you?"

"No—I mean—they're all neighbors—friends."

Colonel Gentry struggled to realize Major Stapleton was paying him a compliment, one soldier to another. One soldier who had also met an enemy bullet and knew what it could do to a man. Was it possible, in his blundering way, Henry Todd Gentry had been courageous? Perhaps he had lost touch with the febrile amateur soldier who had marched to Shiloh dreaming that martial glory might give him the reputation he needed to become a leader who could wrest political control of Hunter County from know-nothings like Andy Conway. Perhaps the amputation, his mother's barely concealed contempt, which the amputation seemed to confirm and deepen, the envy that had snarled and slashed around him all his life, had blurred his vision of himself.

Major Stapleton clumped back up the stairs. Colonel Gentry folded his lamentation and stuffed it into an envelope, on which he wrote:

> A. Lincoln
> Executive Mansion
> Washington D.C.

Gentry decided to put his pistol someplace where it would stop tempting him. He went upstairs to his bedroom and thrust it into the wall safe behind the painting of Alexander Hamilton that hung over his bed. Whatever was going to happen next, he wanted to be around to see it.

ELEVEN

Is this the latest policy of the Lincoln Administration? Negro brutes are encouraged to beat up honest Democrats on the Fourth of July? We call upon the government and the army to answer this question as soon as possible! Every Democrat in Indiana is entitled to know whether he can venture on the streets and roads of the state without fear of assault.

PAUL STAPLETON SAT IN HIS hot room at the Gentry mansion, reading the latest edition of the *Keyport Record.* Editor Andrew Conway was trying to make Rogers Jameson's broken jaw into a major political issue. But Paul found it hard to concentrate on the problem. In his head he kept hearing Janet Todd's sibilant southern voice. His hands yearned to cup those welcoming breasts. His lips longed for that yielding mouth. The wildness of his desire transcended anything his brother Charlie had ever described to him.

Above all Major Stapleton savored the risk, the challenge, of loving her and persuading her to love him, even if he betrayed this febrile plan for a local insurrection. Paul found it hard to take it seriously, no matter how agitated it made Henry Todd Gentry. The Union had a half-million trained soldiers in its ranks. He could not imagine amateurs disturbing the vast military machine that was relentlessly grinding the Confederacy into history's dust. Janet was too intelligent not to see this, eventually. In the end she would be doubly grateful for his loving protection.

"Major?" It was Colonel Gentry outside his door again. Remembering his intrusion three nights ago, for a moment Paul could feel, think, nothing but *Janet.* Her name expanded to fill his mind and body. Paul opened the door to find Gentry looking more than a little agitated.

"We've gotten some bad news from Indianapolis. General Carrington is coming down here personally to court-martial Moses Washington."

Paul had heard little good about General Carrington from people in Keyport. Even Gentry seemed to dislike him. "What's he got in mind?"

"Placating the Democrats—and embarrassing me, I suspect. Andy Conway's editorials have been reprinted all over the state. Carrington never wanted blacks here in the first place. It was my idea. I thought it might convince a few Democrats that they could be good soldiers and good citizens—"

"What can we do?" Paul asked.

"I could write Lincoln. But I hate to bother him with local quarrels. General Carrington says he also wants to court-martial the deserter, Garner, and execute him in the courthouse square if he's found guilty. I may write to Lincoln about that. It would be murder to kill that kid."

Paul had seen more than a few deserters shot. None had sworn allegiance to the enemy like Garner. But he saw no point in lecturing Colonel Gentry on the realities of military discipline. "I'll talk to Moses. Let him know what's coming," he said.

Outside in the ferocious sun, Paul found Sergeant Washington drilling his men in the art and science of the saber. Paul had paid $500 to bail Washington out of the Keyport jail. He was demonstrating his gratitude by honing the men's combat skills.

A stuffed dummy sat on a large wooden horse. One

after another, the troopers charged this scarecrow and hacked off an arm or part of his head with their hissing blades. Watching them, Paul felt the unique satisfaction that comes from commanding men—something civilians would never experience or comprehend. He—and Washington—had made these men into first-rate cavalry. They were as good as any troop Paul had seen in George Armstrong Custer's division.

Paul motioned Washington to join him in the barn. "I just talked to Colonel Gentry. He tells me General Carrington, the federal commander in Indiana, isn't accepting any excuses for what happened on the Fourth of July. He's coming down here to court-martial you. You're probably going to lose your stripes, Moses—and maybe get a reduction in pay and two weeks in solitary confinement on bread and water."

"What that guy was singin' won't make a difference?"

"Not to General Carrington. He's trying to keep the Democrats happy."

Washington sighed. "I knows you done your best for me, Major," he said. "I'll just have to bear it."

"I'll testify for you in the court-martial. I'm just warning you it doesn't look good."

"Thanks, Major."

For a moment Paul heard General John Reynolds lecturing the first classmen at West Point. *Let me quote the wisest man who ever wrote about an officer's role, George Washington's friend, Baron Friedrich von Steuben: "Love is what an officer should feel for his men, what they should feel for him."*

Did he love this man and his fellow blacks? Not the way he loved Janet Todd. But he had developed a rough affection for Sergeant Washington, and with his help he had gotten to know some of the men. They were as varied in temperament and intelligence as any similar group of white men. There were workers and shirkers, wise guys and men eager to obey reasonable orders. Above all he sensed their gratitude for the time and attention he had devoted to training them.

"You better talk to the men. Get them ready for it. We don't want a breakdown in discipline."

"I'll get to work on it, Major," Washington said. There was a weariness—or was it a resentment?—in his voice that worried Paul.

"It stinks, Moses," he said. "But a soldier learns pretty quickly that the army has reasons for doing things that an individual may not like."

Lying for the government again, Paulie, his Gettysburg wound sneered.

Back in the house, dark-haired Dorothy Schreiber, daughter of the colonel of the Lincoln's Own regiment, presented Paul with a scented letter. Dorothy kept close track of his correspondence. It was part of a game of make-believe love Paul played with her. At sixteen Dorothy was old enough to enjoy it but too young for him to take seriously.

"It fairly *reeks* of perfume," Dorothy pouted. "I presume it's from Janet Todd."

"How can you be sure of that, Miss Dorothy?" Paul said. "Haven't I told you I've broken hearts from West Point to New Orleans?"

He ripped it open and read:

Dearest Paul:

I long to see you again. Can you visit me here at Hopemont for a few days? There are matters we should discuss. I had hoped to do so in Keyport, but events prevented us from reaching an understanding I hope will unite us in a bond deeper than ordinary lovers ever know.

Yours,
Janet

"What's she say?" Dorothy demanded.

"She's invited me to Kentucky for a visit," Paul said.

"A *visit*," Dorothy said, puckering her lips as if the word had a sour taste. "There's another letter for you. I left it on the hall table. It smells of the barnyard—or the battlefield."

Shoving Janet's note into the pocket of his shirt, Paul strolled into the hall to pick up the second letter. It did not smell of the barnyard or the battlefield, except perhaps to Dorothy Schreiber's refined nose. But it had the look of a long journey and handling by fingers rougher than those that toil in post offices. Paul ripped it open and read:

Dear Paul:

I'm writing to you by the light of a campfire near Peach Tree Creek, north of Atlanta. I send you mournful news. Jeff Tyler is no more.

I found him among the badly wounded on the battlefield after the Confederates attacked us and were repulsed. I had him carried to our field hospital, but he died before the doctors could do anything for him. He had been hit in the chest by two bullets.

After weeks of defensive maneuvering around half of Georgia, the Confederates gave John Bell Hood command of their army and he promptly launched one of his patented attacks. General Thomas had crossed Peach Tree Creek with about half our corps when Hood struck. The assault was poorly coordinated and they advanced in an oblique line which gave us a chance to enfilade them with devastating volleys from both flanks. Jeff was leading a regiment in Loring's division. I had ridden to the front with General Thomas and saw him go down within twenty yards of our front line.

Jeff asked me to send his love to you and said he was sure you and he would meet again in a better world. I feel as if I have lost a precious friend. I can only imagine how you will feel.

By my count, Jeff is the twentieth of our class to fall in this stupid war. The Confederates show no sign of quitting. They attack with the same reckless spirit that they've displayed from the start. Have you recovered from your wounds enough to join us? I'd be happy to recommend you for a place on General Thomas's staff.

As ever,
Jim Kinkaid

Paul did not know how long he stood there in the silent hall of the Gentry mansion while his eyes mechanically retraced Jim Kinkaid's words on the crinkled page. Behind him he heard Dorothy Schreiber say, "Major Stapleton. I've called you to dinner twice. What can be in that letter that absorbs you so?"

"It's news—from a West Point classmate," he said. "One of my close friends has been killed."

"In battle?"

"Yes. In Georgia."

"Captain Otis is at the table. It's the first time he's come downstairs."

"I'm glad to hear that," Paul said.

"I've begun to think there's something *noble* about him. He cares so much about the outcome of the war. Each day while he was recuperating from his wound he gave me a dollar to buy newspapers from passing steamboats. He wants to know everything that's happening, on all the battlefronts. I read the papers to him—"

Paul found himself grateful for Dorothy's chatter. It saved him from thinking about Thomas Jefferson Tyler.

"You seldom seem interested in the war," Dorothy said. "I've begun to wonder if that suggests a certain lack of grandeur in your soul, Major. Perhaps I'll transfer my affections to Captain Otis. Will that upset you?"

"I'll be devastated, Miss Dorothy. I may issue Otis a challenge."

"To what?"

"Oh, I don't know. Mud pies at twenty paces?"

"If Janet Todd told you that, it would be something more serious than mud pies, wouldn't it."

"I'd let Miss Todd choose the weapons. She'd probably opt for carbines with the hope of eliminating two Union soldiers at once."

They were at the doorway of the dining room. Rotund Millicent Todd Gentry was presiding over a platter of sliced chicken. Cold cider sat before each place in frosted glasses. Colonel Gentry was telling Captain Otis the latest news from the East. General Ulysses Grant had abandoned his costly assaults and settled into siege tactics before Richmond.

Gentry did not approve of this shift in strategy. "Lincoln needs a victory, a very big victory, to win this election," Gentry said. "He needs it soon."

"I hope Frémont runs. He'll get my vote," Captain Otis said. "He favors arming the slaves and making them the rulers of the South. Each one should get a hundred acres in compensation for his ordeal under the lash."

General John Frémont represented the left wing of the Republican Party. The radicals had nominated him on a separate ticket to express their disenchantment with Lincoln. Moderate Republicans were frantically trying to persuade the general not to run.

"Isn't it good to see Captain Otis out of bed?" Gentry said as Paul sat down.

"A pleasant surprise," Paul replied. "I thought he was

ready to claim a furlough wound. It's good to see his ardor for battle has sustained him."

Otis squirmed in his chair. He suspected Paul was mocking his panic at the Fitzsimmons farm.

"What do you hear from New Jersey about Lincoln's chances?" Gentry asked.

"My mother, whose political instincts are keener than most men's, says he won't carry the state—and he'll probably lose New York, too."

"He doesn't deserve anyone's vote," Captain Otis said. "He's been a trimmer from start to finish."

"What will happen to the country if he loses?" Gentry said. "Have you given that any thought, Captain?"

It was impossible. How could he sit here talking politics with these people, when Jeff lay in the earth, his rakish smile forever extinguished, his face empty, like the faces of the dead at Antietam and Fredericksburg and Gettysburg?

"What we need is a leader with principles," Captain Otis said. "Lincoln is not a man soldiers will follow into the cannon's mouth."

"Do you think that's true, Major Stapleton?" Millicent Todd Gentry asked.

"If Mr. Lincoln dared to step onto a battlefield and charge a cannon or two, I'd follow him gratefully," Paul said. "But the moment a ball separated his head from his shoulders I'd proclaim an end to this miserable war. I daresay a veritable chorus of 'yeas' would support me from both sides of the battle line. Even Captain Otis would join it, I suspect—in preference to continuing the charge."

"Major Stapleton, I resent your imputation of cowardice. I resent it deeply!" Otis cried.

Dorothy Gentry was breathless with anticipation. "Are they going to fight a duel?" she asked.

"I'm not imputing cowardice to you, Captain," Paul

said. "On the contrary, I'm paying you the compliment of suggesting that beneath your fanaticism, there exists a fragmentary common sense."

He was chewing chicken and potato salad, drinking cider. He was alive and Jeff Tyler was dead. Killed by northern bullets, fired by men from Indiana, perhaps. Men who had no quarrel with southerners, unlike the maniacs from New England who had started this war by poisoning the country's mind against the South.

"Men with no principles, Major," Otis said, "are quick to call a man a fanatic because he stands for something."

"My test of a fanatic is simple, Major. If his so-called principles lead to bloodshed on a colossal scale and he doesn't recoil, doesn't even show a shiver of regret, that man is a fanatic."

Paul realized he had been aching to say this to Otis for a long time. Was Jeff Tyler's spirit speaking for him? Otis's mouth worked convulsively. "How can a man wearing the uniform of the United States Army say such things?" he said.

"Gentlemen, gentlemen," Henry Gentry said. "Remember we must work together."

"You're right, Colonel. Have you told Captain Otis of the likely fate of Sergeant Washington?"

"Yes."

"What do you think of it?"

"I regret to say he deserves a court-martial and severe punishment," Otis said. "We can't tolerate blacks attacking civilians, for any reason. If we ever hope to civilize these people, they've got to learn respect and obedience."

"Is that how you're going to treat them when they come to Massachusetts? Sounds like it won't be much different from slavery," Paul said.

It was not the first time Otis had betrayed a visceral

dislike of blacks. Colonel Gentry, who had gone to Harvard, had told Paul the attitude was not unusual among the Yankees.

"You don't want to protest? Write to your favorite Republican senator or congressman on Washington's behalf? Or maybe to Harriet Belcher Stovepipe suggesting she produce a novel about him?"

"I have very little political influence," Otis said in a dwindling voice. "I'm not acquainted with Mrs. Stowe."

"Well, at least you're on your feet again. You'll have to command the troop for a few days. I'm going to Kentucky to hear Janet Todd sing 'Dixie.' I trust I have your permission, Colonel Gentry?"

"I don't think the captain is well enough to mount a horse," Gentry said. "But we'll manage."

Paul gulped the rest of his cider, excused himself, and retreated to his room. He took Jim Kinkaid's letter out of his shirt pocket and read it again. *Doesn't this prove something?* a voice whispered. It was not his Gettysburg wound. It was outside his aching head, somewhere in the hot still room.

Jeff Tyler was sitting on his bed, his face a battered mess. He had just fought a bout with hooknosed burly Duane Brainerd of Connecticut, one of the most outspoken abolitionists in their class. Brainerd had remarked that owning slaves was impossible for a man of honor. Jeff regarded it as a personal insult and challenged him to a midnight meeting.

The stairwell and corridors were crammed with cadets in various states of undress. In Brainerd's room, they had moved out all the furniture. He was waiting with his second in a candlelit corner. Paul, as Jeff's second, took up a position in the opposite corner.

Brainerd attacked with a bludgeoning flailing rush. Jeff kept him at bay with jabs and quick combinations.

He bloodied the big Yankee's nose and blackened one of his eyes. But it soon became clear that Jeff lacked the strength to knock Brainerd down or out.

Eventually Brainerd got Jeff in a corner where his boxing skills and his courage did him little good. A terrific blow to the side of his head sent him crashing into the wall. From there the fight became a nightmare. Brainerd knocked Jeff down repeatedly. A final roundhouse right smashed him to the floor and Paul flung a towel into the center of the room, signifying defeat.

Paul lifted Jeff to his feet and he held out his hand to Brainerd. "You've beaten me, Brainerd. But I hope I've shown you I'm no coward," he said.

"You've only shown me you're mentally degenerate," Brainerd said. "I have no interest in shaking hands with you."

"Mr. Brainerd," Paul said. "Either you shake hands with Mr. Tyler immediately, or I'll be forced to fight you."

"When do you want to fight, Stapleton?" Brainerd asked.

Paul stripped off his tunic and shirt and stalked to the center of the room. He was taller than Brainerd and about the same weight. His brother Charlie had taught him to box at an early age. When Brainerd rushed him, Paul dropped into a crouch, stiffened him with a left jab, and demolished him with a right hook. Brainerd staggered to his feet only to find himself on the floor again seconds later. Three more knockdowns and his second threw in the towel. This time the groggy Yankee agreed to shake hands with Jeff Tyler.

Back in their room, Paul applied ice to Jeff's swollen face. "Doesn't this prove something?" Jeff asked, smiling up at him. "Doesn't it prove if the right people in the North stand with the South, we can defeat these fanatics?"

* * *

Major Stapleton looked dazedly around his Indiana bedroom. Thick tears slid down his face. He licked their salt taste on his lips. *Doesn't this prove something?* the voice whispered.

TWELVE

Dear Henry:

Your letter hit me hard in my tired spot. By the time I finished reading it, I was ready to announce I've decided not to run for reelection. Then I rallied a little and thought: maybe this is what God (or the doctor) ordered for me. I was about ready to give up on myself before I got your epistle of doom. I started thinking of answers to your lamentation. The next thing you know I was almost cheerful, in spite of getting handed Grant's latest casualty list. My God how that fellow devours men! But he's killing almost as many rebels—and we've got a big edge on them in the manpower department.

Grant's got the basic idea of this war down pat. You can't win it without killing people. All the other generals wanted to win without spilling too much blood. I freely admit I started out the same way. But now that the war's killed a half million. I've stopped. Maybe I'm turning into Genghis Khan. But I don't think so. I've just stopped hoping to save lives. It's out of our hands, Henry. This whole thing has been out of our hands for a long time. God is running this colossal show. He's placed a terrible curse on this once happy country. I can't think of any other reason for it but slavery. It must have been an abomination in His eyes for a long time.

I know you'll tell me that argument don't scour. There are slaves in the Bible. I can see us getting *into one of our old fashioned brain wrestles, with you ending up calling me the slipperiest animal since God invented a greased hog. You were the believer, Henry, at least until you went to Harvard, and I was the skeptic who couldn't swallow God's goodness when we had so much death and desolation in our lives. My mother's death, for instance. Remember how long I took to get over that? Then came my sister's death for no reason any mortal could discern. But now that I've seen death on a scale beyond our wildest boyhood imaginings, I've developed a whole new theology.*

I've been humbled, Henry. I've finally perceived the vastness, the inscrutability of God in his dealings with individual lives. We can't hope to grasp his purposes or his reasons. We can only glimpse the great wheeling deployments of his dark determinings. But we can glimpse them, Henry. In this job, where I make decisions almost big enough to imagine myself God's coadjutor, I've come to recognize my utter dependence on Him. Now I'm the believer and you're the naysayer. A funny turnaround. I guess I'm telling you that from here to the end of this war, we've got to march on faith, Henry, not reason.

If you want any hope of ending hatred in the heartland—and in the rest of the country—we have to win this war, Henry. If it ends in a stalemate, some sort of armed truce, then you'll see hatred fester on both sides to hitherto unparalleled proportions. In the North, South, West, all those who have lost sons and husbands and brothers will elect demagogues who'll bellow for revenge. In ten or twenty years we'll have another war and it will be a true holocaust.

That's why I've resolved to stop at nothing to win, Henry. Victory is America's only hope. In victory we can be magnanimous, we can restore not

*only the geographical union but the union of hearts
and minds that once bound us together. As for the
blacks, I have no intention of giving the abolitionists an inch on their future. The Emancipation
Proclamation was a promise I made to God before
the battle of Antietam. If we won that battle, I
promised to free the rebels' slaves. We won and I
could not break that promise, no matter what people said. It was my first glimpse of God's purpose
in this thing, Henry. There were some practical
considerations to it, but placating New England
was not one of them, I assure you. Let's not worry
about the blacks now. We can deal with them after
the war too. Strictly speaking we owe them nothing. A half million white men have already died to
free them.*

*Victory, Henry, that's the only thing I want you
to think about, to struggle toward. Anything you or
I have to do to win this war is justified by victory's
transcendent promise. Our reputations, our peace
of mind, yes, even the salvation of our miserable
souls, are mere tinsel in history's hurricane, compared to victory.*

Your old and eternal friend.
Abe Lincoln

Henry Gentry sat in his cellar office, remembering
young Abraham Lincoln. Especially remembering the
way he confronted the large thoughts about God and
destiny and human purpose that challenged his analyti-
cal mind. He wrestled with them exactly the way he
wrestled with an opponent at a husking bee or house-
raising or Fourth of July party.

Men came from Kentucky and a half-dozen surrounding Indiana counties to Keyport to see if they could
throw Abe Lincoln. No one ever did. Afterward, no matter how dirty the man had fought, Abe would buy him a

drink and they would part friends. Could he do the same thing with the rebellious South? For a moment Abe swelled to mythic proportions, those long sinewy arms seizing the seceded states, from the southern border of Kentucky to the Gulf of Mexico, from the eastern border of Kentucky to the Atlantic. His even longer legs were planted like stupendous trees in the midwest earth. He towered against the northern horizon like a creature from folklore—or a nightmare.

"Henry . . . can I interrupt you?"

It was Colonel Lawson Schreiber, the man who had replaced Gentry as commander of Lincoln's Own. He sank into the chair in front of Henry Gentry's desk. Although it was around noon, in the cellar's dim light Schreiber looked spectral. He was close to being a used-up soldier. Gentry poured him two fingers of bourbon and limited himself to one.

"You look like a man with bad news."

"We've only recruited ten men. I guess we'll have to take draftees. When's the next call?"

"In a week or so."

"A drafted man's as good as useless in a fight. He looks for the nearest hole to hide in."

"I guess you'll have to convince them there's no place to hide, Lawson."

"I can't do that, Henry. I can't shoot runaways. I know their fathers and mothers—"

"I understand. I'll wire Indianapolis to increase our quota."

A good man, Lawson Schreiber. He had married Amelia Conway Jameson's sister, Pauline. She had been almost as beautiful as Amelia. Pauline had died last year, some say of worry about her husband. Gentry had taken their daughter, Dorothy, into his house.

"How do things look from the front lines, Lawson?"

"It's become a test of whose devotion to the dead is stronger," Schreiber said. "It's their dead against our dead. But they don't have enemies slandering their dead the way we do. I think you should take a tougher line toward the Democrats, Henry."

"They're my friends and neighbors too, Lawson."

"I don't mean kill them. Just scare them enough to shut them up."

"People like Rogers Jameson don't scare easily."

"I'm glad that sergeant slugged him."

"Speaking of the sergeant, would you consider taking him and his men into your regiment? I think I could arrange it with Indianapolis. It would seem sort of fitting for a regiment called Lincoln's Own—"

Schreiber shook his head. "The men won't fight beside blacks."

"Why not? They're fighting to free them now."

"The sight of a black in a blue uniform drives the Rebs crazy. They come after them like they want to drink their blood. Nobody wants to be near them on a battlefield. They consider them hoodoos."

"I just thought I'd ask, Lawson."

"What the hell is Abe going to do with them after the war? Has he given you a clue?"

"I don't think he has a clue," Gentry said. "He's feeling his way in this thing, Lawson. It's between him and God, a lot of the time."

"God?" Lawson said. "I seem to remember Abe didn't have much good to say about Him—"

"The war's changed that, like it's changed almost everything," Gentry said.

"God," Lawson said. He had once been very devout. Something about the way he said the divine name made Gentry suspect that the war had changed Lawson Schreiber's idea of God.

"Now Abe says we can't begin to understand His ways," Gentry said.

"How true," Colonel Schreiber said. "Let me know when we can expect the draftees."

Schreiber's footsteps thudded up the stairs. Gentry began composing a telegram to the man in charge of the state's draft in Indianapolis. He was interrupted by a softer set of footsteps descending the stairs. A woman's voice said, "Henry—"

Amelia Conway Jameson emerged from the dim center of the cellar. She was wearing a green riding dress, with a mannish hat and a brass-buttoned coat over the flowing skirt. "Amelia," Gentry said. "What an unexpected pleasure."

"I want to talk to you about something that must remain utterly confidential, Henry."

"Of course."

She settled uneasily in the chair in front of the desk. Anxiety clouded her hazel eyes as Gentry lit another oil lamp. He wanted to see her as distinctly as possible. She was still beautiful. The soft supple mouth had the same Cupid's bow curl in the upper lip. Her brow was still as high, as white, as on her wedding day. The only traces of age were lines of care around her eyes and a single wrinkle on her right cheek.

"It's about my son Robert, the one I call Robin," she said. "He was twenty last week. That means he can be drafted."

"His name will probably come up."

"Robin's not a soldier. He's a dreamer, a poet. He's more my son than Rogers'."

"I've sensed that, the few times I've seen him. But there's no need to fret about his safety. Under the law, you can hire a substitute for three hundred dollars."

"Rogers says he won't spend the money. He says soldiering will make a man of Robin, like his brother Adam. I'm certain it will kill him. Robin's not a man's man like Adam. He doesn't get along well with most men his age. They call him vile names like Mary Jane because he prefers to read a book rather than shoot squirrels or drink whiskey—"

She struggled for self-control. "Rogers dislikes Robin because he's taken my part more than once when his father's abused me. I honestly think he'd like to see him dead."

Gentry heard decades of regret in those mournful words. He struggled to keep his mind focused on Robin Jameson. "I'll gladly loan you the money," he said.

"That would lead to more abuse—for both Robin and me. Rogers hates you more than ever now, Henry. He thinks you set that Negro sergeant on him."

"What can I do?" Gentry asked.

"You have some influence in Washington, thanks to your friendship with Lincoln. Can't you persuade someone to take Robin's name off the draft list?"

"My influence is regrettably slight," Gentry said. "Lincoln treats my letters as the ravings of a maniac most of the time. Anyway, the draft is run by the individual states. I don't think anyone from Washington would interfere."

"Please, Henry! There must be something you can do. If he's drafted can't you get him assigned to duty as your aide—or someone else's aide, behind the lines?"

"There's only one way to do that," Gentry said. "You'd have to give the government something valuable enough to persuade them to return the favor."

Amelia looked bewildered. "What could that be?"

"You'd have to become an informer. On your husband. I know he's heavily involved in the Sons of Liberty. We'd want to know everything you can find out—by reading his mail, eavesdropping behind closed doors. In a word—betraying him."

"Are you planting spies in other families this way, Henry?"

"Whenever I get a chance," Gentry said. He could not believe the character he was assuming. The flinty-hearted spymaster, without an iota of compassion in his soul. Should he read her Lincoln's letter? That would be a waste of breath. It was bad enough that he had Lincoln on the wall, gazing at them from the shadows.

"I have another son I love for his own virtues," Amelia said. "He's heart and soul with my husband in this thing. If Adam found out I betrayed them, what would he think of me—of life itself?"

"When you start a war that kills a half-million people, you have to expect some retribution."

"We didn't start this war. It invaded our lives without any consent on our part. Your friend Lincoln started it, if anyone did."

"Adam will never know anything about it," Gentry said. "You have my solemn promise on that."

"But you'll have to tell someone in Washington or Kentucky to persuade them to help Robin."

"I'll do my best to mask your identity. I'll name someone else in the family—perhaps Robin—if they insist on a source."

"No! His father would kill Robin. He'd kill him in cold blood if he ever suspected. Better me. I'll have to trust you—and the faceless bureaucrats above you."

"You can trust me, Amelia. You must know that."

She looked past him at Lincoln's picture, her lips compressed to a bitter line. Her silence stirred a throb of pain in Gentry's amputated arm. Strange, the way pain existed in absent flesh—and in departed affection.

"How should I communicate with you?"

"Write letters to me at my store, addressed to Walter Scott. I want to know the number of men they've raised, where their guns and ammunition are being hidden—above all the exact date on which they plan to rise."

"I understand."

She rose to go. She looked so sad, Gentry wondered if she was mourning this annihilation of the pathetic ghost of their lost love. For a moment he wanted to put his arm around her and ask her to forgive him. But he was afraid she would recoil from his touch.

"Lincoln says after the war we can begin to think about loving each other again."

There was no answer. Amelia vanished into the dim center of the cellar. Gentry listened to her slowly ascend the stairs. *Is that good enough, Abe?* he asked the picture on the wall. *Is that good enough?*

THIRTEEN

THE SULTRY RIVER BREEZE WAS almost tropical in its mixture of heat and humidity. It combined with the current to drive the red-hulled canoe down the Ohio at a swift, almost reckless pace. In the prow, Janet Todd lounged against a set of red leather cushions like an houri in white. But Paul Stapleton, wielding the paddle in the stern, did not see the passionate woman he had held in his arms last week. He was not on the broad Ohio. He was on another river and there was another face, another body in the prow: Jeff Tyler. He was paddling past Anthony's Nose and the other mountains around West Point while Jeff gave him playful orders like a pompous captain on a man-of-war.

Stop, Paul told himself. *That is not death in the prow of this canoe. It is life, woman, vivid with desire—with all the potential for happiness that love can create.*

"There's a cove about a mile from here," Janet said. "Let's stop there for our picnic."

In another fifteen minutes, the prow thrust through a stand of reeds and grated on the sandy shore. Janet sprang out and held the canoe until Paul joined her and dragged it onto the grass. Janet lifted out a picnic basket and led Paul through the trees to a dell surrounded by huge cedars. Their branches formed a canopy against the July sun. Janet set out cold ham and potato salad and a bottle of white wine.

"We can speak freely here," Janet said. "There isn't a house within two miles. My brothers used to come here and pretend to be Indians. They called it the Happy

Hunting Ground. They drank liquor they'd snitched from their parents' cellars and pranced around the fire in breech clouts, doing war dances. Lucy and I crept through the woods one day and watched them."

"I envy them everything except you seeing me in a breechclout," Paul said.

"It's in my brothers' names—and in the names of all the other dead on both sides—that I'm hoping you'll join me in a cause that will unite us in the deepest imaginable way."

She was ignoring what he had told her about a professional soldier's indifference to causes. Once more he tried to evade her determination. "I can't imagine how I can feel more united to you than I am already—"

"It's a way—a plan—to end this abominable war."

"End the war? Janet—how can people our age do such a thing? Our best hope is to survive it—"

"I want you to join me in creating a new nation, a western confederacy that will pursue a separate destiny from the Old South and the Yankee East."

"I hope we're not going to do this all by ourselves."

His attempt at humor went nowhere. Darkness spilled from Janet's eyes, transforming her into a woman from an ancient saga, a prophetess, a sibyl. "Tens of thousands of Democrats in Kentucky, Indiana, Ohio, Illinois, and Michigan have learned they have nothing in common with the hate-filled hearts of the original sections. If they rise up and withdraw from the war, the killing will end. The West, with its immense resources, will hold the balance of power between the old North and South—and insist on immediate peace."

South, whispered Paul's Gettysburg wound. *That's where she's trying to take you. South. This western confederacy is a stalking horse for the other confederacy.*

Doesn't this prove something? whispered Jeff Tyler in the deepest recesses of Paul's heart. *Wasn't south where you wanted to go with me?*

Paul swallowed the cold wine and struggled to regain the cool professional soldier who lived on risk. With almost desperate urgency, he told himself Janet Todd was proposing a fantasy. President Abraham Lincoln was not going to let raw militiamen seize the nations' heartland without a fight. A dozen veteran regiments from Ulysses Grant's Army of the Potomac or William Tecumseh Sherman's Army of the Tennessee would annihilate them in a week.

Suddenly Paul saw himself as Charles Blondin, the daredevil acrobat who had mesmerized the world in 1859 by walking across Niagara Falls on a high wire. But in this version Janet was walking just ahead of him, putting both their lives at risk. The cataract boiled beneath them. It had its own fascination, a weird kind of face and voice. Was it the war, with its ten thousand murderous mouths?

"I wish I could believe in your vision," Paul said. "But won't it lead to even more bloodshed and worse federal tyranny? Won't Lincoln detach men from the armies in the East and West and rout these amateur soldiers? I'm afraid their uprising will only give him the justification he needs to set up a military dictatorship."

"If he tries that, he'll encounter a secret weapon that will reduce Washington, D.C., and every other city in the East to ashes."

"What's that?"

"Greek fire. It's a form of combustion that resists all attempts to extinguish it. It can burn down whole blocks in minutes."

"I've heard the term. It was supposedly used in the Middle Ages. But I thought it was a myth."

Janet shook her head. "A German scientist in Canada has rediscovered it. Hundreds of men are being trained in its use in Canada at this very moment. Hundreds more have already smuggled supplies of it into targeted northern cities."

"These men are from Kentucky?"

"Some are. Others are from the Southern Confederacy. The two confederacies will be natural allies. Though each will retain its independence."

Paul said nothing, but he realized his stare was accusatory. Janet was admitting her real motive: southern independence. For a moment her intensity faltered. She regained it by an act of will. "Other states may break away from New England's grip and join the West or the South. New Jersey, Pennsylvania, Maryland, Delaware. They all despise Lincoln and his war—and loathe Yankees."

"New Jersey certainly does," Paul said, thinking of how often he had heard Boston abolitionists denounced at his boyhood dinner table.

"Paul—if you join me we'll have a love that's united by our admiration, our desire, for each other—and by a cause that will change America's history."

History never made anyone happy. The Stapletons, living and dead, have proved that a dozen times, whispered the Gettysburg wound. Paul's aching head wanted to say it but his heart chose silence. A quarrel now might fatally undo their balance on the high wire.

Janet leaned toward him, her voice gathering fresh intensity in the shadowy stillness. "Say yes and love me here, now, in the daylight," she said. "I want to see all of you and I want you to see all of me. I want our nakedness to be a pledge of absolute honesty between us, a vow to conceal nothing, to hesitate at nothing, to risk everything without shame or fear of disgrace."

A mistake, whispered the Gettysburg wound in Paul's aching head. But in his heart another voice (Jeff Tyler's?) whispered it was *right.* It was exactly right for a soldier who lived on risk. The risk was more formidable than he had imagined it could become. But why should that stop him? Once love became part of their lives, it could change everything.

Slowly, they stripped away their clothes until Janet

was in a chemise and Paul in his underwear. He hesitated and watched her slide the straps of the chemise down her arms and peel it down her body. Naked, she walked toward him across the thick grass and kissed him.

It was not the first time Paul had seen a naked woman. In New Orleans, where French mores reigned in the brothels off Congo Square, nakedness was a given. But those women, even the most beautiful of them, were playthings, creatures of the night. Never had Paul expected to see naked the woman he would call his wife. Like most Americans, he accepted the need for darkness to make love respectable.

This was a new kind of love, infused with war's delirium. "Janet," Paul whispered. "Janet." He placed his hands on her firm, full rump and returned her kiss.

"Now, now," she murmured.

His lips on her mouth, Paul carried her back to where the dell narrowed and the grass was lush. He put her down and knelt beside her, his eyes roving her body, from her small coned breasts to the thick dark hair of her pubis. Above them the summer wind sighed through the topmost branches of the cedars. Sunlight spangled the shadowed grass and her flesh and his flesh, creating a magical aura.

"How beautiful you are," he said. It was not completely true. Janet's body was much like he had imagined it, more stocky than slim, not in accord with the standards of classic beauty. But that only made her supremely beautiful for Paul. A new irremovable crystallization was occurring in his soul. No matter what happened in the unforeseeable future, Paul knew he would never love another woman this way.

Janet touched the ugly scar of his Antietam wound on his chest. "Does it hurt?" she asked.

"Now and then," he said.

"When I saw it the night I came to you, I vowed I'd make sure a bullet would never do that to you again."

"Remember what I said that night? No matter what happens, our love comes first. Nothing can destroy it, failure, defeat, disappointment. Do you believe that?"

"We won't fail."

He kissed her before she could say more. He wanted to bar history and the possibility of its pain from this moment. He almost believed that if he isolated them from time's unpredictable grasp, they could achieve the perfection they needed to armor themselves against future disappointment.

If time did not stop, it unquestionably faltered. The swift shining Ohio became as motionless as a river in a painting; the wind seemed to dwindle in the treetops; even birds fell still. "Love, love, love," Paul whispered with each slow deliberate thrust. His brother Charlie had taught him well. He knew how to bring a woman to the edge of rapture.

Simultaneously, Paul remained Blondin on the high wire, performing an act infinitely more daring than that famous acrobat had ever attempted. To his surprise and secret pleasure, daylight made his performance a drama of conquest and submission that convinced him he was not surrendering. It was Janet who was surrendering. The willful woman who teased and taunted him at the Gentry house vanished before his eyes. She became a creature of the forest, a heaving primitive thing, crying out with uncontrolled delight. In Paul's churning head this transformation promised him that somehow he would extricate them from her commitment to the South's lost cause—in spite of Jeff Tyler's forlorn grave in Georgia.

FOURTEEN

IN HOPEMONT, LUCY LAY ON Janet Todd's bed, gasping for breath. She was covered with sweat yet she shook and shivered like someone who had just fallen into the Ohio River in December. She had run all the way back from her hiding place in the bushes beyond the dell where she had watched Miss Janet and Major Paul Stapleton make love.

It was so unbelievable, Lucy found herself wondering if some evil spirit had cast a spell on her. Was she going to be damned to hell for betraying Miss Janet and Colonel Todd? Were maybe the ghosts of Mister Jack or Mister Andy responsible? She remembered how mad they were when Miss Janet let drop that Lucy had led her down there with her friend Alicia Jameson to watch the boys dancing around that fire practically bare-ass.

Maybe their ghosts were driving her crazy in revenge for that long-ago betrayal. They probably knew all about what she was doing because in the spirit world there were no secrets, everybody knew everything because they were part of God. If they kept torturing her, maybe she'd confess her spying and Colonel Todd would whip her until she died and then Colonel Gentry never would get Maybelle out of that whorehouse in New Orleans.

Thinking of Maybelle steadied Lucy. It was not an evil dream. It was *real*. It was *true*. Miss Janet had taken off her clothes and made love like a fallen woman there on the grass. What could have gotten into her soul, that she'd do a thing like that? No matter how bad Lucy felt about betraying Miss Janet, she never stopped loving and respecting her.

Lucy had lived half her life in Miss Janet's body, imagining how good it must feel to be white and beautiful and have all those men wanting her and being able to say, no, not you or you or you but maybe you, Adam Jameson. And that tremendous man, so big his head kept bumping every doorway he walked through, slobbered and gurgled like a four-year-old whose momma had just said he could have a tiny taste of chocolate cake for dessert.

Having that kind of power over men had made Miss Janet seem like a kind of archangel to Lucy, a creature with huge white wings and a flaming sword. Miss Janet had shown her a picture of an archangel once in the family Bible. Black Joe, the preacher who went through the county saving souls at all the plantations, said that was exactly how they looked and they were the most powerful creatures in the spirit world outside God and the devil.

For a long time Lucy thought Miss Janet could not possibly be human like her, even though she had to go to the jakes like everybody else and her blood came every month and twice she got the summer fever and sweated and moaned and shivered and shook in her bed for a week or two with Lucy wiping her forehead and neck and giving her ice water every five minutes. Still Lucy thought maybe Miss Janet was just pretending to be human and at night she turned into that creature of wings and spirit.

Even when Miss Janet said maybe to Adam Jameson, she never let him near the woman part of her. The most she ever allowed was a kiss at twilight in the garden gazebo and a little squeeze that maybe let him feel her bubbies against his chest. He probably wanted to tear off her clothes and take her right there in the gazebo but he didn't. Instead he went away telling himself he was a no good.

Lucy knew this was the way white men thought about women like Miss Janet because she used to listen to Mister Jack and Mister Andy talk about their love lives. They never minded enjoying niggers and whores bare-ass or any other way but a respectable white woman like Miss Janet was another thing altogether. They almost hated to admit they wanted such women that way. They'd confess to each other how much they wanted someone like Adam Jameson's sister Alicia and how ashamed it made them and off they'd go to Louisville or Cincinnati for another go at the whores.

That was the way white people did it. They divided women up into good and bad and only loved the good ones. Niggers didn't get divided. They were only there to play with when you couldn't find a bad white woman. Adam Jameson loved Miss Janet so much you could see him almost bent over with the pain of it. It was like a knife in his belly all the time. But he never complained because the pain only proved how much he loved her.

Lucy used to look forward to the day when Adam would marry Miss Janet. She would sleep outside their door and listen to the love sounds inside. Even a lady like Miss Janet was bound to make some—and that would be the time when Lucy would creep into Miss Janet's body and find out what it meant to get laid and be loved by someone at the same time.

Niggers didn't seem to know how to do that, at least the niggers she knew. You couldn't blame them, really, because if you loved someone and the master decided to sell one or the other south the poor nigger could go stark crazy with the pain of it and maybe kill himself or herself or do something even worse like putting insect powder in the master's oatmeal and winding up getting hanged outside the county courthouse if the master's people didn't kill him or her first.

No one knew about the trick Lucy had learned of getting into Miss Janet's body. It was easy when you spent so much time with a person, watching her dress and un-dress and talk to you like she was talking to herself and you stood at the windows watching her flirt and dance with men since she was twelve years old and before that sat outside the schoolroom each day and walked her there and home again and made jokes with her about boys and other girls and pretty soon knew almost every-thing Janet thought and felt about the whole world.

What upset Lucy most about the dream or the crazi-ness or whatever she saw in the Happy Hunting Ground today was the way Miss Janet talked that Union major out of his clothes. It was *her* idea. No white lady was ever supposed to do such a thing. Lucy could see the major did not really want to strip. Maybe he knew Miss Janet was acting like a whore and he didn't really like it, no matter what she said about it meaning they'd never hide anything from each other.

Miz Janet, how could you do it? How could you spoil my idea about you? I loved and respected you so much. I never thought you'd get hurt or anything besides dis-appointed from the stuff I've been telling Colonel Gen-try. In fact he told me that it would help him keep you from getting hurt. They'd arrest all those traitors like Rogers Jameson and no one would ever know about Miz Janet but him.

Lucy wrapped her arms around herself and moaned, remembering why she loved Miss Janet. She would never forget the time when they were little and Mrs. Todd caught Lucy with her finger in a chocolate cake while they were entertaining Colonel Gentry and his mother at dinner and Colonel Todd swore he'd whip Lucy but Janet said, *Father, if you whip her I'd feel it as if you whipped me.*

She was remembering that time when they were walking in the woods and Janet told her they had the same soul. She said it was like water poured into two different glasses from the same pitcher. She said

Colonel Gentry (except he wasn't a colonel then) had written a poem about it. She said it was better than anything some Yankee named Ralph Waldo Emerson ever wrote. She said Uncle Henry was a very artistic man, whatever that meant.

Instead of thinking about Uncle Henry and Ralph Waldo Emerson Lucy had thought about the soul and the body. She was almost tempted to tell Miss Janet that she didn't care about the soul, no matter what the preachers said. What she wanted was the same body as Miss Janet, the same white skin and perfume to put on it and beautiful white dresses to wear over it. She almost told her how she lived in her body sometimes. But she was afraid Miss Janet would say she was crazy.

Oh oh oh. None of these thoughts stopped the memory of the crazy dream that turned out to be real. Miss Janet there with Major Stapleton in the shadowy green grass with the sun making spangles on their white skin. Lucy could see something strange was happening inside the major's soul, something was making him hold back a part of himself, while Miss Janet held back nothing, she was as gone as a mare in heat. There was no soul; there was only a kind of blankness, as if her face were a piece of paper with all the words washed off.

Lucy clutched a pillow and wept. She had not been in Miss Janet's body while she watched it. Not for one second. She realized that she could never do that again. They were separate bodies forever now. Miss Janet was no longer mysterious and wonderful in any way. She was just a woman whose skin happened to be white. A woman not so different from Lucy.

That did not mean she stopped loving Miss Janet but it freed her to think about what to do. She had to get over to Indiana to tell Colonel Gentry about this. From what she had heard this afternoon, there was no doubt that Miss Janet was turning Major Stapleton into a Confederate.

Lucy got up, smoothed the bed covers, and went

downstairs. Miss Janet and the major were just getting back from their trip on the river. Miss Janet was telling Colonel Todd how clever the major was, the way he kept close to the shore and avoided the worst of the current and they came home so fast you would swear they were going downriver instead of up.

"Miz Janet," Lucy said. "I been goin' through your clothes. I found I forgot to pack your new blue taffeta dress, the one you bought the last time you went to Louisville. I give it to one of the Gentry niggers to wash and she never give it back to me. I'll be glad to go get it if you gimmy two pennies for the ferryboat."

Lucy could see Miss Janet was pleased to hear about this mix-up. It meant she would not have to worry about Lucy waking up at the foot of her bed if she decided to visit Major Stapleton later in the night to celebrate him joining the Confederacy. The dress was actually hanging in Miss Janet's wardrobe upstairs but Lucy planned to fold it neatly and hide it in a bureau drawer in one of the guest rooms until she got back.

An hour later, Lucy was giving the ferryman a penny and listening to the *whump* of the steam engine in the middle of the long open boat. On the other side of the river it was another half hour's walk to Gentry's. It was almost dark when she got there. Who did she see in the front yard talking to Colonel Gentry but the big sergeant, Moses Washington. He looked at Lucy and she looked at him and she suddenly knew she was going to see him in the barn tonight.

Something in Washington's eyes made Lucy think he might be glad to see her. He looked sad and weary, like someone had turned him from a sergeant into a low-down slave nigger. Colonel Gentry asked her what she wanted. She pulled an envelope out of the pocket of her dress and said she had a letter from Major Stapleton. Colonel Gentry looked pleased. He took it from her and told her to get some supper in the kitchen.

Pretty soon Mrs. Gentry, the colonel's mother, came into the kitchen and asked if Miss Janet and the major were enjoying themselves. "Enjoyin' theirselves?" Lucy said. "They is crazy in love, Miz Gentry. She fusses so over everything she wears for him I'm worn to the bone puttin' on and talkin' off dresses. I got so tired I was *uppity*. It's a wonder I didn't get whipped."

"Janet would never whip you," Mrs. Gentry said. "You have that poor girl wrapped around your little finger."

Lucy ate in the kitchen with the Gentrys' cook, Minnie, and her husband, Peter, the butler. They were both old and gray and had rheumatism. They wheezed and groaned when they had to get up from the table. They were free niggers and considered Lucy such slave trash they did not even bother to talk to her. The two maids were the same way. They just looked at Lucy and laughed at her worn-out dress and bare feet.

"Don't they even buy you shoes?" one of them asked.

Minnie and Peter and the maids talked to each other about the war. The maids had brothers in the Union Army. They wanted the war to end before their brothers got killed and didn't care who won or lost. Minnie and Peter wanted the Confederacy to win. If the rebels lost all the slave niggers would come north and take away jobs from free niggers like them and their children. They had sons and daughters working in Indianapolis and Cincinnati who told them this was the big worry of their lives.

Lucy did not try to understand it. She concentrated on the only thing she wanted, getting Maybelle out of that New Orleans whorehouse. After dinner she went outside and saw Moses Washington walking up and down outside the barn like he had a hundred-pound sack of wheat on his back. "I'm comin' to see you tonight," she said. "Where you sleepin'?"

"Don't bother me," he said. "You didn't bring me nothin' but bad luck, girl."

"I'm comin'. I got somethin' to tell you," she said. "Somethin' important 'bout the major."

"I'll be in the barn."

Lucy waited until it was really dark and Colonel Gentry turned on the light in the cellar. She darted through the vegetable garden and pulled a string that hung outside the cellar door. It rang a little bell in Colonel Gentry's office. He had another string and bell running down the wall from his bedroom, in case she or some other spy came to see him late at night.

The damp cool air of the cellar made Lucy shiver. The colonel stood tilted to one side, as if he could not balance himself because of his missing arm. "What brings you back so soon?" he asked.

"I got some 'portant news. Miz Janet's turnin' the major into a Confederate."

"How do you know?"

Lucy's tongue seemed to swell until it was choking her. She coughed and coughed until she almost strangled and Colonel Gentry gave her some whiskey and water. When she got her breath she realized she couldn't tell the colonel about Miss Janet and the major making love in the Happy Hunting Ground. She couldn't disgrace Miss Janet that way. She lowered her eyes and mumbled like the most stupid nigger in Kentucky, "I just got a feelin', Colonel. I hear Miz Janet say things like the major's goin' to help her win the war."

"The major's a professional soldier. He's taken an oath of loyalty to the government. He's not going to break that for Miss Janet's sake. He's going to let her tell him all sorts of things—and report them back to me."

"I hopes you're right, Colonel. But it sure don't look that way to me. Any news on Maybelle?"

"I'm trying to find her. But I'm only a colonel. No one answers my letters to New Orleans."

He was not a good liar. Lying messed up his eyes

and his mouth. Lucy was glad she had lied to him about Miss Janet and the major. If it turned out Maybelle was dead, she didn't care which side won. She'd be almost glad the rebels won because Miss Janet would be safe and could love the major without anyone arresting her.

Outside in the hot barnyard, Lucy stood in a daze. Her feet began taking her to the barn. At the entrance she almost collided with one of the soldiers. "Where's the sergeant?" she asked.

"He won't be a sergeant much longer," the man said. "If you're lookin' for old Moses, he's in the back."

Groping past the horses snuffling in their dark stalls, Lucy found Moses Washington writing a letter by a flickering lantern. For a moment she could barely breathe. "Where'd you learn to write?" she asked.

"School," he said.

"Niggers go to school in New Jersey?"

"Why not?"

"They don't let'm in Kentucky."

"Too bad."

"Who you writin' to?"

"My daddy."

"What he do?"

"Fishes."

"A man can make a livin' catchin' fish?" The only fishermen Lucy had ever seen were lone anglers on the banks of the Ohio.

"He owns a boat."

Washington stopped writing. He put the letter in an envelope and sealed it. The envelope already had writing on it. He blew out the lantern and walked toward her in the dark. She could feel him looming over her. He was as big as Adam Jameson.

"You only got one thing in your cotton-pickin' little head, ain't you."

"I don't pick cotton. I'm a house nigger. We don't grow no cotton in d' first place."

"You still want to fool with me? I won't be a sergeant in a few days. Just a poor-ass private."

"I'm glad you socked old Jameson. I heard him singin' that song."

"That's why you want to go with me? It's my reward?"

"I noticed you before that. I said to myself, 'There's a nigger I likes.'"

"Why?"

Should she tell him because he was as big as Adam Jameson and she hoped she could imagine she was Miss Janet? She couldn't do that anymore, but he still might enjoy it so much he'd say, Lucy I love you. The words made her heart almost stop. Her tongue got thick again. She was almost choking.

"I—I—hopes you might like me, that's all."

He lifted her dress over her head. "I like you all right," he said. "But you brought me bad luck, girl. That's why I'm gonna take you. So you can pay off the bad luck."

"I don't wanna do it for that," Lucy said.

I wants—to love you. I wants you to love me. Lucy almost said it. But the words got lost somewhere in her belly, where she wanted him and was afraid she'd lose him if she said them.

"I tole you the rebels was comin', didn't I? I was tryin' to save your life."

"But the rebels didn't come. Instead trouble come. Big trouble for me— and for my men. I got a mind to invite them all in here to get a piece of you."

"The rebels'll be comin' now," Lucy said. "They're comin' now for sure. Miz Janet's got the major on her side. He's goin' to play the rebel game."

"How you know this?"

"I seen them today. At high noon. Bare-ass naked in the grass on the other side of the river."

"You ain't lyin'?"

"I ain't a liar!"

"I'll be dammed. I'll be *dammed*."

As he said this his right hand squeezed her bub so hard it hurt. Lucy was glad it hurt. She wanted to be hurt. She had told him what she had never thought she could tell anybody. She had betrayed Miss Janet in a new terrible way.

"You can't tell that to nobody," she said.

"Who says I can't?"

"I do! I'll kill you if you tell it."

"Wow. Dangerous little pickaninny. How you gonna kill me?"

"I don't know. I'll find a way," Lucy said. Tears trickled down her cheeks.

"Hey, hey," Moses Washington said. "It's okay. I won't tell no one. I just can't believe it. I can't believe the major'd sell out the Union. Even for a piece like Miss Janet."

"He's a goner," Lucy said. "But what do I care? Whether the war's won or lost won't make no difference to me. I'll still be a Todd nigger."

"Maybe not," Moses said. "Maybe if we win the war, you'd be free. Then what'd you do?"

"I'd go to New Jersey lookin' for you."

"You would? That's a long way."

"I'd get there. Because I ain't never seen a man I—I—*loved* before."

Lucy stopped, stunned by her own audacity. She had said it. She had said that terrible word.

"I didn't think a nigger like me could love anybody. But I could love you," she said.

"You think so? I'm a pretty bad man. I get mean sometimes."

"That happen to everybody. I wouldn't care."

"You know somethin'? You're a sweet little thing."

He lifted her up as if she were a child and kissed her

on the mouth. Then he slung her in his arms and walked to the back of the stall, where the straw was thick. She could hear the buttons pop as he took off his clothes. They were going to do it in the dark like white folks!

It was better, so much better than Lucy ever imagined it could be. She had done it twice with one of the field niggers but she didn't like it, she kept thinking of what Miss Janet would say. Now she was somehow free of Miss Janet and at the same time she *was* Miss Janet and Lucy and Miss Janet all in a crazy storm inside her. She didn't even care if she had a baby, she was sure Moses would find her and the baby after the war and they'd go to New Jersey and live in a cabin near his father's boat and eat fish and have more babies and die happy a hundred years from now.

"Does you love me?" Lucy whispered when he finished.

"I think maybe I do."

"Say it. I wants to hear it."

"I—love—you."

She heard a kind of smile in his voice. As if he thought they were playing a silly game. Maybe he didn't really mean it. But it was better than nothing.

"I'll pray to Jesus for you every day. That'll change yo' luck."

He drew her down on him for a long hard kiss. Lucy wondered if she could pray to Jesus for him when all her prayers hadn't helped Maybelle. She was so mad at Jesus she had stopped praying to him. Now she'd have to start again. She'd made a promise she couldn't break.

That was a big change for her. But something else even bigger had happened. She could not believe it at first. But it was there, alive and breathing inside her. For the first time Lucy wanted to be free.

FIFTEEN

"I REMEMBER YOUR FATHER WELL," Gabriel Todd said. "A giant of a man. He led us into the Mexican musketry and cannon in our first fight, at Monterrey, as if all that flying lead was no more dangerous than raindrops."

Paul Stapleton's eyes misted, his voice thickened. "I believe his army service was the most satisfying part of his career," he said.

"This old soldier feels the same way about his glory days," Janet said smiling at her father. "Maybe that's why I'm partial to soldiers."

"We went into action that day beside Jeff Davis and his Mississippi boys," Gabriel Todd continued. "There was an New Jersey regiment on our other flank. It was a war that made you proud to be an American. Never did I dream that thirteen years later our sons would be killin' each other."

"My father spent the last ten years of his life trying to prevent the catastrophe," Paul said.

They were in the dining room at Hopemont, surrounded by staring portraits of earlier Todds. Joseph, the gray-haired black butler, was removing the dessert plates. Throughout the meal, every time Janet's eyes met Paul's she felt a shiver of remembered delight from their morning in the Happy Hunting Ground. She was certain he felt it too. When they met in the upper hall on the way to dinner, he had given her a long lingering kiss.

They had been three for dinner. Letitia Todd claimed she was not well enough to join them. Privately, she warned Janet not to dawdle over coffee. She was expecting a visit from her spiritualist, Mrs. Havens, and wanted Janet and her father to join them to complete the so-called caring circle. Janet hoped Mrs. Havens's sulky would lose a wheel or break an axle or her horse would expire from the drought.

"Janet tells me she's convinced you that our plan for a western confederacy has some merit," Gabriel Todd said.

"She only gave me a general idea of it," Paul said. "I'm eager to learn more details."

"Let's start with numbers. We now have fifty thousand men enrolled on the secret membership books of the Sons of Liberty. An early success will enroll another fifty thousand, I'm certain of it."

"That's impressive," Paul said. "Are they organized into companies and regiments? Are they trained and well led?"

"They're organized. Their colonels are mostly Democrats who fought in Mexico, like yours truly," Gabriel Todd said. "The junior officers have been elected by their men, with their colonel's approval. A fair number are federal veterans who declined to reenlist after the Emancipation Proclamation."

"You think they can fight trained troops?"

"With some encouragement from trained troops on the other side, yes," Gabriel Todd said. "This thing has been building for almost two years. Thanks to my son Andy, I was able to put my finger on the men who could inspire them to rise—John Hunt Morgan's cavalry."

"So that was the reason for their raid into Indiana and Ohio last year?" Paul said.

"Yes."

"But it was—if I may use a painful word—a failure. Few if any Democrats rose to support them. Morgan's men were mostly killed or captured. Why do you think they'll inspire a rising this time?"

Colonel Todd's hand shook as he gulped his coffee.

"It would have succeeded the last time—if Robert E. Lee had won at Gettysburg. Morgan's invasion was timed to coincide with Lee's descent on Pennsylvania. When the news of Lee's failure reached here by telegraph on July fifth, Morgan should have retreated. But that was not his style. To him, retreat was synonymous with defeat."

"We have a cavalryman just like him in the Union Army. My classmate, George Armstrong Custer," Paul said.

With a visible effort to control his feelings, Gabriel Todd splashed bourbon into his coffee. "Forgive my vehemence. My second son, Andy, was killed in a skirmish near Corydon, Indiana, during that raid."

"This time a rising will succeed," Janet said, alarmed by the drift of the conversation. "The Democrats of the Midwest are far more exasperated by the Republicans' tyranny. President Davis has promised us as much as a million dollars to buy rifles and ample ammunition. We have the secret weapon I told you about—Greek fire."

Gabriel Todd smiled bleakly at his daughter. "Janet tells me you love her and hope to marry her. If you do, you'll have a wife with a warrior's heart, Major. A Judith, a Joan of Arc. She's been the sinew of this plan of redemption, the courier who's carried the confidential messages that have inspired everyone with that most insubstantial yet precious commodity—hope."

Tears streamed down Gabriel Todd's face. He splashed more bourbon into his coffee. "Forgive me," he said. "It wrenches my heart to think of our lost Union. But I see no other alternative to a rule by men who are violating the very principles on which our country was founded."

"Could you tell me a little more about that side of it—what Lincoln and his followers have done to anger the Democrats of Kentucky?"

Gabriel Todd splashed more bourbon into his coffee cup and leaned back in his chair. "That's impossible, Major," he said.

"Why do you say that, sir?" Paul asked.

"There's no way for any man—at least any Democrat—to tell a *little* more about the outrages we've suffered from these miscreants who call themselves Republicans. I can only tell you a lot. A carload lot. A whole freight train of abuses and usurpations and betrayals of the Constitution of this expiring republic."

Paul's expression grew grave. "I'm ready to hear the whole train, sir."

Gabriel Todd drained his cup and leaned back in his chair. "Let's begin with Lincoln's solemn promise to respect Kentucky's neutrality. Within a few weeks of the great emancipator pledging his word, the federal government set up a training camp on Richard M. Robinson's farm, in Garrard County, ideally situated at the foot of the Cumberland Mountains to recruit the poor of those benighted valleys and knobs and turn them into federal soldiers ready and eager to pillage the prosperous and wellborn. It was nothing less than a revolutionary act, as meaningful in Kentucky as the storming of the Bastille to the French of 1789 or the clash at Concord Bridge to the Americans of 1775. Dick Robinson gave his farm to the federals with the stipulation that he was guaranteed an army horseshoeing contract that's made him rich. In command of these recruits Lincoln placed a three-hundred-and-fifty-pound, six-foot-four bully named William Nelson, son of a Maysville doctor who'd migrated from New England.

"When our Democratic newspapers cried out against this violation of the president's promise, they were brutally suppressed, their presses wrecked, their editors beaten up, jailed, or driven into exile. No less than seventeen newspapers succumbed to this assault. The rest have been reduced to servile docility. When our leading politicians, such as my good friend Charles Morehead, former governor and federal congressman, protested, they were arrested and flung into vile military prisons, where they endured verbal abuse, semistarvation, and demoralizing isolation until their spirits or their bodies surrendered."

Gabriel Todd's cheeks had turned an ominous magenta. Paul exchanged an alarmed glance with Janet. There was more emotion here than an aging body could handle. But Janet could not bear to interrupt her father. More succinctly now, he told how the Republicans ruled Kentucky with troops around the polling places on Election Day, warning all who voted Democratic that their lives were in danger. "Without that kind of terror, the Democrats would have carried the state in 1862 and given our party a majority in the House of Representatives. We could have ended the war by refusing to vote another cent for it."

Clopping, rattling sounds in the drive gave Janet the excuse she needed to interrupt her father. "There's Mrs. Havens!" she said. "I think you've told Paul more than enough to understand why the Sons of Liberty are eager to fight."

Paul's expression was strange. He seemed almost dazed by Gabriel Todd's narration. "Who's Mrs. Havens?" he asked.

"She's a spiritualist my mother has been consulting regularly," Janet explained to Paul.

Paul remarked that spiritualism was popular everywhere. "Even my mother has tried it, hoping to contact my father and my brother Charlie," he said.

"Would you consider volunteering as a fourth at the spirit table?" Gabriel Todd asked. "I consider it pathetic nonsense. It only worsens my grief."

"Of course," Paul said. "I'm sorry we've been interrupted. But I've heard enough from that freight train of yours to become an outraged Democrat of Kentucky by—by marriage."

Gabriel Todd poured bourbon into Paul's cup. "Let's drink to that," he said.

They clinked cups. Janet tossed her hair. "Really, Father. You're making me wonder if you're glad to get rid of me."

"Pay no attention to her, Major," Gabriel Todd said, with a smile that took the sting out of his words. "Todd women tend to be difficult. I'll have the invitations engraved and ready to send out the day peace is declared."

In a few minutes, Joseph led fat red-haired Mrs. Virginia Havens into the dining room. Summer and winter she dressed in white, an affectation that annoyed Janet. From Lexington to the Ohio River, the woman had become a visitor to plantation mansions and to humbler houses where parents, wives, sisters and brothers mourned loved ones killed in the war.

"How are you, Colonel Todd? And Miss Todd?" Mrs. Havens said in her breathless way. She always spoke as if she had sensational news on the tip of her tongue.

"We're fine, Mrs. Havens. This is Major Paul Stapleton," Janet said.

Mrs. Havens acknowledged Paul with a rather frosty nod. She was a devout Confederate. His blue uniform was not a welcome sight. "And how is Mrs. Todd?"

"Not well. We were tempted to tell you not to come," Janet said. "I hope the session won't last too long."

"I wish I could promise you that, Miss Todd," Mrs. Havens said. "But the spirits, not I, are in control of such matters."

Janet offered Mrs. Havens some supper. She declined. She preferred to dine after a session. Sometimes turbulent spirits invaded her body and caused "commotions" in her digestive system.

Gabriel Todd announced that he was going to bed.

Mrs. Havens expressed alarm at the lack of a caring circle until Paul volunteered to replace Colonel Todd. They mounted the stairs to Letitia Todd's bedroom. Janet's mother was dressed in black, as usual, but her mood was almost cheerful. Mrs. Havens's visits had become her only diversion.

"How are you, dear Mrs. Todd?" Mrs. Havens burbled as they kissed.

"I've been in perpetual agony since I saw you. My hip torments me day and night. The doctors forbid me to use more than a third of the laudanum I need."

"We'll see if we can find a healing spirit this time." Mrs. Havens believed that spirits were eager to assist the living in many ways.

Janet and Paul sat down at the small octagonal table on which her mother ate her meals. All the candles in the room were extinguished, except for one in an upright silver holder in the center of the table. In obedience to Mrs. Haven's instructions, they placed their hands on the table's carved edge.

Janet noticed that Paul seemed troubled by this impending encounter with the dead. His eyes were almost reproachful—as if he resented having this experience inflicted on him. Surely he did not believe they were going to contact living spirits.

Mrs. Havens began with an incantation. "O Lord God, master of the world of the dead, we gather here in humble petition to seek an audience with those whom we love. If we can do anything to increase their happiness or remove a care that is burdening them, let them tell us in their own words. For thine is the power and the glory, amen."

After a long pause, Mrs. Havens said, "Let each of us now summon in our souls the name or names of the spirits we desire to reach. We have no assurance that they can reach us. But without our cooperation their efforts will be doubly difficult and even fruitless. Remember with special concentration the power of your love for them and their love for you. Love is the spiritual telegraph down which messages travel. Reflect, pray, but above all love!"

Janet found it impossible to either reflect or pray. She was not a believer in spiritualism. Her brothers were *dead*. Again she was assailed by the almost bewildering totality of their annihilation.

As the war raged and the casualty lists grew, Janet found it harder and harder to believe that the spirit retreated to another place—heaven, purgatory, hell. There was no sense of divine presence in the soldiers' deaths. A transcendental indifference, a God whose eyes were averted from His creatures and His creation, was the only being she could imagine now.

Once this idea of an indifferent God would have shocked Janet. At St. Mary-of-the-Woods, the academy founded by French nuns outside Vincennes, she had been devout to the brink of mysticism. The idea of giving one's soul, one's life, to God, of vowing poverty, chastity and obedience in Jesus' name, had moved Janet profoundly. For a while she had considered becoming a black-robed Sister of Providence. When she mentioned this idea to her father, Gabriel Todd had abruptly ended his daughter's Roman Catholic education.

If the medium's theories were true, Janet was an obstruction on the spiritual telegraph. Yet there was no diminution of Mrs. Havens's performance. Deep sighs followed by theatrical shudders shook her ample frame. "I feel the spirits all around us, but none are familiar," she whispered. "The message I've sent into the void often attracts wandering souls who have no other hope of solace, creatures who have died unrepentant or unloved."

She gasped and clutched her stomach with both hands. "Oh! I feel an entry. I feel—"

Mrs. Havens went rigid in her chair. Expression

drained from her face. She leaned forward and blew out the candle. In the darkened room Janet heard a burst of boyish laughter. "Momma! Momma!" said a voice that was very different from Mrs. Havens's normal voice.

"Oh, who is it? Who is it?" Letitia Todd cried.

"Andy—wants—candy," said the childish voice.

"Oh, the dear sweet boy remembers that little joke," Letitia Todd said. "It's him, reminding me of the perfect love we shared in his babyhood. Ask him if he sees Jack. Are they together?"

"Let us first make certain it's Andy," Mrs. Havens said. "Give us the signal we agreed on, dear boy."

Six sharp raps echoed around the room. They came from the vicinity of the table. But as far as Janet could see in the semidarkness, Mrs. Havens remained immobile.

"It's Andy," Letitia Todd said. "Ask him about Jack."

"Do you see Jack? Are you together?"

"Sometimes," the childish voice said from Mrs. Havens's lips.

"Is he—happy? Are you both—still happy?"

"Yes—Momma," said the childish voice. "Completely . . . happy."

Janet knew Letitia Todd feared her wild son Andy had gone to hell for his drinking and gambling and whoring. "Why are you speaking in your little boy's voice?" her mother asked.

"We—are—still—angels—Momma. Baby—angels."

"As long as you're happy, that's all I care about."

"Your—pain—Momma. Offer—up—your—pain. For—our—souls. Offer—it—to—Jesus."

"I will! I will!" Letitia Todd cried.

Silence. Mrs. Havens shifted in her chair. "He's leaving us," she whispered.

"He's told me all I wanted to hear," Letitia Todd said.

Silence until Mrs. Havens spoke in her sepulchral whisper. "Are there any other familiar spirits here who wish to speak?"

A terrific gust of wind swept through the bedroom, making the white curtains dance. Janet heard glass break as pictures fell off the walls or toppled from side tables.

"Oh my God," gasped Mrs. Havens. "Who are you?"

The wind whirled around them. It felt clammy on Janet's hands and face. "Who are you?" Mrs. Havens quavered.

Silence for sixty seconds. Then another voice took command of Mrs. Haven's lips. "Death!" it said in a guttural growl. "I am Death. I've come to warn all of you. Especially Paul. Don't—do—it—Paul! Don't!"

"That's enough!" Paul Stapleton leaped to his feet. "That's enough of this—this torture! Who is this woman? Is this some sort of test?"

Janet lit the candle. Mrs. Havens was slumped in her chair, saliva drooling from her lips. "Don't—do—it," she croaked in the same voice, dwindling now. If some sort of evil spirit was not possessing her, she was giving a very good imitation of it.

"Get her some brandy, for God's sake," Letitia Todd said. "I fear she's having a stroke."

Janet rushed downstairs to the brandy decanter. By the time she returned to the bedroom, Mrs. Havens had regained consciousness. But she was a very frightened woman. She gulped the brandy and said, "Nothing like that has ever happened to me before. I dealt only with benign spirits. That being seemed about to tear the flesh from my bones."

"Was it a demon?" Letitia Todd asked.

"I don't know," Mrs. Havens said.

"It wasn't a demon," Paul said.

Janet was bewildered to see tears on his cheeks. "It was someone who had recently died—without accepting death. I think I know his name," Paul said.

"One of your classmates?

"Yes. One of my classmates," Paul said. "Will you excuse me?"

He bowed to Letitia Todd. He seized Janet's hand and pressed it to his lips. She listened to the thud of his footsteps in the carpeted hall, the slam of his bedroom door. A nameless fear swept her. What an awful ending to a glorious day.

SIXTEEN

IN HIS ROOM, PAUL FLUNG off his uniform as if it were a straitjacket. Pulling on a robe, he threw himself down on the bed. Was that Jeff Tyler's soul in that spirit medium's body, warning him against betraying his oath of allegiance to the Union?

Or was Jeff telling him not to betray the South's last hope? Don't betray Gabriel Todd's pathetic attempt at consolation for his dead sons? Don't betray the love he saw on Janet's face when she looked at her father? Don't ignore—and thereby betray—the Democratic Party's justifiable anger at the Republicans' outrageous abuse of the Constitution in their determination to hold onto Kentucky?

Beyond these immediate betrayals lay his consciousness of Caroline Kemble Stapleton's secret wish for a Southern victory. It would be her justification, her triumph, in her bitter quarrel with her oldest son, Paul's brother, Jonathan Stapleton.

Paul paced the bedroom, trying to think analytically, reasonably, about the future he was confronting. What sort of Union would there be at the end of this murderous war? Captain Simeon Otis and his fanatic ilk talked of arming the slaves and making them masters of the South. They seemed indifferent to the prospect of a race war. Nothing was too monstrous to punish the South for the sin of slavery.

At the very least, the South would become a sullen desolated part of the Union, perpetually mourning her dead, forever resentful of her conquered status—a kind of geographic cancer in the body politic. Was Jeff Tyler telling him that the only hope of future peace was some sort of settlement that permitted the South to decide its own destiny?

Duty Honor Country. How prayerfully Paul had repeated those words at West Point. They offered a refuge, a guarantee of inner peace, while he was learning how to wage war. But he was a child then, seventeen years old. *When I was a child, I thought as a child,* Saint Paul said. Now he was thinking as a man. Perhaps there were duties beyond the army's rigid regulations and obtuse orders. Perhaps there was a higher code of honor, unwritten, known only to the individual conscience. Perhaps there was another country—a country of the heart that transcended the constitutional nation to which he had sworn his loyalty.

Tears trickled down Paul's cheeks as he thought of Jeff Tyler in his Georgia grave. Jeff had chosen to fight for the South, knowing a nameless grave was part of the risk. Knowing that only a miracle could deliver victory. They had discussed it as professional soldiers and decided each had to follow what Jeff called the imperatives of the heart, no matter what their calculating professional brains concluded. Jeff had gone south rather than take the new ironclad oath of loyalty to the Union that the government required before they permitted anyone in the class of 1861 to graduate. Paul had taken that oath, driven by his own heart's imperatives—his loyalty to his brother, Jonathan, and their father's devotion to the Union.

Now he was trapped between love—or was it pity?—for this Kentucky variant of the South's agony and that oath of loyalty and obedience to duty, honor, country.

Somewhere in the trees beyond Hopemont's lawn, an owl hooted. Wisdom, was he groping for wisdom here in the silence? Was he finally becoming his own man? Not Senator George Stapleton's son or Major General

Jonathan Stapleton's younger brother, not even Major Paul Stapleton, U.S.A., that boilerplated product of the U.S. Military Academy, but simply Paul Stapleton, unranked, identified by nothing but his existence here in the Kentucky night, with the woman he loved lying sleepless in her bed a few dozen feet away.

Tiptoeing down the hall, he tapped on Janet's bedroom door. She opened it in an instant. "I was hoping—praying you'd come," she said.

"To talk," Paul said. "We need to talk."

"Exactly what I want to do," Janet said. She was still wearing her dress, an elaborate green silk affair with a large bow at the waist. It pained Paul to detect coldness, suspicion, in her voice. But what else could he expect? "Let's go out to the gazebo," she said. "We can speak with more freedom there."

A full moon was still riding high. It bathed the lawn with golden light. The old trees cast bizarre shadows on the grass. A night wind, as hot as a sirocco, stirred the branches. They strolled to the gazebo with Paul's arm around Janet's waist.

"You must think you're engaged to a madman," he said.

"I confess to being baffled by your outburst tonight. Did you really think Mrs. Havens was some sort of secret agent who was testing your loyalty to us?"

He told her about Jeff's death and its impact on him.

"Why didn't you share that with me?" Janet asked.

"I thought you were burdened by enough deaths."

"Do you believe the dead survive beyond the grave?" Janet asked.

"I didn't—until tonight."

"I didn't either. I thought Mrs. Havens's spirit talk was nothing but a clever performance. I tolerated her because she consoled Momma."

Janet threw her arms around him and pressed her head against his chest. "Oh, my love. My dearest love."

She was trembling. "Does it make you wonder if there are powers beyond our comprehension? That we have no real control over our fate?"

"So much of what we do is beyond our free choice. I think there are only moments when we're truly free. When we speak or act out of what is truly individual in our souls. That moment by the river today was one of them."

He meant that, Paul told himself. Even though he felt her nakedness—and his desire—had compromised the absolute freedom of his choice.

"What did you mean by accepting—or not accepting death?"

"That's another moment of freedom. The most powerful one I've ever experienced, until I met you."

Paul was back on the bullet-swept field near Gettysburg, kneeling beside General John Reynolds, watching blood ooze from the wound in his heart. Reynolds had been his army father. His death was a devastating blow.

A moment later, George Armstrong Custer loomed above him on his black horse. Defying army regulations, his blond hair cascaded to his shoulders. He shouted above the crash of rifles, the boom of cannon, "Goddamn it, they got Uncle John! I was going to ask permission to charge them. Nothing else will stop them. They're coming on like an avalanche."

"Let's do it. I'll say it was Uncle John's last order."

Paul heard himself telling this to Janet Todd. "Not until I rode toward the Confederates did I realize Custer had only six hundred men. A third of Lee's army, at least twenty thousand men, were coming down the road! That didn't bother Custer in the least. He told his bugler to blow the charge and we rode straight at them. I saw—I *knew*—we were committing suicide. No one but Custer would have done such a thing. He's absolutely convinced of his own indestructibility."

"I'm not sure I want to hear the rest," Janet said,

pressing herself against him. But Paul knew she wanted to hear everything.

"The Confederates deployed into line of battle. Cannon opened on us. Then a blast of rifle fire that emptied saddles all around me. At that moment, I saw my own death. I saw it as something inevitable, ordained, even worthwhile. I saw or thought I saw the whole meaning of my life. I accepted death as something more important, more meaningful, than life. Fear vanished. I chose death, beside Custer, freely, proudly. A moment later a minié ball hit me in the head. I woke up two days later in the hospital."

Janet was silent for a long time. Somewhere in the trees the same owl—or his cousin—hooted. "I hate it," she said. "I hate the whole idea. But I see the wonder of it. The nobility."

"I'm not sure what to name it. I can only tell you it happened."

"And you think your friend Jeff Tyler didn't have a chance to accept his death?"

"I'm sure he knew how desperate the South's cause has become. That alone would make it difficult to die."

The contrast between Jeff's death and his own memories of Gettysburg troubled Paul. "Somehow I didn't feel that way at Gettysburg, although our situation on that first day was about as desperate as soldiers can get. Paul Stapleton seemed to be standing outside the war, playing his part with no sense of being essential to the outcome. Maybe that's all we can hope to do. Honorably play the part assigned to us."

"I've assigned you another part," Janet said. "One that's far more essential to the outcome. I'm sure you'll play it as honorably."

"I'll try. I can promise you that," Paul said, He meant those words, even though he still felt bound by his oath of loyalty to the Union. Somehow he would have to find a way to be loyal both to honor and to love.

"Father is inviting some of the local leaders of the Sons of Liberty to supper tomorrow. He wants them to meet you."

"What's your impression of them?"

"They're good men. I think you'll like all of them—except one you've already met."

"Who?"

"Rogers Jameson. He's the second in command of the Daviess County brigade. He's no thinker but on a battle-field Father says he'll be a fighter."

"He's probably right about that."

They retreated to their separate bedrooms after a passionate kiss. In the morning Paul was relieved to find Mrs. Havens had departed for her next appointment with the spirit world. Gabriel Todd joined them at the breakfast table and asked how the séance had gone.

"Momma felt much better," Janet said. "She heard a voice that seemed to be Andy's. He spoke of how much he loved her."

"Good, good," Todd said. He clearly had neither faith nor interest in the afterlife. Paul was glad there was no need to tell him about Jeff Tyler's intruding voice. After sleeping on it, Paul wondered if there was another explanation. Perhaps Mrs. Havens had picked up a subconscious thought from his own mind. Perhaps that was his own troubled conscience crying out, "Don't do it!" Perhaps people with special sensitivity like Mrs. Havens could pick up emotions on an invisible spiritual telegraph. That would also explain her ability to produce Mrs. Todd's memories of the childhood of her dead son.

The butler brought the day's mail. Colonel Todd shook out his copy of the Louisville *Register*. His eyes widened with amazement at his first glimpse of the front page. "Here's news that could change everything!" he said.

He showed them the headline of the story in the right-hand column:

LINCOLN CALLS FOR ANOTHER
500,000 MEN.
MOST WILL BE DRAFTED.
KENTUCKY'S QUOTA
36,885. GOVERNOR FEARS WIDE UNREST.

"The man is either the greatest fool or the most reckless tyrant on the face of the earth," Colonel Todd said. "Either way, he's playing into our hands. If this doesn't make the Democrats fight, nothing will."

"Grant's casualties in the Wilderness and Sherman's losses before Atlanta must be far higher than the government's admitting," Paul said.

"In other words, they're as desperate as we are," Janet said.

Her smile made Paul uneasy. It was too triumphant. She assumed a Sons of Liberty victory was almost a foregone conclusion when the opposite was more probably the case: the North's desperation made the insurrection an even more enormous gamble. Paul groped for his image of Blondin on the high wire. But the acrobat was nowhere to be seen. The abandoned wire swayed above the cataract in history's hurricane.

SEVENTEEN

"THERE IT IS, GENTLEMEN. A volunteer for our cause whose name will give us political legitimacy in the East and whose West Point training will help us shape our military strategy in the West."

Gabriel Todd's smile suggested he could not imagine a negative response from his five-man audience. Janet was tempted to cast her vote by applauding. Her father had made a masterful case for accepting Major Paul Stapleton in the upper ranks of the Sons of Liberty.

But the man whose vote counted for more than the other four votes combined was not impressed. Rogers Jameson, his broken jaw wired shut, seized a piece of paper and scrawled on it: *I DONT TRUSTE HIM.*

Gabriel Todd had surrendered most of the active leadership of Daviess County's George Rogers Clark Brigade to Jameson. He had recruited most of the junior officers and enlisted men. He knew how to talk to them in the taverns and fraternal societies where they spent their free time. He used his reputation as a fighting captain in the Mexican War to impress them.

Rogers's inability to spell the word *trust* summed up Janet's opinion of him. His marriage to Amelia Conway had elevated him to the company of his social superiors. But he had never made the slightest attempt to acquire any polish or education.

"Rogers," Gabriel Todd said. "Surely you remember his father, George Stapleton. He was the best volunteer general in the Mexican War."

Rogers Jameson seized another piece of paper and

scrawled. *I STILL DONT TRUSTE HIM. HIS NIGER SERGINT BROK MY JAWR.*

"He's a soldier," Janet said. "He's ready and eager to fight—to lead a regiment or a brigade."

"Perhaps I should add that my daughter is considering an offer of marriage from Major Stapleton," Gabriel Todd said. "An offer that's already won my approval."

This drew an even darker scowl from Rogers Jameson. He seized more paper and scrawled: *I THOT SHE WAS PROMISED TO ADAM.*

"Nobody has promised me to *anyone*," Janet said

"Adam has my approval, too," Gabriel Todd said with a genial smile. "When this cruel war is over, I'm sure Janet can settle the matter between the two gentlemen on her terms."

Once more Rogers Jameson glared and scrawled: *FIRST LET HIM SWEAR A SOLUM OATHE. MAKE SURE HE IS A TRU SON OF LIBERTY,*

"Of course he'll swear our oath," Gabriel Todd said. "There'll be no difficulty on that score."

"Of course not," Janet said.

"Is he here?" asked red-haired Colonel Luke Bowman, the most intelligent of the four regimental leaders. He farmed a thousand acres not far from Hopemont. The others were more middling men.

"He's upstairs," Janet replied.

"Ask him to join us," Gabriel Todd said.

Janet found Paul in his room, reading a newspaper. "They're ready to welcome you into the Sons of Liberty. But you'll have to swear an oath of loyalty," she said.

For a moment he looked unhappy. "I can see why they don't trust me," he said.

"Everyone has to swear it."

"Even you?"

"No. They don't think of me as a soldier."

"They should."

She gave him a fierce affirmative kiss.

Downstairs, everyone except Rogers Jameson rose to his feet when Paul entered the dining room. Gabriel Todd gravely introduced him to each of the colonels. With a wry smile, he added, "I believe you know Rogers Jameson."

"I fear I owe him some sort of apology," Paul said. "I want to make it clear that I had nothing to do with Sergeant Washington slugging him."

He held out his hand. Rogers Jameson hesitated for a moment, dislike still flickering in his bulging eyes. But he could not avoid shaking hands.

Gabriel Todd slapped Jameson on the back. "You see, Rogers? You can't help but like this young fellow."

Jameson's beefy face remained sullen. Gabriel Todd ignored his recalcitrance and said, "Major, we're prepared to welcome you into the Sons of Liberty. To join us requires a solemn oath that no honest man can ever repudiate. Are you prepared to swear it?"

"I am," Paul said. His gaze was on Janet. There was not a hint of hesitation in his voice, not a trace of evasion in his eyes.

"We'll proceed to the ceremony," Gabriel Todd said.

He lifted a thick leather-covered book from a serving shelf near the dining room door and opened it on the table. He was immensely proud of this volume. He had written much of it himself and had paid to have it bound by the best bookseller in Cincinnati. Other versions in less expensive covers circulated throughout Kentucky and Indiana and Illinois.

He opened it and began to read: " 'Listen, then, to these principles of government, as I enumerate them, Brother. For they must be the guiding principles of your life, if you hope to join our fraternity—' "

For the next twenty minutes Gabriel Todd recited the fundamental ideas of the Sons of Liberty, all of them derived from the writings of Thomas Jefferson. They stressed liberty above government and the consent of the governed above everything else, as expressed through the votes of originally independent states.

Finally Gabriel Todd studied Paul for a long moment. "How do you respond to the declarations you have just heard?"

He handed Paul the book and he read the oath. "I, Paul Stapleton, fully comprehending and appreciating the declaration of principles I have just heard pronounced, hold them for truth, and promise to cherish them in my heart, to inculcate them in my fellows, to illustrate them, as far as in me lies, in my daily talk and conversation and if needs be defend them with my life."

Again Gabriel Todd studied Paul. He placed both hands on his shoulders and said, "By the power vested in me by the Grand Council, I pronounce you a Son of Liberty."

A beaming Luke Bowman leaped up and extended his hand. "Welcome! Welcome!" he said. "I met your father in Mexico. I'm absolutely certain he'd approve this step. If he were alive, I suspect he'd be the leader of the Sons of Liberty in New Jersey."

"You may be right," Paul said.

Gabriel Todd also extended his hand. "I hope we can do great things together for the cause of peace and justice," he said.

"I hope so too," Paul said.

Rogers Jameson made no attempt to shake hands. Incapable of diplomacy, he continued to regard Paul with patent disapproval. Janet wondered what role this man would play if they succeeded in setting up the western confederacy. It was not a pleasant thought.

Joseph, the Todds' aging butler, announced dinner. They sat down to a feast of roast pork and sweet potatoes. Gabriel Todd poured one of his best clarets and raised his glass. "To the union of all honest men," he said.

"Isn't it time we discussed what Major Stapleton can do for us?" Janet asked.

Paul's eyes assured her they were thinking identical thoughts. "First and foremost I'm offering you my sword, gentlemen," he said. "I don't think what you're hoping to accomplish can be done without some sharp fighting. Do you have a plan for the campaign that I could study?"

Rogers Jameson gave Paul a contemptuous look and reached for his pencil. *WE DON'T NEED NO WEST POINT PLANN*, he wrote.

"I ain't so sure I agree with you, Rogers," Luke Bowman said, passing the note to the other colonels.

"I emphatically agree with Major Stapleton that we need a plan," Gabriel Todd said. "Nothing gives an army more confidence than knowing it has a winning strategy."

OUR PLANN IS TO TAK KEYPORT KILL GENTRY AND HIS NIGERS AND HEAD FOR INDIANAPOLIS, Jameson wrote.

Colonel Todd read this aloud. "I don't call that a plan," Paul said.

The thud of a galloping horse came up Hopemont's gravel drive. Luke Bowman looked uneasily at Gabriel Todd. "Are you expectin' anyone?" he asked.

Colonel Todd shook his head. "Janet, will you go see who it is?"

Janet hurried down Hopemont's candlelit entrance hall to the front door. She opened it and stepped back, astounded. Looming against the darkness was a gigantic black-bearded man in a Confederate uniform and a wide-brimmed cavalryman's hat. He had two huge pistols strapped to his waist. "Janet!" he said.

It was Adam Jameson. His beard made him seem like a figure out of *Rob Roy* or some other historical saga by Sir Walter Scott. He swept Janet against him for a fierce kiss. "For three years I've been dreaming of doing that," he said.

Janet disentangled herself from his arms. "Adam— this is a *total* surprise," she said.

"Is my father here?" he asked.

"He's in the dining room. Along with my father and several other men—"

Gabriel Todd stepped into the hall to greet the uninvited guest. "Colonel Jameson," he said, a broad smile on his face. "What a pleasure to shake hands with one of the South's finest soldiers."

"Thank you, Colonel Todd. I've come a long way for information. Whether I get it or not, seeing Janet has made the trip worthwhile."

"No doubt, no doubt," Gabriel Todd said. "Your father is here. And some other gentlemen you probably know—and one I hope you'll be pleased to meet."

He waved Adam into the dining room. Janet followed him, numb with dismay.

"This is the fellow I'm certain you know," Gabriel Todd began good-humoredly, gesturing to Rogers Jameson. The father gave a strangled cry and lurched to his feet to fling his arms around Adam. Never before had Janet seen the man display such affection.

"What the hell?" Adam Jameson said, shoving his father aside. His eyes were on Major Paul Stapleton in his blue uniform. Adam's right hand was on the pistol on his hip.

"This is Major Paul Stapleton," Gabriel Todd said. "He just took an oath as a Son of Liberty."

"What about the oath he took to Abe Lincoln?" Adam growled.

"That's been superseded. These other gentlemen will be happy to reassure you." Gabriel Todd introduced Luke Bowman and the other colonels. Their names were familiar to Adam, although he had no doubt only seen them at a distance on market days in nearby Owensboro, the county seat.

"I'm no admirer of the Sons of Liberty," Adam growled. "As far as I'm concerned, you're responsible for ruining the best cavalry division in the Confederate

Army. And the best general. John Hunt Morgan has never recovered from our so-called invasion of Indiana. It turned him into a slobbering drunk. He's gone off to Tennessee and left me in command of the division."

"Adam—Colonel—we were given no notice of your approach last year," Gabriel Todd said. "The whole thing was poorly coordinated. Our people were downcast because of General Lee's defeat at Gettysburg—"

"I've heard all the excuses," Adam snapped. "I've just ridden three hundred miles on roads patrolled by Union cavalry to make sure there won't be any need for excuses this time!"

"There will be none," Gabriel Todd said. "This time it's victory or death. That's going to be our motto. The same password Washington gave his men on Christmas night in 1776 when they crossed the Delaware." He pointed to a copy of the painting by Emanuel Leutze in a gilt frame on the north wall of the dining room.

Adam's mouth curled contemptuously. "Washington's ridiculous little army wouldn't last ten minutes on any battlefield I've seen," he said. "Wouldn't you agree, Major Stapleton—assuming you've seen a battlefield—and haven't spent all your time five hundred miles behind the lines in comfortable posts like Keyport?"

"I would agree completely, Colonel," Paul Stapleton said. "At Gettysburg we would have blown him to smithereens, as the Irish say, as totally as we demolished General Pickett's charge."

The hostility etched into both men's voices shivered Janet Todd's nerves. She saw it was doing the same thing to the colonels and to her father and Rogers Jameson.

"I want to know how many men you've got," Adam said. "How many of them are armed and trained. Who's leading them in Kentucky and who's in charge in Indiana."

"There isn't any one man in military command in either state. The men will come out under local commanders in each county," Gabriel Todd said.

"There's no commanding general?" Adam said. "No staff? No army? Just a collection of half-baked civilians?"

"Civilians, Colonel, who've sworn a solemn oath to fight tyranny and dictatorship!" Gabriel Todd said.

"What about deserters?" Adam asked. "How are you treating them?"

"We don't expect any," Gabriel Todd said.

"Excuse me, Colonel Todd, but you're dreaming. Do you know how many deserters the Confederate Army has had, up until now? One hundred and twenty-five thousand. I'm sure the Union Army has had double that. Would you agree, Major Stapleton?"

"Emphatically. I've spent the last six months hunting a lot of them through southern Indiana."

For a moment Janet was in complete agreement with her own generation. She was *one* with these angry knowing young men who had heard bullets hiss and seen men die. But the distress on the faces of the older men shocked her back to reality. What did Adam Jameson think he was doing? He was exactly like his father, a behemoth with a small pugnacious brain. Someone had to rescue this situation before the western confederacy collapsed before her eyes.

"Just a moment!" Janet said. "Adam—you're not giving us a chance to tell you the full dimensions of our plan. It includes an army—several armies—of trained soldiers, men whom you and Major Stapleton here will be proud to command."

Her rebuke had a startling impact on Adam. He rubbed his eyes like a tired child. "I'm sorry," he said. "I haven't had much sleep for the last three days. I've had nothing to think about all day, hiding in attics and barns, but our dead—"

Gabriel Todd tried to regain control of the situation.

"We understand, Adam. We appreciate your concerns. Sit down and let me tell you the rest of our plan—"

"Tell him about the prison camps," Janet said.

"Outside Indianapolis, there are at least ten thousand Confederate prisoners in Camp Morton," Gabriel Todd said. "Outside Chicago, in Camp Douglas, are another twenty thousand. When we free these men and arm them, we'll have thirty thousand trained troops in the heart of the West."

Janet's eyes were on Paul Stapleton. His face remained expressionless, although they had not told him about arming the Confederate prisoners. Janet had decided that revelation could come later. "Do the prisoners know the part they're supposed to play?" Paul asked.

"Yes. Guards have been bribed, messages passed in both camps," Colonel Todd said.

"Do you expect me to free both camps with two thousand cavalrymen?" Adam said. "Fight our way from Indianapolis to Chicago?"

"Of course not," Gabriel Todd replied. "Camp Douglas will be freed by two regiments of Sons of Liberty who are armed and training secretly at this very moment in Chicago. Your column will strike for Indianapolis. With the Sons of Liberty in arms along your route, you should meet very little opposition. What troops the Republicans have at their disposal will be busy fighting the Sons."

"Tell him about Greek fire," Janet said.

"Inside Indianapolis there will be men trained in the use of Greek fire, a form of combustion first used by the Byzantines against the Saracens. It's a mixture of sulfur, naphtha and quicklime—practically impossible to extinguish, once it's ignited. They'll go to work on a prearranged signal as you approach the city. Governor Morton and his crew will have to choose between fighting you and trying to save Indianapolis from burning down around their ears."

This avalanche of information had a peculiar impact

on Adam Jameson. He began to slump in his seat, as if each part of the plan were a weight that had been dumped in his lap without his full approval. Janet sensed he had come here determined to withdraw his men from participation in the plot. What he was hearing made it harder and harder for him to refuse to join them.

While this intuition did nothing to improve Janet's opinion of Adam's intelligence, she found herself moved by the intensity, the sincerity, of his purpose. There was a pathos, even a nobility, to his concern—no, put it more frankly—his love for his men, his grief for his dead that made it impossible to despise him.

"I must confess—I'm impressed," Adam Jameson mumbled. "You gentlemen have given this affair more thought than I imagined. I can see my part in it clearly enough. What will Major Stapleton here do?"

"We haven't decided. He's only joined us two hours ago," Gabriel Todd said.

"I hope he doesn't plan to campaign in that uniform," Adam said.

"Are you appointing yourself the commander in chief of this operation, Colonel Jameson?" Paul asked.

Dislike crackled in every syllable. For a moment Janet felt nothing but anger. She had to remind herself that Adam's tone was almost as obnoxious.

"Not at all," Adam said. "But I strongly urge that one be designated."

"I've already offered them the same advice," Paul said.

"What about money for food, ammunition, fodder for horses?" Adam asked.

"The Confederate government has promised to supply us with a million dollars in gold," Gabriel Todd said.

"Rifles will begin arriving from New York in early August," Janet added.

"It seems as if there's nothing left to do but select the day," Adam said.

"That will require another visit to Richmond,"

Gabriel Todd said. "Their secret agents are coordinating our operation with the people in Illinois. At the moment they lean toward the first day of the Democratic Convention in Chicago—August twenty-ninth. They want the city full of Democrats who'll support them. But we're a bit unhappy with the date because it will draw many of our best leaders out of Indiana and Kentucky. If they stay behind, it may attract the attention of federal agents."

"How can you be sure this fellow isn't one of them?" Adam asked, pointing to Paul Stapleton.

"Colonel Todd—and Miss Todd—have vouched for him," Luke Bowman said.

Adam stared stonily at Janet. "Is that true?"

"Yes," Janet said, feeling her face grow warm. "Major Stapleton has convinced me that his desire for peace is sincere."

"His desire for *peace?*" Adam said, his eyes on Paul Stapleton now. The derision in his voice was unmistakable. He was suggesting Paul desired something—or someone—else.

"That will be the first result of the creation of a western confederacy," Janet said. "We'll call for peace—immediate peace—and both sides will have to accept it. We'll hold the balance of power."

"Excuse me, Janet, but that's the damnedest nonsense I've ever heard," Adam said. "Is this Major Stapleton's idea? Immediate peace? Leaving the Union Army in control of half of Virginia, two-thirds of Tennessee and Kentucky, and a third of Georgia? Not to mention even more of Louisiana and Mississippi? If we get a choke hold on them by cutting off their supplies from the west, I say kill as many as possible before they get out of range."

Rogers Jameson seized his pencil and scrawled: *I AGRE WITH EVERY WURD OF THAT.*

"What do you think, Major Stapleton? Does that idea

upset your digestion any?" Adam asked. "Do you think we can win the war just by proclaiming this western confederacy? Are you a soldier or a politician?"

"I'm a soldier who's been trained to think as well as fight," Paul said, sarcasm again edging his voice. "I believe we can end the war rather quickly if we negotiate from strength and refrain from killing people unnecessarily."

"I don't know what that last word means. When I see a man in a blue uniform, I want to kill him before he kills me," Adam said.

"I begin to think it might be best if you and I served in separate commands, Colonel," Paul said. "I doubt very much if I could ever take orders from you."

Adam stared dazedly at Paul. He rubbed his eyes again. "I guess maybe I ought to get some sleep," he said.

"A good idea," Gabriel Todd said. "We can talk this whole thing over tomorrow in a more even temper."

"Just understand this," Adam said. "I'm ready to do everything and anything—including die—for Southern independence. My men are ready to do the same thing."

"We understand that," Gabriel Todd said. "We understand that perfectly."

Adam staggered to his feet. Rogers Jameson threw his arm around his exhausted son. As the two big men walked down the hall to the door, Adam's knees buckled. He sagged against his father. Janet watched, suffused with the sorrow and the pity of it all.

EIGHTEEN

HENRY TODD GENTRY TOSSED IN his sweaty bed. He was having the dream again. He knew it was a dream but it was also not a dream. It was a wild mixture of history and memory. The Mississippi swept past the raft, tied up to a huge cottonwood tree on the Tennessee shore above Memphis. The river made a gushing, throaty sound as it began its race to the Gulf of Mexico.

On a series of rafts and steamboats, American heroes and cowards, geniuses and fools, acted out their personal stories. Aaron Burr, the personification of the corrupt East, was there pouring coins into the gaping mouths of gullible western volunteers in his doomed foray to seize the gold and silver mines of Mexico. Willard Gentry, Henry's father, was one of the true believers. Did the failure of that fabulous dream rip something out of his heart, reducing him to a mere merchant, making him easy prey for Millicent Todd?

Then came the idol of Gentry's youth, Henry Clay, dueling at ten paces with his nemesis, Andrew Jackson. The gaunt spectral face of the Tennessee demagogue cast a weird glow on Clay's handsome features, revealing his bafflement and fear. Clay pulled the trigger of his pistol but the hammer clicked fecklessly. The gun was empty. A sneering Jackson fired and with a sad cry Clay toppled from the raft to disappear in the Mississippi's silted darkness.

Next came a magnificent white steamboat. On the top deck Amelia Conway stood in her wedding dress, gazing mournfully at Henry Todd Gentry. Beside her stood

Rogers Jameson, triumph on his porcine face. He began undressing her, carefully at first, then impatiently ripping the white gown from her trembling shoulders.

While the pageant sailed past them, Abe Lincoln lay with his head on a burlap bag of wheat, sleeping peacefully. Innocence, nobility, contentment suffused his young face. The veins of thought and furrows of disappointment were in the distant future. This face was the image of his unspoiled questing soul. For a moment Henry Gentry yearned to kiss that supple mouth, to rest his head on that broad chest and confess the love he felt for this unique human being.

A scraping sound swung Gentry's eyes to the shore. Shapes moved there. Someone was hauling the raft closer to the riverbank! The dream was becoming memory—the most vivid memory of Henry Gentry's life. Looming at the far end of the raft were a dozen figures, dark against the moonless darkness of the landscape.

"Abe!" Gentry cried as the intruders rushed toward them.

They were Negroes. Runaways, perhaps, living by their wits in the woods. Or slaves on the prowl for loot. They intended to kill these two white men and appropriate their six hundred pounds of wheat and corn. Henry Gentry seized the pole he used to fend off floating trees and other large debris and swung it at the leader of the pack. He brushed it aside and struck Gentry on the shoulder with a club, paralyzing his right arm. Another club thudded against his head.

"Abe!" he cried one more time as he toppled to the deck.

Lincoln was on his feet, wielding a thick chunk of the driftwood they had collected to cook their dinners. He smashed the face of the first man to come at him. Gentry heard the crunching sound of the wood against bone. With a muffled cry, the attacker hurtled sideways off the raft into the river. The power of that blow drained courage from the rest of the gang. For a split second they recoiled and gave Lincoln the momentum he needed.

With a snarl he waded into them, smashing them left and right, breaking arms and jaws and knees with every ferocious swing. They fought back but there was no defense against the strength in Abe's long arms, toughened by a thousand hours of axwork. Lincoln could make more money in two hours chopping wood than any other man in Indiana could earn in a day. Now he was chopping men with the same devastating results.

Gentry was back on his feet, clubbing them from the flank in spite of his half-paralyzed arm. "Nigger bastards!" he shouted. But Lincoln never made a sound. He just kept swinging that murderous club until there was only one attacker still on his feet.

He was as tall as Lincoln, with a heavier frame. As Lincoln advanced on him, his club ready, Abe lost his footing on the wet deck and fell on his back. The black leaped forward, a knife gleaming in his right hand. Gentry stepped into his rush and swung with all the strength he could muster in his sixteen-year-old arms. He struck the man in the face and he floundered to the left, screaming with pain. Lincoln leaped to his feet and knocked him into the river.

With a collective howl the surviving attackers fled. Several fell off the end of the raft as they tried to get ashore and were swept downstream uttering frantic cries for help. Lincoln stood in the center of the raft, his club hefted for another blow. "Thanks, Henry," he said. "You're a good man in a fight."

Henry Gentry awoke as the dream faded into the dull light of a clouded moon. For a long moment he savored the memory of that compliment, which forever bound him to Abraham Lincoln in the mysterious fellowship of manhood.

Ting a ling. Ting a ling. The alarm system Gentry had

constructed beside his bed to enable his agents to contact him during the night banished sleep. He pulled on his pants and hurried down to the cellar through the dark still house. Over to the storm cellar door he lumbered, calling softly, "I'm coming!"

At the door he held up his candle and was startled to find the light flickering on the gleaming black face of Janet Todd's Lucy. "How did you get here?" he asked.

"I paddled Miz Janet's canoe, Colonel," she said. "I got some *real* important information for you. I'll tell it fast because I got to get back before sunup. Colonel Adam Jameson come to Hopemont tonight. He met his father and four rebel colonels and Major Stapleton and Miz Janet and her father. He kiss Miz Janet and made the major real mad. I guess he come to plan the risin'. I couldn't get close enough to de dinin' room to hear dem talk, but I don' got no doubt they goin' to come after you and your nigger soldiers first thing—"

"Is Colonel Jameson staying at Rose Hill?"

"I thinks so. He lef' with his daddy."

"I'm going to find Maybelle if it's the last thing I do on earth. Get back to your canoe. I've got work to do."

Within five minutes, Gentry was in his uniform, writing a telegram to Major General Stephen Burbridge, the commander of the Union forces in Kentucky

I HAVE SOLID INFORMATION THAT COLONEL ADAM JAMESON IS AT HIS FAMILY'S HOME ROSE HILL IN DAVIESS COUNTY PLOTTING A RAID WITH THE HELP OF INSURGENT DEMOCRATS. SUGGEST IMMEDIATE ACTION TO SEIZE HIM.

Rushing out to the barn, Gentry hitched his fastest trotting horse to his sulky and rode into Keyport. There he roused Western Union telegrapher Clem Mahoney from his bed above his shop on Main Street and ordered him to send the message to Union Army headquarters in

Louisville immediately. There was a troop of cavalry stationed in Owensboro, only ten miles from Rose Hill. He ordered a duplicate sent there.

Back in his cellar office, Gentry poured himself a glass of bourbon and held it up to the picture of Lincoln on the wall. "Maybe this one is good enough, Abe," the colonel said and drank it down as the clock in the upstairs hall struck midnight.

NINETEEN

"Do you still love that fellow?"

Paul's voice hissed out of the gray dawnlight filling Janet Todd's bedroom. She wondered if this was what bullets sounded like in a battle. Within the sibilance was a kind of death or at the very least disaster—crippling wounds, incomprehensible pain.

"I don't think I ever loved him," Janet said, struggling to keep her voice calm.

Gabriel Todd had wisely dissolved last night's conclave as soon as Adam Jameson and his father departed. The Sons of Liberty colonels had ridden off to their farms. Paul had said little or nothing while Gabriel Todd tried to apologize for Adam's hostile behavior. Paul abruptly objected to Rogers Jameson's plan to attack Keyport and kill Henry Gentry and the black troopers. Paul insisted they should be given a chance to surrender. He argued it would turn northern opinion against the western confederacy if the blacks were slaughtered. Colonel Todd agreed with him and they had all gone to bed.

Janet had been awake most of the night struggling with the appalling problem Adam Jameson presented. So, apparently, had Paul. He was standing in the doorway of her room, fully dressed.

"The expression on your face—as he left with his father—"

"I pitied him. Love and pity are very different things. Surely you must have felt some sympathy for him. He was so desperate—so exhausted."

"I was too busy dealing with his unmistakable desire to shoot me."

The war. It was rampant even in Hopemont's chaste dining room when men who had killed in its name met. That only made it more imperative to end the murderous struggle as soon as possible.

"I think you'd better go see him today and tell him very frankly what's happened to your affections," Paul said. "Tell him you're going to marry me as soon as the war ends. Otherwise we'll wind up with pistols at ten paces—and only one of us will walk away."

"I—I wouldn't let either of you do such a thing!"

"Once he issues a challenge there won't be much you can do or say."

She sensed it was time for her to say she loved him. But she found the words curiously elusive: "I'll go see Adam immediately after breakfast. I'll make sure no such horror ever happens."

"While you're there, you might ask him some practical questions. Will he bring any artillery with him, if and when he comes? Will he bring ammunition for the guns and for his cavalrymen? I'm frankly rather appalled at the haphazard way this thing is being planned."

He was profoundly angry with her. Janet found it hard to resist a reciprocal anger. "Do you feel I've been dishonest with you about Adam?" she asked.

"I think you might have been a bit more explicit about your arrangement with him."

"I never dreamt he'd appear this way. I thought I had time."

"Maybe you thought the war would solve your problem."

"You mean—one of you might be killed?"

"One—or both. There's something of the adventuress in you. I sensed that from the start. It was another reason for loving you, as far as I was concerned. I've never had much interest in subservient women."

He strode to her bed and lifted her in his arms for a possessive kiss. She did not—or could not—respond. "Please go back to your room," she said. "I'm sure you've already awakened Lucy. If Father or one of the other servants found you here it would be very embarrassing. He wants to believe you're risking everything for a promise."

"Lucy's not here. I *am* risking everything for a promise. The promise of years and years of happiness to come."

Again, she sensed he wanted an affirmation from her. He wanted her to say she shared that wish. He was trying once more to center their love on itself, to remove it from this conspiratorial web she had woven around it. But something in the droop of Adam Jameson's big head as he trudged down the hall prevented Janet from responding. She let Paul go back to his bedroom without another word.

Ten minutes later, Lucy slipped into the room. She told Janet she had gone to see her mother, Lillibet, after Janet went to bed. "She's feelin' so poorly I stayed de night with her."

Janet told Lucy to get out her gray riding habit and tell Sammy, Hopemont's groom, to saddle her favorite horse, the big roan named Trumpeter. At breakfast, Paul had little to say to Colonel Todd and his devious daughter. Her father talked of getting to work on a plan of campaign. He had maps of Indiana in his library. He would tell Paul where the Sons of Liberty planned to gather in each county. With minimal enthusiasm Paul agreed to join him.

Sammy had Trumpeter waiting at the front door. Janet rode along the river road, hoping to catch a few breaths of cool air from the Ohio. But the July sun was relentless. Even at a walk, Trumpeter's neck and flanks were soon streaming sweat. Her riding habit became a kind of hair shirt. She found herself wishing she were twelve years old again. Until that age, she rode astride like a boy, her skirt hiked up to her knees. Then her mother decreed it was time to make a lady of her and she was ordered to sit sidesaddle in these hot riding habits.

At last Rose Hill appeared on its knoll overlooking the Ohio. She rode up a driveway of cottonwoods a generation older than Hopemont's. Amelia Conway Jameson's family had been one of the first to settle this part of Kentucky. The stately brick mansion, with its eight limestone chimneys, had replaced an earlier house around the same time that Janet's grandfather built Hopemont.

Janet was greeted in the front hall by Robin Jameson, Adam's younger brother. Two beings more unlike would be hard to imagine. Robin was about half Adam's size, with a slim almost fragile body and a face that had an uncanny resemblance to Thomas Jefferson—the same high cheekbones, red hair and sharp features. One of Jefferson's nephews had emigrated to Kentucky before the turn of the century and married into the Conway family.

"Janet darling!" Robin said. "What brings you here in such a *fetching* outfit?"

"I've come to see Adam," she said.

"The family hero is still snoring. He and Father stayed up until dawn killing a bottle of bourbon."

"Is your mother at home?"

"She's down in the slave quarters administering the latest formula for worms. We're having an epidemic."

"Could you tell Adam I'm here?"

Robin summoned one of the house servants and told her to wake up Colonel Jameson. "In the meantime you can entertain *me*," he said, gesturing Janet into one of the small parlors off the front hall. "What's this I've heard about you being plighted to a Yankee?"

"Who told you that?" Janet asked.

"One of your niggers told one of ours. Your Lucy, I suspect. She's down here all the time. It's all over the county by now."

"There's absolutely nothin' to it. He's not a Yankee, in the first place. He's from New Jersey, a very pro-Southern state. He's been payin' some attention to me—that's all."

Her face was hot. She was blushing. She was a wretched liar. Was she regretting what she had done with Paul? She suddenly saw the moral side of it. She had *wanted* him. She had yielded to that desire as much as to the wish to bring him into the conspiracy.

"Methinks you doth protest too much, dear Janet," Robin said with a skeptical smile.

"I intend to do more than protest to Lucy. She's likely to get the whipping of her life."

The front door slammed. Amelia Conway passed down the hall in an old calico dress. "Mother!" Robin called. "Look who's turned up for a visit."

"Janet!" Amelia rushed into the parlor and kissed her on the cheek. "What a rare pleasure. You should have given me fair warning so I could put on some decent clothes. You've come to see Adam?"

"Yes," Janet said.

"He'll be so pleased. I suppose he found you at your house last night?"

"Yes," Janet said, growing more and more embarrassed. Amelia was beaming at her as if she were practically her daughter-in-law.

"He can't go out of the house in the daytime. Awful to think it, but there are people around here who would be glad to betray him."

"The federals are offering two thousand dollars for him, dead or alive," Robin said.

Scrunching his shoulders and slipping his hands between his legs, Robin smiled as if he found this idea more than a little amusing.

"It's not funny, Robin!" Amelia said.

"Of course not, Mother," Robin said, hastily assuming a grave expression. "I just find it hard to believe—that anyone would want to kill my dear sweet brother."

"I've told you many times, Robin—he loves you in spite of your—your oddities."

Not for the first time, Janet sensed there were secrets inside the Jameson family that she did not want to explore. The father clearly detested his second son. At sixteen, their sister, Alicia, had married a forty-year-old Keyport merchant, and she seldom if ever visited her parents. Janet could not comprehend how someone as elegant, as refined as Amelia Conway had married an oaf like Rogers Jameson.

Maybe she had just wanted him, whispered the voice that had just convicted Janet of sinning with Paul. She angrily rejected this inner antagonist. She was a leftover from her devout teenage years at St. Mary-of-the-Woods.

"I sent Betsy up to wake Adam," Robin said.

"I'll make sure he got the message," Amelia said.

She left them in the side parlor. Robin pulled a book off the shelf and offered it to Janet. "Have you seen these poems by the marvelous new English poet, Algernon Swinburne?"

"I'm afraid I haven't read much poetry lately," she said.

"There's one that could be an elegy for the South. It's a lament for Itylus, the child accidentally slain by his mother, Aedon, the queen of Thebes. If you remember your mythology, she mourned him so bitterly, the gods changed her into a nightingale. Listen to this.

" *'O swallow, swallow, O fair swift swallow*
Why wilt thou fly after spring to the south
The soft south whither thy heart is set?

Shall not the grief of the old time follow?
Shall not the song thereof cleave to thy mouth?
Hast thou forgotten ere I forget?' "

"There's no need for elegies yet," Janet said.

"Oh no? Why is my brother hiding in his own house like a fugitive?"

"Wars are won by the winner of the last battle," Janet replied.

"I didn't realize you'd become so bloodthirsty, dear Janet. Maybe you and the behemoth will make a perfect match, after all. I see the whole thing as mass insanity on both sides."

"I see it as a struggle for civilization! Our civilization, the one our parents, our grandparents, our ancestors created—"

"You're wrong, dear Janet. Utterly, totally wrong. I hope you don't end up singing—"

He glanced at the book.

" '*O swallow sister, O fleeting swallow*
My heart in me is a molten ember
And over my head the waves have met.' "

Unnameable fear swept Janet's mind and body. Was she moving into a future beyond her control? She gazed into Robin Jameson's Jeffersonian face and wondered if he was one of those prophets who are not honored in their own country.

"What the hell's this?"

Adam towered over them in his worn gray uniform. He snatched the book out of Robin's hand. "Algernon Swineburn?" he said, pronouncing the last name as if the writer were part pig. "There's a good name for a poet."

"He's quite talented," Robin said.

"Get out of here, little sister," Adam said. "Janet and I need to talk."

"Sticks and stones can break my bones—and words can also hurt me," Robin murmured. "I hope you can stay for dinner, Janet."

"I doubt if I can, thank you," she said.

Adam slouched in the chair Robin had vacated, engulfing it. His beard made it impossible to read his expression. "Sorry about the way I acted last night. I was a little out of my head."

"I came over to clear up certain things, Adam."

"You don't have to clear up anythin'. I'm going to take care of that myself."

"What do you mean?"

"Pompey's on his way to Hopemont with a challenge for Major Stapleton. It expresses my contempt for a man who'd seduce the affections of a woman while the man she's pledged to marry is fightin' a war he's too cowardly to go anywhere near."

"I insist you retract that letter. Immediately!"

"I doubt if that's possible. You can't take back the kind of insults I wrote. They can only be wiped out by gunpowder."

"Are you out of your mind? This man has come over to our side, heart and soul."

"I know all about his performance. It was worthy of John Wilkes Booth. A lot of people wrote me about it."

"I won't let you kill him."

"He may kill me. It'll be a fair fight."

"We need you both! Your men won't come without you."

"This is more important than the war, Janet. This is a question of my honor—and his honor, if such a thing exists in the northern mind. I can't lead men into battle if they know I failed to repay this insult."

"There was no insult on Major Stapleton's part. He barely knew of your existence—at least in relation to me. I saw no need to mention you because I regarded the promise I made to you as no more than an agreement to reconsider your—your—affection for me—when the war ended. I never agreed to marry you or to deny myself the attention of other men. I didn't retire from the world to await your return like some creature from a romance."

The black eyes in the bearded face remained as opaque as moonstones. This was a very different man from the overgrown boy she had seen off to war with a halfhearted kiss.

"That was not my understandin'. It was never my understandin'. I don't believe it was yours until you met this Yankee double-talker."

"You're wrong. You know things were not well between us, Adam, before the war. You must have known I was putting you off with patently weak excuses—"

"I don't pretend to understand the female mind—"

"The female mind! I consider that an insult. My mind is no different from yours. It tries to make realistic judgments on the world around me. It tries to be honest with itself—and with others."

"Then why weren't you honest with me?"

"That would take a volume to explain. I was flattered at first by your attention to me—"

"Colonel!"

Pompey, Adam's burly black body servant, stood in the doorway, streaming sweat. "Federal cavalry. Met'm on the road to Hopemont. A hundred of'm at least!"

"Jesus Christ!" Adam was on his feet, a tower of fury. "Get my gun. I'm gonna die fightin'. They ain't goin' to lock me up in some prison for the rest of my life!"

Janet was transfixed. She was going to be in a battle. There would be bullets flying everywhere. Perhaps she would die. As Pompey raced upstairs screaming, "Federal cavalry!" she realized Adam was acting like a madman. Was it her fault? Did he want to show her how ready he was to die for the cause?

"Don't be ridiculous," she said. "You're needed. You've got to hide. Or run."

"I can't run. My horse is spent. There ain't another decent horse left on the farm. The federals took them all and paid in their rotten greenbacks."

Rogers Jameson rushed into the room in his nightshirt, hefting a shotgun. Pompey was on his heels with Adam's pistol.

"You can't fight them! They'll kill you both," Janet said.

"Six to one your goddamn Union major set them on us!" Adam roared.

"You have to hide! There must be somewhere you can hide!" Janet said.

"Janet's right." Amelia Jameson stood in the doorway, white-lipped. "In my bedroom there's a window seat. Adam could curl up in that. Janet and I will have a visit. She'll sit on top of it."

Rogers Jameson shook his big head. Strangled words drooled from his wired jaw. "Gdum. Rathr die—"

In the distance the thud of hooves became audible. The federal horsemen were no more than five minutes away. Adam's rage vanished. It was miraculous. In an instant he was cool, collected and decisive. "They're right, Pap," he said. "It's my only chance. Will the niggers stay loyal?"

"Of course," Amelia said.

"Th-dmn-wll bttr," Roger Jameson growled.

TWENTY

AMELIA JAMESON'S BEDROOM HAD DEEP blue window DRAPES, a pale green Oriental rug and a canopied bed with sky blue hangings. The rest of the furniture was fragile Chippendale. An Italiante painting of Venus and Adonis hung on the south wall. For a moment Janet imagined Rogers Jameson in this room, in that bed. A Kentucky version of Beauty and the Beast. No wonder they hated each other. For a moment she saw the whole inner drama of the marriage: Amelia's attempts to civilize Rogers, his even stronger determination to remain untamed.

Adam Jameson flung the cushion off the window seat and flipped up the lid. Robin Jameson smiled up at them. "I thought you were going to fight it out, Big Brother," he said.

Adam picked Robin up by the front of his shirt and flung him across the room. His head struck the rug with a sickening thud. Amelia rushed to him with a frantic cry. Insanity!

Adam seized Janet's arms. "If they find me," he said, "I'm comin' out shootin'. Go flat on the floor. I don't want the last thing I see in this world to be you with a bullet wound."

He kissed her. The pounding hooves of the federal cavalry mounted to thunder. They were turning in the drive. Adam climbed into the window seat. He had to lie on his side, his legs curled. He clutched the pistol to his chest and looked up at her. "I love you," he said.

Janet slammed the lid. Was it his coffin? she wondered dazedly. Was she wishing for his death? Or simply the obliteration of his relentless affection? Pompey was dragging a groggy Robin Jameson out of the room. Amelia Jameson watched him go and whirled, resolution suffusing her face. By an act of will she seemed to transform herself from hand-wringing mother to mistress of herself and the situation. Was this where Adam had inherited his decisiveness?

"We must look utterly casual," Amelia said. "You've come down to see me. Do you knit or sew?"

Janet shook her head.

"I'll manage for both of us," Amelia said. She rushed to a bureau and pulled out a needle and thread and a dimity apron. "Here," she said and handed Janet a year-old edition of *Godey's Lady's Book,* the popular magazine. "We're discussing the latest styles."

Janet flipped *Godey's* open to a display of French Empire dresses. Was this what she would be doing every afternoon if she married Adam Jameson? She had never had much interest in fashion. But it was a central part of a woman's sphere, as the experts called the female share of a marriage. Men and women had separate spheres. Why was she so eager to invade the man's sphere? Was it because the woman's sphere was so brainless?

Downstairs a fist thumped on the front door. It was presumably opened and a man's voice roared through the house: "Where's your son, Jameson? We've had eyewitness reports that he's here. If you don't produce him we'll burn the place around your ears. I have no patience with you disloyal bastards anymore. You're all outside the protection of the law."

"That's General Burbridge," Amelia said. "It shows how badly they want Adam—when the Grand Inquisitor himself leads the hunt."

Kentucky's Union commander was easily the most hated man in the state. A few months ago he had issued Order Number 59, declaring that four Confederate captives would be executed for every Union soldier killed by rebel guerrillas.

Amelia put down her sewing and went to the head of the stairs. "General Burbridge," she said. "You may recall me as Amelia Conway. Your father and my father were friends when he served in the Congress. Please calm yourself. I haven't seen my son Adam for three years. My other son, Robin, is upstairs, much indisposed by a fever. Adam's fianceé, Miss Todd, is visiting me. I can't believe you'll carry out such a barbaric threat."

"I'm going to search every nook and cranny of the house and barns!" General Burbridge roared. "If we find him, I'll most definitely burn the place as a just punishment for concealing a known desperado."

"I won't bother to defend my son as a courageous soldier of the Confederate Army," Amelia said. "I'll only assure you that he isn't here."

She returned to the bedroom and picked up the dress and the sewing basket again. "I hope you and Adam had a chance to talk last night," she said, her manner as composed and serene as if Janet were merely a welcome guest and the house were not swarming with Union soldiers.

"I'm afraid we only talked about our plans for our— our hopes to win the war."

"This grand conspiracy I hear hints about now and then?" Amelia said, ignoring Janet's evasion. "My husband wouldn't dream of confiding in me. What have you learned about it?"

"Enough to give me hope," Janet said.

"What a cross your poor mother and father must be bearing. Losing those two wonderful sons."

"My mother is very low. I wonder if she'll ever recover."

"I'm not sure I could bear the loss of even one son. Will Adam play a part in this insurrection?"

"A vital part," Janet said.

"Do you think it has a chance of succeeding?"

"Mrs. Jameson! You'll excuse me. We must search this room as well."

General Burbridge stood in the doorway. Short and slim, with a blond Vandyke beard, he exuded energy— and arrogance. His blue uniform was pressed and immaculate. The black leather holster on his hip gleamed. His boots had a similar shine. He wore a pair of white leather gloves that added a touch of luxury to his appearance. Janet thought of Adam Jameson's faded and patched gray uniform and almost wept.

Amelia introduced Janet. Burbridge scowled. "I'm familiar with Miss Todd's name. You and your father entertained this desperado last night at Hopemont. That in itself could be grounds for arrest."

"I don't know what you're talking about, General," Janet said.

"We have an eyewitness ready to testify."

"I didn't know you arrested women," Amelia Conway said.

"I've arrested several. A few nights in prison had a wonderful effect on their loyalty."

Behind Burbridge loomed two big cavalrymen with carbines. The general turned and snapped, "Where's that nigger?"

One of the troopers shoved Pompey into the room. "We know your son is here. This is his body servant," Burbridge said. "He never goes anywhere without him. What's he doing here without your son?"

"Pompey was ill. Adam sent him home to recuperate," Amelia said.

"Pompey's too damn faithful for his own good. We've offered to make him a contraband. Under the terms of the Emancipation Proclamation, any nigger who's forced to serve the Confederacy in any way is free."

"He didn't say nothin' about bein' sick," one of the soldiers said. "He said he come home because he got tired of the war."

"Tell us where your master is and you're a free man. We'll free every slave on this place," Burbridge said.

Could any black resist that offer? Janet could almost feel Adam's finger tightening on the trigger of his pistol. "I tole you—I don' know where the colonel is," Pompey said. "Someplace in Virginia's all I recollect."

General Burbridge growled in disgust. "Search this room. Every inch of it," he said, waving Pompey out the door ahead of him.

Looking embarrassed, the troopers prowled the bedroom. They pulled back the hangings of the bed. They looked under it. They peered into a large armoire and poked the muzzles of their guns among Amelia's dresses.

Suddenly Janet was *inside* the window seat on which she was sitting, her arms around Adam Jameson. She was pressing her lips against his bearded mouth, murmuring, *Don't don't*. She could feel the tension building in his big body toward an explosion that would catapult him into the center of the room, gun blazing. He would kill these two troopers but the others would kill him before he got out of the house.

She could feel the heat of his body, taste his breath. *Don't,* she begged. Wanting had nothing to do with it, but she was ready to say, *I love you.* She was ready to say and do almost anything to defeat these obnoxious federals.

The troopers found nothing in the room and departed. Downstairs, Janet heard an exasperated General Burbridge shout, "Get all the house niggers together! I want to question them! One may tell the truth!"

In a few minutes they could hear Burbridge making a sonorous speech to Rose Hill's servants. He offered them the same freedom he had dangled in front of Pompey.

"You're sure they'll stay loyal?" Janet asked.

"I've devoted a good deal of my life to winning their affection," Amelia Jameson said.

For Janet, the words summarized hundreds of hours spent in the slave quarters. Thousands of southern women had done the same thing with their slaves, from the northern border of Kentucky to the Gulf of Mexico and the Rio Grande. It was an exhausting, often demanding task, utterly beyond the competence of men. They were the reason that the South's slaves had remained loyal while almost every able-bodied white man served in the Confederate Army.

General Burbridge was back, growling in the doorway. "Mrs. Jameson, Miss Todd," he said. "Would you come downstairs for a few minutes?"

"For what purpose?" Amelia asked.

"I'm under no obligation to explain myself. Come with me, immediately!"

"General Burbridge, I'm relying on you to preserve some remnant of your family's reputation as gentlemen while you're in my house," Amelia said.

"Mrs. Jameson, if your house was not being used to conceal a desperado, wanted for murder and reckless destruction of private property, I would be intimidated by your high tone."

Don't, don't, Janet pleaded. She was back in the window seat, desperately trying to control Adam Jameson's rage and simultaneously trying to control her own anger.

"What in the world do you want me to do downstairs, General Burbridge?"

"I want you both to testify in front of the servants that you haven't seen Adam Jameson today. I want them to see you both lie—if that's what you choose to do—so they'll know the morality of the people who are denying them their freedom."

Suddenly Janet knew with unbelievable clarity what

was going to happen next. Was she somehow connected to Adam Jameson's mind and heart by that mystic plunge into his hiding place? She stood up, saying in an extra-loud voice, "We'd better do what General Burbridge says."

Amelia gazed at her, startled, almost affronted. In the same moment, Adam flung up the window seat and leaped into the room, his pistol leveled. "If you make a sound, Burbridge, you're a dead man," he said.

The shock and fear on Burbridge's face produced an explosion of pleasure in Janet's mind and body that she could only compare to the moment of climax with Paul Stapleton in the Happy Hunting Ground. It was bewildering—and appalling. Was she falling in love with war and death?

"Take his gun," Adam said.

Janet removed Burbridge's pistol from the holster on his hip and handed it to Adam. "Now, Burbridge," Adam said. "You're going to call your second in command upstairs. You'll tell him to bring Pompey with him. When your man gets here, we'll disarm him too and then you'll tell him to order every man in your command to throw their guns into the Ohio. Pompey will march them down there and make sure they do it."

"How do I know you won't kill me anyway?" Burbridge said.

"That's a chance you'll have to take, Burbridge. I don't know another man I'd enjoy killing. I'm inclined to do it for your murder of innocent prisoners of war, not to mention your insulting remarks to my mother and Miss Todd. But I have compunctions about killing an unarmed man. However, if you attempt to retaliate against my family or Miss Todd's family for this embarrassment, I'll come back to Kentucky and kill you, armed or unarmed. Is that perfectly clear?"

General Burbridge glared at him. Adam jammed his pistol into his chest. "Is it?"

"Yes," Burbridge said.

"Let's begin the game," Adam said. He seized Burbridge's arm and walked him to the door.

"Colonel Haldeman!" the general called. "Would you come upstairs, please? And bring that nigger, Pompey, with you?"

Adam dragged Burbridge out of sight, to the left of the door. Colonel Haldeman soon appeared—a stocky redhead who walked with a swagger. He had Pompey by the arm.

"General?" Haldeman said at the head of the stairs.

Adam prodded Burbridge with his pistol. "I'm in here," he said.

Colonel Haldeman walked into the room to find Adam with his pistol pressed against General Burbridge's head. "Give your gun to the lady, Colonel. If you don't want to kill the general—and yourself."

A shaken Haldeman surrendered his gun to Janet. She waved Pompey into the room and shut the door. Another prod from Adam produced Burbridge's order to throw the cavalrymen's guns into the Ohio under Pompey's supervision.

"When you come back, Pomp, I want you to pick the three best horses from their supply and bring them around to the front of the house. You and I and General Burbridge will need them for a trip we'll soon be taking. Tell your sister Missy to pack as much grub as we can carry in your knapsack and mine."

"Yes sir, Colonel," Pompey said, his sharp-featured black face impassive. Janet wondered if he had been hoping Adam would be caught so he could accept Burbridge's promise of freedom. She could not blame Pompey for the feeling. In spite of it, he had remained loyal. So had the other servants. Didn't that prove something?

"Get going, Colonel. You've got twenty minutes," Adam said.

"You won't get away. We'll have a thousand men on your trail in two hours," Haldeman said.

"Better not if you want General Burbridge back in one piece," Adam said.

Haldeman and Pompey departed. They could hear Haldeman shouting orders downstairs. Adam shoved Burbridge into a chair and grinned cheerfully at Janet and Amelia. "Don't worry, Mother. Everything will go beautifully," he said.

Janet realized she was still holding Colonel Haldeman's pistol. "What shall I do with this?" she asked.

"Maybe you ought to keep it and ride off with me. I begin to think you'd make a first-rate soldier," Adam said.

"I wish I could," Janet said.

She stared dazedly at this bearded giant. Could he possibly know what she had been thinking and feeling while he was in the window seat? What did it mean? Was she in love with two men?

In less than twenty minutes, Pompey returned with Colonel Haldeman. "All them guns is at de bottom of de ribber," Pompey said. "I got de horses ready and Missy done loaded us with eats."

"Good," Adam said. "Now, Colonel Haldeman, where are your men?"

"On the lawn."

"Get them around to the slave quarters. I don't want anyone near enough to throw a rock or a stick and try to rush us. If I see a move from any direction, General Burbridge better start saying his prayers."

They watched from the window while Haldeman formed his 100 troopers into a column and marched them off the lawn to the slave quarters, a quarter of a mile from the main house.

Adam tucked General Burbridge's gun into the waistband of his trousers and gave Haldeman's gun to Pompey. He kissed his mother on the cheek and turned to Janet. "Maybe it's just as well Pompey didn't deliver my letter. Tell a certain person I apologize for my atrocious conduct last night," he said.

He swept her against him and kissed her as if he knew his new power over her. Janet did not return the kiss but she did not resist it either. She was in a daze. She felt as if her mind, her self, were splitting into fragments.

"We'll pray for you," Amelia said.

"Thanks, Mother."

With Burbridge in the lead, the muzzle of Adam's gun against his back, they departed. Janet and Amelia watched them ride down the drive and disappear among the trees lining the river road.

"Adam's magnificent!" Janet said.

Amelia Jameson did not respond to this praise of her son. "They have a way to retaliate," she said in a leaden voice. "Robin will be drafted now, for certain."

"You can hire a substitute."

"I doubt if his father will pay the money. He wants Robin to join Adam—but I won't stand for it. He'd be dead in a week."

Janet said nothing. She was too absorbed in her own dilemma to offer Amelia any sympathy. "You don't understand. You're too young," Amelia said. "A mother loves all her sons. A woman loves—can love—many different men."

Into the bedroom rushed an old black woman in a near frenzy. Janet recognized her as Aunt Rachel, the mother of Adam's body servant, Pompey. Her breath came in gasps; her mouth worked spasmodically; she clawed at her face. "Oh, Mistress!" she cried, sinking to her knees in front of Amelia Jameson. "It's all my fault. I tole Pompey and he tole me t'fess to you and I wouldn' get whipped, but he wouldn' promise nothin' for that scamp Lucy."

"What in the world are you talking about, Rachel?" Amelia asked.

"Them letters that Miz Janet writes to Colonel Adam.

I done read them for Lucy and she must've tole them Union soldiers and that's why they come here and like to catch him and Pompey. I felt so awful, Mistress, I had to tell somebody. You won't whip me, will you, Mistress? You won't let Masser whip me? Lucy said it wouldn' mean no harm to Miz Janet it would jus' help get h'sister Maybelle back from that whorehouse down de river where she's liable to kill h'self."

Aunt Rachel flung herself facedown on the carpet and wept and wept and wept. *It can't be true,* Janet thought. The words reverberated in her head like the crash of a pistol. *It can't be true.*

TWENTY-ONE

IS SHE STILL HALF IN love with Adam Jameson? If so does that oath you swore last night mean anything? As oaths go, it did not mean very much in the first place. You had no trouble adjusting your conscience to swearing allegiance to a Southern version of liberty. It's more or less the basic credo of the Democratic Party, to which you already belong by birth, blood and conviction.

These thoughts paraded through Paul Stapleton's head as he sat at a table in Hopemont's oak-paneled library listening to Gabriel Todd describe the routes that the various county brigades of the Sons of Liberty were planning to take for their march on Indianapolis. He made random notes but he was not paying serious attention to Colonel Todd. He kept seeing the expression on Janet's face as she watched Adam Jameson stumble down the hall to Hopemont's front door. Jealousy mingled with an unnerving realization that the Sons of Liberty were a far more serious conspiracy than he had imagined. The confidence with which Gabriel Todd was reeling off the number of recruits on the enlistment books of each brigade was impressive. Adam Jameson had an electrifying impact on the colonels of the George Rogers Clark Brigade. After he left they had talked in awed tones of their admiration for him and the confidence his presence would give their amateur soldiers.

The sound of hoofbeats on Hopemont's drive brought Paul to the window. Instead of Janet, it was one of his black troopers from Keyport. He handed Paul a message from Henry Gentry: *General Carrington has arrived.*

He wants to complete the court-martials as soon as possible. He is in an extremely unpleasant frame of mind. Please return immediately.

Paul showed the message to Colonel Todd, who agreed he had no alternative to a rapid departure. "I hope you can come back without delay. We have a great deal to discuss," he said.

Paul assured him he would do his best to return swiftly. He packed his small valise, strapped it on his saddle and rode down the hot dusty river road to the steam ferry across the Ohio. He caught the clumsy boat just as it was leaving the Kentucky shore. Within an hour he was at he Grange. Gentry met him in the hall and led him into the front parlor, where General Henry Carrington was pacing the room, indifferent to the magnificent view of the river. Two submissive-looking staff officers sat on a love seat, along with a shaggy-haired civilian in a dirty white suit.

Gentry introduced Paul and they shook hands. The officers were both colonels, the first a gray-haired heavy-jawed man named Slocum, the second a short rotund redhead named Brewer; the civilian was named Dawes—a reporter from the Indianapolis *Journal,* the state's chief Republican newspaper.

General Carrington's lean bony face was decorated at the chin by a scraggly black beard. His torso was similarly lean. He emanated a foxy quality, especially around the eyes. He looked like a man who knew what it was to be both predator and quarry.

Carrington got to the point immediately. "Your jaw-breaking Negro sergeant has created a serious political problem at the worst possible time," he said. "Governor Morton's extremely upset about it."

"He was provoked by an extremely insulting song, General," Paul replied.

"Colonel Gentry told me all about it in his report. I don't think the song alters the case one whit. We're going to court-martial him and give him the maximum sentence permitted by military law. Then we're going to court-martial that deserter you caught on Independence Day and shoot him in the courthouse square. The two things will communicate the sort of message the Democrats need to hear. The Union will protect them from unruly blacks. But the war is a fight to the finish, and we won't tolerate anyone who takes an oath of loyalty to the Confederacy."

Paul glanced at Colonel Gentry. As the senior officer in Keyport, it was up to him to disagree with the general. Paul had tried to defend Sergeant Washington; an officer was obliged to support one of his men if he thought he was being treated unjustly. But the general had the last word—unless the colonel wanted to contest it.

Gentry fussed with his empty sleeve, which he had pinned across the chest of his uniform. "General," he said, "if I may speak informally, I think you're all wet."

Carrington's beard bristled. The staff officers gazed at Gentry with astonishment, although Paul caught a glimpse of covert agreement on Colonel Brewer's ruddy face. Reporter Dawes was equally amazed but he did not reach for his pad and pencil. He was not here to tell a story of Republican dissension.

"Punishing Sergeant Washington sends the wrong message to the Democrats—that they can insult Negroes to their faces with impunity," Gentry said. "That will only lead to more broken jaws and maybe some broken heads on both sides. As for shooting a pathetic dimwit like Private Garner, it's likely to make him a martyr to Republican ruthlessness."

This was a different Gentry from the mild-mannered slightly pathetic cripple of Paul's recent acquaintance. General Carrington, clearly not used to hearing contrary opinions from lower-ranking officers, was nonplussed.

"Colonel Gentry," Carrington said. "I'm not here to solicit your opinions! I'm issuing orders, not subjects for debate."

Gentry tugged at his empty sleeve, as if it was a reminder that he had nothing to lose by continuing the argument. He had no hope of further promotion in the
U.S. Army.

"Sergeant Washington's military record is impecca-
ble. He's played a vital part in capturing over one hundred deserters in the past four months. More than any
other unit in Indiana."

"You have more to catch," Carrington snapped.
"Down here on the Ohio, four-fifths of your so-called
citizens are disaffected traitorous Democrats. It's hardly
surprising that their sons cut and run."

"All the more reason not to give their brothers and fathers an excuse to start an insurrection by announcing
that we're going to shoot every runaway we catch. I've
told you about the Sons of Liberty, General. I think they
represent a serious threat to Lincoln, the war effort and
the nation's future."

"Colonel Gentry, I repeat, I'm not interested in your
opinion!" General Carrington snapped. "Everything I
hear through my agents testifies to the incompetence,
the almost criminal passivity, you're displaying in this
military district. You allow Democrats to slander the
government and the army, to undermine, to conspire—"

"Who are your agents, General? Isn't a man entitled
to confront his accusers?" Gentry asked.

"I wouldn't trust you or anyone else with their
names," Carrington said.

"General—I'm trying to tell you something your
agents don't tell you. Your policies aren't working. By
my count, you've smashed up and closed down thirty
Democratic newspapers in Indiana. You've got at least
three hundred political prisoners in your Indianapolis
bastille, all Democrats held on spurious charges, with
no hope of release thanks to the suspension of habeas
corpus. To what end? The Democrats are more rebel-

lious, more hostile to the war than ever. You're turned a difficult situation into a gigantic mess!"

Carrington's irritation escalated to fury. "Be careful, Colonel. Your friendship with the president doesn't render you immune to retaliation."

He wheeled on Paul, who was listening to this exchange with growing disgust. It confirmed everything he had heard about Republican contempt for the Bill of Rights from Gabriel Todd two nights ago. "I take it you agree with Colonel Gentry, Major Stapleton?"

"On the whole, yes," Paul said.

Carrington glowered. "I know who you are and who your father the *senator* was—and who your brother, the much-wounded major general, is. I'm impressed by none of these things. A professional soldier tainted by family ties to the Democratic Party had better give unquestioning support to the government's policy—if he wants to retain any hope of future promotion in the U.S. Army."

"General Carrington," Paul said. "I resent that remark *extremely*. On behalf of myself and my father and my brother. There's no family in this country who has given the Union stronger support."

Up until now, the Gettysburg wound whispered.

Carrington pulled on his gloves. His two aides stood up, both looking somewhat embarrassed by the general's performance. "I expect to see you at the courthouse this afternoon at three P.M. with both prisoners. I want both men convicted by five o'clock."

The general stalked out to his horse, trailed by his colonels and the reporter. Paul stared after him, shaking his head. "I'll—be—damned," he said.

"That son of a bitch is a walking, talking explanation for a lot of the hatred loose in Indiana," Gentry said. "Last year, when the Democrats held a state convention in Indianapolis, he unleashed a regiment of troops on them. He put a dozen men in the hospital and the rest fled the city by horse, foot and train."

"Has he seen any action?" Paul asked.

Gentry shook his head. "He went from a desk in Washington to a desk in Indianapolis. Last summer, when Morgan's cavalry crossed the river, Carrington rushed here with twenty-five hundred men. He sat in this very parlor and got drunk while Morgan rode east into Ohio. At nightfall Carrington marched west, into Illinois."

Gentry realized Paul was staring at him with something close to amazement. He was revealing more about the way the Republicans were operating in Indiana than a visiting Democrat should know.

"I've become exasperated with idiots who think Americans can be intimidated by arresting them and smashing up their newspapers," Gentry said.

"What a shame you can't convince General Carrington of that," Paul said. "Maybe he's encouraged by the Union commander in Kentucky, General Burbridge. He apparently thinks the same way."

"I know," Gentry said mournfully. He waited a strategic moment and asked, "How was your visit to Hopemont?"

"Relaxing," Paul said. "Colonel Todd and his wife are very hospitable people."

"Did you meet anyone else at the house?" Gentry asked.

Paul said nothing.

Gentry waited another strategic moment. Paul had no doubt the colonel could see reluctance in his wary eyes, on his tightening mouth. But Gentry could not know the reluctance mingled with the memory of the expression on Janet Todd's face as she looked at Adam Jameson. Major Stapleton was asking himself if his betrayal was motivated by the clarion call of duty, honor, country or jealousy of that headstrong behemoth.

"I have other sources of information, Major," Gentry said in a low hurried voice, glancing over his shoulder to make sure other members of the household were not approaching. "I've been told that Rogers Jameson and four colonels from the Sons of Liberty's Daviess County brigade were dinner guests—and you were joined by Colonel Adam Jameson of Morgan's cavalry."

"If you know so much already, Colonel, why are you asking me for information?" Paul snapped.

"I presume you learned a good deal from an evening with these gentlemen."

"Actually I learned very little," Paul said. "Beyond the rough estimate of their numbers—fifty thousand. Their organization is extremely haphazard. That figure could be off by ten or twenty thousand either way."

"Did they mention a date?" Gentry asked. "That's what we need to know. The date of the uprising."

"They don't seem to have settled on one yet."

A lie. Or at least an avoidance of the truth—by refusing to mention the August 29th date the Confederate government recommended. Was that a violation of his West Point oath? A betrayal of duty, honor, country? Or was it only a delaying tactic, to give him time to make sure Janet belonged to him—and he had the opportunity to extricate her from this doomed drama before merciless men like General Carrington and his Kentucky counterpart, General Burbridge, took charge of the situation?

Yes yes yes. A delaying tactic. The idea gave Paul time to breathe, to think. Henry Gentry's glum expression suggested he knew he was getting less than the truth. "Hadn't we better get the prisoners ready for the court-martials?" Paul said.

TWENTY-TWO

"WHERE'S MAJOR STAPLETON?" JANET TODD asked Joseph, Hopemont's butler, as she pulled off her sweaty riding coat in the front hall.

"Gone back to Keyport."

Relief flooded her body. She had no desire to tell Paul about the federal raid on Rose Hill and Adam's hair-breadth escape. She was not at all sure she could describe it without revealing emotions better kept to herself.

"Where's Lucy?"

"Upstairs in your room, I 'spect," Joseph said.

Janet's first reaction to Aunt Rachel's revelation echoed in her mind: *It can't be true.* She still half-believed those words. If there was one human being in the world she trusted absolutely, it was Lucy. Distrusting her was tantamount to distrusting herself.

She found Lucy in her room, ironing a dress, and told her to sit down in an armchair by the window. "Something terrible happened at Rose Hill just now, Lucy. Federal cavalry raided the house to capture Colonel Jameson. He got away by outwitting the Union general and forcing his troopers surrender. The uproar made Aunt Rachel, Pompey's mother, go crazy. She ran into Mrs. Jameson's bedroom and said it was all your fault. You had made her read my letter to Colonel Jameson and reported it to someone in Indiana. I didn't believe her. It couldn't be true. Why did she say such a thing?"

Lucy clutched at her hair, then pulled at her calico dress as if she wanted to rip it off. "Miz Janet, I didn't mean no harm! I never meant harm should ever come to you in this business!"

"What in the world are you talkin' about?"

"The war you're fixin' to start with them federal niggers in Keyport. The one you want Colonel Jameson to come into no matter what! And Major Stapleton. You loves him but you got him in it too. I tole that much to Colonel Gentry but I never said a word about you goin' to the major's room at night or—or—"

Her voice dwindled to a mutter. "Or to the Happy Huntin' Ground."

Janet's first impulse was more disbelief. "Lucy, have you gone crazy?"

"Maybe I have, Miz Janet. Maybe I been crazy ever since your daddy sold Maybelle to that whorehouse in New Orleans. I knew it was wrong to get Aunt Rachel to read your letters but Colonel Gentry told me he'd make sure nothin' happened to you."

"My father would never sell Maybelle to—to someplace where she'd be unhappy. Who told you that?"

"Colonel Gentry. Mr. Jameson too. They both said it was as sure a thing as the grass bein' green. Colonel Gentry said he'd get her out of the place if I helped him stop this war of yours 'fore it started. That way you wouldn't get hurt and no one would ever know what I done."

Tears streamed down Lucy's cheeks. She dropped to her knees and buried her face in Janet's skirt. "Oh Miz Janet forgive me please I won't do nothin' like it again ever. I'll be as good and true to you as I ever was in spita Maybelle. I'll jus' pray she don't kill herself in that place, that somehow she'll find a man to take her out of it—"

For a moment Janet saw the life into which she had been born as an unjust sentence handed down by some malevolent invisible persecutor. She had never asked for this black presence in her life. Any more than her mother and her father had asked for this plantation on which a hundred black women and children were eating them into debt while their able-bodied kin worked at half-speed because they knew they could join the Union Army any time they chose and there was nothing Colonel Todd could do to retrieve them. The Todds, Kentucky, the whole South were sinking into ruin because no one knew what to do with these people. To free them risked anarchy, to keep them in bondage produced betrayals like this one—and worse.

"I have never been so disappointed with anyone in my entire life," Janet said.

It was true. Lucy's betrayal resounded in Janet's mind as a kind of death knell to the whole southern system. She could no longer bear the thought of a lifetime with these people. But she also could not tolerate the thought of admitting it to obnoxious Yankees like Captain Simeon Otis.

"I couldn't help it, Miz Janet! I loved Maybelle so! She was so beautiful and sweet and kind to me. As kind as you!"

"How could you be so stupid! Colonel Gentry lied to you. So did Mr. Jameson. My father never sold Maybelle to a—a—whorehouse."

The idea was so loathsome, she could barely pronounce the word. "I know, as surely as I know this house is standin', that Maybelle is living in Mississippi or Alabama or Louisiana in the house of some respectable family, working as a cook or a nurse to their children."

Lucy rubbed her streaming eyes. "What you gonna do to me, Miz Janet?"

"I don't know. I'm going to talk to my father about this. You'll be punished, I can promise you that."

Lucy flung herself on the floor at Janet's feet, in a pathetic imitation of Aunt Rachel. "Oh, please don't, Miz Janet. I'll kill myself first. Don't tell your daddy."

Janet left Lucy sobbing on the floor and rushed downstairs, ignoring her mother's call from her bedroom for an explanation of the racket Lucy was making. In the gazebo she found her father well into his daily quart of bourbon. She seized the bottle and poured the last third onto the grass.

"It's time for clear heads," she said. "Clear heads and hard hearts."

She told him what Lucy had done. With a roar Gabriel Todd struggled to his feet. "I'll whip her personally. I'll whip her till she dies."

"That won't accomplish anything," Janet said. "The damage is done. It's more important to find out what she's told your dear old cousin Colonel Gentry."

"I'm going to whip him too. I'll whip that one-armed bastard till he begs for mercy."

"You're sounding like Rogers Jameson. The Todds are thinkers, Father. Didn't you tell me that a long time ago?"

He sank back into his chair, struggling to clear the bourbon haze from his head. "You're right," he said thickly. "But what can we do?"

"Did you sell Maybelle to—to—one of those houses?"

"I sold her to a trader in Lexington for a thousand dollars. He was sure he could get fifteen hundred for her in New Orleans. I didn't ask him who'd pay it and he didn't tell me."

So it's true. The words were like a knife thrust or a bullet in Janet's body. Not a fatal wound but a painful one. What was this crime compared to the monstrous things Lincoln and his crew were doing? An act of weakness, at worst.

"First we have to find out as much as possible about what Lucy's told Gentry. Then see if we can befuddle him some way."

"First we'll whip her. Then we'll ask questions."

"No, Father. I don't think I could stand that. I still love her in a strange irreversible way."

He gave her a consoling hug. "Where is the black traitoress? We'll both question her."

They strode back to the house. "Lucy!" Janet called up the stairs. "Come down here."

No answer. Janet mounted the stairs, thinking she might whip her personally, after all. In the bedroom she found Lucy unconscious on the floor, fluid drooling from her mouth. Beside her right arm spread a pool of blood from a slashed wrist.

"Janet?" her mother called. "Janet!"

Janet rushed to her mother's room. Letitia Todd was frantic. "Lucy came in her and snatched my medicine off the bureau. My laudanum. She took a scissors too—"

Janet raced back to her bedroom and tied a tourniquet around Lucy's arm. "Father!" she called. "Father! Come quickly."

In sixty seconds a winded Gabriel Todd was in the doorway. Together he and Janet hauled Lucy over to the commode. Janet thrust a finger down her throat and she vomited up a half-pint of green laudanum. Janet slapped her hard in the face and she came half-awake. When she saw Colonel Todd she struggled to free herself from their grasp.

"Lemmy die!" she wailed. "Why didn' you lemmy die?"

"You're not going to die until you tell us every single thing you told Colonel Gentry," Janet said.

They propped Lucy against the wall and demanded answers. What they heard appalled them. Lucy had opened every letter Janet and Gabriel Todd had sent for the past year and with the help of Aunt Rachel had recited their contents to Henry Todd Gentry. That meant Gentry knew the plan for the creation of the western confederacy and the southern confederacy's role in it.

"They could arrest us anytime," a staggered Gabriel Todd said.

Janet paced the room, groping for self-control. "Maybe not, Father. They don't have the letters. Just the contents—and Lucy's testimony would never be admitted in any court. Slaves have no legal standing. They don't know the date of the uprising because we haven't decided it. They don't know the names of most of our leaders. We've been chary with names because the letters had to travel through so many hands."

"All true," Gabriel Todd said. "But with habeas corpus suspended, they could still throw us in jail for a long time. They wouldn't hesitate to arrest you. That swine Burbridge is no respecter of women."

"But they haven't done it," Janet replied. "Their hesitation makes me think we've got them in a kind of checkmate."

They locked a weeping Lucy in Janet's bedroom and went downstairs to confer on the veranda, where no house servant could eavesdrop. Gabriel Todd remained unconvinced that they were at least temporarily safe. He wondered if other Hopemont slaves were working for Gentry and feared there might be a conspiracy to kill him and his wife and daughter with poison or a midnight uprising—the unmentionable nightmare that haunted every slave owner.

Janet discounted this possibility. Lucy's pleas that she never meant to harm her were convincing. She doubted if anyone else on the plantation was involved in the betrayal. Compared to nearby plantations, few of their blacks had run away since the war started. They were fundamentally loyal.

"I think the letters have revealed to Gentry just how volatile the situation is, how strong we are," Janet said. "He's afraid if they began arresting people on the say-so of an illiterate slave it would only drive more Democrats into the Sons of Liberty's ranks. We could and would deny the existence of the letters and attribute the whole thing to Lucy's lurid imagination and the money Gentry was paying her. We might even suggest that he was carrying on a liaison with her."

"I like this, I begin to like it very much," Gabriel Todd said, stalking up and down the veranda in the ferocious heat.

"As long as they don't know the exact date of our insurrection, we have the upper hand. I suspect boldness is our best defense. I'm inclined to leave for Richmond as soon as possible with Major Stapleton to set a date and get the money to buy the rifles. I suggest you send Lucy to Colonel Gentry with orders to deny everything, to say she made it all up. You could even give her a sarcastic note urging him to stop spying on his near relations."

"By God, they need you in Richmond to run this war!" Gabriel Todd said.

A rush of pleasure coursed through Janet's body—not dissimilar to the one she had felt as she witnessed Adam Jameson's triumphant escape and savored the part she had played in it. What was she discovering about herself? Did making history mean more to her than anything else? Was Paul right, she was an adventuress at heart? Was that kind of woman capable of loving anyone?

"I better start packing," Janet said. "I'd like to catch a steamboat that will get me to Cincinnati before dark tomorrow."

Upstairs, Gabriel Todd removed a still-tearful Lucy from Janet's bedroom. "Come along, you lyin' little piece of dirt," he said, twisting her arm behind her.

Lucy gasped with pain. "Miz Janet, tell me you forgive me, please!" she wailed.

"I don't forgive you," Janet said. "I'll never forgive you."

"Nor will I," Gabriel Todd added. "Tomorrow I'll show you just what unforgiveness means to your damned black skin."

For a moment Janet was about to remind her father

that she did not want Lucy whipped. But the thought of her spying at the Happy Hunting Ground froze the words in her throat.

You wanted him, whispered the reproachful voice in Janet's head. Was that the deepest reason for her anger at Lucy—knowing she had seen and understood that? When Lucy claimed she had not told Gentry about it, wasn't she implying that she believed Janet had disgraced herself? Even if Janet resisted feeling any shame for it, Lucy felt it.

So what if I did want him? I'm not an ordinary woman. The rules don't apply to me. Especially when I'm fighting a war.

Spoken like an adventuress. But that undeniable fragment of Lucy's loyalty suddenly made Janet unable to bear the thought of her being whipped. She ran to the head of the stairs and called, "Father—don't whip her! Just send her off—"

"You leave her to me," Gabriel Todd said. "Go catch your boat."

TWENTY-THREE

SABRINA, A SMALL WHITE STERN-WHEELER, steamed energetically down the Ohio River's channel, ignoring the sandbanks spreading from either shore. The sand meant "La Belle Riviere" was going into one of her midsummer funks. As the drought continued, the water level had dropped so low, the big two-stack side-wheelers had to proceed with caution, if at all. Paul Stapleton stood in the prow, savoring the breath of fresh air Sabrina's progress stirred from the overpowering humidity.

It was not only the heat that made Paul uncomfortable. He was wearing a dark blue civilian suit. It was the first time he had appeared in public without a uniform since he entered West Point eight years ago. He felt shorn of his chosen identity—not a bad thing, perhaps, for a man in the espionage business.

He had attended the court-martials General Carrington had decreed for Sergeant Moses Washington and the deserter Garner. They went precisely as the general wished. His two staff colonels sat with Gentry on the three-man board and voted with one voice. Paul testified in Washington's defense but the colonels were unmoved. Ignoring Gentry's vote for acquittal, they reduced Moses to private, fined him six months' pay, and sentenced him to fourteen days in jail on bread and water. As for the hapless Garner, he was condemned to death by the same 2–1 vote in less than five minutes.

Back at The Grange, Paul found a letter from Janet Todd, delivered by Adam Jameson's younger brother, Robin. A talkative young man, he told Paul about General Burbridge's raid and his brother's narrow escape. Janet's letter was a combination of love and intrigue, with the emphasis on the latter. Word had arrived from Chicago, Janet wrote, proposing a date for the Sons of Liberty rising far earlier than they had anticipated. It was imperative that they leave for Richmond immediately to obtain the money to buy rifles in New York. She wanted Paul to meet her in Cincinnati the day after tomorrow.

Portray yourself as an unemployed actor, she wrote. *It's worked nicely for me on my previous trips. I'm traveling as Janet Carew.*

Paul had sent Robin on his way with a scribbled note, confirming the rendezvous. That night after dinner he had coolly informed Gentry that Janet was going to Richmond to confer with the Confederacy's leaders and she wanted him to come with her. Gentry muttered about leaving a semi-invalid, Captain Otis, in charge of the troop without the support of Sergeant Washington. But he could hardly object to Paul's acceptance of Janet's invitation.

Paul could see Gentry was uneasy about Major Stapleton's loyalty. Minutes before he left for the Keyport dock, the colonel showed him a telegram from Abraham Lincoln granting a stay of execution to the deserter Garner. Gentry said this virtually guaranteed a pardon. The colonel clearly hoped Lincoln's leniency would make an impression on Paul.

Beside Paul on the prow of the *Sabrina* stood a short potbellied Union Army captain named Wallace whom he had met at dinner. Wallace had entertained him with stories of his travails as a paymaster for the federal troops stationed in Tennessee. All his money had to travel over the Louisville and Nashville Railroad, which was under constant attack by Confederate guerrillas. Twice in recent months he had cowered in the bushes while the Confederates made off with several hundred thousand dollars in greenbacks. The government's inability to provide safe transit for him and his cash had convinced Captain Wallace that the war was unwinnable.

Wallace despised Lincoln—"the Illinois baboon" was among his kinder epithets—and had worked hard to win this year's Republican nomination for Salmon P. Chase, the dignified deep-browed secretary of the treasury, who was from Ohio. But the Lincoln forces had what Chase lacked—money. The hundreds of millions the government was pouring into war contracts had won Lincoln a legion of loyal businessmen who were eager to finance his campaign. Simon Cameron, the Republican boss of Pennsylvania, had used business money to "buy up" the entire Pennsylvania legislature, Captain Wallace claimed. They had backed Lincoln in a public letter and Chase's candidacy had gone into a swoon. Captain Wallace's dream of becoming assistant paymaster of the forces with a big office on Pennsylvania Avenue in Washington had gone with it—along with his hopes of a Union victory.

That left Wallace with only one reason for staying interested in the war—money. He talked at length about how much a man could make if he borrowed enough to buy a few hundred bales of cotton in Mississippi or northern Louisiana for 20 cents a pound and sold it in New York for $1.90 a pound. "I could name you a half-dozen Union generals who've gotten rich doing it," Wallace said, with a fine show of righteous indignation.

The captain was one more proof, if Paul needed it, of the moral bankruptcy of Lincoln's war. Paul escaped him into that recurrent source of wonder, the western landscape. As they approached Cincinnati, majestic hills receded and advanced, here glowing with green pasturage, there crested and ribbed by beeches that seemed transplanted from a world of giants. But Paul had begun to think too many of the current inhabitants were moral pygmies.

Finally the city loomed out of the twilight like a fairy metropolis, myriad eyes blinking welcome. In Paul's mind only one welcome was relevant: Janet Todd's. The uneasiness he had felt since Adam Jameson blundered into their lives persisted. Paul still wanted proof—or at least evidence—that there was no calculation in Janet's love. At the same time he was uncomfortably aware that he might be asking the impossible.

As Paul descended the gangplank beside Captain Wallace, he found his nose assailed by an overwhelming odor. It permeated the smoky humid twilight. "What in God's name is that stink?" he asked. "It's worse than an army camp."

"Hogs," Wallace said. "Millions of hogs in a state of transit from hoggish nature to boots, saddles, sausages and ham. Slaughterin' hogs for the Union Army is makin' Cincinnati rich—and smelly."

The captain offered to share a hack to the Gibson House, the hotel to which Janet had directed Paul. As they jogged through the busy streets, Wallace wondered where Paul was going and why. He tried out his unemployed actor's routine on the captain, who immediately wanted to know if Paul had ever performed with John Wilkes Booth. Wallace considered Booth the best actor in America.

Paul said he had never had the privilege of sharing a bill with Booth, who like his father, Junius, and brother Edwin, was a luminary of the American stage. "You might find some work here in Cincinnati," Wallace said, disappointed by Paul's lack of celebrity. "We've got six theaters goin' full blast."

The Gibson House was an imposing brick pile. Paul gave Wallace a half-dollar as his share of the cab ride and the captain went on to army headquarters to pick up his next cargo of cash for the troops in Tennessee. Paul signed the register as Robert Nash and wrote "actor on tour" in the column where an address was requested. "Has my sister, Mrs. Carew, arrived?" he asked.

The toothless gray-haired clerk peered at the guest list. "Nope."

"Give her the room next to mine," he said.

"I'm afraid I need cash in advance. That's our policy with actors," the clerk said.

Paul paid him six dollars for the two rooms. He bought a copy of the Cincinnati *Gazette,* one of the West's most influential Republican newspapers, and the Democratic Cannelton, Indiana *Reporter* and read them in the hall bathtub while he soaked off the perspiration of his journey. The *Gazette* had supported Chase against Lincoln and remained convinced that the president could win neither reelection in November nor the war. It described Sherman as hopelessly bogged down before Atlanta and Grant as mired in blood and mud before Richmond.

Far more space was given to Horace Greeley, the editor of the Republican New York *Tribune,* who had gone to Niagara Falls to see if peace could be negotiated with Confederate "commissioners" in Canada. The results were zero. The southerners demanded recognition of Confederate independence and Lincoln insisted on restoration of the Union and the abandonment of slavery. The paper lamented Lincoln's unwillingness to offer a solution to the diplomatic deadlock.

The Cannelton *Reporter* did far more than lament Lincoln's intransigence. They quoted from a statement the Confederate commissioners in Canada had given the Associated Press. The Southerners accused Lincoln of sabotaging the peace negotiations by setting conditions he knew were unacceptable. They called on the voters of the North, "appalled by the illimitable vistas of private misery and public calamity" that Lincoln's policy of endless war unveiled, "to vindicate the outraged civilization of their country" by kicking him out of office.

The *Reporter*'s editorial page took Lincoln to task in equally ferocious terms. They said Negro emancipation was the real stumbling block to peace. The South was ready to accept political reunion but never with four million free blacks at their throats. "Tens of thousands of white men must yet bite the dust to allay the Negro mania of the president," the Democratic editorialist declared.

There were moments when a man could almost feel sorry for Lincoln. Most of his own party seemed to despise him as much as the Democrats did. He had the impossible task of satisfying the vengeful abolitionists of New England and the upper Midwest, the wavering moderate Republicans like Greeley in New York and the other middle states and millions of instinctively hostile Democrats. Was it possible that Lincoln was as much a victim of this war as everyone else?

The president's clemency for the deserter Garner gnawed at Paul's mind. It was not the gesture of a cold-blooded mass murderer. But the war Lincoln had unleashed on America was mass murder. Perhaps he too secretly yearned for a way to stop it. Maybe he would almost welcome a truce, forced on him by a western confederacy.

Back in his room, Paul was half-dressed when a hand knocked on the door. "I'll be there directly!" he said. He pulled on his pants and rushed to the door, barefoot.

Janet stood there, smiling. She was wearing a flowered green bonnet and a darker green traveling suit. The curve of her breasts was visible beneath the suit coat. "How clever of you to adopt me as your sister," she said.

He drew her into the room, kicked shut the door, and kissed her for a long tender minute. "I've been thinking of nothing but you," he said.

"You've had time to take a bath," she replied, gazing past him at the damp towel on the floor. "I can't wait to imitate your pristine example."

They agreed to meet in her room in a half hour. He found her lying on the bed in a lacy peignoir. She was on her right side, her head resting on her arm. An oil lamp on the bed table cast a soft glow on her dark hair. "This time you don't even have to undress me," she said.

Paul was surprised to discover he did not like this blasé invitation. Was it Cincinnati's hoggy stench, which wafted through the open windows, an unromantic contrast to the air of the dell beside the Ohio? No, there was an element of willfulness in this unadorned offer that struck him as inappropriate and even disturbing. Did she feel haste was somehow necessary to reassure herself as well as him? Was she trying to conceal a lack of genuine feeling?

Something even more disturbing caromed through Paul's head as he forced a smile and began to unknot his tie. In New Orleans, on his never-to-be-forgotten visit to his brother Charlie, when he walked into his first bordello bedroom, the woman had been waiting for him in much the same position and state of undress. He could see her as vividly as he now saw Janet. Celeste. Satiny tan skin, gleaming dark hair, a ruby in her ear.

For a moment Paul almost cursed himself and Charlie for that memory. Was this what the preachers meant by the wages of sin? Did he really think Janet Todd was a whore?

Of course not. But he still felt the need to retreat a few paces, to perform some of the arabesques of the lover. He wanted to experience a certain resistance— and transform that resistance into surrender. He wanted to go from hinted negation to unmistakable affirmation. None of these things were possible if he merely stripped off his clothes and—

He banned the word that leaped from his soldier's vocabulary. "I know what I'd like to do first," he said.

"What?" she asked, a flicker of irritation compressing her lips. It reminded Paul of the way his mother expressed annoyance when she did not get her own way. But he had learned to ignore those signals.

"Order some champagne."

"A nice idea. But I hate to spend the little money we have on luxuries—"

"I'm paying for it. I'm loaded with Mr. Lincoln's greenbacks. There's practically nothing to spend them on in Keyport. Colonel Gentry's refused to take a cent for my room and board—"

He rang the room service bell. A moment later a green-uniformed bucktoothed boy of about fourteen was at the door. "Bring up a bottle of Moët et Chandon," Paul said.

"What's that, mister?" the kid asked.

"Champagne. French Champagne."

"You better write it down."

In ten minutes the boy was back, his eyes wide, balancing a tray with a bottle in an ice bucket and two fluted glasses. "This costs five bucks!" he said. "That's more than you're payin' for the room!"

"Put it on the bill," Paul said.

"The boss says you gotta pay cash. You're an actor."

Paul gave him five dollars and a quarter tip. He unwound the wire around the cork; with one twist it popped and shot to the ceiling. "The campaign has begun!" he said, pouring the pale foaming wine.

Unfortunately, the champagne too reminded him of his visits to Charlie's favorite bordellos in New Orleans. Gentlemen were expected to buy champagne to entertain their girls. What was happening in his erratic head? Was his Gettysburg wound trying to sabotage him?

They clinked glasses and discussed their steamboat rides. Paul described Captain Wallace's jeremiad against Lincoln. "I met a Kentucky woman who hurled equally atrocious insults at Jefferson Davis," Janet said. "She called him a military ignoramus."

"He's a graduate of West Point," Paul said. "I'd like to

defend him. But I fear the lady is right. His strategy, especially in the West, has been ruinous."

Janet took a large, somewhat unladylike swallow of her champagne. "I made the most awful discovery about Lucy," she said. She described Lucy's betrayal, her confession and her suicide attempt.

It was Paul's turn to gulp his drink. "I wondered where Gentry got his information about you."

"He has information about me?"

"He says you're a Confederate agent."

"Why would he tell you that?"

Paul poured himself more champagne. "He's tried to seduce me—I suppose *persuade* is a better word—into spying on you."

"You didn't tell me this? You were aware that he knew my father and I were involved in the Sons of Liberty?"

"I don't recall him mentioning them. I saw no point in disturbing you—"

"Disturbing me! Paul—we could have taken precautions. We could have met Rogers Jameson and his colonels at some less obvious place. How could you treat me like this? As if I were a child. Is this what you think about women?"

She left the bed and sank into a chair, clutching the peignoir about her. Paul put down his champagne glass. It was amazing—and dismaying. She was penetrating the ambivalence in which he had been living and thinking and feeling. He took a deep breath. But all he got was Cincinnati's stink, further unraveling his composure.

"At first I didn't take Gentry seriously. I thought you were planning a trivial little local uprising. But when I saw the real dimensions of your plan—"

It was not working. She put down her champagne glass. Their celebration was evaporating with the bubbles.

"Janet," Paul said, taking her hand. "Those moments

by the river are the most precious memory of my entire life."

"But you still didn't tell me about Gentry."

"There? You wanted me to bring something that ugly into our act of love?"

"Afterward! On the way back to Hopemont? Or anytime in the next two days!"

"I—I was in the process of changing my loyalty. That's not easy for a man who takes his oaths of allegiance seriously."

"You mean there was still a time when you might have changed your mind—and become another of Gentry's spies?"

"That was never an option. But I might have decided to do nothing for you—or him. I would have volunteered for the front immediately. I told you I was thinking about it."

"Would you have done that before—or after—we visited the Happy Hunting Ground?"

"That changed everything. You know that as well as I do."

Suddenly Paul felt confident again—in control of the situation. "Tell me about Adam Jameson," he said.

Janet held out her glass for more champagne. She walked over to the window, as if she wanted to put distance and shadows between them. "You're jealous of him? I suppose I should be flattered."

"Or ashamed."

"Of what?"

"Of keeping two soldiers enslaved to you."

She said nothing. His attempt at raillery expired. Janet studied him for a long moment. Her expression, her manner, softened. "I—I—was amazed by my feeling for Adam when I saw him. He was so totally different from the awkward oversize boy I'd last seen in 1861. But it wasn't remotely like what I've felt for you.

From the first time I saw you I was *attracted* to you. Women aren't supposed to have such feelings but I did. There was something *elemental* about it, something almost shameless. I find myself asking, Is it part of love or does it interfere with love?"

"It's part of love. I felt exactly the same thing."

He poured her more champagne. Suddenly everything was evolving exactly as he had hoped. They were healing the wound Jameson had inflicted. "In vino veritas," he said, raising his glass.

"Yes," she said. "Veritas."

To his dismay she looked unutterably sad. "What's wrong now?" he asked.

"I was thinking of Lucy. I fear Father will beat her terribly."

"Blame it on Gentry. He seduced the poor creature into the game."

She shook her head. "I begin to think love and war don't mix."

"We'll make them mix. We'll challenge fate!" He drew her to her feet and kissed her tenderly. "Undress me," he said.

He was trying to replicate the memory of the Happy Hunting Ground. But it was impossible in the thick foul humidity of midsummer Cincinnati. As she fumbled with the buttons of his shirt, he sensed, he saw, her inner reluctance. What irony. Now she was the unwilling one.

Naked, they lay together on the bed and Paul began caressing her. "Janet, dearest Janet," he murmured. "There's so much happiness in store for us. We can't let it escape us."

"I want that happiness. I want it as much as you do!"

The words were almost a cry. Paul heard desperation in her voice. Was it anxiety for the southern cause or an inner struggle between him and Adam Jameson? Were they the same thing?

In his head, his Gettysburg wound whispered, *How do you like the imperatives of the heart, Paulie? Are you ready to go back to the real world?*

Jeff Tyler challenged that mocking adversary: *Doesn't this prove something? Doesn't this prove something?*

While around them Cincinnati, Queen City of the heartland, reeked with the war's stench.

TWENTY-FOUR

THE CLATTER OF A WAGON on the road outside his house awoke Henry Gentry. He struck a match and peered at the clock. It was 4:00 A.M. An odd time for anyone to be riding around Hunter County. He lay awake in the humid darkness, brooding on the stalemated war, reports of draft resistance in a half-dozen nearby towns, and the probable defection of Major Paul Stapleton to the enemy. Not even Lincoln's clemency for the deserter Garner had seemed to impress him. A week or ten days on the way to Richmond back with Janet Todd would very likely turn him into every intelligence director's nightmare, a double agent. Gentry could see Paul telling him in his best duty, honor, country style the wrong date for the Sons of Liberty uprising.

Uhhhhhhhhhh. A sound not unlike the autumn wind in the branches of the beeches on the lawn puzzled Gentry. There was not a breath of wind stirring. *Uhhhhhhh-hhh.* There it was again. It seemed to be coming from the veranda, directly below his bedroom. *Uhhhhhhhhhhhh.*

Gentry shrugged into his night robe and lit a candle. Downstairs the sound was louder. It was definitely coming from the veranda. He opened the door and gazed in stupefaction at Lucy. She was lying on her side, wearing her usual calico dress. The back of the dress was soaked a dark red. Flesh hung in ribbons off her bare arms, where the lash had curled around them as it struck her back. On her breast was pinned a note: <u>HEREBY CONSIGNED TO YOUR INFAMOUS CARE: ONE TREACHEROUS LYING NIGGER.</u>

"Lucy—what happened?" Gentry gasped.

"They whupped me, Colonel. They whupped me bad. I tole'm everything but Master whupped me anyhow."

She shuddered and seemed to go into a convulsion. "Lemmy die, Colonel," she said. "Miz Janet hates me and I wants t'die."

Gentry rushed upstairs and awoke Captain Otis. He in turn awoke two of the black troopers in their tents beyond the barn. Together they carried Lucy upstairs to Major Stapleton's bedroom. She was breathing in slow spasmodic gasps. Otis volunteered to ride into town and fetch Dr. Yancey. With the blacks' help, Gentry forced some brandy down Lucy's throat.

Yancey arrived as dawn was breaking. With Otis's help he stripped off Lucy's dress. "My God," he said, gazing at the mass of deep welts on her back. "This will putrefy if we don't do something immediately."

"What do you recommend?"

"I remember reading that in the eighteenth-century navy after a man was lashed they washed his back in brine. Can you spare a pound of salt?"

"Of course," Gentry said.

In the kitchen, Minnie, his aging cook, was beginning breakfast. Gentry asked her to stop everything and prepare the brine. As Minnie concocted this potion, Millicent Todd Gentry loomed in the kitchen doorway. "Henry, what in the world is happening?" she asked.

"We have a medical problem, Mother. Lucy, Janet Todd's slave, has been badly beaten."

"By whom?"

"I'm not sure. I fear it was by your nephew, Gabriel Todd."

"Todds don't beat their slaves. Where is she?"

"In Major Stapleton's bedroom."

"You've put a nigger in one of my beds? A nigger who's probably a bleeding mess?"

"Yes, Mother."

"Take her to the servants' quarters immediately."

"I'm afraid I can't do that, Mother."

"Henry, I'm ordering you to do it."

"Mother—I have news for you. I own this house. It's my property. It was left to me in Father's will, along with the rest of the estate."

"That was a mere legalism!"

"I don't care what you call it. That poor girl stays in that bed."

Millicent Todd Gentry whirled and stormed upstairs to the bedroom. By the time Gentry got there, she was standing over Lucy's bed, demanding to know who had whipped her.

"Master," Lucy said. "I deserved it, Miz Todd. I never should've had nothin' to do with Colonel Gentry—"

Dr. Yancey was busy soaking cloths in the brine. But he was listening to this byplay. Gentry saw his cover as an intelligence officer vanishing. "Mother," he said. "Will you please get the hell out of here?"

"How dare you speak to me that way?" Millicent Todd Gentry cried.

Something very akin to pleasure coursed through Henry Gentry's flesh. "I'm in charge here, Mother. Go or I'll have Captain Otis drag you out."

Millicent Todd Gentry departed, wailing, and Dr. Yancey proceeded to drench Lucy's back in brine. It was hellish work. She screamed with every application and begged them to let her die. When Yancey pronounced himself satisfied, he ordered Lucy to remain in bed, without a nightgown or dress, until the wounds started to heal. A liquid diet of whiskey and water was also prescribed.

"How'd she get here, Henry?" Yancey asked. "I can't imagine anyone that badly beaten swimming the Ohio—or even rowing herself in a boat."

"I have no idea," Gentry said. "I found her on my porch."

"So someone dropped her there. Someone who wanted to send you some sort of message, it would seem."

"So it would seem. But I can't imagine why," Gentry said.

Yancey put on his coat, a knowing smile on his face. He had figured things out; Gentry was sure of it. "I know you're not a neutral in this war, Walter. But I hope you'll keep quiet about this," he said.

"I don't discuss my patients, Henry," Yancey replied.

"I hope that extends to their circle of—acquaintances."

"Absolutely, Henry. Is she pregnant?"

For a moment Gentry was too astonished to say anything. "I don't know," he said.

"Shame on you, Henry. I know you must be hard up. But if you told me, I could have imported Steamboat Lil or one of our other old friends from Louisville."

"Beggars can't be choosers, Walter. As a friend I hope you'll say absolutely nothing."

"Absolutely," Yancey said, complacently certain that Gentry had told him the truth. It proved his cynical view of human nature was still on the mark.

Retreating to his cellar office to escape his mother's wrath, Gentry tried to think intelligently about his situation. His cover was unquestionably blown across the river in Kentucky. He could be sure that Gabriel Todd would tell Rogers Jameson about Lucy and arouse that behemoth to a new pitch of fury. But there was not much Jameson could do, as long as Colonel Gentry had a hundred armed men on his farm.

He told himself not to worry about his own skin but about the clandestine war he was fighting. He had no difficulty getting the message that was delivered with Lucy's bleeding body. What could he or should he do about it? *Think, Henry,* he told himself. *Think like a soldier. You have spent four months listening to Major Paul Stapleton discuss the war from the point of view of an*

*intelligent West Pointer and aide to several generals.
What have you learned about military science?*

The most important word in Major Stapleton's vocabulary was *initiative*. The general who retained the initiative, forcing his enemy to fight where he chose, was the man who won the battles and wars. How could he apply that idea here? The Sons of Liberty retained the initiative as long as no one knew the date of their insurrection. That was why they could arrogantly dump Lucy on his veranda, in effect telling him that they were still in control of their piece of the war.

He could not do much about the Sons. If he arrested leaders such as Rogers Jameson and Gabriel Todd, other men, harder to track, would replace them—and the disaffection of their Democratic followers would be confirmed. Their resolution to sink the Lincoln ship of state would only harden, making them even more difficult to defeat if it came to shooting.

But there was one part of the Sons' plan that was not only visible—it was vulnerable. Adam Jameson's cavalry, waiting up there on the mountainous border between Virginia and Kentucky, was essential to the insurrection. Could he persuade the Union Army in Kentucky to attack it? A successful assault would cripple the Sons of Liberty. The news would spread through Kentucky and Indiana, taking the steam out of the proto-rebellion.

Henry Gentry decided to begin at the top. He composed a long coded telegram to Abraham Lincoln, explaining the urgency of his request. Thanks to the telegraph's lightning communication, he had reason to hope that the assault could be organized quickly—if he persuaded the president. For a clincher he suggested that the expedition be described as an attempt to destroy the Confederate saltworks in the town of Saltville, near Jameson's camp. There would be no need to reveal any knowledge of the existence of the Sons of Liberty.

As twilight descended, a messenger arrived from the

telegraph office. Gentry pinned the envelope under an encyclopedia on his desk and cut it open with a scissors. It was one of the many little maneuvers a one-armed man learned to do without thinking about it.

> YOUR MESSAGE RECEIVED. I THINK IT MAKES EMINENT SENSE AND HAVE ORDERED GENERAL BURBRIDGE TO TAKE AS MANY MEN AS HE CAN SPARE WITHOUT LOSING CONTROL OF KENTUCKY AND LAUNCH THE ATTACK ON JAMESON AS SOON AS POSSIBLE. I HAVE ADVISED HIM THAT YOU WILL JOIN HIM TO FURTHER INFORM HIM OF THE PURPOSES AND IMPORTANCE OF THE ASSAULT. I SUGGEST YOU LEAVE FOR LOUISVILLE IMMEDIATELY SINCE TIME IS OBVIOUSLY OF THE ESSENCE IN THIS THING. GOOD LUCK. A. LINCOLN

For a moment Gentry felt dazed. He was getting back into the fighting war. Almost immediately he started to worry about General Burbridge. Everything Gentry had heard about the military commander of Kentucky made him think he was as bad as Indiana's General Carrington, or worse. Maybe Lincoln was obliquely telling him what he had painfully learned in the last three years: once a war begins, you have to work with whatever turns up, including generals.

Gentry had other worries—notably his favorite spy, Lucy. Minnie told him she was refusing to take any nourishment—not even the whiskey and water Dr. Yancey had prescribed to prevent fever. His mother was immured in her room, refusing to speak, much less eat, with her order-giving son. Gentry sought out his houseguest, Dorothy Schreiber, in the music room. At the grand piano that he had tormented for a few youthful years she was playing the most popular song of 1864, "Weeping Sad and Lonely, or When This Cruel War Is Over."

> *"Weeping sad and lonely*
> *Hopes and fears how vain!*
> *When this cruel war is over*
> *Praying that we meet again."*

Tears streamed down Dorothy's pretty face. Gentry asked her why she was so upset.

"I've just come from a visit to that poor boy, Garner. He expects to be shot tomorrow or the next day. He doesn't believe President Lincoln will pardon him. Nor do I. Why should he worry about one life more or less?"

"I'm sure Mr. Lincoln will pardon him," Gentry said. "He worries about individuals whenever he gets a chance. Most of the time he's overwhelmed by the war. We're the ones who have to apply his principles to individual lives."

Dorothy's sixteen-year-old mind struggled to absorb this thought. "Have you heard what's happened to Lucy, Janet Todd's slave?" he asked.

"I heard she was whipped almost to death for doing something bad. Why did they send her over here?"

"She was whipped for doing something good, Dorothy. She was trying to help us win the war by telling me secrets that she'd learned in Kentucky."

"Secrets about what?"

"I can't tell you. I can only tell you she's a heroine and needs your help. She needs to feel someone cares about her."

"What do I have to do?"

"Just sit and talk to her for a while each day. Get her to eat and take her medicine."

Dorothy wrinkled her nose. "I wouldn't know what to say."

Gentry did not blame Dorothy for her reluctance. She was the granddaughter of a Democratic congressman. Her mother had been an ardent Democrat, who had opposed her husband's decision to volunteer for the army.

Eight years ago, Dorothy had watched her older sisters march in a Keyport Democratic parade during the election of 1856, carrying placards: SAVE US FROM MARRYING NIGGERS. Negrophobia was very strong in the Indiana Democratic Party.

"Ask her what she wants to do now that she's free. Suggest things. Read her stories from the Bible or some other book."

"Maybe I'll read her *Uncle Tom's Cabin,*" Dorothy said, a nasty light in her eyes. Harriet Beecher Stowe's novel was not a favorite among Democrats. Dorothy seemed to be hoping Lucy would say the book was nonsense.

"Wouldn't it be interesting to find out what she thinks about it?"

"I guess it might," Dorothy said.

"I want you to do it, Dorothy," Gentry said. "Even if my mother says not to, I want you to do it anyway. Think of it as your contribution to the war. Maybe it will bring your father home faster."

Upstairs they found Lucy lying facedown in the big four-poster bed like a corpse on a battlefield. She was staring at the pillow, tears trickling down her face.

"Lucy," Gentry said. "Dorothy came to me and said she felt so sorry for you, she wants to visit you and help you get over your whipping. She wants to be your friend."

Lucy's eyes roved to Dorothy's blank startled face. Did she see the evidence of Colonel Gentry's fat lie there? "I sure could use a friend," Lucy said.

"She'll be as much of a friend as Miss Janet was, I promise you," Gentry said. "But you won't have to wait on her. You're a free woman now, Lucy. You can be friends without being a servant."

Lucy's disbelief was almost visible. "Is this because you knows I'm goin' to die, Colonel?"

"You're not going to die!" Gentry said.

"There's someone I'd like to see. Sergeant Moses Washington."

Gentry saw no point in telling her that Washington was no longer a sergeant and would be in jail for another ten days, dining on bread and water. "He's—he isn't here, Lucy. He's on detached duty."

"Then I'd like to send him a letter. Maybe Miz Dorothy could write it for me," Lucy said.

"She'll be delighted."

Gentry left Dorothy sitting beside the bed, taking down the letter, and rushed to his room to pack for his trip to Louisville. When he came downstairs a half hour later, Dorothy was at the piano again, weeping violently.

"Now what's wrong?"

"Oh, it's so sad, Colonel Gentry," she said. "That poor little thing's in love. I never knew a nigger could fall in love. She loves Sergeant Washington and told him she was going to heaven, where she'd pray for him and protect him from Confederate bullets. It's the saddest story I've ever heard. It beats anything in *Uncle Tom's Cabin*."

Gentry asked her for the letter. "Tell her I'll personally deliver it to Sergeant Washington," he said, slipping it into his pocket.

Gentry led Dorothy to a chair by the window and wiped her eyes with his handkerchief. "I hope you'll keep visiting Lucy. This is your chance to grow up, Dorothy, to become a woman instead of a girl. You don't know how much kindness can do for a human being. When I lost my arm, I thought about dying too. I thought about killing myself. But I didn't do it, because Abe Lincoln proved he was still my friend. With the whole war and the presidency on his back he found time to write me a long letter telling me how bad he felt when he heard what had happened to me. He told me he wanted me to keep working for him. He made me realize he still cared."

Dorothy looked as if she thought this tear-choked one-armed man sitting opposite her was about to go berserk. She nodded violently and said, "I'll try, Colonel Gentry. I'll try to help her."

Outside, Gentry asked one of the black troopers to drive him into Keyport in his buggy. At the courthouse he hurried into the wing that included the jail. Sheriff Monroe Cantwell greeted him with a cordial nod. Monroe may have lost his enthusiasm for the war but they were still friends.

"How's our bread-and-water prisoner doing?" Gentry asked.

"He ain't complainin' if that's what you're hopin' to hear. He just takes what we give him and puts it down his gullet. He's one tough nigger."

"I'd like to see him."

Cantwell led Gentry to a cell in the rear of the jail. It was so small, Moses Washington seemed to fill two-thirds of it. Gentry handed him Lucy's letter and told him what had happened to her.

Washington ripped open the letter and read it in a single swift glance. "She says she's dyin'. Is that right?"

"She might be, Moses. I'm hoping you'll answer her."

"Ain't I got enough trouble, Major? You want me to start playin' nurse to some poor little pickaninny who 'magines I love her?"

"Think it over, Moses. It may turn out she's done more to help us win this war than a whole brigade of infantry. She's got guts—and she really loves you. I don't know why. That's your business."

"I'll think about it," Washington said.

"While you're at it, think about this. I'm suspending your sentence and restoring your rank. I want you to get back to your men and make sure they're ready to march on an hour's notice. We're going to war, Sergeant— against real soldiers."

In a half hour, Moses Washington was out of jail and on his way back to The Grange in Gentry's sulky. A half hour later, Gentry was on a steamboat heading down the Ohio to Louisville to explain to General Stephen Burbridge the importance of attacking Adam Jameson and seizing the initiative from the Sons of Liberty. He saw Lucy as the centerpiece of his argument: *Let's make sure they've lashed their last slave.*

If Gentry stopped to think about it, he might have heard Lincoln saying, *Whoa there, Henry. You have a tendency to get carried away.* But Colonel Gentry was not in the mood to listen to that shrewd cautious voice.

TWENTY-FIVE

SOOT AND THE ACRID ODOR of burning coal blew in relentless gusts through the open windows of the Baltimore and Ohio main line train as it rumbled through western Maryland at twenty-five miles an hour. The summer heat made it impossible to close the windows. Beside Janet Todd in the clanking metal box on wheels, a dozing Paul Stapleton had a patina of the ubiquitous grime on his angular face. Through his rumpled blond hair she could see the full dimensions of his head wound—a reddish ridge of scar tissue that ran down the center of his skull from his hairline to the back of his head. It made Janet think of her reaction to his chest wound the night she saw it for the first time.

For a moment she was swept by a terrible sadness. Was she risking the love she had confessed to this damaged man in odoriferous Cincinnati by insisting he join her in this conspiracy? She was forcing him to sacrifice his honor, the only god he worshiped. But it was in the name of another kind of honor, the violated trust that her father and her brothers and the other Democrats of Kentucky had offered the great betrayer, Abraham Lincoln.

Janet saw all too clearly what Paul was trying to do: make their love more important than the success or failure of the western confederacy. During the long uncomfortable night hours on the train, while Paul slept beside her, Janet had decided not to let that happen. She was going to insist on an absolute equality of purpose. One could not succeed without the other.

That meant she would have to diminish, if not eliminate the ecstatic impulse to surrender that she felt in Paul's arms. It threatened her control of the situation. She told herself she would regain the ability to experience it later. If she could will it out of existence, she could will it back to life when she chose.

In panels on the ceiling of the railroad car were paintings of great moments in American history: Thomas Jefferson, John Adams and Benjamin Franklin presenting John Hancock with their draft of the Declaration of Independence; George Washington arriving in New York to take the oath of office as first president; Andrew Jackson defeating the British at New Orleans. She had noticed Paul staring up at these memorials to the Union. Was he thinking they would soon become as meaningless as the heroic statuary in the Roman Pantheon, the Greek Acropolis?

Paul had told her that his great-grandfather Hugh Stapleton had stood beside Washington on the balcony at Federal Hall when he took the oath as the first president. Paul's father had been proud to call Andrew Jackson his friend. Janet replied that the Todds had fought in half the battles of the Revolution and beside Jackson at New Orleans. She insisted that if their mission succeeded and the western confederacy was born, they would still value the history of the original country and use it to inspire their children. Paul agreed halfheartedly, at best semiconvinced.

Paul awoke and brushed mechanically at the layer of soot on his blue suit. He peered out the window at the well-tilled farms and consulted his watch, first wiping off the soot; the stuff even penetrated pockets, not to mention eyes, mouths, lungs. "Nine twenty-five," he said. "We should be in Baltimore before noon."

"And Washington by three o'clock if the B and O stays on schedule."

"The Stapletons are stockholders. If they fail us, I'll complain to the chairman of the board."

Janet studied him for a moment. "I don't think you're comfortable as a secret agent."

"I'm a little uneasy about meeting one of my West Point classmates or friends in Washington. Or worse, my brother or one of his staff officers."

"We shouldn't be there more than twenty-four hours."

Janet had made the trip to Richmond several times. She assured Paul that Washington, D.C., was honeycombed with southern sympathizers. There was a well-worked-out system for escorting travelers to the Confederate capital. Her contact was a Maryland woman named Mary Surratt, who ran a boardinghouse on H Street that served as a kind of headquarters for secret communications with Richmond. Mary's son, John Surratt, was one of the coolest, most dependable couriers.

They rumbled into Baltimore at noon and found the train for Washington, D.C., waiting for them across the platform. By three o'clock they were in the capital's busy station. The heat was almost unbearable and it was accompanied by a suffocating humidity that made Indiana's muggy drought seem almost benign.

Janet decided it would be best if they traveled to the boardinghouse on H Street separately. That way, Paul would have no need to explain her presence if he met someone who recognized him. He would simply say he was in Washington to talk to the adjutant general about returning to active duty with one of the Union armies.

In a half hour they were both in Mrs. Surratt's genteel parlor, sipping iced tea served by the small plain dark-haired owner of the house. She listened eagerly to Janet's assurance that the Democrats of Kentucky and Indiana were united in their detestation of Mr. Lincoln. "Will they dare to vote?" Mrs. Surratt asked. "In Maryland they feel the same way but most don't have the courage to go to the polls. It's a dictatorship, pure and simple."

"The Democrats of the Midwest are going to express

themselves in a more direct way. They've given up on the ballot box," Janet said.

"The sooner the better," Mrs. Surratt said. "We badly need a sign of hope."

John Surratt, a tall fair-haired young man with a short goatee, joined them and greeted Janet warmly. Mrs. Surratt introduced Paul as Robert Nash and said they were bringing good news from the West. Surratt clapped his hands with enthusiasm when Janet reiterated the plan for an uprising. The young man said they could begin the trip to Richmond that night, if they were ready. The journey now took an extra twelve hours because General Grant kept extending his siege lines around the city.

"Why not?" Janet said, although she had slept very little on their two-day trip from Cincinnati. Paul wanted to get out of Washington as soon as possible. Mrs. Surratt suggested they take a nap and she would serve supper at seven o'clock. They could be on their way by nine. She led them upstairs and gave Janet her own bedroom and Paul her son's room. Janet decided she needed a bath more than she needed sleep and spent most of her naptime soaking in the hall tub and dressing in a clean outfit. At supper she felt light-headed but refreshed and confident. She wore a smart deep blue traveling dress with a pleated skirt that added to her self-assurance. Paul had washed off his grime in a bedroom washbowl and was looking more like his calm steady self.

John Surratt wanted to know if they thought Atlanta could hold out against General Sherman's army. "I'd say yes, if Jefferson Davis could make a copy of Robert E. Lee and send him out there to take charge," Paul said.

Mrs. Surratt and her son looked dismayed. "Everything we hear in Kentucky suggests General Sherman's army may end up trapped and starving before the end of summer," Janet said. It was a total lie but she did not think these people should be discouraged.

As they finished dinner they were joined by a handsome black-mustached man with a theatrical air. John Surratt introduced John Wilkes Booth and said he was on his way to Richmond. Janet was suitably impressed and Paul too seemed pleased to meet the famous actor. Young Surratt told Booth they were Confederate agents traveling as actors and would appreciate Mr. Booth vouching for them if sentries or federal officials on the road to Richmond raised questions.

"Of course," Booth said. "Anything I can do to assist our sacred cause will be done be done with pleasure, including, if necessary, this!"

He whipped a small pistol from beneath his coat. "I would love to remove a Yankee abolitionist from the face of the earth," he said. "But I'd probably shoot some poor kid who's been drafted into the ranks by our Murderer in Chief."

"I hope that isn't loaded," Paul said, eyeing the pistol, which Booth waved excitedly at them as he talked.

"Fear not, my friend," Booth replied, putting the gun back in the holster under his coat.

"Have you brought more quinine?" John Surratt asked.

"A hundred pounds," Booth said. "It's in my luggage."

"I'll put it in the safe place in the carriage," Surratt said and hurried out of the room.

"This wonderful man has spent thousands of his own dollars to smuggle quinine into Richmond," Mrs. Surratt said, beaming at Booth. "Heaven knows how many fever-stricken women and children he's saved. It's unobtainable in the South, thanks to Mr. Lincoln's cruel blockade."

"The swine makes war on infants in the cradle," Booth said. "Has there ever been a war as vicious as this one? Not even the Mongols under Genghis Khan could match it."

In an hour they were in John Surratt's comfortable carriage, their luggage lashed on the roof. Booth's quinine and some dispatches for the Confederate secret service were in a concealed compartment under their feet. At the Potomac River bridge, they met their first test. Sentries and a junior lieutenant asked to see Surratt's permit to operate a carriage and demanded proof of the identities of his passengers.

Booth stuck his handsome head out the window and smiled genially. "I trust you don't have to ask who I am," he said. "These other two, Bob Nash and Janey Carew, are brother and sister from New York and old colleagues of mine. We're on our way to Richmond to perform *Macbeth* and *Julius Caesar.* Nash will play Caesar. I look forward to assassinating him in thirty-six hours or so."

"I'm honored to meet you, Mr. Booth," the awed lieutenant said. "I'm honored to meet you too, Mrs. Carew and Mr. Nash."

As they rumbled into Virginia, Booth muttered, "There's only one tyrant I'd like to assassinate. It wouldn't be as difficult as some people think. Lincoln is incredibly careless. He rides around Washington without a military escort. He goes to the theater without a bodyguard."

Booth swigged from a bottle of brandy and offered it to them. When they declined, he laughed and said to Paul, "You'd better take at least a swallow. An actor without liquor on his breath is like a Yankee without a Boston accent—unconvincing."

Paul obliged him and said it was very good brandy. "I always buy the best," Booth said.

As a reward for his protection, Booth demanded to know why they were going to Richmond. Janet told him about the western confederacy. The actor was enormously excited. He said it was the first hopeful news he had heard since Gettysburg.

At several points along the route they were challenged by federal sentries. Booth vouched for Janet and Paul with ever more extravagant claims for their theatrical talents. Soon they were his dearest friends and famous from Pittsburgh to Chicago to San Francisco. As he downed the brandy he grew more inquisitive about their identities.

"You're not brother and sister."

"No," Janet said.

"Let me guess where you come from. You, Mrs. Carew, are from Kentucky. Mr. Nash is from New Jersey."

"How can you tell?" Janet asked, amazed.

"Accents are an actor's stock-in-trade. Almost every state has its own voice." He advised them to have a plausible story ready if they encountered a federal sentry or secret agent with an ear for accents.

For an hour he entertained them with imitations of New York, Boston, Charleston and Chicago speech patterns. He added Jewish, Irish and English accents. He even threw in some Chinese pidgin and American Indian patois. Finally the brandy took effect and Booth slept. Janet and Paul tried to imitate his example, but it was not easy in the lurching jouncing coach. The roads of Virginia were in atrocious condition after three years of war.

The rising sun struck the carriage with an almost supernatural intensity. Everyone awoke. Booth procured another bottle of brandy from one of his suitcases and began discoursing on what a sad place Richmond had become. "Once the happiest city I've ever visited," he said. "Others may surpass it in architecture but not in the gentility, the gaiety of its people. Now desperation is stamped on every face."

"What plays are you planning to perform, Mr. Booth?" Janet asked, deliberately changing the subject. The last thing she wanted Paul to hear was Richmond's desperation.

"Hamlet," Booth said. "My insufferable older brother, Edwin, is performing it in New York at this very moment, to immense applause. I'm not one of the applauders. It's a *Hamlet* of the brain, without belly or bowels or—"

He swigged more brandy. "If Mr. Nash and I were alone, I'd add another anatomical detail that would amuse him, I think."

A tremendous explosion ended Booth's jollity. The ground trembled beneath the carriage's wheels. An invisible force struck the vehicle, sending it lurching to the left. The horses screamed with terror and bolted. "Mr. Nash, Mr. Booth—help me!" John Surratt shouted. Paul climbed out the door onto the box and helped him get the animals under control. The carriage jolted to a stop and Janet leaped out, followed by John Wilkes Booth. They stared in the direction of Richmond as an immense mushroom cloud rose a thousand feet into the air, the stem seemingly composed of fire and the head of black smoke.

"What is it?" Janet asked.

"I have no idea," Paul said. "I've never seen anything like it on a battlefield."

"It looks like it was created by Satan himself," John Wilkes Booth said.

"That's Petersburg under that mushroom cloud," John Surratt said. "Richmond's a few miles further north. Grant's been tryin' to grab Petersburg for months. It would cut General Lee's last railroad line."

As he spoke dozens of cannons crashed in unison, making a noise almost as loud as the original explosion. It was followed by the distant sound of cheering and the staccato stutter of rifle fire. "That sounds like an attack," Paul said.

They climbed back in the carriage and Surratt took them down back roads in a wide arc around the battle raging in front of Petersburg. It was another hour before he called out, "Richmond ahead!" They peered from the coach windows at the capital of the Confederate States of America.

Houses and an occasional church spread up and down a wide hilly amphitheater with the majestic pillared capitol, designed by Thomas Jefferson, on the highest hill, dominating the view. White porticoes gleamed through the trees on neighboring hilltops. But the sylvan effect was marred by smoke pouring from the stacks and blast furnaces of the Tredgar Iron Works, visible beyond the capitol.

"There's a good sign," Janet said. "Tredgar is still making cannons."

"Not very good ones, unfortunately," Paul said.

"Good enough to kill sixty thousand of Grant's Yankees," Janet said.

In an hour they were in the center of the city. Everywhere were signs of panic bordering on frenzy; it undoubtedly had something to do with the explosion. Surratt was forced to wait at several cross streets while straining six-mule teams hauled wagon trains of ammunition to the men in the lines. Guns and caissons clanked over the cobblestones behind sweat-caked horses that were mere racks of bones. Regiments of gray-clad soldiers trotted on the double down side streets toward Petersburg.

They said good-bye to John Wilkes Booth at the corner of Twelfth Street. He was staying at Richmond's best hotel, The Exchange. Janet and Paul trudged up the sloping street to the three-story brick house that was the headquarters of the Kentucky delegation to the Confederate legislature. Although Kentucky had not seceded, after northern troops occupied it southern sympathizers had set up a shadow government and sent delegates to Richmond.

A black servant led them to the house's sunny rear portico, where John and Elizabeth Hayes were finishing dinner. He was a former Lexington lawyer in his forties, with curly red hair and a friendly freckled face; she was one of Janet's Breckinridge cousins, purportedly a look alike of Letitia Todd in her youth, down to the deep wave in her dark hair. There were exclamations of pleasure and the warmest possible welcome.

Janet introduced Paul as Robert Nash, adding that it was not his real name. "Can you tell us what that explosion means? Was it an accident? Did someone touch off an ammunition dump?" Paul asked.

Hayes shook his head angrily. "It was a federal mine," he said. "It was set off without warning and blew a huge hole in our siege lines. It killed over a thousand men. But we seem to be containing the follow-up attack."

"They don't have the courage to fight us in the open." Elizabeth Hayes said. "They burrow under our soldiers like vicious moles. Has there ever been a more loathsome enemy?"

John Hayes asked Janet why she had come to Richmond. "I can't tell you much," she said. "We must see President Davis as soon as possible. Can you get a message to him?"

She handed Hayes a letter she had written on the train to Baltimore. He said he would take it to the Confederate White House, on the corner of Twelfth and Clay Street, immediately. They might catch the president home for dinner. He left them with Elizabeth Hayes, who insisted they eat something while they waited.

Mrs. Hayes apologized for the quality of the food she served them. "It's impossible to buy a decent piece of meat," she said. "The most one can hope for is something that won't poison you." With the stringy tired meat were side dishes of equally tasteless vegetables and potatoes. While they ate, Mrs. Hayes treated them to a lamentation on life in Richmond.

The price of food was astronomical—ten times what it had cost in 1862, when they arrived. She had sent their four children back to Kentucky to live with their grandparents. The Confederate dollar was rapidly approaching worthlessness. People were selling their furniture and clothes for food. The shops along Main Street were mostly auction houses, where war profiteers—blockade runners mostly—were buying up goods and jewelry at bargain prices.

"But the spirit of the people is what counts. Surely they can tolerate hardship when they consider what's at stake," Janet said.

"They've tolerated a great deal," Mrs. Hayes replied. "But lately everyone has begun to lose hope. General Lee killed seventy-five thousand federals in May and June, but Grant's army is bigger than ever. When we lose a man, he isn't replaced."

This was not what Janet wanted Paul to hear. She hastily changed the subject to John Wilkes Booth. Mrs. Hayes's pretty oval face came aglow. "He's the most gorgeous male creature I've ever seen. I'm so glad to hear he's in town again. I'll make John buy tickets, no matter how much they cost."

Hayes's footsteps sounded inside the house. "Good news. President Davis says he'll see you before supper, if the attack on Petersburg fails—as it seems to be doing, catastrophically. General Lee has taken personal command of the situation."

"Can't you let us in on your secret?" Elizabeth Hayes asked.

"The Sons of Liberty are about to rise," Janet said.

The Hayeses exchanged excited smiles. They knew about the conspiracy. John Hayes went off to an afternoon session of the Confederate Congress. Janet was grateful when Elizabeth Hayes suggested they catch a few hours of sleep. The sun was low in the west when her husband returned. Elizabeth Hayes awoke them and they went downstairs, eager to hear what he had learned about the great explosion.

"The whole thing is almost unbelievable," Hayes said, his eyes wild with angry excitement. "They say the federals tunneled under two of our forts and exploded at least four tons of gunpowder. It stunned their troops as much as ours. When they recovered, they rushed forward to discover the explosion had made a huge crater, as much as twenty feet deep, in the earth. Our men let them crowd into the thing, then poured in volleys of rifle and cannon fire. It was the most perfect slaughter in the history of warfare. They must have lost five thousand men!"

"Incredible," Paul said.

A black servant came to the Hayes front door with a message from President Davis. He was ready to see Janet and Paul. The black man led them down Twelfth Street to Clay, where the Confederate White House commanded both streets. It was a wide-fronted mansion of brick that had been plastered over. White marble steps led to a small entrance porch. A sentry box stood on the sidewalk beneath poplar and sycamore trees. Inside, a black servant led them through stately rooms with Carrara marble fireplaces to a wide colonnaded balcony overlooking a garden.

There sat two gray-haired, gray-bearded men, one in a rumpled civilian suit, the other in an immaculate gray uniform, with the stars of a general on his epaulets. "President Davis," Janet said. "This is so good of you to see us on such short notice. I'm honored to meet you, General Lee."

Davis's smile was somewhat bleak; a nerve twitched in his furrowed cheek; he looked weary. He introduced her to Robert E. Lee as the daughter of Colonel Gabriel Todd. The general rose and took her hand and said he remembered her father from the war in Mexico. But even as he spoke he was looking with far greater interest at Paul.

"Is this who I think it is?" Lee asked. "Cadet Private Paul Stapleton of Company A?"

"You have a remarkable memory, General," Paul said, shaking hands.

"That was his rank in his plebe year at West Point—my last year as superintendent," Lee explained to Janet with a bemused smile.

"The son of Senator George Stapleton?" Jefferson Davis asked.

"Yes, Mr. President," Paul said.

"This is a delightful surprise. What brings you into our ranks?"

Paul hesitated. He looked vaguely embarrassed. For a panicky moment Janet thought he was going to apologize. "Perhaps I can speak for Major Stapleton better than he can," she said. "I've been watching him slowly realize he could no longer tolerate the brutality of the Lincoln regime in Indiana and Kentucky."

Lee frowned, clearly wishing Paul had spoken for himself. "You feel this change of heart supersedes the oath you took to the federal government when you graduated from the military academy?"

"Yes, General," Paul said.

Lee nodded but Janet sensed he was not entirely satisfied. "He's taken another oath, to the Sons of Liberty," she said.

The general glanced at Janet for moment, without turning his head. She sensed this information was unwelcome. He continued to speak to Paul. "You were wounded at Gettysburg, I believe?"

"Yes, General. And at Antietam before that."

"You were on John Reynolds's staff?"

"Yes."

"I was saddened by his death."

"We all were, General."

"A great loss," Jefferson Davis agreed.

Janet was bewildered. They were talking as if they were all members of the same army! She was learning the power of the invisible fraternity of West Point.

"I gather you've had a busy day, General," Paul said.

"An understatement. I've just finished reporting the event—if we may call it that—to President Davis. It was a clever idea that might have ended the war. Fortunately for us, General Grant put General Burnside in charge of the enterprise. He managed with his usual skill to turn it into a fiasco."

Paul nodded. "I saw General Burnside in action at Antietam and Fredericksburg. A more stupid man never wore general's stars."

"I consider it the epitome of good fortune to have had him as an opponent," Lee said. "But I fear his reputation won't survive the crater."

"So you're here to tell us that we can expect good news from the West," President Davis said.

"We hope so, sir," Paul said.

"I'm not sure I should even hear about such secret service matters," Lee said.

"Of course you should. I want your opinion," Davis said. "Can you give us a succinct summary, Major?"

Paul told them the Sons of Liberty's plan as he had heard it at Hopemont. He emphasized the importance of Adam Jameson's cavalry division and the hope of freeing the Confederate prisoners outside Indianapolis and Chicago. He estimated the Sons of Liberty's numbers at thirty thousand. "They claim to have fifty thousand men on their rolls, but like most militia, they'll be lucky to turn out two-thirds."

Janet was appalled. Paul had never mentioned this pessimistic estimate to her. Worse, both Davis and Lee nodded in agreement! They were talking as professional soldiers, acting as if she did not exist.

"Who'll command the Sons of Liberty?" Lee asked.

"Local colonels. They don't have an overall commander."

"I dislike that," Lee said. "They could easily degenerate into a mob. That's the last thing we want in defense of our cause."

"I've urged them to appoint a commanding general. So has Colonel Adam Jameson, I might add," Paul said, giving Janet a brief smile that she thought was almost sly.

"What we need more than a general are decent rifles," Janet said. "That's why I'm here. Will you give us the money to buy them immediately? We've learned that informers have been reporting on our plans. The sooner we act the better."

She was speaking to Jefferson Davis. He was no longer a professional soldier; he was a politician who had encouraged the Sons of Liberty with words and money. Davis glanced uneasily at Lee; Janet wondered if he was wishing he had not asked the general to stay and give his opinion on this adventure.

"We'll have no public link with the insurrection," Davis said. "Colonel Jameson, if he's captured, will have orders to say he asked his men to go as volunteers. It's important not only from the viewpoint of the honor of our cause but also from the politics of the thing. We'll want people to believe this western confederacy is a spontaneous creation."

"It will be spontaneous!" Janet said. "People are truly aggrieved and angry! They're in a revolutionary frame of mind!"

"What about Major Stapleton?" Lee asked. "Can we offer him any protection if he's captured? He may be considered a traitor and face execution."

"I don't intend to be captured, General," Paul said. "The motto of the Sons of Liberty is victory or death."

Lee frowned but said nothing. Jefferson Davis's lips compressed to a harsh line as he reached the decision that only he could make. "You'll have the money. It will be waiting for you in New York, along with the names of the men who'll sell you the guns. Our secret service people will give you the details tomorrow morning. There are some other matters they may want to discuss with you, such as newspaper support."

Robert E. Lee still said nothing. But his disapproval of the western confederacy pervaded the portico with unmistakable force. It apparently did not meet his lofty standards of honorable warfare.

For a moment Janet almost screamed in his face, *Damn you and your honor! Does the federal government care about honor, jailing Democrats without charges in Kentucky and Indiana, perpetrating monstrosities like the crater?* But she was a mere woman, disqualified from discussing such subjects. Instead, she asked Davis if they could advance the date of the uprising to the middle of August.

The president shook his head. "I'm afraid not. The people in Chicago want August twenty-ninth. It would be unwise to quarrel with them."

"So many of our best people will be in Chicago for the Democratic Convention—" Janet said.

"I told your father from the start of this business that the Sons of Liberty army should be independent from its political side," Davis replied.

Janet heard not a little irritation in his voice. She realized their conspiracy was only one of a hundred problems on this tired man's mind. Further argument would obviously be futile. They shook hands with President Davis and General Lee and retraced their steps through the stately rooms to the street.

"I'm convinced all over again," Paul said.

"Of what?"

"That General Lee is the greatest man I've ever met. He emanates moral authority."

In the distance cannons rumbled. The Confederate

sentry in his box stared morosely at them. He was a skinny boy of about seventeen, his uniform was a web of patches. He looked as if he had not eaten a decent meal in months. Janet thought she saw desperation stamped on his face. She wondered if it would soon be stamped on her face.

Never, Janet vowed. She would show these professional soldiers what angry civilians could accomplish with guns in their hands. She would help them revolutionize America's heartland and ask, *Now do you believe me?*

TWENTY-SIX

HALFWAY UP THE STEEP MOUNTAIN road, Moses Washington turned his head to look back on the Army of Kentucky, a blue column two miles long, laboring behind the 100-man Keyport garrison that Gentry had volunteered for battle. The first half of the column were Negro regiments. The Keyport men were at the head of the column because their seven-shot carbines would be potent weapons in a skirmish with a Confederate patrol.

The continuing drought had left a layer of dust an inch thick on the road, and the soldiers' marching feet stirred it into a haze that hovered around the column in the fierce summer sun. Washington's throat felt raw. He gulped from his canteen and heard Captain Simeon Otis call, "Save your water, men! We'll need it up ahead! The creeks are all dried out!"

Captain Otis was on a fine white stallion, well above the dust level. He had not been inhaling half of Kentucky's topsoil for the last six hours. But he meant well. He had given them a speech that was practically a sermon this morning before they started their march. He had told them they were going into battle. They were going to get a chance to prove they could fight as well as white men.

Otis had received a telegram from Colonel Gentry three days ago ordering them to join the Army of Kentucky on the march into Virginia. Otis made it sound as if they were going to get to Richmond ahead of General Grant. When they reached the column, a colonel had ridden up to them and cursed for a full minute. He said there was no way they were going to let them take their horses on this march. There was barely enough water for the men—and the officers' horses.

So here they were, infantry. Jasper Jones, Washington's New Jersey sidekick, was marching next to him. Only half Washington's size, Jasper was having trouble with the forty-five-pound pack on his back. "At least I don't have to worry about drinkin' my water," he said. "I finished my canteen an hour ago."

Washington gave him a swig from his canteen. "You gonna write that letter to juicy Lucy?" Jones asked.

Last night, they had run into Colonel Gentry in their roadside camp. He had asked Washington if he answered Lucy's letter. Washington had been too busy drawing rations for his men to think about it last night. Now, with nothing on his mind but putting one foot after another, he doubted if it was a good idea. He did not want to get involved with a slave nigger. Lucy's heart was warm and tender. But there was no point in encouraging her to think he had fallen in love with her.

"You ain't gonna write her?" Jasper said. He knew Washington well enough to read his silences.

"It'd just lead to trouble for both of us. She might follow me to New Jersey."

"How do you know we're ever gonna see New Jersey again? I don't like the look of this country we're marchin' into," Jasper said. "I sure hope we don't have to go up one of these hills to kick some Confederates with rifles off it."

Washington said nothing but he mentally brushed aside Jasper's words. Jasper had been worrying about what the white man was going to do to them since they volunteered. So far the man had turned out to be pretty fair, especially Major Stapleton. There was an officer who really cared about his men. He had made sure they had the best food and medicine in Hunter County, Indiana. He had spent hours and hours training them to be cavalrymen. It was not his fault that they were fighting as infantrymen. Washington wished Stapleton was around to give them some advice. He had thought it over and decided he did not believe Lucy's story that the major had switched to the rebel side.

Washington could not imagine himself getting killed in a battle. In their two dozen fights with armed deserters, a few bullets had whistled close. Other men had been hit. But he simply could not believe a bullet was going to turn him into a corpse or one of the gasping groaning wounded. It had something to do with seeing himself as a good soldier, tough enough to fight, smart enough to duck.

"Write the girl a letter, Moses," Jasper Jones said. "It won't cost you nothin'. Won't even have to pay to mail it. Colonel Gentry'll deliver it. Maybe it'll bring us luck. I got a hunch we're gonna need it."

"How come you're suddenly so worried about her?"

"I heard what Gentry told you. That girl's been fightin' the war for us while we sat on our asses eatin' good in Indiana."

"You think it takes guts to be a spy?"

"Sure as hell does. Sometimes they hang spies. Write Lucy a letter. She deserves it."

Lucy a hero? A female slave nigger a hero? Washington scoffed at the idea. But Jasper had gotten him thinking about that night with Lucy. He heard her saying, *I loves you*, and promising to pray for him. He was going into a battle. Bullets would be flying close to him. When they stopped marching to eat dinner, Washington pulled a piece of writing paper out of his pack. He had been meaning to write his parents a letter. He'd take care of Lucy first.

Dear Lucy:
  We're marching off to fight a battle. Colonel Gentry told me about your bad luck. But at least

*now you're a free woman and can begin to think
about living like one. I hope you feel better soon.*
  Your friend,
  Moses Washington

He put the letter in an envelope and went looking for
Colonel Gentry. He found him in a circle of officers,
eating hardtack and cold beans like the rest of the army.
Washington saluted and said, "Here's that letter for
Lucy, Colonel."

"Thank you, Moses," Gentry replied. "I'll see that she
gets it. How are your men doing in this heat?"

"No one's dropped out so far, Colonel. But we're
mighty low on water."

"Everyone is. All the mountain streams have dried up
in the drought. I've never seen anything like it. No rain
for sixty days now!"

"We gettin' close to these rebels?" Washington asked.

"We'll be there this time tomorrow. I'm afraid it's going to be bloody. I hope you and your boys do well."

"We'll sure try, Colonel."

Almost exactly twenty-four hours later, Washington
and his men, still marching at the head of the column,
saw the white buildings of Saltville in the distance. It
took them another hour of slogging up and down some
smaller hills to get close to the town, which was
perched on a ridge at least 500 feet above the road. By
this time everyone was desperately thirsty. Almost
every canteen was empty. They told themselves there
would be wells in the town where they could drink
their fill.

Then they saw the Confederates. They were in a series of forts on a hill overlooking the road. Their red battle flag with its white stars and blue cross was flying
over the topmost fort. As the column approached, a cannon boomed in the lower fort and a ball hissed over their
heads. *Craaack!* Rifles crashed a second later. Their aim

was better. A half-dozen men cried out and crumpled into the dust. *Craack!* Another blast of rifle fire hit the column and more men went down.

The column disintegrated. Men ran off the road and threw themselves flat in the grass. Washington and Jasper Jones and the others from Keyport stayed in the road. "What'll we do, Moses?" Jasper shouted. He was scared.

Washington stayed calm. He was still convinced no bullet could hit him. *Craack!* Another volley laid more men low. Captain Otis and other officers rode up and down on their horses, shouting, "Fall back! Fall back!" They retreated down the road, leaving the wounded behind them.

Washington thought that was wrong. He stepped out of the column and called to Captain Otis, "Shouldn't somebody get them wounded boys out of there?"

"They've got the road covered!" Otis shouted. He was scared silly.

"I'll go back with ten men and get them," Washington said.

Otis shook his head and rode for the rear of the column. *Craack!* Another volley from the Confederate riflemen. By this time they were out of range and the balls whistled over Otis's head. He flattened himself on his horse and galloped away. Some of the wounded staggered to their feet and followed the column down the road. About a half-dozen lay there, dead or too badly hurt to get up.

After retreating about a half mile, The Army of Kentucky halted. Wild confusion reigned. Some officers ordered their men to form a battle line. Others insisted their companies should stay in the road. Captain Otis ordered everyone to load his gun. Washington didn't know what was going to happen next, but he started to fear the worst. Beside him, Jasper Jones was saying, "Jeeesus, what a mess!"

About a hundred yards away, under a big chestnut tree, the general in charge got off his horse and started talking things over with a half-dozen colonels. Colonel Gentry stood outside their circle, as if he knew a one-armed man had nothing to say about how to fight a battle.

"I sure hope we don't have to go up that hill," Jasper Jones said.

"Can you think of another way to get at them rebels?" Washington asked.

"Starve them out," Jasper said.

"Real good. While we die of thirst down here on the road. We got to get rid of them so we can get water, fast," Washington said.

Sure enough, within a half hour the Army of Kentucky was in line-of-battle formation, ready to go up the hill. In the center, the 125th Indiana Colored Volunteers were in a compact column. Ahead of them were Moses Washington and his 100 Keyport troopers. They had orders to blaze away with their carbines as they got close to the fort to keep the rebels' heads down. On either wing, two more black regiments were in the lead, their white colonels and officers determined to be the first over the walls of the rebel forts. That was what Captain Otis told Washington and his men, anyway, before they formed up for the charge. Behind the blacks came two ranks of mostly white soldiers in long lines that curved at both ends.

In the rear were a half-dozen light cannons that teams of horses had dragged up the mountains. The guns flung a round at the enemy fort. Firing uphill, the artillerymen's aim was atrocious. The black iron balls vanished over the top of the mountain. They fired another round with the same result. "Can't they hit anything?" Jasper Jones said.

The colonel of the 125th Indiana Volunteers gave them a version of Captain Otis's speech. He told them they were going to show the world what black soldiers could do in a battle. He talked through his nose the same way Captain Otis did. He had the same funny shine in his eyes.

"What a lot of horseshit," Jasper Jones said as the colonel drew his sword and trotted to the head of the column.

A cannon boomed and the whole line surged forward, cheering. Captain Otis strode beside Washington and his men, waving his sword. They were still a long way from the lower fort when the wall erupted in a sheet of flame and smoke. Bullets hissed everywhere and men screamed in pain and went down in the drought-brown grass. Others toppled without a sound, unquestionably dead.

"Forward boys, show everyone—" the Indiana colonel shouted.

Two bullets hit him in the head, tearing off most of his face. He fell backward onto the grass and the already thinned front ranks faltered, terrified by the sight.

"Keep going forward boys!" Captain Otis shouted. "We'll be on top of them in no time."

Those were Otis's last words. Again the Confederate fort erupted with flame and smoke and a half-dozen bullets thudded into the captain's body. He toppled without a sound. The men near him shuddered and groaned. Some cried to Jesus. What kind of a battle was this? Washington wondered. You got killed before you could fire a shot at your enemy.

"Forward! Forward!" shouted the Indiana regiment's major, a fat, stumpy man. He looked terrified. He was not going forward. He was whacking men with the flat of his sword, trying to get the line moving again. Everyone was frozen with fear. Another blast of gunfire killed the major and at least thirty of the Indiana Colored Volunteers.

"They're crazy!" Jasper shouted. "These white men are goin' to kill us all!"

"Come on!" Washington said, breaking into a run. Most of the Keyport troopers were dead or wounded. Washington shoved that fact out of his mind. They were proving they were soldiers. They were ignoring bullets, dead colonels and majors and captains. They were driving home the attack. That was what war was all about.

Another eruption from the Confederate fort. Something smashed into Washington's chest. *What the hell?* he thought. Were these rebels throwing rocks? He wanted to keep running forward. But his legs refused to obey him.

"Moses!"

Washington turned and saw Jasper Jones on his knees, clutching his belly. Dark red blood spurted around his fingers. Simultaneously Washington realized something strange had happened to his chest. A pain worse than anything he had ever experienced in the prize ring was taking root there. He put his hand on it and the hand came away wet with blood. Jasper got blurry, as if someone had turned him into a smudged photograph. Cheering white soldiers ran past them into the smoke shrouding the battlefield. That was the last thing Moses Washington remembered for a while.

Blam Blam. What was that noise? Gunshots. Single gunshots. The pain in Moses Washington's chest was worse. It jangled through his whole body every time he breathed. *Blam Blam.* He raised his head and saw about twenty Confederate soldiers on the far side of the battlefield, shooting the wounded men lying there.

"Here's 'nother one!"

"Send him to nigger heaven!"

Blam.

They were shooting the wounded blacks. They walked past the white wounded without touching them. Jasper Jones was lying only a few feet away from Washington. He was curled up on his side, his fingers still clutching his bloody belly.

"Jasper," Washington whispered. "They're gonna kill us."

He took a better look at Jasper. He was dead. For another five minutes Washington lay there, breathing in small gulps to reduce the pain, trying to figure out what to do. His shirt was soaked with blood. He felt so weak, he was afraid he'd fall down if he tried to run.

Behind him he heard someone shout, "Stop! Stop! I demand you to stop!"

It was Colonel Henry Gentry. He was on a big black horse. He was all by himself. There was not another federal soldier in sight. Several of the Confederates walked toward him, their rifles leveled on their hips.

"What'n hell do you want?" asked one of them, a short red-faced boy. He did not look more than fourteen years old.

"I want to see Colonel Jameson. I'm a friend of his mother's. I'm Colonel Henry Gentry."

"You wait here. I'll see what the colonel says."

The boy vanished into the fort. A wounded white soldier rolled over and cried, "Water! Jesus won't someone give me some water?"

One of the Confederates handed the man his canteen. The wounded soldier gulped it greedily. This Confederate was not a boy, though he was almost as short as one. He had a scraggly brown beard.

"What you tryin' to do? Stop us from killin' these niggers?" he asked Gentry.

Gentry said nothing.

"We took a blood oath. Every nigger we see in a blue uniform is gonna get kilt," the veteran said.

The boy emerged from the fort. "Colonel Jameson says he's got nothin' to say to you!" he called. "He told me to tell you he'll see you in Indiana!"

Gentry turned his horse and started down the hill. Moses Washington realized the one-armed colonel was his only chance. In Keyport he had seemed like a pathetic imitation of a soldier but he had come up here to try to stop the killing. Maybe he would help him.

Washington sprang to his feet and staggered after Gentry, calling, "Colonel!"

Gentry looked over his shoulder and slowed his horse. Washington clung to the pommel and they went careening down the hill. Washington's feet dragged on the ground but somehow he kept his grip.

"Hey!"

"He's got that nigger!"

"Kill him!"

The shouts were followed within seconds by a scattered volley. The bullets whistled high and only inspired the horse to increase his speed. In sixty seconds Gentry was on the road, heading for the Union camp. A few more bullets followed them but they were soon out of range. In another two or three minutes Union soldiers were helping Washington into a hospital tent, full of groaning men and cursing doctors.

A white-bearded doctor gave Washington a half-glass of whiskey. Two orderlies jammed a rag in his mouth and held him down while the doctor probed for the bullet with some sort of long wire. The whiskey did not do much for the pain, which was ten times worse than the original wound. Finally the doctor growled, "Got it," and held the bullet in his bloody fingers for Washington to admire.

"You're one lucky nigger," the doctor said. "It missed your lung and didn't break any bones. You'll live if it doesn't get infected."

The orderlies bandaged the wound and Washington stumbled into the hot July sunshine. A swirl of darkness forced him to lean against a tree. Around him lay about two hundred wounded men, screaming and moaning for water. Washington realized he was desperately thirsty himself.

"Moses!" It was Colonel Gentry holding out a canteen. There were tears on his face. "They shot us to pieces," Gentry said.

Washington realized the colonel was talking about the Keyport troopers. He swigged from the canteen. It was brandy. "We done our best, Colonel."

"I know you did. If only we had a better general. I told him a frontal assault was crazy. I wanted to send a flying column up the road to seize Saltville. That would have given us water—"

"Wish we'd done it, Colonel."

"Can you come with me? I want you to tell General Burbridge what you saw."

Washington felt too weak to walk more than a step but he managed to follow Gentry down the road to where General Burbridge was standing with his colonels. Gentry said he had rescued a witness to mass murder. He wanted Burbridge to file charges against Adam Jameson and every other officer in his command. He wanted them prosecuted after the war.

"Get out of my sight, Gentry," General Burbridge said through gritted teeth. "Haven't I got enough to worry about without you making me responsible for a lot of wounded niggers? This is your mess as much as mine. I don't think you'll telegraph Lincoln about it."

Gentry turned away from this humiliation as if Burbridge had kicked him in the stomach. For the first time it dawned on Washington that the man really cared about black people. "I'm sorry Moses," he said as they walked slowly back to the hospital.

"Nothin' to be sorry about, Colonel. I knows it wasn't your fault."

"I'm still sorry," Gentry said. "Sorry as hell." He gave Moses the canteen full of brandy and wandered into the trees.

At sundown the Army of Kentucky retreated. Moses Washington spent the night in a jolting wagon with about two dozen wounded blacks who had been lucky enough to stagger off the battlefield. Every rut in the road sent a bolt of pain through his chest. Only one of the wounded belonged to the Keyport troop. They had been wiped out almost to the last man. Washington grieved for Jasper Jones. They had been friends since grammar school. Jasper had been his cornerman in his prizefights.

"Oh why did I ever leave Mas'r?" cried the soldier next to Washington. The doctors had cut off his leg below the knee. He was a typical slave nigger, ready to crawl back to the plantation.

Wait a second, Washington thought. Once and for all he was banishing that idea from his mind. Every time he thought about the way he had used that phrase to make himself feel superior, his chest seemed to hurt worse. Slave or free did not make any difference to those Confederates who had vowed to kill every colored man in a uniform. Moses Washington was part of their fight for freedom now.

This change of mind made Washington think of Lucy. They had whipped her almost to death because she had stopped being a slave nigger and tried to win the war for her people. Washington told himself he was going to write her a real letter soon. He was going to tell Lucy that her people were his people now.

Twenty-Seven

WILL, PAUL THOUGHT, GAZING AT Janet Todd as they stood on the prow of a Baltimore and Ohio ferryboat, crossing the Hudson to New York. The sheer intensity of this woman's determination was carrying them deeper into this conspiracy, in spite of the portents of failure. She simply refused to listen to anyone, from John Wilkes Booth to Robert E. Lee, who intimated that the South was losing the war and the western confederacy was a desperate gamble.

Love. That was the other reality in the equation. Did *will* negate it, producing zero? For some men, that sort of mathematics might be persuasive. They might fear their manhood was at risk with such a woman. But Paul had never seen Janet Todd as sweet-tempered or submissive. This formidable will only multiplied the risk of love somewhat beyond his original estimate.

There was now another factor in the equation that Major Stapleton was juggling in his aching head: The Crater. Before they left Richmond, Paul had accepted an invitation from their host, John Hayes, to visit it. They had ridden by back roads from Richmond to Petersburg. Hayes knew the Confederate commander, Pierre Beauregard, and he had allowed them to go into the fort adjacent to the site of the explosion. The scene beggared anything Paul had seen at Antietam or Fredericksburg. Thousands of dead Union soldiers, many of them African-Americans, were piled on top of one another in the huge hole. The sickening stench of decaying flesh rose in the humid air. A swarthy Confederate major about Paul's age said, "They've sent a flag of truce, asking permission to collect them. But we're going make the bastards part of the foundation of a new fort."

Stupidity, Paul thought. How long could a professional soldier remain loyal to an army that committed such colossal acts of stupidity? The word kept echoing in his head all the way to New York. He did not know how this idea functioned in the equation he was trying to construct. He only knew it was acquiring ominous power.

From the ferry they hurried onto cobblestoned West Street, where they hailed a hack to ride uptown. It was the first of August; the temperature was in the nineties, with a soggy humidity that almost matched Washington D.C. Gotham's streets were a tangle of hacks, wagons, carts and carriages. Dense crowds surged along the sidewalks, the faces a mixture of white and black, Irish and German and English. Prosperity was visible everywhere, in the freshly painted buildings, the shops crammed with goods, the expensive clothes of the passersby. It was an almost cruel contrast to Richmond's bleak poverty.

Janet was thinking different thoughts. "How nice to be in the most pro-Southern city in the North," she said.

"It was until the draft riots last July," Paul replied. "Now I fear they take a dim view of the Confederacy."

In the summer of 1863, New York had erupted in violent protests against the draft. For almost three days the city was in the hands of a mob. Only the intervention of federal troops had restored order.

"Why do you constantly have something *negative* to say about our cause?" Janet asked.

For a moment Paul almost admitted he was trying to make her see the South's cause was hopeless. "I'm only being negative about mob rule. Like General Lee, I don't think mobs accomplish much. Here in New York the Democrats murdered every Negro they could find. They hanged them from street lamps—it was ugly."

Mentioning Lee only increased Janet's irritation. They had quarreled about the general on the train from Washington, D.C. Janet had complained that he had not even tried to understand what they hoped to do in the western confederacy. Paul had insisted that Lee's concern about the Sons of Liberty turning into a mob was a legitimate worry. He declined to abandon the argument now. "You can't support an honorable cause with dishonorable acts," he said.

Janet said nothing. She looked away from him at the crowded sidewalks.

"I thought we were going to be absolutely honest with each other. I assumed that meant I should say exactly what I think about everything, from Colonel Adam Jameson to General Lee."

She clearly thought that clause of their contract should be either revised or revoked. Paul stubbornly continued, "The night before my roommate, Jeff Tyler, left the military academy, we agreed that the South's only hope was to fight an honorable defensive war. They should portray themselves as people being invaded by fanatics who were trying to change the fundamental structure of their society. It was their best hope of winning the world's sympathy."

"What has that wonderful idea accomplished?" Janet said. "France, England, have toyed with us. Taken our money and sold us blockade runner trash. While we've neglected our natural allies—the Democrats of the North."

At the Astor House, a huge granite pile on lower Broadway, they registered as brother and sister actors and obtained adjoining rooms without the slightest difficulty. Once more they were forced to pay in advance.

"I begin to feel sorry for theater people," Paul said as they went up in the hydraulic elevator. "They seem universally distrusted."

The elevator operator was a white-haired black man who stared straight ahead, paying no attention to them. "It's almost as bad as being a southerner in the North," Janet said.

"Or a northerner in the South, I suppose," Paul replied.

"What do you mean?"

"I wonder where we'll live, when all this is over."

"My father is leaving me Hopemont. I'd be happy there, if you would be."

"I'd be happy anywhere that you were happy."

The elevator stopped at their floor, and the black operator opened the door to reveal a fat redfaced man and his equally fat wife. The woman stared at Janet's hand and gave Paul a glare as she and her husband stepped back to let him and Janet off. The whine of the descending elevator seemed to underscore the woman's disapproval.

"Did you notice her looking for a wedding ring?" Paul said. "I can imagine them telling friends over dinner about these two terrible young people on their way to an *assignation*. It's an old New York custom."

"Have you ever done it?"

"Not until today."

He thought his tone was playful but Janet's response was a frown.

In an hour, bathed and in fresh clothes, they were riding uptown in a horse-drawn trolley to a brownstone off Fifth Avenue on 36th Street. Paul handed an envelope to a short swarthy butler. He examined its contents and escorted them to a booklined study. A man with a distinctly Jewish-looking face and gray hair sat playing solitaire on a card table. He did not look up as they walked into the room.

"I'm told you need money," he said with a brief

smile. "Something in the vicinity of two hundred thousand dollars?"

In Richmond, the morning after their meeting with Jefferson Davis and Robert E. Lee, they had conferred with Judah Benjamin, the tall brilliant Jew who was serving as the Confederacy's secretary of state. He had given them this address and told them they would get additional instructions here, along with the money.

"We're buying thirty thousand rifles," Paul said. "They could easily demand twenty dollars a gun."

"If they want more money, we'll pay the balance later. A lot will depend on the kinds of guns that are on the market at the moment."

The man opened a wall safe and counted out the money in $500 bills. "I'm adding another twenty-five thousand to buy yourself some newspaper coverage," he said. "If your western revolution gets going it wouldn't hurt to have a New York paper backing you."

Paul put the money in a belt around his waist. The mere act made him feel uneasy. He had sensed General Lee's disapproval of his decision to join the Sons of Liberty's conspiracy. Accepting this money as an agent of the Confederate government meant he had crossed the line from treasonous words to treasonous action. If the business ended in a court-martial, he would have only Henry Gentry's testimony to exonerate him—and he might be strongly inclined to say he had begun to distrust Major Stapleton.

"Do you have a newspaper in mind?" Paul asked.

"The *Daily News*. Fernando Wood backs the Southern Confederacy, thanks to the annual stipend we pay him. He'll be behind the western confederacy for the right price."

There was more than a hint of sarcasm in the way he balanced the two confederacies. Paul suspected he believed in neither of them.

"Don't Mr. Wood's convictions have anything to do with it?" Janet asked.

"Fernando Wood has no convictions."

The man resumed playing solitaire. The butler led them to the front door. "At least he could have wished us good luck," Paul murmured.

As they boarded another horsecar, Paul bought a copy of the New York *Daily News* from a newsboy. *MORE ABOUT THE CRATER FIASCO!* was the headline over the lead story on the right-hand side of the page. The reporter described the disaster in grisly detail. He confirmed Lee's estimate that the Union troops had exploded more than four tons of gunpowder under the Confederate forts. He told how General Ambrose Burnside had been ordered to cancel the attack shortly after the explosion, when it became evident that the crater was an obstacle, not an open sesame to victory. But he had sat in his bombproof shelter and done nothing for five hours while his men blundered into the slaughter pit. Two other Union generals cowered in similar bombproof shelters, drunk, while their men died.

Stupidity. The word gnawed at Paul's brain.

He paged through the rest of the paper. Toward the back, he saw a smaller headline: *Another Union Repulse.* The writer described the Army of Kentucky's attack on the Confederate saltworks near Saltville in western Virginia and its rout by the men of General Morgan's division under the command of Colonel Adam Jameson. An editorial tied this minor disaster into the crater fiasco and ended with a call for Ulysses S. Grant's dismissal as commander in chief of the Union Army: *How much longer are the American people expected to tolerate such gross incompetence? How many more men must die to support this failed president and his ruined administration?*

"Doesn't that make delightful reading?" Janet asked.

"What?"

"The mess Grant is making," Janet said.

Paul had almost forgotten she was sitting beside him, reading the same stories. He had instantly grasped the significance of the Union attack on Saltville. It was an attempt to destroy Adam Jameson's division before he could march to support the Sons of Liberty uprising.

The last paragraph of the Saltville story included a list of Union casualties. Paul was startled to find Captain Simeon Otis among the dead. He pointed out the name to Janet. "Colonel Gentry must have been involved," he said.

"That makes me feel even better," she replied.

Henry Gentry's intelligence network had obviously learned a great deal about Gabriel Todd's conspiracy. It meant an incursion by Adam Jameson was unlikely to have the advantage of surprise. Should he point this out to Janet? No, it would only lead to another argument.

They left the horsecar at Washington Square and hurried across the green park to a side street shop with an innocent name: GREYSTONE'S RARE BOOKS. Inside, a muscular balding man with a brown handlebar mustache was behind the counter. He studied them warily.

"I've been told you'd have this order ready," Paul said, handing him another envelope. This one had been given to them by a Confederate secret service official in Richmond's Treasury Department, across the street from Thomas Jefferson's capitol.

"I'll be with you in two minutes," the man said.

The message was in cipher. He undoubtedly had the codebook in the back of the store. He returned in a moment and held out his hand to Paul. "Miles McDonald's my name," he said. "We've been expecting you."

Paul introduced him to Janet. "She's the real commander of this expedition," he said. "I'm only along as an ordnance expert."

McDonald sent a clerk racing off to summon three

other members of the group. They soon joined them in the back room, where McDonald served everyone bitter coffee into which the men poured stiff shots of Irish whiskey from an open bottle on the table. Two of the new arrivals had Irish names and looked it; the third, a short, potbellied sidewhiskered Englishman named Bartholomew Mason, described himself as a Jeffersonian Democrat from the slums of London. But there was no trace of cockney in his accent.

When McDonald introduced Paul, the two Irishmen reacted with disbelief to his surname. "Are you related to the general?" one asked.

"He's my brother."

"Last summer he killed about a thousand good Democrats over on Second Avenue around Fourteenth Street," the other Irishman said.

"Are you talking about the draft riots?" Janet asked.

Mason nodded. "We were within an inch of capturing the city when General Stapleton's division arrived from Gettysburg, complete with cannons, which they didn't hesitate to use. He smashed the secession out of this city in about ten minutes."

"The poor fellows never had a chance," Miles McDonald said. "It was clubs against rifle bullets and canister."

Paul avoided Janet's eyes. Was she wondering why he had not told her about his brother's role in the draft riots? If so, she chose to conceal it. "Here's another Stapleton," she said, "ready to tell his murderous brother and everyone else it's time to stop the slaughter."

The Irishmen looked skeptical. But Mason said, "If you've convinced Jefferson Davis, that's good enough for me. Here's the deal. Tonight at eight o'clock, you'll have dinner with Fernando Wood in the Astor House and find out how much he wants to put the *Daily News* behind you. Tomorrow we'll show you the guns."

"The *News* is goin' broke, so don't think you're gettin' a silk purse. It's a lot closer to a sow's ear," Miles McDonald said.

"Pay no attention to him," Mason said. "He's an old Tammany Democrat. They all hate Fernando because he kept too much of the graft for himself when he was mayor."

"I'm a man who believes in the Southern Confederacy," McDonald said. "It's our one hope of escaping the dictatorship of the Republicans. If they win they'll run the country for the next hundred years and no Irish-Catholic will get a decent job anywhere. Our children's children will be lugging bricks and digging ditches beside a bunch of niggers, probably for less money than they get."

The other two Irishmen remained stony-faced before this impassioned speech. Paul read nothing in their faces that suggested they could think a hundred years ahead. They were mercenaries, working for Mason.

"Where are the guns?" Paul asked.

"On a railroad siding over in Jersey City. We'll take you there tomorrow," Mason said.

"Where did you get them?" Paul said.

"The less you or anyone else knows about that, the better," Mason replied.

"We've got a line on something hotter than rifles," Miles McDonald said. "Gatling guns."

"What are they?" Janet asked.

"A rapid-fire gun that can shoot over a hundred rounds a minute," Paul said. "I saw a demonstration of one in Washington in 1862. General John Reynolds and a dozen other top officers urged the government to buy it. But the idiots in the army ordnance department refused to approve it—"

Paul stopped, embarrassed by the anger in his voice. He was talking as if he wished the Union Army had bought the clumsy murderous weapon and won the war. Did he really wish that had happened? He would never have received his Gettysburg wound—or met Janet Todd. Life was a very confusing equation, crammed with pluses and minuses.

"The inventor's joined the Sons of Liberty," McDonald said. "He gave us the plans. We're having the guns made in Europe."

"Will they be here in time for us to use them?" Janet asked.

"Maybe," Mason said.

"With or without them, we'll show the world that tens of thousands of Democrats are sick of Lincoln," Janet said.

For a moment Paul almost rebuked her. He had begun to think Janet did not care whether the Sons of Liberty's insurrection succeeded. She would be satisfied with an upheaval—days or weeks of turmoil that would prove Lincoln had no support in the American heartland. It was more than a little ironic to see the way she and Henry Gentry agreed that the mere fact of an insurrection would wreck Lincoln.

The trouble with that idea was the way it left the men with guns in their hands exposed to capture and possible execution for treason, as General Lee had pointed out. As a professional soldier, Paul's instinctive loyalty was to these fighting men. He suddenly heard Henry Gentry saying, *Janet Todd is a Confederate agent.* Was his seduction, his enlistment in the Sons of Liberty, part of a coldhearted plan? No, he rejected that demoralizing idea.

They rode downtown to the Astor House through the terrific heat and humidity. Janet quizzed him about Fernando Wood. Paul knew little beyond his stormy tenure as mayor of New York—he had fought with the reigning Democratic bosses of Tammany Hall—and his 1861 proposal that New York should secede from the Union and became a free city, in which North and South would trade as equals.

At eight o'clock in the Astor House's opulent Merchants Room restaurant, they met the owner of the *Daily News*. Fernando Wood had a face that seemed to narrow to a knife edge around his aristocratic nose. Beneath shrewd knowing dark eyes was the precisely curled black mustache of an English gentleman. Wood was wearing a creamy white summer suit with a large purple handkerchief in the upper pocket, matched by a purple tie. Beside him sat a handsome redheaded woman in a white lace dress that displayed a remarkable amount of her snowy breasts. Wood shook hands and introduced Gertrude McAfee.

"Gertrude's from the South," he said with a smile. "I thought she'd like to be in on our dastardly plot."

"What part of the South?" Janet asked.

"New Orleans," Miss McAfee said in a heavy drawl.

"Her father is an old friend. He sent her up here to protect her from Lincoln's liberators. She wrote a wonderful series of articles for the *News* about the insults women have had to endure in New Orleans since the federals occupied it."

Miss McAfee was a little too voluptuous and her smile too clever for Paul to swallow this. She reminded him of several women he had seen on the arms of Union generals in Washington. They listened while she described New Orleans women being dragged into doorways and violated by drunken Union soldiers, many of them Negroes.

Meanwhile they enjoyed New York's favorite dish, oysters on cracked ice. Wood ordered champagne and suggested lobster in a poached cream sauce for the main course, followed by chocolate mousse for dessert. It was a feast and Paul began to wonder who was going to pay for it. He suspected it was not Fernando Wood.

"So," the ex-mayor said as the coffee was served. "What do you want me to do for twenty-five thousand dollars?"

"Support the western confederacy," Janet said. "Call it the noblest work of political genius you've ever seen. Print everything we send you about our declaration of independence, our constitutional convention." She described the thousands of angry Democrats ready to revolt in Kentucky and Indiana, their plan to create a new country backed by the liberated Confederate prisoners outside Indianapolis and Chicago.

"I like it," Wood said. "I'll put every ounce of ink and every inch of type in the building behind it. The moment you succeed, I'll call on Lincoln to resign."

Paul took an envelope containing $25,000 from the inside pocket of his coat. "Why do you want all this money to do that, Mr. Wood?" Janet suddenly asked. "I've just come from Richmond. The South needs every cent it can find to buy uniforms, ammunition, food. They're close to starvation."

Wood stared at them in undisguised amazement. "*I* need it because the *Daily News* isn't making a profit, Miss Todd," he said. "And Miss McAfee needs a few new dresses. And I need several new suits. And a bargain's a bargain. What's going on here? You people are just supposed to deliver the money and fill me in on the details."

"Here's your money, Mr. Wood," Paul said, handing him the envelope. "Although I agree with Miss Todd's sentiments, I also understand your necessities."

"Those insufferable Republicans at the *New York Times* have been trying to put Fernando out of business," Gertrude McAfee said. "It would be a tragedy if they succeeded. The loss of one of our few courageous Democratic voices."

Wood ordered another bottle of champagne to try to restore their good humor. The ex-mayor also ordered another chocolate mousse, which he shared with Miss McAfee. A gob of chocolate dropped onto her left breast. There was much giggling as Wood wiped it off.

Miss McAfee's profession was becoming more and more apparent. Whether she practiced it in New Orleans or had assumed it in New York was an interesting if somewhat moot point.

Miss McAfee said she hoped Wood would let her write about the Sons of Liberty uprising. "These two should be the stars of the story," she said. "I can even see a title: 'For Love and Liberty.'"

"Not bad," Wood said. He scribbled it on a pad he pulled out of his inner coat pocket.

"Once things get going, I hope you'll tell us your story, Miss Todd," Wood said. "We'll make you famous—or infamous, depending on the reader's political orientation. I hope you'll include how you persuaded Major Stapleton to change sides and risk his reputation and his life for your cause."

The edge of sarcasm in Wood's voice made it clear that he was getting even for Janet's suggestion that he support the western confederacy free of charge. He was practically saying she had made sure Paul was being well rewarded for his southern sympathies.

"I'll consider it," Janet said with a defiant toss of her dark hair.

The idea of making their love a story in a cheap newspaper like the *Daily News* horrified Paul. Wood and Miss McAfee departed wishing them success, and the waiter presented the check. Paul paid it and he and Janet took the elevator to the sixth floor of the Astor House.

"You're not serious about letting him use our story in his rag of a newspaper, are you?" Paul asked as they walked down the red-carpeted corridor to their rooms.

"Why not?"

"Janet—what we have between us can never be shared with anyone."

"Come now. Don't you think everyone knows we're lovers? John Wilkes Booth, the Hayeses, Jefferson Davis? Even your wonderful General Lee?"

"I don't know about the others. But I'm quite certain General Lee thinks I'm conducting myself like a man of honor with you."

"But you're not. At least on his terms. On my terms—and I hope on your terms—you are. Why not tell the world about us? It might win us thousands of Democrats who remember your father's name."

"No!"

They stood there in the silent corridor, suddenly no longer lovers but antagonists. For a moment Janet seemed tempted to defy him. Instead, she pressed herself against him and said, "I'm sorry. You're right, of course. It's unthinkable."

Paul kissed her with a violence that confessed how close he had been to repudiating love—and the western confederacy. "Can I come to you tonight?" he asked

"Of course."

A half hour later, when he knocked on her door, she called, "It's open!"

She was in bed beneath a sheet, wearing a pale blue nightgown. A faint breeze stirred the curtains but did little to alter the almost suffocating heat and humidity. In the yellow lamplight, there was a sheen of perspiration on Janet's forehead. Her expression seemed welcoming, but Paul sensed something strange in her manner.

"Are there many women like Gertrude McAfee in New York?" Janet asked.

"A great many. They're in Washington too. Some people call them adventuresses. But I'm afraid they soon sink to another level."

"You called me an adventuress a while ago."

"It had a different meaning," Paul said.

"I hope so," she said.

Paul sat down beside her on the bed. "Tomorrow morning, why don't we go to city hall and get married? No matter what happens, we'll know we love each other for better or for worse. We'll have testified to it in a public way."

"I'd say yes in a moment if Adam Jameson wasn't involved. I think he'd react badly to the news. So badly he might find reasons to stay in western Virginia."

There it was, the southern cause, personified by Adam Jameson, standing between them as long as the war lasted. The only solution was a swift end to the war—something the western confederacy might accomplish.

Paul lay down beside Janet on the outside of the sheet and kissed her gently. "Let's forget them all for a while," he said.

He took off his night robe and slipped under the sheet. Untying the bow on her nightgown, he began undoing a half-dozen smaller bows that ran down the center of the lacy garment.

"I love you," he said. "You love me. It's the only thing that matters."

"If only that were true," Janet murmured.

"It *is* true," Paul said.

For a moment he saw himself trying to extricate Janet from the clutching hands of Gabriel Todd, Rogers and Adam Jameson, Jefferson Davis, Fernando Wood. They had to get beyond argument, beyond interfering voices that inflicted doubts and wounds. "Come to me," Paul whispered. "Don't hold anything back."

Within minutes, Paul saw this was exactly what Janet was doing. She was no longer the woman who had surrendered in his arms at high noon beside the gleaming Ohio River. Whether it was willed or unwilled, he sensed a determination to enjoy him without the gift of herself that he needed and wanted to reassure him that he was still in control of their lives.

Why wasn't it happening? In this gigantic hotel, stripped even of their surnames, they were primary selves, simply Paul and Janet. Family and history should be vanishing in a gathering ritual of gift and acceptance, wish and desire, hope and faith. But the Janet he was kissing and caressing remained Janet *Todd*. Was there something even more irreducible beyond that formidable family name: *Confederate agent?*

"Now Janet, now," Paul whispered as he entered her. "Give yourself to me as I'm giving myself to you. Tell me how much you love me. Say it."

She would not or could not say it. Instead she tried to give him her physical self, the inner flesh that accepted his manhood, the breasts and thighs and tongue and lips that created this terrific wanting in his body. *You can have all of this, Paul, but not the other thing, not Janet without Todd.*

The clatter and cries of Broadway's voices and vehicles drifted into the room. They evoked memories of the Confederate moneyman's dry amorality and Fernando Wood's lecherous greed and Gertrude McAfee's commercial sensuality. The August heat bathed Paul in sweat as he struggled to annihilate these enemies of love.

But he could not overcome Janet's refusal to abandon *Todd.* Suddenly he was Blondin, falling from his wire into a cataract of wish and desire that was a sort of death. He refused to accept it and simultaneously in his deepest self accepted it as he had accepted that other death at Gettysburg. It was too real, too huge, to escape. It was his fate.

"I love you," he whispered as he cradled her in his arms.

She answered him with a kiss. But the words he wanted to hear remained unspoken.

They slept.

TWENTY-EIGHT

JANET TODD AWOKE WITH A start in the hot humid room in the Astor House. Thick beams of morning sunlight filled the windows. Below on Broadway a policeman's whistle shrilled again and again. It sounded vaguely ominous.

Beside her Paul was lying awake, staring at the ceiling. His chest was bare. The Antietam wound was like an evil purplish stain, only inches from her eyes. His expression was mournful. Janet struggled to convince herself she had done the right thing last night. He would have to wait until the western confederacy declared the war was over and victory was proclaimed in Indianapolis or Chicago. Then he would have all of her, body and soul.

Abruptly Janet was back ten hours, sitting opposite Gertrude McAfee, Fernando Wood's girlfriend. Janet watched him scoop that daub of chocolate mousse from her breast. She saw the cool sensuality in McAfee's eyes. Was she becoming one of those women? She only knew she liked the word that defined her: *adventuress*.

She lay there, savoring the idea of rescuing the South from defeat, of changing the course of history. She wanted that triumph as much as she wanted Paul Stapleton. She wanted it so much she was ready to risk becoming a woman like Gertrude McAfee. A woman who did not care what respectable people thought of her. A woman who ultimately did not care what Paul Stapleton thought of her.

No. That possibility stirred pain. But it was an endurable pain. She was not selling herself for new dresses, to see her name in cheap newspapers. It was for the South's tormented cause. For her father's violated honor. For their sacred dead. There was a difference, a vast moral difference, in her version of the adventuress role.

For another moment Janet studied Paul's brooding face. She still saw the same troubling mixture of innocence and maturity there. She understood the maturity now—it was the pride, the courage, the devotion to the ideal of soldierly honor that had twice returned him to the war in spite of his wounds. She exulted in her power over this man. She loved him but she also loved the power. She had *captured* him. She had overcome his loyalty to his homicidal Republican brother; she had forced him to admit that duty honor country were meaningless in a nation on the brink of dissolution—no matter how much the loss of those ideals wounded his spirit. She had persuaded him to commit treason for her sake—and the sake of her cause.

Knuckles rapped on the door. "Who is it?" Janet asked.

"Bart Mason," said a gruff voice.

Paul gestured to the door, seized his nightrobe and stepped into the closet. Janet shrugged into a nightrobe and peered through the half-opened door. The bewhiskered Englishman gazed sardonically at her. "We're looking for Major Stapleton," he said. "We can't seem to wake him up."

The smirk on the face of his Irish henchman made it clear that they knew where Major Stapleton was. "He's an early riser. He must have gone out for a walk," Janet said.

The Irishman and Mason exchanged sly smiles. "We'll wait in the lobby," Mason replied. "We want to leave for Jersey City within the hour. We need to finish the business with the guns today so we can start shipping them."

"I'm sure Major Stapleton will be back directly."

Adventuress, echoed in Janet's head as she slammed the door. To Mason and his friends she was no different from Gertrude McAfee. Janet told herself she did not care. "You can come out. They're gone," she said.

Paul emerged from the closet looking truculent. "What the devil are they doing, barging up here?"

"They want to start shipping the guns."

"I bet they do. I think those fellows are like Fernando Wood. More interested in making a quick buck than in helping the cause."

"What makes you say that?"

"Intuition, mostly. Little things, like Mason refusing to tell me where the guns came from."

Why was he always so critical of Southerners and southern sympathizers? For a moment suspicion flared in Janet's mind. Was Paul an immensely clever double agent? Had Gentry sent him across the Ohio to confuse and demoralize them—and incidentally to enjoy Janet Todd? No, it was impossible.

Downstairs, they invited Mason and his friend to join them for breakfast in the Merchants Room. Mason demurred. They could save time by having coffee and rolls on the ferryboat. Outside the Astor House he hailed a hack, and they clopped rapidly downtown to the Battery, where they boarded a Baltimore and Ohio ferryboat. At a table in the dining salon, they gulped hot coffee and fresh rolls.

Mason asked them how things had gone with Fernando Wood. "We agreed on terms," Janet said. "We gave him the money."

"Does he always come equipped with women like Gertrude McAfee?" Paul asked.

"I have no idea," Mason said. "It's none of my business. Or yours."

"He practically admitted a lot of our cash would be traveling around New York on her back," Paul said.

Mason exchanged a sour look with his Irish friend and said nothing. In Jersey City they walked through the ferry terminal into the railyards beyond it. Never had Janet seen so many boxcars. There must have been 5,000 of them. The ground was covered with black cinders that seemed to redouble the heat of the blazing August sun. Around them steam engines chugged and hooted, moving cars from one siding to another.

They saw no one but a few trackmen and the engineers and firemen in the steam engines. Several waved greetings to Mason and the Irishman. Finally they reached a siding at least a mile from the terminal. The Irishman slid back the doors of a red boxcar and Paul climbed inside. He stood in the doorway and helped Janet up. It was well over a hundred degrees in the car. Around them were dozens of boxes marked: CONTENTS: BOOKS.

The Irishman boosted Mason into the car and stayed outside to make sure no one interrupted them. Mason produced a screwdriver and pried open one of the boxes. There were at least two dozen guns inside. They looked murderous to Janet. Their long black barrels, their dark brown stocks gleamed in the dim light. They seemed to be in good condition. She wondered if this hot wearisome trip to Jersey City had been necessary.

Paul picked up one of the guns and hefted it. He walked to the open door of the car and peered down the barrel. He studied the firing mechanism and clicked the trigger several times. "You got these from Mexico, didn't you," he said.

"I told you not to worry about where we got them," Mason snapped.

"They're not rifled. They're muskets the Mexican army used until the French took over the country two years ago. They brought rifles and the Mexicans started selling these old guns all over South America—and North America, it now appears."

"What the hell's the difference?" Mason growled.

"Rifled or smooth, it still spits out a bullet that can kill a man."

"The rifle does that at three hundred yards and these things do it at eighty. It's like sending a man into a fight with one hand tied behind his back."

"Who the hell gave you the authority to pass these judgments?" Mason said.

"A lot of people. Janet's father, Colonel Todd. President Jefferson Davis."

"I knew Jeff Davis before you were born," Mason said. "He knows I wouldn't sell him a defective gun. Every one of these weapons is in perfect working order."

"I'm sure they are. The Mexicans know how to take care of guns. They've been using them to shoot each other for the last forty years," Paul said. "That's not the point. These are second-rate guns. The worst possible weapons to give amateur soldiers like the Sons of Liberty."

Their strident voices brought the Irishman to the door of the boxcar. His face was not friendly.

"I talked you over with Miles McDonald last night," Mason said. "We agreed someone named Stapleton was damned hard to trust. McDonald told us to take care of you if you tried to pull any tricks. I'm tempted to do it right now."

The Irishman pulled a pistol from under his coat. It was a big gun, with a silver barrel and a bulging magazine.

"That isn't going to get you your money," Paul said.

"I think maybe it will. I think maybe your lady friend here will want to keep the story of your visit to her room secret from Jeff Davis, her father, and a lot of other people."

Paul laughed in his face. "Janet Todd isn't going to let you shoot me and then hand over two hundred thousand dollars to keep you quiet. She's a woman of honor. If I visited her last night, it was because I love her—and she loves me."

"We're not above shooting both of you," Mason said. "The Confederates aren't going to win this war. It's every man for himself these days."

"You're a real hero," Paul said. "First you're going to shoot an unarmed man, then a defenseless woman."

He strolled over to the open door. "Would a foine young fellow like you do such a thing?" he said, mimicking an Irish brogue.

Janet saw he was exactly like Adam Jameson. War had given him a kind of contempt for death. "Wait a moment," she said. "There has to be a better answer to this."

The Irishman's gaze shifted to Janet. In a motion so swift she saw only a black blur, Paul kicked him in the face and slammed the boxcar door shut. Spinning, he drove his fist into Mason's face, sending him crashing into a stack of boxes. Paul sprang on top of him and pulled a pistol from inside his coat.

"Open the door," he said to Janet, crouching beside it.

She pulled back the door and Paul leaped into the opening, gun leveled. The Irishman was sprawled on his back, both hands clutching his bloody face; his gun was a good yard from his hand. Paul gestured with his pistol, and Mason hastily exited the boxcar.

"Give me his gun," Paul said. Mason obeyed.

Paul shoved both pistols into inner pockets in his coat and helped Janet down from the boxcar. "We'll see what President Davis says when we tell him about this," he said to the two gunrunners. Mason pressed a handkerchief to his bruised cheek and said nothing.

Back in New York, they headed for Miles McDonald's bookstore off Washington Square. The Irishman was behind the counter as usual. His smile vanished when Paul drew one of the guns and jammed it under his chin. "Did you give Mason and his boyo permission to kill me—and Miss Todd—if we refused to buy those second-rate guns?"

"I swear to God I never said any such thing," McDonald said, his eyes bulging with terror. "I don't deal in guns, just in intelligence. I never trusted the little limey bastard that much in the first place—"

"Can you communicate quickly with Richmond?"

McDonald shook his head. "It takes at least forty-eight hours. We can telegraph a safe house in Washington, but they have to take the message and the answer overland by courier."

"Here's the message. It's for President Davis. 'GUNS INFERIOR. BARTHOLMEW MASON UNTRUSTWORTHY. WISH FURTHER INSTRUCTIONS.'"

McDonald wrote it down. "I can send this," he said. "But I've got a better idea. I'll show it to Mason. I wouldn't be surprised if it gets you the best guns he can find."

"It's worth a try," Paul said.

Walking beside Paul into Washington Square Park, Janet felt bewildered. Her sense of power over him had vanished. More important, she no longer felt any need to control him. The doubting negativist had vanished. He had taken charge of their future in a new unassailable way. They sat down on a bench in the park and he took both her hands. "We're going to make this *work*," he said. "Trust me."

TWENTY-NINE

YOU'VE JOINED THEM. THE WORDS blazed in Paul Stapleton's head. That moment in the stifling boxcar, when he saw those third-rate Mexican muskets, swelled in his mind and heart to a historic dimension. Everything had coalesced. Honor and love and The Crater. The Republican abuse of the Constitution in Indiana and Kentucky. The loathing for Lincoln everywhere, even among his own detestable party. Robert E. Lee's elegiac moral grandeur, Jefferson Davis's desperation. All these realities became part of an equation that produced a new solution.

Paul saw with his trained soldier's eyes the disaster Janet Todd's military innocence and Mason's disillusioned greed were about to create. He also saw with equally overwhelming intensity the futility of his attempt to love Janet without accepting her as a Todd, as a woman with unalterable loyalty to the desperate all-but-doomed South. The heart's imperative had flung duty, honor country into history's dustbin. He was part of this conspiracy now, part of their despairing motto, victory or death.

He sensed, he saw, the new power this commitment gave him. When Janet hesitantly asked what they would do if they could not find any other guns, Paul said, "We'll find some. The country's awash in guns."

Instead of arguing angrily, she accepted his judgment. They were partners now in a new electrifying way that sent energy coursing through Paul's body. "Let's visit our old friend Fernando Wood and see if we can get some advice for our twenty-five thousand dollars," he said.

They took a horsecar to Printing House Square, near New York's elegant city hall, and found the *Daily News* building at the bottom of a crooked street. Outside it looked dilapidated and inside it was not much better. Editors and reporters hunched over battered desks that looked like relics of the previous century. Only Fernando Wood's office had any trace of style. His big desk was gleaming gold-trimmed mahogany. In a corner were several oversize armchairs, covered with red plush velvet. On the walls were photographs of Wood shaking hands with governors and presidents and a framed copy of the *Daily News* hailing his speech to a massive "Peace Convention" he had organized in the city a year ago.

Paul told the ex-mayor what had happened in the Jersey City railyards. "Without the guns there's no western confederacy. We may have to ask for our money back," he said.

"I know Bart Mason. I'll talk to him. You'll get the best goddamn guns available. I guarantee it," Wood said.

He took them upstairs to show them the *Daily News's* steam-driven presses spewing out an extra reporting that a group of Republicans senators were meeting in New York to find a candidate to replace Lincoln. "They're shooting themselves in both feet," Wood said. "It makes your move in the West look better and better."

Paul and Janet walked down Broadway toward the Astor House in the almost suffocating heat of the early afternoon. Maybe Wood was right. The United States of America seemed on the brink of collapse. Maybe the western confederacy's declaration of independence would be all that was needed to kick out the last props. Maybe there would be no need for any shooting.

"Do you think we should change hotels?" Janet asked.

"Mason won't bother us," Paul said. "He knows I've got their guns."

"Paul! Paul Stapleton. Am I seeing things?"

The female voice came from a hack, standing in the traffic. Before he turned his head, Paul knew it was his mother. Caroline Stapleton was framed in the hack's open window. She was wearing an expensive green silk bonnet decorated with ostrich feathers. Her beautiful face was delicately rouged, her mascaraed eyes wide with astonishment.

"Mother," Paul said. "What a nice surprise."

Caroline paid the driver and descended from the hack. She was wearing a black plush pelisse and a green silk dress with a lingerie collar. She embraced Paul without so much as glancing at Janet. "What brings you here?" she asked, stepping back. "Why didn't you tell me you were coming? Who is this?"

"Janet Todd, Mother. She lives in Kentucky, just across the river from Keyport," Paul said. "She's visiting friends here in the city. I'm here to see a doctor about my Gettysburg wound. I've been having terrible headaches. I didn't mention them in my letters—I didn't want to worry you."

"How dreadful," Caroline said, her white-gloved hand gliding down the side of his face in a gesture that was both maternal and possessive. "I'm so glad to meet Miss Todd." She gave Janet a conspiratorial smile. "Paul mentioned you in one of his letters."

"Favorably, I hope," Janet said.

"He said he was in love with you," Caroline replied. "Are you still, Paul dear?"

Some young men would have been flustered. But Paul was used to his mother's directness. "I only mentioned I had hopes, Mother. Miss Todd remains as elusive as I gather you were at her age."

"I'm so *pleased*," Caroline said. "I don't think any woman should simply *succumb* to these arrogant males. Can we go someplace for a lemonade or some iced tea? According to the newspapers, this August sun can kill old ladies."

In ten minutes they were in the relatively cool Rotunda Bar of the Astor House, sipping iced tea. Caroline confessed that she was in New York to see a doctor too. When Paul asked why, she dismissed the question with a wave. "It's nothing immediately fatal. Who is this head doctor you're seeing?"

"To be completely honest, Mother, I'm here on secret service business. I can't tell you a word about it until after you read it in the newspapers."

Caroline turned to Janet with another conspiratorial smile. "My youngest son has grown up. Are you part of this secret business, Miss Todd?"

"As a matter of fact, I am," Janet said.

"How fascinating. How *thrilling*," Caroline said. There was the tiniest edge of mockery in her tone. She seemed to be suggesting that she had a very good idea what their real business might be. Or at least had no difficulty imagining it.

"I don't want to know a thing about it. If I've learned anything as a parent, it's the necessity to let each generation pursue its own version of happiness. I can only tell you this, Miss Todd. Of my three sons, Paul's the one who's never disappointed me."

Sitting between two women who assumed they controlled him, Paul sardonically contemplated his fate. He decided he was glad he had become a soldier. No matter how doomed he was to be overpowered by these formidable creatures, a barracks, a battlefield still guaranteed him a reasonable amount of independence.

"What do you think of the political situation?" Janet asked. "Paul's told me there are few people in the country with better judgment—"

"I'm retired from politics, Miss Todd. A mere bystander. But I find it hard to see how Mr. Lincoln will be reelected. Does it look that way in Kentucky?"

"Decidedly," Janet said.

In the front of the bar a pretty brunette began playing

an upright piano and singing "Weeping Sad and Lonely, or When This Cruel War Is Over."

"The sheet music of that song has sold a million copies," Caroline said. "It gives you an idea what people are thinking."

"It's very popular in Indiana," Paul said.

"And Kentucky," Janet said.

"I was disgusted by this war from the start," Caroline said. "Its effect on New York has only confirmed my original intuition. It's created what they call 'The Shoddy Aristocracy.' Thousands of people have gotten so rich they don't know what to do with their money. Women are powdering their hair in gold dust and silver dust. The men spend enough on a single dinner with their mistresses at Delmonico's to feed a soldier and his family for a year."

"It makes you wonder if the Republicans started it with money in mind," Janet said. "If they were real patriots, they would have trusted the essential goodness of the American people to solve the problem of slavery. Eventually I'm sure the South would have found a way to free the blacks in gradual steps, so people didn't feel threatened by a race war."

"My sentiments *exactly,*" Caroline Stapleton said.

Caroline Stapleton smiled at Paul in that elusive, somehow mocking way. "I see you've found a woman in my image, Paul. I'm flattered. Can I lure you both to New Jersey for a few days?"

"I'm afraid we don't have time. The situation in Indiana is very tense. They want me back as soon as possible," Paul said.

Caroline's eyes told Paul she understood—and approved—what was happening between him and Janet. Would she also approve the western confederacy? Paul was almost certain the answer would be yes. Encountering her in this way seemed to validate the choice he had made in the boxcar.

"I have a train to catch," Caroline said. She kissed Paul on the lips. "Write and tell me *everything* as soon as you feel free to do it."

She bussed Janet on the cheek and hurried out of the bar.

"I like her *tremendously*," Janet said.

"I'm not surprised," Paul said wryly. "You have a lot in common."

"What do you mean?"

"She has the soul of an adventuress. But she married a rich Democrat and became respectable."

Janet's lips curled into a pleased but impudent smile.

As they strolled into the Astor House lobby, Bart Mason pushed through the hotel's brass front doors. With him was his second Irish partner—the one who had not gone to Jersey City with them. Mason waved to them and they sat down on an overstuffed sofa. There was a bluish bruise on Mason's right cheek. The Irishman remained standing, glowering at Paul.

"I've found some first-class guns. They'll cost you a lot more money," Mason said.

"What kind?" Paul asked.

"Spencers."

"Let's go look at them," Paul said.

In three minutes they were in a hack, riding toward the East River docks. "I hope I didn't hurt your Irish friend too badly," Paul said.

"You broke his nose. He brought it on himself. I didn't tell him to pull that gun."

Remembering Mason's threats, Paul thought this was rather far from the truth. Perhaps Mason was just trying to cover himself with the Irishman's friend. Either way Paul was glad he had two pistols inside his coat.

In a half hour they were in a warehouse on New York's East River—a hot dim cavernous place. On an upper floor were more stacks of boxes, ten times higher than those in the railroad car. A man about Mason's age, of no distinguishable ancestry, opened a box.

A glance told Paul the guns were Spencer repeating rifles—longer-barreled versions of the carbines he had obtained for his black troopers in Keyport. They had the same linseed-oiled wood stocks, case-hardened frames, locks and hammers in mottled colors and rust-blued barrels. The small work was brightly polished and heat-blued. On the frame was stamped: SPENCER REPEATING RIFLE CO. BOSTON, MASS.

Paul peered down the barrels of a half-dozen guns. They had the standard three-groove rifling. He pulled the triggers to check the firing mechanisms, inspected the seven-bullet magazine. They were in perfect condition.

"They're direct from the factory," Mason said. "They were going for export. The federal idiots in Washington are still buying mostly Springfields."

"This is the right stuff," Paul told Janet. "They fire seven shots a minute. A regiment armed with these things can take on a whole division armed with single-shot Springfields. You have to load them down the muzzle. With these, you just slap seven bullets into the magazine."

"Wonderful," Janet said.

"How soon can you get them to us?" Paul asked Mason.

"I'll have them in Indiana in a week. From there you'll have to take charge of them."

"What city will you send them to?" Janet asked.

"It depends on which railroad we can bribe. Probably Evansville," Mason said.

"You've got thirty thousand?" Paul asked.

Mason shook his head. "Fifteen thousand. But they're worth thirty thousand muzzle loaders."

"How much?"

"Four hundred thousand."

"It's a deal," Paul said. He took the wad of $500 greenbacks out of his money belt and counted 400 of them into Mason's hands. "There's two hundred thousand. You'll get the balance in a few days," he said.

For a moment the Englishman's eyes smoldered. Would he have ordered his Irish henchman to shoot yesterday if he had known Paul had the money on his body? It no longer mattered. They had found the right guns for the Sons of Liberty. Were they too part of his fate? It looked that way.

Janet picked up one of the guns. "You must teach me how to use this," she said to Paul.

"Never," Paul said.

"General Burbridge isn't going to throw me into a stinking jail if he catches me," Janet said. "I want to put up a fight."

"It looks like you've got a woman warrior on your hands, Major," Bart Mason said.

"Our motto is victory or death," Janet said.

Was she telling Paul that he was in love with an adventuress who was determined to invade all parts of his male world—including the battlefield? This was neither the time nor the place to argue about it. But Paul silently vowed to make sure Janet never got near enemy gunfire. From now on, he was in command of their perilous partnership.

Stop kidding yourself, Paulie, whispered his Gettysburg wound.

THIRTY

FIASCO. THE WORD HUMMED THROUGH Henry Gentry's head like a swarm of Confederate minié balls. Behind him, the beaten Army of Kentucky plodded through the heat. Half the wounded had died, mostly for want of water on the torturous descent from the mountains.

Just ahead on his big bay horse, Major General Stephen Burbridge slumped in his saddle down, a veritable condensation of gloom. Knowing how much he was hated by nine out of ten Kentuckians, he could easily imagine the derision that would be flung at him in the newspapers, the laughs that would be enjoyed behind his back for the disaster at Saltville.

In Louisville, they found Burbridge's headquarters in turmoil. Confederate guerrillas had burned a steamboat at the docks. Guards had captured two men running away as the boat caught fire. In a valise were a half-dozen hand grenades that exploded and burned furiously, resisting all attempts to douse them. Burbridge ordered the two incendiaries shot immediately.

The general wondered if anyone could tell him what these flaming grenades contained. "It's Greek fire," Gentry said. "The Sons of Liberty have been talking about it as a secret weapon."

"Why have *you* kept this a secret?" Burbridge asked.

"I sent a report on it to Washington," Gentry said. "I thought they'd warn you about it."

"They don't give Kentucky ten seconds of thought in Washington," Burbridge raged. "Lincoln doesn't want to know the kind of war we're fighting here. Surrounded by traitors and guerrillas and secret agents."

Gentry let General Burbridge stew in his self-pity for a few hours, then returned to his headquarters. Burbridge was at his desk, dictating a report on Saltville to one of his aides. He let Gentry wait until he finished a completely imaginary account of the battle, in which he estimated Adam Jameson's force at eight thousand men, equipped with heavy cannon. He was practically daring Gentry to send Lincoln an accurate version.

"General," Gentry said, when they were alone. "I know you don't want to see or hear from me again. But there's a favor I'd like to ask."

"A favor?" Burbridge growled incredulously.

"I'd like you to put Adam Jameson's brother, Robin, at the head of the list for the draft in Daviess County. If certain things transpire as I think they might, I'd like you to take him off the list when I send you a two-word telegram: 'All's well.' Can you arrange that? I presume you have some influence with the draft commissioners."

"There isn't anyone or anything in this miserable state that I don't have influence with," Burbridge said. "What's supposed to happen? Will your 'all's well' mean anything? Or will it be a repetition of your brilliant idea for an attack on Saltville?"

"We can only hope for the best, General," Gentry replied.

"And fear the worst, with fools like you around," Burbridge said.

With those warm words, the director of federal intelligence for southern Indiana and the military commander of Kentucky parted. The next day Gentry was back in Keyport. He walked from the ferry to his house through the blazing noon heat. At the door the first person he saw was Dorothy Schreiber. "How is Lucy?" he asked.

"Come up and see for yourself," Dorothy said.

Upstairs in Major Stapleton's former bedroom, Lucy

was sitting in a chair, wearing a blue robe that Gentry thought he had last seen on Dorothy. The ex–slave girl seemed thin and sickly but her smile was bright. In her lap was a book. She was painfully moving her finger from word to word, trying to sound out each one.

"Lucy's learning to read," Dorothy said. "I'm having such fun teaching her. I never thought teaching could be so enjoyable. I've always hated school."

"Have you gotten a letter from Moses Washington?" Gentry asked Lucy.

She held up three fingers.

"Three! That's even better news," Gentry said. He gave her an exaggerated report of Washington's heroism in the battle. "He was at the head of the attack. He's a brave man."

Lucy glowed. "He says he loves me. That's the best news I've heard in my whole miserable life."

"Eins, zwei, drei, vier!" The stentorian voice drifted in the open bedroom window.

"What's that?" Gentry asked.

"General Carrington heard about the casualties at Saltville," Dorothy said. "He's sent us a hundred Germans to replace the nig—I mean the colored troopers."

"You heard about Captain Otis too?"

"Yes," Dorothy said. "Did he run away again?"

"No. He died at the head of his men," Gentry said.

"Eins, zwei, drei, vier!" roared the German voice.

"They're goin' to be the best soldiers in the world," Dorothy said. "They drill all the time. Every day at least one of them falls over from sunstroke."

"Have you heard from your father?" Gentry asked.

"Yes. He's stayin' in Tennessee, thank goodness. They're not goin' to join Sherman in Georgia. Maybe they think Lincoln's Own has had enough hard fightin'."

"I would certainly agree with that idea," Gentry said.

"I wrote him a letter. I told him about Lucy. I told him I was glad he was fightin' to free the slaves. It's the first time I've been able to say anything good about him bein' in the army. Momma hated it so much. I hope she won't feel bad if she hears about it in heaven."

"I don't think she will, Dorothy," Gentry said. "That letter will mean a lot to your father." Dorothy had matured amazingly in the ten days Gentry was away on the expedition to Saltville.

In the front parlor, he found his mother reading a copy of the *Keyport Record.* "This report of the battle of Saltville convinces me all over again that your friend Lincoln is an idiot," she said.

Gentry glanced at the story. "COLORED TROOPS ROUTED" was the headline. There was not a word about the murder of the wounded blacks. His old friend Andy Conway was continuing the great tradition of the Democratic Party, lying to the American people at every opportunity.

"The Africans weren't routed. They were slaughtered. Thanks to the stupidity of General Burbridge."

"When are you going to get that little nigger out of Major Stapleton's bedroom?"

Gentry chose to ignore the question. "Have you heard from Major Stapleton?"

"Not a word. How long was his leave?"

"I didn't set a number. His mother was quite ill."

Down in his cellar office, Gentry pondered the calendar. Today was August 5. Sometime between now and November, when the voters would go to the polls to decide Lincoln's and the country's fate, Adam Jameson and his cavalrymen would head for Kentucky and the Sons of Liberty would rise. Unless he knew the exact date, he would be helpless to prevent it.

Roads could not be patrolled indefinitely to challenge Jameson's invasion. There were too many possible routes. They did not have the manpower to cover them all. If he arrested Gabriel Todd and the others before they struck, he would have no evidence of an act of treason and they could only be held by ignoring habeus corpus à la General Carrington. Gentry had spent a good year damning Carrington in his letters to Lincoln. He could not change his mind at this late date and adopt the general's deplorable tactics.

Gentry sat there, sipping bourbon, thinking of Amelia Conway Jameson in her bedroom at Rose Hill, fingering the notice that Robin Jameson was subject to an immediate draft into the Union Army. He imagined her pondering one more plea to her snarling husband and winced at what might happen during that interview, remembering the time he had seen Amelia in Keyport with bruises on her face. With his jaw wired shut Rogers Jameson would be even more likely to consider his fists the best available answer.

Could he bear the thought of another bruise on Amelia's cheek? With the help of a steady supply of bourbon, he would try. Amelia was his one hope now. Gentry was sure Major Paul Stapleton was gone beyond recall. Ten days in hotels with Janet Todd would make him a confederate in every possible meaning of that word.

Gentry grieved for Paul. There were so many young men like him, torn between the atavistic pull of the Democratic Party and the Emancipation Proclamation. Lincoln's switch from a war to save the Union to a crusade to abolish slavery would be debated by historians for generations. If the South won, it would be described as a cynical trick that failed. If the North won, it would become a brilliant stroke that drove the South from the moral high ground the Confederates possessed as defenders of their invaded country.

Neither would be true, of course. Only Gentry and a few others knew the real author of that transforming proclamation: God. Gentry tried to think about the word, the idea, and failed. Lincoln's new theology bewildered him. God was in charge of this cataclysm?

What kind of a God slaughtered his followers on both sides of the battle line with such seeming indifference? Yet here was Abe Lincoln, the man whose soul exceeded in range and capacity any that Gentry had ever seen, testifying that God had guided him and America in this completely unexpected direction.

If, as Jesus said, God was love, it was a very terrible brand of that commodity. In the name of God's war, Gentry was forcing the only woman he loved to choose between her sons, to betray one son and her husband— to covertly confess to a man she would henceforth loathe that she had been living a lie, she had made a stupid mistake when she left Henry Gentry keening laments into the Ohio River's mists and married Rogers Jameson.

Amelia was southern, Democratic, to the core of her soul. She could only see her choice as something inflicted on her by Gentry's arrogant possibly diabolical friend Lincoln, for whom her erstwhile lover Gentry was only too happy to play smirking surrogate.

Henry Gentry gulped his bourbon. He wished he could pray to someone for forgiveness. But he had no hope or faith in such a possibility. Since Harvard, he had never been a believer in much of anything beyond Ralph Waldo Emerson's careless God, Brahma, the blind slayer of the evil and the good.

We're doing it the hard way, Abe.

THIRTY-ONE

PAUL STAPLETON STOOD BESIDE JANET Todd on the deck of the small paddle wheeler as it approached Hopemont. The mansion's chimneys rose above the trees like dumb sentinels. Along the shore, the Ohio River was still a procession of sandbars and puddles. Colonel Todd had laid down a floating walkway of planks on barrels to enable passengers to debark from the channel. The drought continued; the deck was so hot you could feel it through the soles of your shoes.

"I wish I could go ashore with you. But I'd better report to Colonel Gentry. I'm still in the Union Army, you know," he said.

She kissed him on the lips. "Come over as soon as possible," she said. "There's a great deal to discuss."

Janet no longer even considered the possibility of failure. The Spencer repeating rifles that were rumbling toward Indiana in anonymous boxcars guaranteed the birth of the western confederacy. Paul had to admit she might be right. Even in the hands of amateurs, Spencers were formidable weapons. The Confederates called the Spencer "the horizontal shot tower." They had learned never to charge a regiment equipped with Spencers.

Fifteen thousand men with Spencers would easily demolish the second-rate federal troops in Indiana and the third-rate state militia, all of whom still used muzzle-loading single-shot Springfields, thanks to the colossal stupidity of the U.S. Army's ordnance department. It would be their just desserts if the war was ended by Rebels with guns that every Union soldier should have been using by now. It was of a piece with the way the war had been fought. The ugly carnage of The Crater was like a final exclamation point in Paul's mind, proving every negative he had ever thought about Northern generalship.

Paul carried Janet's bags along the floating walkway to the Hopemont dock. One of the Todd slaves, a boy of about thirteen, greeted them and followed Janet up the hill to the house with the luggage. On the rear second-floor porch, Colonel Todd waved to him. Paul waved back. Janet would soon be telling him the story of Major Stapleton's heroism in New York.

Why didn't he feel like a hero? Because he was a traitor? No, he rejected that idea. It had something to do with General Lee's concept of honor as a commitment from which a man never wavered. His love for Janet had become a new kind of honor—but part of his soul still longed for the older simpler ideal. Maybe General Lee had similar conflicts. The imperatives of his heart's devotion to Virginia had sundered his oath of loyalty to the United States of America.

Two miles down the river on the Indiana side, Paul debarked at the Keyport town landing. He paid a boy wearing a wide straw hat twenty-five cents to walk two miles to the Gentry house and ask the colonel to send a buggy. Paul retreated from the ferocious sun to the comparatively cool interior of Kingsley's Saloon, on the main street. There he found Andrew Conway, editor of the *Keyport Record,* nursing a tall ice-filled glass.

"What's in that thing?" Paul asked.

"Gin and bitters."

Paul told the bartender to bring him one.

"You've been east, I hear," Conway said.

"My mother was ill."

"Better, I hope."

"Much."

"What's New Jersey saying about the war?"

"They're as sick of it as they are in Indiana."

"Someone told me they saw you on the street in Cincinnati with Janet Todd."

"They must have bad eyes or hallucinations from the heat."

Conway stroked his drooping black mustache. "It's all right. I've been told certain things and figured out one or two others. But I don't think you're free and clear. Not if Adam Jameson gets in your vicinity. I'd still devote an hour or two a day to pistol practice."

"I was the best shot in my class at the military academy."

"Then maybe you got nothin' to worry about."

Conway looked around the barroom. There was only one other drinker, an old man at a table in the back, mumbling to himself. The bartender was serving him another stein of beer. "Poor Smitty hasn't been sober since his boy was killed at Chickamauga," Conway said. "Do you think the Sons of Liberty will succeed?"

"If the men in the ranks are led with determination, they have a chance."

"Have they given you a command?"

"Not yet. I expect to hear from them in a day or two."

Conway raised his glass. "I've got an edition set in type proclaiming the rise of the new confederacy."

"I can't wait to read it."

"Paul?" It was Colonel Gentry in person, come to transport him to The Grange.

"I thought you'd send someone—"

Gentry waved aside his apology. "I needed some fresh air. If ninety-eight degrees leaves anything fresh. How are you, Andy?"

"Just fine, Henry. I've been wanting to ask you what part you played in the battle of Saltville."

"Dismayed spectator."

"According to some things I hear, it was your idea."

"One-armed men don't go looking for battles."

"I wouldn't say that. Look at General Hood. I hear he's given Sherman another licking in front of Atlanta."

"That sounds about as accurate as your story on the battle of Saltville."

"I used only eyewitness accounts, Henry."

"Why didn't you call me? I would have told you what happened to the blacks."

"I don't publish Republican lies, Henry."

Outside, Paul threw his bag in the netting at the back of the gig and climbed in beside Gentry. "So you were at the battle of Saltville," he said as they headed down the river road. Waves of heat shimmered in the air ahead of them.

"Yes."

"Was it your idea?"

"I tried to seize the initiative," Gentry said. "Someone told me that's how West Pointers are taught to fight battles."

Paul smiled briefly. "Sometimes it works. Sometimes you get a bloody nose."

"We got a very bloody nose."

"You used Negro troops?" Paul said.

"Yes."

"How did our boys perform? I read that Otis was killed."

"They performed well. But it didn't do them any good. General Burbridge fought an idiotic battle. Bodies against riflemen in fortifications. It was a little Fredericksburg."

"They—took some losses?"

"They were wiped out, almost to a man. Only Washington and a half-dozen others survived. They're all in the hospital."

"How could that be? Didn't they do anything for the wounded?"

Paul knew there were four men wounded to every

man killed in almost any battle. This gruesome arithmetic had become an axiom for any veteran of the war.

"The Confederates shot the wounded."

"They—shot—the—wounded?" Paul said.

"Only the blacks. They shot them. I saw it. I rescued Washington when I rode up to protest it."

"They shot the wounded," Paul said.

"Yes."

They shot my men. That was what Paul wanted to say. *They shot my men.* The men he had trained to be soldiers. The men he had taught how to shoot, how to ride, how to wield a saber. *They shot my men.* How could he fight for people who did something like that? He had heard reports of a massacre of black troops in the Confederate attack on Fort Pillow, Tennessee, last year. But he had suspected it was exaggerated by civilians who did not know the wild things soldiers did when they stormed a fort.

But no one had stormed anything at Saltville. As Gentry described it, the Union troops never got near enough to fire more than a few random shots. They had been cut to pieces by well-aimed volleys before they came within two hundred yards of the fort.

"How was your trip?" Gentry asked.

"Uneventful."

"Completely uneventful? You have nothing to report?"

"Nothing."

The ferocious heat combined with the appalling news of Saltville to all but shut down Paul's brain. He could only stumble forward like an infantryman in an attack that had failed, waiting for the bullet that would finish him.

"Did you buy guns? There's a rumor about guns arriving any day."

"I'm sorry, Colonel. I don't feel free to continue this conversation."

The gig rattled and swayed along the rutted road as Gentry absorbed the meaning of Paul's refusal. "I hope you won't mind sleeping on the third floor. I've given your room to Janet Todd's Lucy. She's not strong enough to climb stairs—"

"What's she doing in your house?"

Gentry told him how Lucy had arrived on his doorstep, her body a mass of bleeding welts. "I think they presumed she was going to die. But Walter Yancey outdid himself to save her. He was inspired by my promise of a five-hundred-dollar bonus."

"Who beat her?" Paul asked.

"Gabriel Todd and Rogers Jameson."

"I'm amazed—that Janet Todd let such a thing happen."

"I am, too," Gentry said.

"Why did they do it? And then send her to you?"

"I suspect it was a kind of bravado. Lucy was spying for me. They found out about it somehow. They wanted to let me know they didn't care what I found out. They had plans that were immune to my prying."

"Plans," Paul said dazedly.

The gig rattled on. Gentry stared straight ahead at the sunbaked road. "I don't think Lincoln can survive it."

"What will he do?"

"Quit, I imagine. He's written to me about doing it more than once. The job's beyond his capacity. Beyond any man's capacity, I suspect."

"What's happened to Private Garner?"

"Lincoln pardoned him. He's returned to his regiment, where he'll probably desert again if he gets a chance."

Soon they were jogging up the long curving drive of the Gentry mansion, beneath the shade of the stately beech trees. In the house, Paul lugged his bag up to his new room on the third floor. Under the sunbaked roof, it was an inferno.

On the bed were several letters. One was from his mother, written a week before their meeting in New York. It was full of her usual equivocations about the war. She predicted Lincoln's defeat in November if the Union Army lost another battle. She described how unhappy his brother Jonathan's two sons were; their father had not been home in a year. His wife's health was deteriorating from the perpetual dread of seeing his name on a casualty list.

Wormwood, Paul thought. That was all Jonathan could expect from Caroline Kemble Stapleton for the rest of his days. He had refused to listen to her counsel of neutrality in 1861. He had insisted on lending the Stapleton name to Lincoln's war.

Paul ripped open a letter from Major General George Armstrong Custer. It described his victory over their classmate, Confederate Brigadier General Tom Rosser in the Shenandoah Valley. *I captured Tom's wagon train with his full dress uniform in it. Naturally anything cut for that behemoth didn't fit me. I sent him a note under a flag of truce, telling him to make the tails shorter next time.* Custer closed urging Paul to join him immediately, if he felt up to it: *I need a fighting brigadier and I can't imagine a better one than you.*

The third letter was from his brother, Jonathan, a scribbled note written in the trenches before Richmond. He gave him some grisly additional details about The Crater, embellished by a ferocious denunciation of General Ambrose Burnside. General Stapleton raged against the folly of keeping such a discredited birdbrain in a command position because he had good political connections. He ended with the hope that all was quiet in Indiana.

Suddenly Paul was spurring his horse into Antietam Creek to show the infantrymen how shallow it was. General Reynolds had sent him forward to find out why the Union attack was stalled. He found General Burnside was destroying regiment after regiment, trying to cross a narrow bridge. Riding back, Paul encountered his brother leading his division forward. Paul had urged him to avoid the bridge and cross the creek downstream.

Seconds after Paul plunged into the creek, a Confederate bullet smashed him out of the saddle. "Paul!" he heard Jonathan cry as hundreds of guns fired in unison from both sides of the creek with an ear-shattering crash that sounded like the entire world had exploded.

Hands seized him. Brave men, ignoring the bullets. One toppled with a cry and slid beneath the creek's now muddy surface. They labored up the bank while Jonathan roared for a stretcher. Paul's body felt like a sack of oats. He did not seem to have arms or legs. The sun whirled in the vibrating sky to be suddenly replaced by Jonathan's long lean visage. It was streaked with tears. "Paul, Paul," he said.

His big hand touched Paul's face. A gesture of love. It was astonishing to discover Jonathan loved him. Growing up Paul had half feared him. He was ten years older, a man of twenty when Paul was still a boy. Jonathan's love had sent him to Indiana in a forlorn attempt to get him out of harm's way. The love was as real as Jonathan's guilt for his colossal misjudgment of how long the war would last. Did he owe something to that guilt-ridden love?

There was a postscript to Jonathan's letter:

I saw this poem by my favorite writer, Herman Melville, in a newspaper. It was inspired by that Michigan regiment who goes into battle with a live eagle chained to their standard.

THE EAGLE OF THE BLUE

Aloft he guards the starry folds
Who is the brother of the star
The bird whose joy is in the wind
Exulteth in the war

> *Amid the scream of shells, his scream*
>   *Runs shrilling; and the glare*
> *Of eyes that brave the blinding sun*
>   *The volleyed flame can bear.*
>
> *The pride of quenchless strength is his*
>   *Strength, which though chained, avails*
> *The very rebel looks and thrills—*
>   *The anchored emblem hails.*
>
> *Though scarred in many a furious fray,*
>   *No deadly hurt he knew;*
> *Well may we think his years are charmed*
>   *The eagle of the blue.*

Paul sat down on the bed and read the poem again. He dimly realized he should get out of this oven of a bedroom. He was being roasted alive. Sweat ran down his forehead into his burning eyes. He rubbed his streaming neck.

They shot your men, whispered his Gettysburg wound. What did his Antietam wound, his emancipation wound, say to that? Nothing, apparently. What did Jeff Tyler say? Also nothing. What could Jeff say?

Paul stripped off his sweat-soaked civilian clothes and put on his uniform. Henry Gentry's servants had washed and ironed it. There was a crispness, a freshness to the blue cloth that was momentarily pleasurable.

Did Janet and her father expect him to wear this uniform when he returned to Hopemont to take command of a Sons of Liberty regiment or brigade? He suspected they would like that very much. But it was impossible.

He was trapped between impossibilities. He had sworn an oath to join the Sons of Liberty, he had pledged his love to Janet Todd. He could not escape those obligations. But they did not include this uniform.

He would not dishonor the uniform in which he had trained his dead troopers.

Maybe this proves something, whispered a voice. It was not Jeff Tyler. It was Paul's Gettysburg wound, sardonic as usual. Suddenly Paul felt death all around him in the hot silent bedroom. How it would come he had no idea. But he saw it was inevitable. It was his only exit from this labyrinth of impossibilities.

$\underset{\text{\large\textbackslash\textbar\textbar\textbar/}}{}$

THIRTY-TWO

THE FIRST THING JANET TODD noticed inside Hopemont was the absence of the servants. The place was like a haunted castle. The curtains were drawn against the August sun. In room after dim room there was not a sign of a familiar black face. Upstairs she found her mother in bed. Letitia gazed at Janet with only minimal recognition on her haggard face. Her hair was uncombed. The room smelled of urine and feces.

It was eleven o'clock in the morning. Normally, Letitia would be bathed and dressed and sitting in her chair. "Mother—what's wrong? What's happening?" Janet asked.

"Nobody comes when I call," she said. "I've been calling you and your father and Sally. Nobody comes."

Sally was Letitia's personal maid. "Why? What's going on?"

"Ever since your father whipped Lucy—"

She found her father in the gazebo in the garden, almost too drunk to speak a coherent sentence. She asked for Lucy. His face darkened. "Whipped the spyin' black bitch! Whipped'er till there was 'n' inch of blood on th'barn floor and shipped'er t'Gentry. Rogers' idea. He took her over th'river. Tole Gentry we were ready to fight any time he was, see?"

"Father I asked you not to whip her."

"Not whip'er? Janet darlin', women don' know how t'fight war. War is blood. Soldier doesn' l'people insult'm. Fights back—"

"I asked you not to do it!"

"Had to—Rog Jameson said had to. He wanted to kil-l'r. I said no. Let'r die on Gentry's hands."

"Why are you sitting here drunk while Momma is up in her room, neglected? She looks half-starved! Is this how we're going to win the war?" She grabbed the half-open bottle of bourbon and smashed it against a tree.

Do you know what I've been doing, Father? I've been letting Paul Stapleton have me. Night after night after night. I've been selling myself for your stupid cause, ruining my reputation and my self-respect.

She did not say it. She could not inflict another wound on this man. Besides, she had not lost her self-respect. She was not a typical woman. She was an exceptional woman. An *adventuress.* That justified everything she had done, from bedding Paul Stapleton to plotting to overthrow Lincoln's government. Maybe even whipping Lucy. She had known Gabriel Todd was going to whip Lucy. The most she tried to do was limit the number of stripes.

Janet strode down to the slave cabins and found a half-dozen women sitting around, staring disconsolately into space. Beyond them lay empty fields.

"What's going on? Where are the hands?" she asked.

"Run away," Milly, one of the housemaids, said.

"Where's Lillibet?" Janet asked.

They gestured to the open door of her cabin.

"Where's Sally?"

They gestured in the same direction.

She plunged into the hot cabin. Lillibet lay in bed, looking like a black mirror image of Letitia Todd in the main house. Her face was wasted, her eyes dazed with pain or woe or both. Sally sat beside her, bathing her forehead. She jumped up, trembling, when she saw Janet.

"What are you doing here while Mistress is up in her bed with nothing to eat or drink and her night stuff not emptied for the last week, from the smell of it?" Janet said.

"Momma's been sick," Sally mumbled. "She been sick since Master whipped Lucy so bad."

"She deserved it!" Janet said. "Do you know what she did? She spied on me. She took money to spy on me!"

It was obvious Sally did not know what *spy* meant. She stared at Janet as if she were insane. "It tore up everybody, Miss Janet. We couldn't understand it. We still don' understand it. Everybody went sorta crazy. The hands all run away. No one lef' but us poor women. Master—your daddy—got drunk and stayed that way. What's happenin' to us? We was the happiest niggers in Kentucky a lil while ago."

Something seemed to collapse inside Janet. She could not retain her rage. It crashed through her body and lay in ruins around her. "Terrible things are happening to all of us," she said. "Go up to the house and take care of Mistress. I'll stay with Lillibet."

She sat down beside Lillibet and dipped the cloth in the dish of water beside the bed. She bathed the mournful black face. "Lillibet, I'm so sorry. I asked Daddy not to whip her. But the war—the war has us all half-crazy."

"Is Lucy dead and gone?"

"I don't know."

"She looked mighty near dead when Jameson took her away in his wagon. He throw her in the river?"

"No! He took her across the river to Colonel Gentry's house."

"Why?"

"I don't know," she lied. "Maybe they thought he'd take care of her. She's free now, one way or another."

"If she ain't dead."

"I'll find out."

By nightfall she had restored a semblance of order to the house and the slave quarters. Her mother had been bathed and dressed in clean clothes and her bed changed. Sally prepared a halfway decent dinner of fried chicken and yams for them. Janet had no idea what to do about the runaways. Neither did her father.

Gabriel Todd had sobered up enough to discuss her trip. She did not tell him about the desperation in besieged Richmond, the sordid deal with Fernando Wood, the nearly fatal negotiations with the gunrunners. She cast a glow of hope over everything, especially the Spencer repeating rifles. After dinner he sent for Rogers Jameson, who galloped to meet them with only one question on his lips: "Did you get any guns?"

"Fifteen thousand Spencer repeating rifles."

Rogers gave her an exultant bear hug worthy of his son Adam. His broken jaw had mended. He was his voluble self once more. He said he had 3,000 men ready to cross the Ohio the moment Adam and his men appeared. They had bribed the ferryboat captains at Owensboro. They had made a trial run last night. They could get everyone across in four hours. He wanted to know when the Spencers would arrive, what date Richmond had set for the insurrection.

When Janet told him Jefferson Davis had been immovable about keeping August 29 for the date, Jameson smashed both his huge fists on their dining room table. "I wish we didn't have to depend on that broken-down old fool. You should hear what Adam says about him!" he roared.

"He has his reasons. Everything has to be coordinated with the men in Chicago and elsewhere."

"Where's your West Point hero?" Jameson asked. "Did he decide to stay in New Jersey with his momma?"

"He's in Keyport. He had to report to Colonel Gentry. I wish you'd think better of him. Without Paul we would have gotten old worthless muskets from Mexico."

"Get him over here. We've got this army about organized," Jameson said. "We want to fit him in."

The next morning Janet sent Sally across the river with a note to Paul, urging him to come as soon as possible. Sally returned with a scrawled promise that he would be on the noon ferry.

Something is wrong, Janet thought the moment she saw Paul standing at the prow of the ferry as it approached the landing. For one thing, he was not wearing his uniform. Had he quit the Union Army? She wanted him to appear before Rogers Jameson's Sons of Liberty brigade in that uniform. It would have an electrifying impact on the men in the ranks. She had never mentioned it to him. She had assumed he understood the value of such a gesture.

The grave expression on his face was wrong too. It was not the look of a man who was about to be welcomed back to a daring conspiracy by the woman he loved. She decided there was only one thing to do. She kissed him boldly on the mouth as he walked up to her. At least a dozen heads turned. Everyone on the ferry landing knew Janet Todd. But she did not care. She had stopped caring about everything except victory.

On the way to Hopemont in the buggy, Janet asked him about Lucy. "Is she all right? I asked my father not to whip her but—"

"But he did," Paul said. "She's still a mass of welts. Her arms are swollen. She can't walk very well. Dr. Yancey thinks they damaged some nerves in her back."

"How awful."

"You can say that again," Paul replied.

Janet refused to say it—or think it. "In a way she deserved a beating, don't you think? She was spying on us. She watched us in the Happy Hunting Ground. She was in the bushes. Do you know that?"

"My God," Paul said. She could not tell whether he was admitting she was right or was simply appalled by the ruin of that beautiful memory.

"In spite of that, I honestly tried to prevent her being whipped. But I had to meet you in Cincinnati—"

Paul nodded. They rode on through the suffocating

heat. Thank God the buggy had a top that gave them some protection from the relentless sun. "The slaves got into a state. Most of the field hands ran away."

Paul did not seem to be listening. He stared into the sunbaked distance. They passed neighboring farms where other slaves were working. "If we don't bring off this insurrection, every slave in Kentucky is going to run away. The handwriting is on the wall. Ours were just looking for an excuse," Janet said.

"I heard about the battle of Saltville from Colonel Gentry," Paul said. He spoke in a hurried way, as if he knew he was crudely changing the subject.

"Was it as bad as the newspapers said? For the federals, I mean?"

"Worse. He told me something else. Something I still can't believe."

"What?" Janet asked, feeling, sensing, it was going to be something similar to what Sally had said to her, something that would send things crashing inside her.

"They shot the black wounded. Murdered them in cold blood after the Union Army retreated. They killed all my men from Keyport—except for a handful."

The horse, a big roan named Caster, continued his steady pace down the road. More fields with slaves hoeing and grubbing. A house or two in the distance. Above a distant copse a hawk wheeled slowly. The sky remained mercilessly blue. There was not a cloud anywhere.

"Isn't that—just one more terrible thing—in this awful war?" Janet said.

Paul stared straight ahead. "When I see your friend Adam Jameson, I'm going to ask him for an explanation," he said. "If he doesn't have a good one, I may kill the bastard on the spot."

"I'm sure—absolutely sure—he'll have an explanation."

"I doubt it."

"Paul—calm down. You're not even sure it happened.

You only have Gentry's word for it. You know what a lyin' sneakin' scum he is. Who else but a Lincoln lover would set a slave to spy on his own kin? These people will do anything to get their vile way."

"You may be right about that," Paul said.

"Don't bring this up with my father or Rogers Jameson, please. They won't know how to deal with it."

"I have no intention of mentioning it. I only wanted you to know about it."

Why? she wondered. Did he enjoy tormenting her? No. Paul was remembering the night in New York when she had become an adventuress, when she had married her soul and body to the cause. Now the cause had been ruined for him by the slaughter of those nameless blacks at Saltville. Was that true for her, too?

No. No such obscenity could or would have been committed by a white Kentuckian before the abolitionists created hatred between the blacks and the whites. The Yankees had ignited this murderous rage against the blacks, the innocent source of the South's woes. It only made stopping the war, giving the South a chance to deal with the blacks in an atmosphere of peace and forbearance, all the more essential. Why couldn't Paul see that? Why was he letting this one unworthy act threaten their victory?

If she was wrong, Janet dared God to contradict her. She dared God to prove the South's cause was wrong. She dared him to prove giving herself to Paul was wrong. She was ready to risk her soul as well as her body for *victory*.

At Hopemont, Rogers Jameson was waiting with her father. Gabriel Todd was sober and clear-eyed. Janet wondered if she was responsible for the change. Did she restore his sense of paternity, his hope for a future shaped around her children? Or was Rogers Jameson's crude vitality the explanation?

On Hopemont's broad veranda, they talked about the

guns. Jameson chortled about the damage a regiment of men could do with the seven-shot Spencers. "Them Yankees will dirty their pants, I guarantee you," he said.

Gabriel Todd said the Sons of Liberty had issued commissions to the principal officers. He was a major general in command of the Kentucky troops. Rogers Jameson was a brigadier general in command of the Daviess County troops. They had appointed an overall commander in Indiana, a doctor named William Bowles. He had commanded a regiment in the Mexican War. The army's top commander was the former chief justice of Kentucky, Joshua Bullitt.

"I'm hoping that you'll serve as my chief of staff," Gabriel Todd said to Paul. "That's the best way we can all draw on your training and battle experience. You'll have the rank of colonel."

"I'm honored," Paul said. "I've had some experience on staff. I think I can be of service. Who's your quartermaster? Do you have a chief of artillery? A medical department? We should begin assembling supplies as soon as possible. How much ammunition do you have in reserve?"

"Whoa now!" Rogers Jameson said. "This ain't no West Point operation, Colonel Stapleton. This here's goin' to be a quick campaign. A sort of rampage, you know? Every man's got orders to bring a week's rations with him in his haversack. We 'spect to be in Indianapolis in five days, where we can dine off the federal government. The town's full of warehouses with all the chow an army can eat for a good year."

"They're only shipping five hundred and forty rounds of ammunition per gun," Paul said. "That's not a lot for even a week's campaign."

"We'll capture all the ammo we need in 'Napolis the same way we'll get the grub," Jameson replied. "The town's crammed with everything an army needs. Once we free the Confederate soldiers they got locked up there, our boys can relax. There'll be a trained rebel army in the heart of the state, ready to operate. My boy Adam will have the cavalry."

"What about artillery?"

"We'll get that in 'Napolis too," Jameson said.

"Is this your thinking too, General?" Paul asked.

"Substantially, yes," Gabriel Todd said.

"How many men do you estimate Governor Morton and General Carrington can put in the field?" Paul asked.

"We guess about six thousand," Gabriel Todd said.

"Is this based on observation? Actual knowledge?" Paul asked.

"On the best information we have," Gabriel Todd said.

"They'll have artillery?" Paul asked.

"We'll have Greek fire," Jameson said.

"I don't think much of that as a tactical weapon," Paul said.

"There he goes again with the West Point lingo," Jameson said. "You think people are gonna fight if we can send their houses up in smoke?"

"It might make them fight very hard. You might find Democrats and Republicans from Indianapolis fighting for General Carrington."

"I don't think so. General Todd don't think so. Neither do the other leaders," Jameson said.

"I consider myself overruled," Paul said.

"With them Spencers, our worries are as good as over," Jameson said. "The federals have got a coward for a general. Carrington won't fight. He'll run for cover and his army will follow him."

"You talked of putting thirty to fifty thousand men in the field. Will any of them bring their own guns? We don't have enough Spencers to go around."

"A lot of'm have got guns," Jameson said. "We'll get the rest in 'Napolis."

"What about battlefield exercises?" Paul asked. "Have you maneuvered your brigade as a unit?"

"How can I do that without givin' the game away to every sneakin' federal spy in the county?" Jameson said. "There ain't goin' to be any real opposition. We don't have to worry about maneuvers."

"I'm sure we can give adequate orders depending on the situation," Gabriel Todd said. "The men are in high spirits. They're eager to strike a blow against the Lincoln dictatorship."

"I see we have almost nothing to worry about," Paul said.

He looked at Janet, his face grave. She was back in New York, hearing him tell her the Mexican muskets were worthless. Was he telling her, silently, that her father's and Rogers Jameson's plans were also worthless? No—there was something more subtle in his voice. With an inner tremor, Janet recognized it. Paul did not *care*. He did not care if their plans were worthless. He did not care if the Sons of Liberty won or lost. The bodies of those murdered blacks had become a wall between them. She realized he was here for only one reason: because he still loved her.

"How do you plan to get the Spencers to the men?" Paul asked. "Fifteen thousand rifles are a lot of metal."

"Each regiment'll send wagons to rendezvous points along the river on certain nights," Jameson said. "We'll move 'em from Evansville in flatboats. We can transport two or three thousand a night. By August twentieth we'll have 'em completely distributed."

"You've got the boats and the oarsmen?"

"Yes."

"Aren't there federal gunboats patrolling the river?"

"They haven't been seen since the water went down," Jameson said.

"God is on our side," Janet said.

"I'm more certain of it every day," Gabriel Todd said.

Almost mechanically, her mind still gripped by her insight into Paul's uncaring, Janet noted her father was lying. Gabriel Todd did not believe in God. He was a man with nothing to lose. That was why he did not criticize Rogers Jameson's haphazard plans. He wanted to do something, anything, to defy the raging futility the war had inflicted on him. She wondered if he hoped to die in this rampage—and fling in fate's face a final snarl of defiance.

Janet trembled. Why did she always see so much, understand things it would be better to ignore? Her throat swelled with pity. She would somehow sustain Gabriel Todd—and Paul. Father and lover, she would sustain them both with her adventuress's indomitable heart. Somehow.

THIRTY-THREE

COLONEL HENRY GENTRY PONDERED THE calendar on his desk. It was August 15. General Grant was still stalemated before Richmond. General Sherman was not doing much better before Atlanta. In Sherman's rear, a Confederate cavalryman named Nathan Bedford Forrest was doing fearsome damage in Tennessee, burning railroad bridges, capturing railroad trains loaded with supplies and money, routing a Union force sent to stop him. Guerrillas still rampaged through Kentucky. In retaliation, General Burbridge had executed another twelve captured men.

Still not a word from Amelia Jameson. Was his plan going awry? It was exactly what he deserved, Gentry mused. He was acting like a swine. Perhaps that was another word for intelligence officer. He imagined Amelia, watching the clock hands, the calendar, as time plodded inexorably toward the date when Robin would be drafted: September 1. His stomach twisted with disgust at himself, the war, General Burbridge, General Carrington, President Lincoln.

Every other day, Major Stapleton invented another excuse that took him across the river to Kentucky. Janet Todd was ill. It was her father's birthday. Janet's mother was ill and had taken a great fancy to him. None of these was a very clever lie. But Gentry made no attempt to challenge him. From other informants, such as Luther Sprague, the typesetter at the *Keyport Record,* he knew that they were moving toward the moment of explosion. Sprague had sent him a surreptitiously printed front page of the *Record* proclaiming the birth of the western confederacy.

From one of the Keyport ferry hands he learned that there was a great deal of activity on the Ohio River after dark. The man had been offered twenty dollars a night to pull an oar. He had pleaded a bad back and rushed to Gentry, who paid him twenty-five dollars for the information. Did he know what was in the boats? "Guns," the man said.

Gentry telegraphed the commander of the federal gunboat flotilla in Louisville, asking him why he was not patrolling the river at night. He was told it was too dangerous. The low water created unexpected sandbars and shallows that could only be detected by the naked eye. Charts were next to useless.

Gentry sipped his bourbon and wondered if he should do something. Perhaps advise Burbridge to arrest Rogers Jameson? That would remove Amelia's fear of immediate retaliation. He decided it would be superfluous. Gentry knew why she was unable to act. She was torn between Adam and Robin. Between the ape and the angel. She loved both of them.

Another day passed. The drought, the heat wave, continued. The temperature dropped below ninety-five only for an hour, between dawn and sunrise. Gentry responded to a choleric letter from General Carrington demanding to know if he had anything to do with getting the deserter Robert Garner pardoned. Gentry blamed Lincoln's mercy on Major Stapleton. Gutless coward that he was, Carrington would think twice about attacking the younger brother of a major general.

A hobbling Lucy brought him a letter for Moses Washington. She had written it herself! The handwriting was at about the third-grade level but she had decorated it with a string of hearts—no doubt at Dorothy Schreiber's suggestion. Moses was still in a federal hospital in Louisville, fighting an infection that had developed in his wound. Gentry's mother continued to make nasty remarks about a Negro sleeping on the second floor of her house, just down the hall from her. Gentry continued to ignore her.

At noon on August 16, Dorothy Schreiber called down to Gentry in the cellar, "Colonel, Mrs. Jameson is here! Can she visit you for a moment?"

Gentry lumbered to the foot of the stairs with a candle. "Be careful," he said. "The last step is higher than the others."

Amelia let him take her hand. The touch of her moist palm ignited strange sensations in his body. Not exactly desire. Something closer to longing. That made him certain she was here to tell him once and for all that she despised him.

Amelia declined a drink of water. Arranging her skirts, she wiped her face with a handkerchief. "Now I see why you hide out down here. It's cool."

"And Mother can't negotiate the stairs."

She almost smiled. "Robin's been drafted," she said.

"I—I had no idea. It's done by each state—"

"I begged you to do something for him."

"I tried. But General Burbridge has a hard heart."

Tears trickled down her cheeks. "Henry, I can't do it! I can't betray Adam."

"I understand."

"But you still won't do anything?"

"It's out of my hands, Amelia."

"Pompey came down the other day with a message for Rogers."

"Did he say anything about Saltville?"

"The battle? Only that you got whipped."

"I'm surprised."

"What do you mean?"

"I thought he might have said something about the blacks. What Adam's men did to them."

"What?"

"They shot the wounded. One by one. They must have shot two hundred of them."

Amelia just sat there. In the distance, Gentry heard the German sergeant, Adolf Schultz, drilling his men: "Eins, zwei, drei, vier!" The German had a voice that could be heard in Chicago. Still Amelia sat there. Upstairs, Dorothy Schreiber began playing "Weeping Sad and Lonely, or When this Cruel War Is Over" on the piano. The tinkling notes fell around them like snowflakes. Still Amelia sat there.

Finally she said, "You're lying."

"I wish I were. I saw it, Amelia. I rode up the hill and asked Adam to come out and tell them to stop it. But he ignored me. He said he'd see me in Indiana."

"Adam," she said.

She sat there. A steamboat hooted on the river. Bees droned around a hive under the eaves. Birds chirped in the hedges just outside the cellar door. Once the hedges had been part of a maze his father had constructed for want of something better to do in his middle age. Gentry remembered wandering through the leafy labyrinth with Amelia on his seventeenth birthday. He made her kiss him every time she got lost. Only he knew the way out. Now they were in another labyrinth but he was not at all sure he knew the way out of this one.

"This war is evil. I knew it from the start."

"So did I."

"But you didn't try to stop your friend Lincoln from starting it."

"Like him, I thought it would be over in a month."

She sat there. "I believe I will have a drink of water," she said.

He poured it for her. She sipped it. "What do you want to know?" she asked.

"As much as possible," he said. "Above all—the date."

"What if I don't know it?"

He opened his hand helplessly.

"I don't know it."

He opened his hand again. "Anything will be better than nothing."

"I understand."

Was she trying to bargain with him? Or was she telling the truth? He preferred the latter judgment. Naturally. He was still a fool in love. Gentry's heart swirled with longing for a time forever lost. He ordered himself to say nothing. He sat there, waiting, watching. She was still beautiful. Perhaps only to him. The patina of beauty was visible beneath the lines of care on her face.

"I really don't know," she said.

She left him. He listened to her footsteps mounting the stairs. He went out in the yard through the cellar door and watched Schultz drilling the poor Germans in the heat. A man crumpled to the ground. Two of his friends carried him into the barn. "By the right flank, vorwärts!" roared Schultz. "Eins, zwei, drei, vier!"

Sheriff Monroe Cantwell rode into the yard on a small gray horse. Gentry noticed Democrats preferred small horses. The party of the people. "Henry," Cantwell said. "I just got a report of two deserters at the Murray farm."

"You have work to do, Sergeant," Gentry said.

In a half hour, Schultz and his hundred Germans clattered out of the yard. Gentry went back to his cellar and wrote another letter to Lincoln, reporting his latest information about the Sons of Liberty. He told the president about the guns moving up and down the Ohio at night. He enclosed his copy of the *Keyport Record*'s front page announcing the western confederacy. He recommended detaching 10,000 men from Grant's army. If Lincoln put them on trains, they could be here in two days. Ten thousand veterans would squelch these amateur desperados in a day.

The railroad has revolutionized warfare. Why not

take advantage of our mobility? No. Portentous. He was talking to a man who had been running a war for three years. Lincoln knew all about mobility. The problem was manpower. He remembered what Lincoln had told him a year ago. Desertion alone was costing the Union fifty thousand men a year. Yet it would be worth weakening Grant to stop this explosion before it occurred. The men leading it were not stupid. They knew it did not have to succeed to bring Lincoln down. The mere fact that twenty or thirty thousand men had taken up arms—the Democratic newspapers would swell it to a hundred thousand—would be enough to ruin Lincoln in November.

The thing had to be *suppressed.* Why couldn't Lincoln see that? His tired brain had fallen into a military groove. Victory had become something won with the gun. The man who said he was against appealing from the ballot to the bullet was now relying on the bullet. *Abe, Abe, we're doing it the hard way.*

An hour after the Germans departed, Major Stapleton returned from his latest foray to Kentucky. He was upset to discover there was work to be done in Indiana. "You should have sent for me," he said.

"I didn't know where you were, Major," Gentry replied.

"At the Todds'. You knew that."

"I've had reports of you riding far afield."

"Janet has decided to ride each day for exercise."

"Ah."

The Major galloped off to the Murray farm. Two hours later, one of the Germans rode wildly into the yard. *"Eine grosser Schlacht!"* he shouted. "Many *Feinde!* Many *tod.* Wagons, *bitte! Schnell!"*

Gentry translated: "A big battle! Many enemy! Many dead. Wagons please! Quickly!"

He sent the German galloping to the fields with a message to his farm manager. In a half hour ten of his hands were in the yard. They hitched horses to six wagons and lumbered toward the Murray farm, which was at the far end of the county. Gentry rode with them, after dispatching a messenger to Dr. Yancey. As they approached the farm, a spiral of smoke curled into the blue sky. Major Stapleton galloped down the road to meet them, his face flushed.

"It was another ambush. Much bigger, this time. At least forty men. When Schultz charged them they stood their ground around the farmhouse for a half-dozen volleys. Then they vanished through the corn. It was over by the time I got there."

"How many men did we lose?"

"At least twenty," Stapleton said.

"Did they catch any deserters?"

Stapleton shook his head. "I don't think there were any."

"Who set the Murray house on fire?"

"The Germans. They're angry about their losses."

As Gentry rode into the Murray yard on the lead wagon, a tearful Margaret Murray rushed up to him. She was his age. They had danced together at more than one youthful hoedown. "Henry, they're burning our house! We didn't do anything! The Sons of Liberty came from nowhere and took over the farm—"

Flames were gushing from the second floor windows. It was much too late to save the house. Stout Stephen Murray stood to one side, glaring at him. "Is this the kind of protection you're giving citizens who've tried to stay neutral?" he shouted. He was a Democrat, like his father before him. He had three daughters and no sons. It was interesting, the way people's neutrality or partisanship reflected what they stood to lose in the war.

The dead and wounded were in the dust in front of the Murray barn. Sergeant Schultz dragged a tall thin boy of about seventeen over to Gentry. The boy was groaning and whining with pain. His right leg was drenched in blood. "Do you know this man, Colonel?" Schultz shouted.

Gentry shook his head.

"He says he's a member of a regiment of the Indiana Sons of Liberty! He wants to be treated as a prisoner of war." Schultz's face was streaked with black powder. "What craziness is this? They shoot my poor fellows for no reason." He babbled about getting a doctor for his men.

"There'll be one waiting at my house," Gentry said.

On the ride back Schultz wanted to know where the Sons of Liberty got their guns. "They had repeating rifles. No wonder they shot us to pieces."

"I have no idea," Gentry said. "Do you, Major Stapleton?"

"No," Stapleton said. Gentry thought he sounded uncomfortable, telling that lie.

"They could have bought them in New York and shipped them out here. The country is awash in guns," Gentry said. "The federal government can't keep track of them all."

Yancey worked all afternoon and into the night on the wounded. There were several amputations, including the captured Son of Liberty's shattered leg. He was from nearby Cannelton. His name was Theodore Stearns. He died about an hour after the operation. Yancey said amputees sometimes died from the shock. *Or the grief of it,* Gentry thought. *The idea of a crippled future.*

The next morning, Gentry pondered the coffins of eight dead Germans recruited from distant Europe to die in Lincoln's war. Somehow that had meaning for him. A world war fought to free America from the stain of slavery. But most Americans did not think slavery was a stain. The majority party, the Democrats, said it was perfectly all right. It was in the Constitution, wasn't it? If it was good enough for Washington and Jefferson, what's wrong with it now? Was this new birth of freedom Abe Lincoln had proclaimed at Gettysburg worth dying for, a year later? Theodore Stearns and his friends apparently did not think so.

Major Stapleton joined him for the funeral service. Gentry read sonorous words from his mother's Episcopal prayer book. Sergeant Schultz wept. Gentry thought Major Stapleton looked downcast. They buried the Germans in the Gentry family graveyard about a half mile from the main house, beside the two blacks who had died in the earlier ambush.

After dinner, Gentry retreated to his cellar office to write a telegram to Lincoln describing the ambush: *This demonstrates how serious the situation is. Again, I urge you to detach ten thousand veteran troops and get them here as soon as possible.* He had just finished putting this into code when Dorothy Schreiber called, "Colonel, Mrs. Jameson is here!"

Once more he greeted Amelia at the foot of the stairs. In his office, she asked him for a drink of water. From an embroidered bag on her wrist she took two folded pieces of paper. "Here is what you want, I suspect," she said.

She withdrew it from his reaching hand. "First I must extract another promise. If Adam is captured, he will *not* be executed as a guerrilla. He will be treated as a prisoner of war."

"Agreed," Gentry said.

Amelia handed him the paper. He spread it on the desk:

The date of the Sons of Liberty attack is August 28. The Rogers Jameson brigade will cross the Ohio late that night to occupy Keyport and join regiments from Hunter County for a march on Indi-

anapolis. They expect to have at least 10,000 men.
Rose Hill is the rendezvous point.

The names of Rogers' colonels are:
George Mooney
Henry Travis
Arthur Haliburton
Luke Bowman

The Kentucky commanding general is Gabriel Todd. His chief of staff is Colonel Paul Stapleton. Rogers is a brigadier general. The soldiers will be met in Keyport by Judge Joshua Bullitt with a month's pay in greenbacks for every man. Judge Bullitt is coming from Canada with the money on the Cleveland and Great Western Railroad.

"Thank you, Amelia. You've done a brave thing. A good thing, I hope."

"Why don't I feel good? I feel soiled. I think I'll always feel soiled."

"Amelia. Don't say that."

"I will say it, Henry. I think you should know it. You above all."

He sat there in the silence, listening to Amelia's footsteps on the stairs. All these years she had known about his longing. All these years she had nurtured the possibility in her heart that someday somehow she might satisfy it. Now she was telling him that hope, that possibility, was gone forever.

With a sigh Colonel Gentry tore up the telegram to President Lincoln and sent another one to Major General Stephen Burbridge in Louisville. *All's well. Additional information will follow in code. I will await your early reply.*

Gentry telegraphed another coded copy of Amelia's letter to General Henry Carrington in Indianapolis. He had no doubt that he and Burbridge would take the credit for defeating the Sons of Liberty. Gentry wanted it that way. He would not accept a medal from Lincoln if he offered one. You do not want a medal for doing something you will be ashamed of for the rest of your life.

We're doing it the hard way, Abe.

THIRTY-FOUR

IN THE HOT CLAUSTROPHOBIC DARKNESS of his room under the Gentry eaves, Paul Stapleton tossed in his bed. He kept seeing the dead Germans in their blue Union uniforms, killed by the Spencer repeating rifles he had bought in New York. He kept seeing the wounded blacks, murdered at Saltville because they too were wearing Union blue. He kept seeing Jeff Tyler in his grave outside Atlanta, the bloody gray uniform his shroud.

Above all he saw Janet Todd beside him in his bed. His love for her had achieved ultimate crystallization in his soul. The way she clenched her small hands when she disagreed with him, the stubborn way she bowed her dark head when he argued with her, the straight-backed way she sat in chairs and rose with an abrupt decisive motion, the mournful light that filled her blue eyes when she talked of the war, everything stirred overwhelming desire. He had no one to blame but himself, of course. He had cultivated this process; he had submitted eagerly to the growth of this exquisite mixture of pain and pleasure. He had wanted a love that was more intense than ordinary affection. Now it was destroying him.

It was the guns, the mixture of the guns and love, that was ruining his sleep. It was the image of the 15,000 repeating rifles flooding into Kentucky and Indiana. Those linseed-oiled stocks and gleaming rust-blued barrels and seven-shot magazines were transforming this amateur rebellion into a continental-size nightmare.

The ambush of the overconfident Germans was a

graphic glimpse of what Spencers could do. The shoot-up had been Rogers Jameson's idea. He had not bothered to tell Gabriel Todd or Paul Stapleton about it. That was the way Jameson operated—with minimal regard for rank or courtesy. Paul suspected Jameson was concealing grandiose ambitions to become the president of the western confederacy, a man who would sit down as an equal with Abraham Lincoln and Jefferson Davis to work out the destiny of North America. He saw himself as a latter-day version of his famous ancestor, George Rogers Clark. Already Jameson talked about the "Revolution of 1864" as if it were his personal invention.

Paul sensed that Gabriel Todd realized he had created a potential monster in Rogers Jameson but did not know what to do about him. Colonel Todd's mind tended to operate in the abstract. Collisions with reality were difficult for him. More often than not, he retreated to his bottle. Paul had not met the other leaders of the Sons of Liberty, Dr. William Bowles, Judge Joshua Bullitt, and an Indiana lawyer named Lambdin Milligan, but he suspected they were similar to Todd. Abstract thinkers with only minimal ability to lead men.

That was how revolutions developed. The abstract thinkers started them and the men of action finished them. Rogers Jameson was not an elevated example of a man of action. George Washington he was not; nor was he even Andrew Jackson. Jameson's ego was much larger than his brain. But a large ego can take a man quite a distance, when it was backed by 15,000 repeating rifles in the hands of infuriated young Democrats.

While pretending to ride out with Janet Todd to enjoy her company as a lover, Paul had been doing his duty as Gabriel Todd's chief of staff. They had visited the colonels of Sons of Liberty regiments along both sides of the Ohio, where their numbers were thickest. All had told him with wide-eyed enthusiasm how the Spencers had increased the ardor and confidence of their men. Janet would inform these excited gentleman that Colonel Stapleton (his Sons of Liberty rank) had been instrumental in obtaining the rifles.

Paul saw what she was trying to do. Janet wanted to build up him and her father as counterweights to Rogers and Adam Jameson if the western confederacy became embroiled in an internal power struggle. For the moment, that remained secondary to the rising hope that the rebellion would succeed. A coded message from Richmond reassured them that Judge Bullitt was arriving from Canada with a million dollars to pay the troops. That news too brought exultation to the lips of the regimental officers.

A number of the colonels were former Union Army officers who had resigned when Abraham Lincoln issued the Emancipation Proclamation. They knew how to handle troops in a battle. They talked confidently of flank attacks and skirmish lines. They nodded knowledgeably when Paul traced their routes of march on a map of Indiana. Meanwhile, the calendar peeled inexorably toward August 28, the night they would gather for the rising the next day.

Other actors were moving into place. Confederate veterans were infiltrating Chicago with suitcases full of Greek fire grenades. Two Sons of Liberty regiments were supposedly inside the city, ready to support them. Chicago would be full of other Democrats, there for the national convention. They could be counted upon to back the Sons when they liberated the Confederate prisoners at Camp Douglas, just outside the city, and took over the metropolis.

At breakfast in the morning, Henry Gentry regarded Paul with a contrite expression. "Major Stapleton," he said. "I can see you're not sleeping well. I wonder if Lucy should give you back your bedroom."

"No thank you," Paul replied. "I'm perfectly contented with the room. It's quiet. I'm sure the heat will break soon."

"I've been told this spell is likely to hold until the end of August," Gentry said. "Unless there's some sort of big battle in our vicinity. I've heard that often brings on a thunderstorm. Has that been your experience, Major?"

"I've heard it mentioned by old soldiers. But I haven't experienced it," Paul replied.

Gentry's smile was much too self-satisfied. Paul was sure the colonel knew exactly what he was doing in Kentucky. "How is Mrs. Todd?" Gentry asked.

"She's much better. Though the family is greatly distressed. All their field hands have run away."

"What a shame. Have they joined the Union Army?"

"They don't seem to know where they've gone."

"It must be exasperating. The sort of thing that might drive a man to desperate measures."

"Like hiring free men and paying them decent wages?" Dorothy Schreiber said. Her experience with Lucy had turned her into something close to an abolitionist.

"That might be a desperate measure if you have to mortgage your property to pay the wages," Gentry said. "The next time you visit, Major Stapleton, I hope you'll tell Gabriel Todd I'd be happy to loan him any amount he needs until he readjusts things."

Paul could easily imagine Gabriel Todd's reaction to the idea of putting his property in the hands of Henry Gentry's lawyers. Was the colonel toying with all of them? For a moment Paul's sense of solidarity with the Todds ignited.

"I'm serious," Gentry said. "When the war ends, I plan to open a bank here in Keyport. Its sole purpose will be to help friends and relations like the Todds cope with the change from slave to free labor."

"I think their land should be confiscated and distributed to their slaves in part payment for generations of unpaid labor," Dorothy said.

"The Emancipation Proclamation doesn't apply to Kentucky, Dorothy. They haven't seceded," Paul said. "What would you say, Colonel Gentry, if the Todds used your money to buy more slaves?"

"Lincoln will abolish slavery throughout the Union soon after the war," Gentry said. "With victory in his pocket, Abe will be an irresistible political force."

"I wonder," Paul said. "He certainly won't be popular in Kentucky. Or in Indiana, as far as I can see."

"Well—he hasn't been reelected yet. And he hasn't won the war," Gentry said in his irritating inconclusive way. Paul was again convinced that the colonel was toying with him.

The butler handed Gentry the morning newspapers. He subscribed to a half-dozen, including the anti-Lincoln New York *Herald.* On its front page was a shocking story. The *Herald* had gotten its hands on a letter that Henry Raymond, editor of the *New York Times* and chairman of the Republican National Committee, had written to Lincoln. Gentry read it aloud to the breakfast table:

"Republicans Throw In Towel.

"'The tide is setting strongly against us,' writes Republican boss Henry Raymond to President Lincoln. 'Congressman Washburne tells me that Illinois is certain to go Democratic. Senator Cameron of Pennsylvania predicts a similar verdict for his state. Governor Morton reports that nothing but the most strenuous efforts can carry Indiana. Here in New York, we expect the Republican ticket to lose by more than fifty thousand votes.

"'Too many voters are complaining of the want of military successes. Others lament that we are not to have peace in any event during your administration until slavery is abandoned. Nothing but the most resolute and decided action on the part of its friends can save the country from falling into hostile hands.' "

As Gentry finished reading this gloomy prophecy, his mother appeared in the doorway of the dining room. She sat down at the breakfast table and said, "I never had any confidence in that oversized lout Lincoln from the start. He was *common* as a boy and he's *common* as a man."

"If I was a member of this supposedly revolutionary party I keep hearing about, the Sons of Liberty, I'd put away my guns and wait for the ballot box in November," Gentry said. "Don't you agree, Major Stapleton?"

"It sounds reasonable. But people aren't in a reasonable mood, Colonel Gentry. Not after three years of war and Republican usurpation here in Indiana and across the river in Kentucky."

"If only someone could talk sense to these people," Gentry said.

Sure he was being needled, Paul's reply was curt: "Why don't you try it, Colonel? Don't you know who they are?"

"I have a name or two," Gentry said. "Not enough to make a difference."

"What a shame. We may have that epic battle yet. At least we can look forward to cooler weather after it."

"Every cloud has a silver lining," Gentry said.

That afternoon, Paul departed for Hopemont. There was no military reason to stay in Indiana. Sergeant Schultz and his men could handle the occasional deserter. There was no longer any danger of the Sons of Liberty staging another ambush. Paul had persuaded Gabriel Todd to forbid further experiments along that line.

As Paul mounted his horse on the Kentucky side of the ferry crossing, Moses Washington walked toward him in a well-pressed blue uniform. He looked rested and healthy. Paul leaned from the saddle and shook hands with him.

"What brings you to Indiana?"

"I got a week leave," Moses said. "I thought I'd pay that little girl Lucy a visit. I hear she's had a pretty hard time."

"Very hard," Paul said. "I've heard you had your troubles, too, up in western Virginia."

"Yes, sir," Moses replied. "Sure wish you'd been there, Major. Maybe you could have talked some sense to them officers."

"I heard about the rebels shooting the wounded," Paul said.

He did not want to say it. The words spoke themselves.

"Yes sir."

"I'm glad you got away. Colonel Gentry told me about it. Did your pal Jones make it?"

"No sir. He got it in the belly goin' up the hill. Died before they could shoot him again."

"You'll fight again another day, Moses. Maybe even the score."

"I sure hope so, Major."

"Good luck, Moses."

"Same to you, Major."

Paul shook hands again and rode on to Hopemont. All the way down the hot dusty road, the conversation reverberated in his brain. *You had to say it,* his Gettysburg wound mocked.

It didn't mean anything, Paul replied. *It was just two soldiers talking about a battle.*

Why doesn't Janet Todd ever mention it? She's never said a word about it since the day you told her. What does that mean?

I love her, Paul replied. *It doesn't mean anything.*

Dust settled in his throat. He swigged from his canteen. There was not the hint of a breeze. Birds perched disconsolately in the oaks and cottonwoods along the way, too weary to sing. The road was empty. Only a handful of slaves were in the fields. There were stories in the newspapers about farm hands in Indiana dying of heat prostration.

At Hopemont, Janet met him with a kiss. But that was all he was going to receive. She had made it clear that she no longer relished furtive lovemaking in the middle of the night. She wanted a husband, not a lover, now. A husband who was her partner in victory.

"The last of the rifles have been distributed," Janet said. "We're ready to march. Adam Jameson's men will start down from the mountains tomorrow. They'll be here in two days."

"Good," Paul said.

"Promise me you won't ask him anything about killing the wounded blacks."

"I can't do that," Paul said. Again, the words spoke themselves. "I promise not to shoot him. But I feel obligated to ask him for an explanation."

Janet looked more than a little unhappy.

Paul followed her out to the gazebo, where Colonel Todd was sitting with a tall glass of bourbon. The colonel had read the Republican tide-is-setting-against-us letter in one of the Kentucky papers. His optimism was soaring. "I think this is going to be easier than we ever expected. Lincoln seems as good as finished, even without the push we're going to give him."

"It looks that way," Paul said. "Have you thought of waiting him out? Letting events take their course—without launching this attack?"

"Why in the world should we do that?"

"It might be better for everyone if this was settled politically."

Colonel Todd and Janet were both gazing at Paul with hostile eyes. "After going this far, at so much risk and trouble, that doesn't make much sense," the colonel said.

"Politics aside," Janet added, "we've got a moral obligation to the Confederate government. They've supplied us with the money and guns. To take all that help and do nothing would amount to betrayal, in my opinion."

A moral obligation to the Confederate government. The western confederacy, if it came into existence with Gabriel Todd or someone like him as its president, would be a southern satellite. Paul had known that since their visit to Richmond. Why was it troubling him now? Did seeing Moses Washington have something to do with it?

Suddenly Paul was back five months, his Gettysburg wound making him unsure of his balance on a horse, teaching the black troopers how to use a cavalry saber. He saw the excitement, the pride, on their faces when they discovered they could wield this fearsome instrument. He remembered everyone laughing when Jasper Jones confessed, "I was afraid I was gonna cut my own damn head off the first time I swung that thing." Soldiers. He had made them soldiers and they had made him a soldier again.

Janet suggested a walk before dinner. They strolled down Hopemont's long curving drive. "Why don't you want to *fight?*" she asked. "I thought we were *together,* heart and soul, in this thing."

Paul struggled to be honest and persuasive at the same time: "I've seen battles, Janet. Seen the dead—and the wounded, who are a lot worse to look at than the dead. A battle should be fought only if it's absolutely necessary."

Janet whirled on him. "I'm going to share this battle with you. I'm riding with the troops. Father doesn't know it. I've arranged it with Rogers Jameson. I'm going to cross the Ohio with his men."

Paul saw what Janet was doing. She was challenging him to match her commitment to the conspiracy. She was testing his love. That was almost as demoralizing as what she was proposing to do.

"Janet—you can't. I absolutely forbid it."

"On what grounds? You have no authority over me, Colonel Stapleton."

"Surely love gives a man some kind of claim."

"Not if you abandon the most important part of the compact we made that morning beside the Ohio."

There it was again, the fatal entanglement of their love and the sacred cause, the dream of victory. Desperately Paul told himself he forgave her. She was like any soldier on the eve of battle. Wildness was rampaging in her soul.

"I can't protect you," he said. "No one can protect another person in a battle."

"I don't want to be protected," Janet said. "Once and for all, you must stop treating me as your *possession*. I've shared so much of this business—I want to be there for the victory. I want to see Indianapolis burn—or surrender. I want to hear bullets whistle."

"They don't whistle. They hiss—or hum like swarming bees. Sometimes they snap like firecrackers."

"I want to hear them."

Did she see what she was doing? What she was forcing him to do? No. In her rising battle fury she thought she could test him and he would obey her. But he had another alternative. He could betray her in the name of love. Even though he knew the betrayal might annihilate love's future.

Rogers Jameson came to supper. He drank Gabriel Todd's whiskey and they debated strategy and tactics for the march to Indianapolis. Rogers still resisted anything that sounded like a complicated plan. Paul let Todd do most of the talking. Predictably, they got nowhere.

Afterward, Paul followed Rogers Jameson onto the lawn and stopped him as he was mounting his horse. "General," he said. "Miss Todd tells me she plans to cross the river with you and your men. I don't think it's practical—or necessary."

"She's perfectly welcome as far as I'm concerned," Jameson said. "I'm sure Adam will greet her with open arms."

"If you have any hope of deserving the title of general, you'll retract that remark immediately," Paul said. "A general's first responsibility is to resolve conflicts between his ranking officers, not encourage them."

Contempt mingled with dislike on Jameson's fleshy face. "Calm down, Colonel," he said. "I won't let her go beyond Keyport. That won't be dangerous. The town'll surrender without a shot. Them stupid Germans of Gentry's will run for their lives. We'll give Colonel One-Arm a taste of Greek fire and send Janet back here 'fore we head for Indianapolis."

The next morning, one of the German soldiers brought Paul a message from Gentry: *Please return. Urgent military problems require your attention.* He showed it to Janet and they decided it would be best for him to obey the summons; a refusal might arouse suspicions. They were only twenty-four hours away from the great explosion. "We'll meet you in Keyport," Gabriel Todd said.

In his cellar office, Gentry greeted Paul with a cheerful hello. "How are things at Hopemont?" he asked.

"Fine," Paul said.

"You won't be able to say that tomorrow night. I'm putting you under arrest, Major."

At first Paul thought Gentry was joking. But it was clear that he was extremely serious. "I'd like to hear the charges, Colonel," he said.

"I've got a document—and a living witness—that you're the chief of staff of a rebellious army organized by the Sons of Liberty. But I have a better reason for arresting you now. I don't want you shot for treason."

Gentry spun his chair and stared up at the picture of

Lincoln on the wall of his office. "Believe it or not, Major, an old fool like me still believes in love. I'm trying to help you preserve it in spite of how defeat and her father's disgrace will affect Janet Todd's feeling for you. It's your only chance—and mine—to rescue something valuable from this stinking war."

"If I wanted any romantic advice from you I'd have asked for it!" Paul said.

"This isn't romance. It's reality. Tomorrow night, General Burbridge is going to surround Hopemont with a thousand cavalrymen. He's going to arrest Gabriel Todd, Rogers Jameson, and the colonels of the George Rogers Clark Brigade."

"I should be there. There may be gunfire. Janet has taken to seeing herself as a soldier—"

Gentry shook his head. "You're staying here."

"Like hell I am. I'll go where I damn please as long as I've got this gun in my holster!"

"Sergeant Schultz!" Gentry called. He jerked a string on his desk, and a bell tinkled outside the house.

The storm cellar door clanged open. Boots clumped toward them. Schultz appeared in the office doorway, a pistol in his hand. Behind him loomed three of his biggest men, hefting rifles.

"I'm arresting Major Stapleton for insubordination," Gentry said. "Take his gun away from him and lock him in your office in the barn until you hear from me."

"I hope you know what you're doing," Paul said as Schultz pulled the pistol from the holster on his hip.

"So do I," Gentry said.

THIRTY-FIVE

TETHERING THEIR HORSES TO A sapling, Janet Todd and her father walked into the hot, still woods at the far end of their property. Birds twittered listlessly around them. The drought continued, all but extinguishing life from the land. In a valise Janet carried the folded figure of a man that she had cut from an old bedsheet. She had given him a face and a soldier's kepi and a pair of epaulets on his shoulders.

She pinned the figure to a tree and retreated a dozen steps. From the valise she took the Colt repeating pistol her father had used in Mexico. Since she insisted on riding to Indianapolis with the Sons of Liberty, Gabriel Todd had decided she should know how to use a gun.

Janet flipped open the chamber and inserted six bullets while her father watched approvingly. He had all but stopped drinking two weeks ago. The change in him was marvelous. Janet thought he already looked five years younger. As the calendar marched toward their day of deliverance, Janet had felt renewed love and admiration for this man.

Feet planted firmly, she raised the silver gun with two hands. She had been amazed by how heavy it was when she first hefted it. "All right," Gabriel Todd said. "Remember, squeeze, don't pull. Fire one bullet at a time."

Blam! The gun exploded and the figure fluttered slightly.

"Good shooting. That hit him in the chest."

Blam!

"Even better. That hit him in the head."

Would she be able to hit a living man that way? Janet was not sure. If he was wearing a blue federal uniform, perhaps. But what if he was some ordinary Republican farmer, trying to resist their revolution? She told herself it was kill or be killed—and in her case possibly raped as well.

She put six bullets into the sheetman. The last four were in his arms and legs. She had let those wandering thoughts distract her aim. In a battle, if there was one, there would be no time for thoughts. Paul's description of Gettysburg and Antietam made that clear.

They rode back to Hopemont through the empty fields. None of their hands had returned. They had probably joined the Union Army—a guaranteed refuge for runaways now. General Burbridge had issued a proclamation assuring every black who joined up protection from his hapless master.

"Will the western confederacy legalize slavery?" Janet asked.

"I doubt it," Gabriel Todd said. "We'll simply tolerate it in states where it already exists, like Kentucky and Missouri. It would be a mistake to bring that question before the legislature."

Janet sensed his discomfort and dropped the subject. Every time they discussed the future confederacy, problems like slavery loomed. Janet had gradually become aware that her father was concealing grave doubts about his brainchild. The northern tier of Illinois, Indiana and Ohio had been settled by New Englanders and other migrants from the East. The settlers of the Ohio Valley had been from the South. The two sections were divided on almost everything, from religion to slavery to politics.

But the calendar, that relentless agent of change, had already carried them beyond doubts. It was August 28. Everything was in place. The Confederate armies were still holding their own before Atlanta and Richmond.

For fifty miles on both sides of the Ohio River the Sons of Liberty were oiling their Spencer repeating rifles. At this very moment, perhaps, additional Confederate agents were arriving in Chicago with their valises of Greek fire.

"I wish you'd give up this idea of riding with us," Gabriel Todd said.

"My mind is made up, Father," Janet said.

"I'm not just worried about your safety. I'm thinking of your mother. She'll be left alone—"

"The servants are still loyal. They've gotten over Lucy."

She had spent hours in the slave quarter nursing Lucy's mother, Lillibet. Janet told her Lucy was alive and free— and she was sorry her father whipped her so badly. Janet also said her father never should have sold Maybelle. She promised he would never do anything like that again. Lillibet returned to her kitchen and the other house servants also went back to work.

Gabriel Todd abandoned the argument. "Just promise me you'll do exactly what I tell you if any shooting starts."

"What will that be?" Janet asked.

"I don't know. It depends on the situation."

I'm not a mere woman, Father. I'm an adventuress. She wanted to say something like that to explode his image of her as a creature who needed and wanted protection. But he would never understand. *Adventuress,* with its overtones of sexual license, would shock him.

On Hopemont's veranda they discovered Rogers Jameson waving an envelope. "Adam's in Kentucky with his men!" he said. "He sent Pompey ahead with this letter for Janet."

The letter had gotten badly crumpled in the hours it had spent in Pompey's pocket. Janet smoothed it against her thigh while Jameson talked about how eager his Sons of Liberty brigade was to begin the march on Indianapolis. He peered into Hopemont's open front door and added, "Good thing that Yankee chief of staff of yours ain't on the premises. This letter could turn him green."

"I'm sure Colonel Stapleton and Colonel Jameson will let Janet choose between them when peace is at hand," Gabriel Todd said.

Janet was glad she had never mentioned Adam's aborted challenge to a duel during his July visit. Her father obviously favored Paul and would be dismayed by Adam's preference for a violent solution.

"I suspect your ambush last week has scared the liver out of Colonel Gentry," Gabriel Todd continued. "I bet he's got Stapleton designing redoubts all around his property."

"We'll toss a coin to see who gets the pleasure of shooting that one-armed two-faced scum," Jameson said.

In the front parlor, Janet smoothed Adam Jameson's letter again and again. She did not want to open it. She did not want her mind and heart confused by anything but the machinery of victory. She only wanted to think about men and guns, about guns and men. She would think about love when the killing ended.

But she had to open the letter. There might be important information in it.

Dearest Janet:

We're on the march at last. I have a plan to augment our ranks. When I reach the Bluegrass, I'm going to declare that region of Kentucky part of the Confederacy and announce we're drafting every man of fighting age. I have a feeling a lot of young men are only waiting for a push to declare for the South. It will also be a first step toward combining or at least connecting the southern confederacy with the western confederacy. My men will be the link between the two countries. I like that idea, don't you?

I keep thinking of the loyalty, the courage, you displayed on my behalf the day Burbridge raided Rose Hill. I'm looking forward to repaying that swine for his insults to you and Momma. The humiliation we inflicted on him that morning is only a down payment on the full punishment he deserves for that and all the other crimes he's committed against southern supporters in Kentucky. My men are in superb shape. We've spent every day of the last month training to fight from the saddle or dismounted.

In regard to our route, I've decided to swing west of Daviess County into Henderson County and join you from that direction. The federals have pretty large detachments blocking the more direct and obvious routes. I'll ride ahead with forty picked men and join you and your father and Pap for a final talkover the night of August 28.

Whatever happens, the thought that you and I are together in this thing heart and soul has given me the rarest of gifts for a southern soldier at this point in the war: hope. God is involved here somehow, Janet, bringing us together in His own way. I believe that with all my soul.

Love,
Adam

Hot tears rose in Janet's throat. Paul Stapleton had never linked their love to God and the southern cause that way. His love for her had enlisted him under its banner, had opened his eyes to its justice. But other sentiments—his West Point oath, the looming figure of his brother, the general—made such simple enthusiasm impossible.

She knew all this. She had accepted it as part of the bargain she had forged with herself, with Paul, with God. Why did Adam's words shiver her resolution? Was it that accuser's voice, whispering, *You wanted him?* Did she feel some sort of obscure need to expiate a sin? Adventuresses did not worry about such things.

As they sat down to dinner about three o'clock, hooves clopped in the driveway. Janet opened the front door to discover Mrs. Virginia Havens descending from her carriage. The spiritualist seldom kept a consistent schedule. She showed up pretty much as she pleased, once she was sure of a warm welcome.

Janet rushed into the dining room. "It's Mrs. Havens, of all people. Shall I send her away?"

Gabriel Todd thought for a moment. "No, let her come in. Maybe it's time I joined you for a session. It might make your mother feel better if something happens to me on our adventure."

They were all riding into the valley of the shadow of death. Janet remembered Paul's warning that Lincoln and the Union Army were not going to accept this revolution in their rear passively. She nodded and invited Mrs. Havens to join them for dinner.

Mrs. Havens was dressed in white as usual—and was as spherical as ever. She clutched a Bible in her hand and chattered about a "perturbation" in the atmosphere. Some sort of large spiritual event was about to occur, she was convinced of it. "It may well be a kind of gathering of the souls of the dead," she said in her husky voice. "I begin to think there's a kind of intermediary world where the newly dead await their loved ones. Especially soldiers who die violently."

"I believe the ancients called it the shore of the River Styx," Gabriel Todd said, glancing wryly at Janet.

Mrs. Havens had never heard of the River Styx. Or of Charon, the ghastly boatman who ferried the dead across its dark still waters to Hades. Janet was thoroughly familiar with the myth. Although St. Mary of-the-Woods's nuns were French Roman Catholics, they gave their graduates an excellent classical education. It was one of the reasons that her father had selected the school for her. This pagan faith of the old Greeks and Romans was all Gabriel Todd really believed.

Odd, how formal a father's relationship with a daughter was. Gabriel Todd never shared his inmost thoughts about so many things—love, sex, marriage. When it came to God, Janet realized with a pang that she could not escape St. Mary's. Beyond or beneath all her doubts and her defiant embrace of an adventuress's role she still believed in the vast mysterious being they had worshiped there.

As Mrs. Havens labored up the stairs ahead of them, Gabriel Todd whispered in Janet's ear, "Do you think she'd stay with Mother if we offered her enough money?" Janet nodded yes.

In her bedroom, Letitia Todd embraced Mrs. Havens. Her mother was totally unaware of their plans for tomorrow, of course. That made it more poignant when Gabriel Todd said, "Darlin' wife, Mrs. Havens here has convinced me I ought to join you for this excursion. I almost hate to admit it but she's put a patch of faith on my heathen soul. I don't know how she did it—"

"I've prayed and prayed for something like that to happen," Letitia said.

Mrs. Havens beamed and Janet drew the window drapes, reducing the room to semidarkness. Mrs. Havens lit a single candle in a silver holder in the center of the table. She recited her incantation to the God of the dead and urged the Todds to concentrate on their loved ones to facilitate communication from the spirit world.

They waited in silence. Nothing happened. The spirits remained silent. "Lord God of the dead, your servants are here, looking for wisdom and consolation," Mrs. Havens said. "Are you listening to our plea?"

More silence.

Mrs. Havens renewed her plea three more times with the same negative result. "I can't understand it," she said. "We seem to be in some sort of vacuum. I can sense my messages are not going beyond this room. Yet as I rode up the drive I sensed a spiritual host hovering around me. I was certain that there would be rich communication."

Was it possible that Mrs. Havens was not a fraud? The medium apparently did not concoct those spiritual voices in which she spoke. She waited humbly for some sort of power to take possession of her vocal chords. That was why the voice that had taken command at the end of her previous visit had frightened her so badly.

"Why is this happening, Mrs. Havens?" Letitia asked.

"There's another presence here, more powerful than the voices of the dead. Someone or something who is determined to deny us the consolation we seek. Some kind of angelic emissary, I think. I sense anger emanating from him, sealing up the windows of the room like shutters of steel."

"Why—oh why?" Letitia Todd wailed. "I've prayed and prayed for the boys' souls, exactly as you told me."

"I'm sure you have. But you are not alone here, dear Mrs. Todd. We come together as a band of seekers. Alas, one of us must be wishing for something that's forbidden."

Janet trembled. Damn the woman! Was she wishing for the freedom to love Paul Stapleton and Adam Jameson? Wasn't that what an adventuress would do? Love them on alternate nights, keep them both in her power?

"Maybe there's another explanation, Mrs. Havens," Gabriel Todd said. "Maybe the silence is telling us the boys are happy in Abraham's bosom. They're no longer concerned with the trifling woes of us earthbound mortals. Maybe we're being told it's time to trust in faith and abandon signs and wonders."

"It's never happened to me before, Colonel Todd. I swear it!" Mrs. Havens said.

"I have an idea. Why don't you stay here with Mrs. Todd for a few days? We'll pay you for your time. Perhaps the spirits will return when two doubters like me and Janet are out of the house. We're planning a trip to Cincinnati."

"Cincinnati? Why in the world?" Letitia asked.

"We've got to find some hands to work this farm, Letty. I've been told there's a raft of unemployed Irishmen down there that can be hired cheap. Strong boyos who can do the work of three slaves. I want Janet to come with me. They may want to bring wives with them and she can talk to the women."

"Can we afford it? We barely made a profit with slaves."

"We'll have to try. We'll leave you and Mrs. Havens now. Rogers Jameson and some friends are coming in for cards. The servants will bring you supper in a few hours."

Janet and her father went downstairs. "I hope that didn't trouble you," Gabriel Todd said.

"Of course not," Janet lied. "I never took Mrs. Havens seriously."

"Good. Let's prepare for our trip to Indianapolis tomorrow. We won't have a minute to spare once Jameson and his colonels arrive."

In the kitchen, Janet asked Lillibet to fill two haversacks with enough salted ham and dried beef to last two or three days. Also enough cornmeal to make cakes in a skillet over an open fire and plenty of bread. In her room, Janet took the pistol from the valise and slipped it into a holster she planned to carry on a leather shoulder strap, concealing it beneath a light cloak. Beyond an extra dress, she saw no need to burden herself with clothes.

Hoofbeats thudded on the twilit drive, soon followed by male voices downstairs. She found her father and Jameson and his colonels in the dining room, helping themselves to drinks from the sideboard. She offered to bring them anything they wanted from the kitchen but they all said no. For the time being they would fortify themselves with good old Kentucky bourbon and eat something just before they began the march to the ferry. She sat down at the table with them, contenting herself with a glass of water.

They were all Rogers Jameson's age—about fifty, with faces weathered from years spent in the sun and wind and rain on their farms. They looked durable but not terribly bright. None of them had Jameson's forcefulness. Once more Janet wondered if he could or would obey orders.

Gabriel Todd unrolled a detailed map of Indiana, revealing all the roads and rail lines. He and Paul had been thinking a good deal about their march to Indianapolis. They had decided it might be useful to commandeer the railroad and put as many men as the available cars could carry on a train that would roar ahead of the main army and outflank enemy attempts to block the roads and river crossings.

Rogers Jameson shook his head. "It's too risky, Gabe. There ain't enough cars to carry more than a thousand men. That's not enough to handle a heavy attack. They could get surrounded and cut up before we got to them."

"There's plenty of Sons of Liberty up ahead who'll come out to help them," Gabriel Todd said.

"They ain't got Spencers," one of the colonels said. "It's them guns that've given our boys confidence. Nobody wants to fight the federals with a squirrel gun."

The colonels all nodded in unison. They were backing Rogers Jameson. Janet found herself wishing Paul were here to support Gabriel Todd. Her father was thinking like a cavalryman. He knew the value of lightning strikes in the enemy rear. Such bold moves cut communications and created fear and disorder.

A strange tinkling sound interrupted them. Janet realized it was coming from the cut-glass chandelier above their heads. Something was shaking it. What? Surely not the wind. Then Janet heard a deeper sound, a kind of muffled thunder. She realized it was the hooves of hundreds of horses.

Janet rushed to the front parlor window, followed by Rogers Jameson. They gazed out at a terrifying sight. Coming down the drive and across the lawn was a tidal wave of federal cavalrymen, rank after rank. The lead horsemen carried pine torches. Just ahead of them rode Major General Stephen Burbridge.

"My God!" Janet gasped.

"Jesus Christ!" Rogers Jameson snarled.

He raced back to the dining room. "Guns!" he roared. "Where the hell are your guns, Gabe? There's a thousand federals on the lawn. Someone's ratted us!"

"In the case—in the library," Gabriel Todd said.

They raced into Hopemont's library. Around them loomed the books that Gabriel Todd had enjoyed all his life. With trembling hands he tried to open the gun cabinet. Rogers Jameson snatched the keys away from him and opened it. He handed shotguns to the colonels. They shoved shells into the chambers.

"I'll fight, too!" Janet cried. "I've got a pistol."

"GABRIEL TODD AND ROGERS JAMESON AND YOUR FELLOW TRAITORS!" General Burbridge was using a metal speaking trumpet. "WE KNOW YOU'RE IN THERE. WE'VE ALREADY SEIZED THE WEAPONS AND SUPPLIES YOU HAD STORED AT ROSE HILL. SURRENDER IMMEDIATELY. THE HOUSE IS SURROUNDED."

"There ain't enough of us to make a stand, Rogers," one of the colonels, Sam Davidson, said. Fear drained manhood from his face. His words had a similar effect on the other colonels.

"If we hold out until midnight, the brigade will start arrivin'," Rogers said. "They'll take'm in the rear."

"That's four hours away," Davidson said.

"You want to rot in some federal jail? It's our only chance!" Jameson roared.

"DO YOU HEAR ME? IN EXACTLY ONE MINUTE WE WILL STORM THE HOUSE!" Burbridge said in his tinny voice of doom.

"Wait a moment!" Gabriel Todd said. "Wait—a—moment! We are not goin' to fight them. My wife is upstairs an invalid. My daughter, my only survivin' child, is standin' next to you. I'll go out on the veranda now and surrender to them. If you fellows want to try to get out the back way, go to it. I'll do my best to keep them occupied for a few minutes."

"I always knew you had no guts," Rogers Jameson snarled. "All we got to do is kill a few and they'll keep their distance for the rest of the night. They're third-rate soldiers. If they were any good they'd be with Sherman in Georgia."

"WE'VE GOT SOME OF YOUR GREEK FIRE OUT HERE! WE'RE READY TO USE IT," Burbridge said.

"See what I mean? He don't want to storm us," Rogers Jameson said.

"Janet," Gabriel Todd said. "Go upstairs and get your mother down to this floor."

Janet raced upstairs. In her bedroom she slung her pistol and holster over her shoulder and tied the gray cloak at her throat. She was going to defend herself. She was not going to surrender. She was not going to prison.

In her mother's room, Mrs. Havens was standing at the window, terrified. "Miss Todd, what's happening?

Are those horsemen real? They look like spirit riders of
the apocalypse!"

"They're all too real. Help me get my mother downstairs."

"What is it, Janet? What's happening?" Letitia Todd
cried.

"I'll explain later, Mother," Janet replied.

Together Janet and Mrs. Havens hoisted Letitia to her
feet and labored down Hopemont's curving staircase.
As they reached the bottom step, Gabriel Todd joined
them. "Janet, I want you to come out on the veranda
with me," he said. "We'll insist on our innocence. The
other fellows are goin' to run for it through the garden.
Mrs. Havens, stay here with my wife."

Mrs. Havens nodded numbly and helped Letitia to a
large Tudor chair a few feet from the door. Gabriel Todd
opened the door and stepped into the flickering torchlight. As Janet followed him, she realized she was carrying her gun. She could only pray no one noticed it
beneath her cloak.

"I have no idea what you're here for, General Burbridge," Gabriel Todd said. "I hope you do."

"I'm here to arrest you for treason! Where's the rest
of them?"

"There's no one in the house but me, my daughter
here, and my invalid wife and a guest," Gabriel Todd said.

The drumming sound again. Not quite as heavy. It
was coming from the darkness beyond Burbridge's
mass of mounted men. Janet's eyes leaped past the federal phalanx and saw a line of gray-uniformed cavalrymen emerging from the darkness. Leading them was a
huge black-bearded man. It was Adam Jameson and his
horsemen.

It was a miracle of deliverance. Janet's heart leaped
into a stratosphere of fierce gratitude that transcended
love and desire. The Confederates pulled up about ten

yards from the federal horsemen. Suddenly there were shotguns in every gray-uniformed rider's hands. A blast of flame tore a terrific gap in the federal ranks. Men screamed and toppled; horses bolted. Adam drove his horse through the opening toward the Todds on the veranda, firing left and right with two pistols. He pulled up at the foot of the steps and shouted, "Come on!"

Janet realized he was talking to her. He could do nothing for her parents or Mrs. Havens. She was the one he wanted to rescue from a federal prison. He leaned down and she leaped from the steps onto his arm. He slung her into the saddle in front of him as if she weighed no more than a doll.

Bullets whizzed around them. The federals were firing back. Adam's men were answering them with pistols. She saw how few the Confederates were—and remembered what Adam had written about riding ahead with forty picked men. He was taking a desperate gamble to rescue her.

A federal cavalryman charged Adam with upraised saber. He shot him out of the saddle, hauled his horse's head around, and started for the darkness at the end of the drive. Just ahead of them Janet saw a dozen Confederates flung out of their saddles by bullets. Riderless horses dashed left and right, whinnying with terror. General Burbridge was shouting commands. The night was livid with booming guns and roaring cursing troopers.

"I've got a gun!" Janet said and tried to pull it out of the holster.

Chunk. An alien sound. The horse lunged ahead. But Adam was no longer in control. The hand that had been holding the reins was clutching his head. The horse slewed drunkenly. Adam was wounded! Janet grabbed for the reins. Sprawled against him, sitting sideways, she could exert no control. Adam regained the reins and hauled the horse to a stop.

"My eyes," he said. "My eyes are gone."

Hooves pounding. A dozen federal cavalrymen surrounded them. Head drooping, Adam sat motionless in the saddle. Janet reached for her gun. They would die together here. But something froze her hand on the butt. What was the point of dying now? The western confederacy had been betrayed. Victory had dwindled to a forlorn dream. Adam needed help.

She jumped to the ground. "This is Colonel Adam Jameson," she said. "He's wounded. We must get him to a doctor."

To her amazement, the cavalrymen sheathed their sabers and holstered their pistols. "So that's Adam Jameson," one said.

"Never thought I'd see him alive," another one said.

"We'll do what we can for him, Miss," a third said. "We've got ambulances down the road."

For a moment she was bewildered by the code of the soldier. She realized that three years of war had created a separate world for these men in which they did unto the enemy what they hoped the enemy would do for them. Maybe the hatred did not go as deep as she had thought. Maybe there was still some kind of bond in the word American.

She took the reins of Adam's horse and walked back toward Hopemont. The troopers rode on either side of her. When they were about halfway there, the lower floor of the house exploded into bright yellow flame. "No!" she cried.

"What? What is it?" Adam asked.

"They're burning Hopemont."

"The general's usin' that Greek fire stuff. He swore he'd do it," one of the federal troopers said.

When they reached the gravel drive in front of the porch, Janet saw the bodies of the four colonels. They had all been shot many times. Their faces, their chests, oozed blood. But there was no sign of Rogers Jameson.

"Is Pap here?" Adam asked. His tongue was thick, as if he were drunk.

"No," Janet said. "I think he got away."

General Burbridge strode up to them. "Who's this?"

"Colonel Adam Jameson," Janet said.

"And you're Janet Todd, I suppose?"

"Yes."

Hopemont was burning furiously. The flames licked out the lower windows. Orange light glowed in the upper windows. Beyond Burbridge, Janet could see her father's blank dazed face. Her mother clung to him, weeping. There was no trace of Mrs. Havens.

"You deserve to go to jail like the rest of them," General Burbridge said. "But an agreement is an agreement."

"General," one of the federal soldiers said. "Colonel Jameson's wounded bad. Hit in the eyes. Can we take him down to our ambulances?"

"I suppose so," Burbridge said. "Personally, I'm inclined to hang him. But I've been reprimanded by Washington, D.C., for hanging and shooting too many people. Our idiot president apparently thinks I'm supposed to win this goddamn war without killing anyone."

Adam was led away by an escort of four soldiers. A half-dozen of his men, all badly wounded, went with him, along with a dozen federals. The rest of Adam's men were dead or had escaped into the night. Commandeering a horse from Hopemont's stables, General Burbridge ordered Gabriel Todd to mount it.

"Where are you taking him?" Janet asked.

"To the federal prison in Louisville."

In another five minutes they were gone. Janet was left with her dazed mother and the bodies of the four Sons of Liberty colonels and the dead Confederates, looking like creatures from a nightmare world in the glare of blazing Hopemont.

Mrs. Havens reeled out of the darkness and wailed over the dead. "I knew it, I knew it," she said. "I knew something terrible was about to happen. Not even the spirits of the dead could stand it! No wonder the angels have turned their eyes away from this war!"

"Come, Mistress," said a dark Negro voice. "Come down to my place now. Come along. I'll fix you some coffee."

It was Lillibet, inviting Letitia Todd to her slave cabin. Numbly Mrs. Todd obeyed her servant.

Janet gazed in bewilderment at the dead men, the roaring pyre of Hopemont. Slowly, words penetrated her numbed brain. *An agreement is an agreement.* General Burbridge had said that. He had agreed with someone that she would not go to jail. Who was it?

Paul Stapleton. Who else could it be? He was the betrayer of victory. The seductive destroyer of her dream. Janet's hand went to the butt of her pistol. If she ever saw him again she would kill him.

THIRTY-SIX

A SLEEPLESS PAUL STAPLETON lay on a cot in Sergeant Schultz's office, alternately cursing Colonel Henry Gentry and ruefully admiring him. If Paul had followed his instincts and headed for Kentucky, he might be dead at this very moment—or on his way to court-martial and execution in Louisville. Death had no terror for him. But he recoiled from inflicting disgrace on his brother, Jonathan, and on his father's reputation as a defender of the Union.

Paul's watch read 3:00 A.M. when Sergeant Schultz and his rifle-carrying escort opened the office door. "Herr Colonel Gentry wishes to speak with you," the sergeant said.

They marched Paul to the storm cellar door and let him make his own way across the darkened interior to Gentry's office, where a single oil lamp cast a yellow glow. The colonel had already done a lot of damage to the bottle on his desk. He poured a hefty slug for Paul.

"You're worried, I suppose."

Paul nodded.

"That makes two of us."

"Any news of Adam Jameson's men?"

"They passed south of Lexington yesterday. I suspect they're heading for Henderson County. Trying to get west of us. Where we're less likely to expect them. It will make it easier to trap them against the Ohio. They'll never get back to Virginia."

"How many men does Burbridge have?"

"About fifteen thousand. They shipped him ten thousand from the Tennessee garrison by railroad."

"Taking no chances."

"As Lincoln said in 1861, to lose Kentucky is to lose the whole game."

"They'll arrest Colonel Todd?"

"I'm afraid so."

"You're arresting the other leaders?"

"All over Kentucky and Indiana. I hate to admit it but General Carrington has done a good job. He had double agents working with the top people."

"What about the rank and file? They've got fifteen thousand Spencer repeating rifles I found for them in New York."

"We'll issue a proclamation offering amnesty to anyone who turns in his gun."

Blam! The noise was so unexpected, they both took a sip of bourbon before reacting to it. "That sounded like a shot," Gentry said.

"It was," Paul said.

They had sentries patrolling the property. Since the ambush of the Germans, Gentry felt they were under semisiege. Gentry handed Paul the pistol he had taken from him yesterday. Together they stepped cautiously into the night.

Sergeant Schultz rushed up to them. "Major, Colonel," he said. "Private Bockman has been shot! He's dying."

They rushed to the gate, where poor Bockman lay groaning. He had been hit in the chest by a shotgun blast. He died before they could get him back to the barn.

"The Sons of Liberty?" Paul said, gazing around them into the darkness.

"It's possible," Gentry replied. "Though it would be twelve hours ahead of their schedule. I hope it doesn't have anything to do with events across the river."

They calmed down Schultz and the other Germans by giving them several bottles of bourbon from Gentry's seemingly inexhaustible liquor cabinet. The colonel and Paul went back to the cellar. The first hints of dawn were beginning to gray the eastern sky. Gentry lumbered ahead of Paul toward the office.

As Paul closed the storm cellar doors, a voice whispered from the darkness to his left, "Put up your hands, Major." He felt the muzzle of a shotgun against his back.

It was Rogers Jameson. He removed Paul's pistol from his holster and shoved him toward the office. Gentry saw them at the door and slowly sat down in the chair behind his desk. Paul sat down in the chair on the other side of the desk. Jameson covered them both with the shotgun.

"Hello, Rogers," Gentry said.

"Hello, Henry," Jameson said.

Jameson was not in very good shape. He had been shot in the shoulder. A big bloodstain covered the top right side of his blue work shirt. His face and hands were smeared with Ohio River mud. He must have fallen several times as he waded through the shallows.

"Your sneakin' coward's plan worked pretty well, Henry. You sicced Burbridge and his hounds on us and killed and captured just about everyone," Jameson said.

"I'm sorry to hear that," Gentry said. "I was hoping no one would get hurt."

"That sounds just like you, Henry."

"I hope Janet Todd's all right," Gentry said.

"The last I saw, Hopemont was burnin' bright. Burbridge used Greek fire on it. If Janet was inside, she sure as hell ain't all right."

"Burbridge promised me he'd protect the women and servants," Gentry said.

"I couldn't care less, Henry. But I can tell you this much. You and your Yankee hero here ain't gonna be protected unless you give me two or three thousand dollars, fast."

"I'm not sure I have that much money in the house."

"A thousand will do the trick. I'm headin' west. Nobody puts Rogers Jameson in jail."

"I don't have the money here, Rogers. It's upstairs in the safe."

"The Yankee hero here will go get it. If he brings back a dozen Germans, I'll blow you away, Henry, and go down fightin' like my boy Adam. He attacked Burbridge as I was gettin' out of the Todd garden. If you know as much as you seem to know, I don't guess he has much of a chance."

"That's about right, Rogers. Burbridge has fifteen thousand men in Kentucky."

"You're so goddamn smart, Henry. I'm tempted to blow a hole in you now and forget the money."

"Major Stapleton will get you the money, Rogers."

Gentry took a set of keys out of the desk drawer and handed them to Paul. He pointed to a delicate brass key. "That'll open the wall safe in my bedroom. It's behind the Hamilton portrait. Bring down whatever's in there."

Paul took the key and climbed the cellar stairs to the first floor. The house was silent. He went up to Gentry's bedroom and opened the safe. There was a lot of money in there, wrapped in elastic bands. Beside it was Gentry's pistol. What a nice coincidence. Should he leave the gun here and give Jameson the money, hoping he would go away?

No, Paul decided. Jameson was almost certain to kill Gentry and probably him. He would give them each a single barrel of the shotgun at close range. Another possibility was an order to Sergeant Schultz to surround the house. That would guarantee Gentry's death, followed by Jameson's. No one would reproach Major Stapleton for it.

But he would reproach himself. He owed something to Gentry. Exactly what Paul chose not to define. He checked the chambers of the gun. Six bullets. He tiptoed down the hall and woke up Lucy. She was still sleeping in his bedroom. "Go out the back door and tell Sergeant Schultz to surround the house," he whispered. "Rogers Jameson is downstairs with a shotgun, getting ready to kill Colonel Gentry."

"Yes *suh*," Lucy said.

Paul pulled off his boots and descended the cellar stairs as quietly as possible. Staying beyond the glow of the oil lamp, he tiptoed to the left until he could see into the office. Gentry was still in his chair behind the desk. Jameson was sitting in the chair on the other side of the desk with the shotgun leveled at Gentry's chest.

If Paul shot Jameson from behind, his fingers would convulse on the shotgun's triggers and blow a very large hole in Gentry. Paul decided to try to get Jameson to turn in the chair, hoping he would move the shotgun in the same motion.

"I hated you the first time I saw you, Henry," Jameson said as Paul walked softly toward the door, the greenbacks in his left hand, the pistol in his right hand—concealed behind his back.

"The feeling was mutual, Rogers," Gentry replied.

Just inside the door, Paul stopped and held out the money. "Here's your greenbacks, Jameson."

Exactly as Paul hoped, Jameson turned his head and moved in the chair. The shotgun moved with him until the muzzle was pointing at the wall to Gentry's left. Paul shot Jameson twice in the middle of the forehead. The shotgun boomed, a terrific crash in the low-ceilinged cellar. But it only blew a hole in the wall.

A flicker of dismay passed over Jameson's face. His hand scrabbled at the shotgun. Paul shot him again. Jameson slid out of the chair and thudded on the floor, dead.

"I was wondering how you were going to do that," Gentry said.

Paul pulled his Navy Colt pistol out of Jameson's belt and returned it to his holster. "I'm heading for Kentucky," he said.

Gentry nodded mournfully. "Tell anyone who's willing to listen that I'm sorry about Hopemont."

"I don't think they'll be interested."

"I suppose not," Gentry said.

Mounting his horse, Paul rode for the ferry. It was 6:00 A.M. by the time he got there. The three-man crew had just shown up to start the day. Paul paid them five dollars to take him across on an unscheduled trip. He rode down the river road while the sun rose spectacularly over the Alleghenies, Kentucky's eastern rampart.

At Hopemont the air was heavy with the smell of burnt wood and cloth. The big house was a gutted shell. Most of the front wall had collapsed. A few spasms of flame danced against the side and rear walls. There were at least a dozen dead Confederate cavalrymen on the lawn. Paul dismounted and walked past their sightless stares. In the driveway before the porch he found the riddled bodies of the four Sons of Liberty colonels. He had no trouble figuring out what had happened. He only wanted to know one thing: was Janet alive?

Almost as if he had shouted the question, she appeared around the west side of the house. She was wearing a gray cloak over a green riding dress.

"Janet! Thank God," Paul said, walking toward her, his arms open.

Janet's right hand went under her cloak. When it emerged there was a large silver pistol in it. She gripped it with both hands and aimed it at his chest.

"Traitor," she said.

"No," Paul said.

"You betrayed us. I'm going to kill you."

"Janet, I didn't! I swear to God I didn't—"

She shook her head. "You planned it with General

Burbridge. I can see you in Louisville, telling him every detail."

"Janet—it was Gentry. Someone told him everything. The date, the names. He put me under arrest."

"Liar," Janet said, still holding the pistol with both hands. "Say your prayers, if you have a conscience."

"Janet, I love you. You love me. This whole thing was madness—a passing madness. I always knew something like this could happen."

"Burbridge wanted to arrest me. But he said he couldn't. An agreement was an agreement. What else could that mean but an agreement with you? Why would Henry Gentry worry about me?"

"Because you're a woman. You're his blood relation. He's a decent man. He knew about us."

"Liar."

"All right," Paul said. "I'm a liar. Shoot me. Get it over with. I've only got one more thing to say. I love you."

Hot tears ran down Paul's face. It was ending exactly as he had feared. But disaster only seemed to intensify the love he felt for this woman. He would never love another woman with the unique blend of desire and exaltation Janet Todd had created in him.

Silence. The woman—was it really Janet, with that hate-twisted face?—continued to aim the pistol. A part of Hopemont's back wall crashed into the flickering debris. The sunrise was filling the sky with red and gold and amber light. Hands at his sides, Paul waited for her to pull the trigger.

The gun thudded to the ground. "I can't kill you," Janet said. "I still love you. I'll love you for the rest of my life. But I'll never let you touch me again. I'll never let myself touch you."

"No!" Paul said.

"In some way, shape, or form, you knew this was going to happen."

"I *didn't* know. Gentry told me and then arrested me. There was no way I could have warned you."

"Why has he let you go?"

"Because he hoped our love for each other could survive this insanity. Maybe he's trying to make some amends for Lucy."

She saw it. She saw it now exactly as he saw it. Paul was sure of it. Their love was more important than this patch of mad murderous history in which they were still trapped. Could they escape it?

Paul realized he had to tell her one more thing. She had to know it in the name of the honesty they had pledged beside the Ohio. "I didn't want you to win," he said. "It was because of the blacks—because of Adam Jameson shooting my men at Saltville. I stayed because I loved you but I didn't want you to win."

She nodded. "I half knew that. But I hoped I was wrong."

"Can't we—somehow—get beyond it, Janet?"

Slowly, sadly, she shook her head. No. They could never get beyond it. Instead, each week, month, year it would only grow more insurmountable, more intolerable, more irreversible. Paul saw the shape, the substance of the doom that was descending on him. Like his father, he had become the figure in the foreground, the unintending culprit who bore the burden of history's refusal to fulfill the deepest desire of a woman's heart.

"Go away," she said. Tears were on her cheeks now. "Go—away. I'll always love you. But I never want to see you again."

Another chunk of Hopemont crashed into the ruins. "Janet, I can't bear that thought," Paul said.

"I can't, either. But we'll have to try."

She picked up the pistol and walked away from him and from ruined Hopemont, down the path toward the slave cabins. She left him standing there among the dead.

"Janet!" Paul cried.

She did not look back. The last thing Paul saw before he turned away was the forlorn figure in the gray cloak, her head bowed, the unused silver pistol in her hand.

THIRTY-SEVEN

JANET TODD SAT OUTSIDE HER hut in Hopemont's slave quarters, shelling peas. Spring was greening the verdant earth. Trees were budding, cows and sows were in heat, larks were singing in the garden. But she felt nothing, neither joy nor sorrow. It also happened to be Easter Saturday. That meant nothing to her, either.

A few hundred yards away, Hopemont's charred ruins lay untouched. She had no money to rebuild the house. Her father had died of dysentery in the fetid federal prison in Louisville before they could bring him to trial for treason. Other Sons of Liberty leaders had been convicted before military courts and sentenced to death. But President Lincoln (influenced, some say, by Henry Gentry) had declined to hang them. They were still in prison; some were appealing their convictions.

This was only a dollop of the deluge of history in the last eight months. A week after the Sons of Liberty uprising had been crushed, General Sherman had telegraphed electrifying news from Georgia: *Atlanta is ours and fairly won.* Overnight, Lincoln's chances of getting reelected had been transformed from improbable to near certainty. In November he had been returned to the White House by a hefty majority.

Meanwhile, General Sherman launched his 70,000-man army on a march through Georgia from Atlanta to the sea, cutting a swath of destruction through the heart of the Confederacy. In desperation, the Confederate Army of Tennessee, too small to stop Sherman, marched in the opposite direction, hoping to chew up scattered Union garrisons in Tennessee piecemeal and reach Kentucky, where a harvest of new recruits would enable them to invade the upper west.

But General George H. Thomas, the Union commander in Tennessee, had used the telegraph and the railroads to concentrate every available man at Nashville. There, ten days before Christmas, he routed the Army of Tennessee in a two-day battle that many called the death knell of the Confederacy. In that tremendous clash, Colonel Paul Stapleton had been killed. In the *Keyport Record* Janet read how he had been mortally wounded breaching the Confederate defenses at a crucial point at the head of his regiment of black soldiers.

Janet knew Paul had volunteered to command black troops. Henry Gentry told her this in a letter assuring her that Paul had not betrayed her. She had understood the implications of Paul's choice. She wondered if Caroline Kemble Stapleton also understood it. She did not try to find out. She was beyond sympathy, beyond grief, beyond everything human except mere survival.

Her mother was an even more pathetic zombie, living with Amelia Jameson at Rose Hill, cared for by her faithful maid, Sally. Mrs. Jameson spent most of her time grieving over Adam. He was permanently blind. That single bullet had destroyed both his eyes.

When Janet visited her mother, she sometimes sat with Adam. She let him hold her hand. She told him what she heard about the dwindling war. She knew he still loved her. More than once she had to stifle an impulse to scream, *It's impossible! I don't love you! I'll never love anyone again!*

Most of the time, Janet stayed on the Todd plantation, trying to get in a crop. She had hired some Irish laborers from Cincinnati who were working about a third of the acres for five dollars a week. She did not know why she was trying to survive. She was an automaton, going through the motions of life without a spark of human feeling inside her. She had been that way since the night the western confederacy died.

Over the horizon, the war churned on. Every newspaper made it clear the South's collapse was imminent. Last week General Lee had surrendered the battered remnant of the Army of Northern Virginia at Appomattox. Janet no longer cared. Not even President Lincoln's second inaugural address, calling for reconciliation and peace, reminding everyone that both sides had prayed to the same God and neither side's prayers had been completely answered, meant anything to her. She was beyond all those ideas.

"Miss Todd?"

A big black man in a blue uniform was standing in the lane between the huts. He had sergeant's stripes on his sleeve. He had doffed his kepi and was holding it in both his large hands.

"I don't know whether you remember me. I'm Moses Washington. I was stationed over the river at Colonel Gentry's house."

"I remember you," Janet said, continuing to shell the peas.

Sergeant Washington cleared his throat. "Miss Todd. I got a message for you—from Colonel Stapleton. It was the last thing he said to me before he died at Nashville."

"What is it?"

"He said—to tell you he never stopped lovin' you."

No. No. No. She did not want to hear those words. But she had heard them. What did they mean? She knew the answer. It was exhaled from her empty heart. "I never stopped loving him, either."

"He said—to tell you he accepted it. He said you'd understand what he meant."

"Yes," Janet said, gazing up at the earnest black face. "I understand."

"He said—he hoped you did too. Accept it."

"I'll try, Sergeant. What brings you here?"

"I'm fixin' to marry Lucy and take her west to Fort Leavenworth. With the war almost over, the Army's recruitin' two regular Negro regiments to keep the Indians quiet out that way."

"How is Lucy?"

"She's pretty much all right, ma'am. Walks with just a little limp now."

The sergeant paused and fiddled with his kepi. "Lucy asked me to give you a message, too, Miss Todd."

"What?"

"She said she still loves you and always will. She knows you didn't mean to have her whipped that way."

"Tell her—I didn't. Tell her I'll always love her too."

"She'll be mighty glad to hear that, Miss Todd."

"Did Colonel Gentry ever find Maybelle?"

Sergeant Washington shook his big head. "He went to New Orleans himself but he never found her."

"I'm sorry."

"I'll tell Lucy that too, Miss Todd."

"Good luck at Fort Leavenworth."

"Thanks, Miss Todd. Good luck to you, too. I hopes you get things back to normal here soon."

The words were so earnest—and so ludicrously far from reality—Janet did not know what to say. Perhaps Sergeant Washington realized that. He forced a smile, put on his kepi and strode away toward the ferry landing.

Janet sat there in the spring sunlight and tried to imagine Paul saying those words with his last breath. *Accepted it. Hoped you did too.* She remembered his description of accepting death on the battlefield. He was talking about that—and something more—a great deal more. He meant accepting everything. Their love. The war. The ruin of their love by the war.

Paul was telling her from his soldier's heart what he had learned about accepting death—trying to make her see what this new more terrible acceptance meant.

When a soldier accepted death, he was freed from fear. He was able to go forward, to be a man of courage in a new transforming way. Was Paul telling her that he wanted her to be free that way, too?

What was the use of transforming herself? From what to what? From Automaton Janet to Acceptance Janet? Her life would still be as empty as a shelled pea pod.

No, it wouldn't, whispered a voice in her heart.

Who was it? Janet took a deep slow breath and realized it was Paul. Sergeant Washington had brought him here to say good-bye to her. Here to Hopemont, where they had pledged unflinching honesty and perpetual love.

Slowly, dazedly, Janet saw what acceptance would free her to do. She would be able to marry Adam. She would bring him here and build a house suitable for a blind man. Not a Hopemont with a winding staircase worthy of a palace. A simple one- or two-story house. Acceptance Janet would try to love him. She would slowly, painfully, help him see the terrible implications of the way God had answered their prayers. Together they might learn to see a different world from the one they had inherited from their fathers.

Janet put aside the peas and walked down the road to Rose Hill. Adam was sitting in the parlor, huge, black-bearded, immobile. "Adam," Janet said. "I've been thinking. Now that your wound has healed, isn't it time we got married?"

He trembled. "Janet. Oh Janet. Do you want an over-size cripple on your hands for the rest of your life?"

"I want a man who loves me," Janet said. She kissed him on the lips. It was amazing. A half hour ago she had been sure she would never kiss a man that way again.

"Mother!" Adam shouted. "Come here. I've got some good news."

Amelia Jameson stopped at the parlor door, her face brightening, her eyes widening with hope. She knew what Adam was going to say before he said it.

"Janet dearest," Amelia said, embracing her. "I can't tell you how long I've wanted you as a daughter."

Robin Jameson rushed into the parlor. Before anyone could speak, he blurted out news of his own: "I was down at the steamboat dock. A Bible salesman from Cincinnati got off. He says Lincoln's dead. The actor— John Wilkes Booth—shot him. Why would he do a crazy thing like that?"

"Dear God," Amelia Jameson said.

Two days later, on the other side of the Ohio River, Henry Gentry sat in his cellar office, staring up at the photograph of Lincoln with his hair mussed. On his desk, a headline in the *Keyport Record* reported the president's assassination. What did it mean? Gentry did not know. He could not begin to fathom the undertakings of Abraham's God. All he knew was an overwhelming sense of loss, as if the foundations of the earth beneath the house had given way and he was alone here, inhabiting a ruin.

Where could he turn for consolation? Paul Stapleton, with whom he had begun a wary father-son-like friendship, was dead. He could not think of another person who did not secretly gloat that Henry Gentry had been deprived of his powerful friend. Everywhere Democrats were silently rejoicing at this sign of God's righteous wrath.

Struggling against tears, Gentry took a deep breath and noticed an unusual odor outside his office—one he seldom encountered in his dank dungeon: perfume. Amelia Conway Jameson stood in the doorway in a blue dress.

"Henry," she said. "I felt almost a need—or at least a wish—to come over here and tell you how badly I know you must feel about the president."

"Thank you."

"All these months I was hoping you might visit Rose

Hill. I suppose you were embarrassed because of Adam. He's going to marry Janet Todd. She's going to build a house on her property—"

"I'm—I'm so glad."

"Robin's going to college in the fall. Yale, I think. I want him to get out of Kentucky."

"A good idea."

She sat down in the chair beside his desk. In the dim light he could not see a single line on her lovely face. The silken voice was exactly the same as it had been thirty years ago.

"Maybe you were worried about your—your wound. It doesn't trouble me, Henry."

"Amelia."

In ways too mysterious to comprehend, love had returned to the heartland.

Afterword

THIS BOOK WAS WRITTEN FROM hundreds of pages of notes compiled by a well-known newsman of the nineteenth century, Clay Pendleton. In the late 1880s, Jonathan Stapleton hired Pendleton to go to Keyport and find out what had happened to his younger brother in Kentucky and Indiana in the summer of 1864. These notes were intended to supplement a cryptic letter Paul wrote to Jonathan shortly before he was killed at Nashville. Janet Todd Jameson was especially forthcoming. By the time of Pendleton's visit, she had became a well-known novelist, distinguished by her sympathetic characterizations of black as well as white Americans. She also helped her husband, Adam Jameson, write a best-selling book about his Civil War adventures, *Morgan's Partisan Rangers*. Amelia Gentry, by that time a widow, gave Pendleton access to Henry Gentry's papers, including his letters to and from President Lincoln. Pendleton also tracked down Moses Washington in California, where he and Lucy retired after his service with the U.S. Army.

All the principals required Pendleton to promise that nothing would be published during their lifetimes. The interviews lay in a vault in the Stapletons' New Jersey home, Bowood, until last year, when novelist and historian Thomas Fleming put the material into the form you have just read. He worked under a grant from the Principia Foundation, set up by the late Paul Stapleton (the grandnephew of the protagonist in this tragic story) to make his descendants—and other Americans—more aware of their family's and their country's complex and often conflicted history.

James Kilpatrick,
President,
Principia Foundation